Cinnamon Bun

· Volume 5 ·

Cinnamon Bun

· Volume 5 ·

RavensDagger

Podium

Podium

Cinnamon Bun

· Volume 5 ·

· **Chapter One** ·

Game of Groans

We need to go over everything, then plan out what we'll be doing while we stay in Goldenalden," Amaryllis said. She slapped her book onto the surface of the room's dining table, then pulled out a map from her bag and unrolled it on the tablet.

"I thought we just had to deliver some letters," I said, bunny ears twitching. "And maybe snoop about, have some fun? Play tourist."

Amaryllis huffed, a very particular huff that I think meant something like "this is going to take some explaining." "Things are more complicated than that. I don't have a good lay of the situation either—until then, everything I'm about to say is entirely speculative."

Awen and I glanced at each other, then back to the table. It felt like she should have been doing this in the *Beaver* instead of the Dewdrop Inn, but if Amaryllis thought this was the right time . . . "Okay," I said. "What do you want to explain, and what will we be doing?"

"The situation first," Amaryllis said. She tapped the world map with the tip of a talon, something that I'd noticed she liked doing. "There are four bigger players here and quite a few smaller ones."

"I'm guessing Mattergrove isn't one of the bigger ones," Awen said, her expression somewhat pained.

I supposed she was worried about her home.

"I'm afraid you're correct," Amaryllis confirmed. Her talon moved to the west and down, settling over the Seven Points. "Mattergrove has economic ties with Deepmarsh and the Harpy Mountains and deeper ties with the independent cities to its north, but otherwise, I don't think they have a big enough stake in things to truly get involved. If a war breaks out, they might be a source of supplies for the harpies and grenoils, but I don't think they'll be any more involved than that."

"Oh, all right," Awen said. "That's probably good."

"So who are the big players?" I asked. "And what's that mean, anyway?"

"The big nations to watch out for are the Nesting Kingdom, Deepmarsh, the Trenten Flats, and Sylphfree." She tapped each nation's capital as she named it. "Deepmarsh is the smallest of these, but they are well situated. Their marshland is inhospitable to large troop movements, and the grenoils are capable of having big population booms if they so choose."

"They can?"

Amaryllis nodded. "You've spent some time in their kingdom. I'm surprised you didn't know how they're born."

"I never asked," I said. "Do they do it like . . . frogs?"

"Essentially, yes. They have pools where eggs are laid by the hundreds. The fittest of these are chosen and then raised to become tadpoles and, eventually, members of whichever family they're from. Most eggs are never hatched, though."

"Huh," I said. I didn't know what to think about that.

"It's an important factor to consider in the grand scheme," Amaryllis said. "But we're going off topic. The next country to consider is the Nesting Kingdom."

"Your home," I said. "Would they go to war?"

"Against the sylphs or the cervids? Definitely. We've skirmished against the cervids before, and the sylphs are longtime enemies." She touched the mountain between the two nations. "The Golden Peak is a natural wonder that both of us want. Not only for the gold found there but the ancient dungeons as well. Right now, it's ostensibly owned by both sides, with everyone having claims over the same area. In reality, it's neutral, unclaimed territory."

"That's not great," I said.

"It isn't," Amaryllis agreed. "Having fought the sylphs before means that we—the Nesting Kingdom, that is—don't think the idea is impossible. The last war was a long time ago, though. Now there are proper airships and new weapons to account for. The populations of both nations are quite a bit larger too."

"Does that make it more or less likely that they'll want to fight?"

"I don't know. People have been at peace for a while. They might not want that changed. And some of the xenophobia has settled down a little."

I nodded. That was good to hear. "What about the other two? The Trenten Flats and Sylphfree."

"The Trenten Flats are a problem regardless of whether a war is started or not. They've been expanding a lot. They nearly have cities spanning the central continent. They're stretched thin across most of that, though. A lot of wide, barren swatches with nothing but plains and a few forests. Still, they have by far the largest military, though it is also the least advanced."

"Advanced how?" Awen asked.

"Cervid airships, as far as I'm aware, are still two generations behind anyone else's. Their bodies also mean that piloting isn't as easy for them as it is for a harpy or sylph. Their enchantments are generally of lower quality, as is most of their spellcraft. Really, their greatest advantage is their numbers."

"There's a lot of them," I said.

Amaryllis nodded. "Plenty more than any other nation can field. If it comes to a wide-scale battle, it doesn't matter that their mages are weaker. A modern, academy-educated harpy war mage will run out of mana long before the cervids run out of poorly trained novice mages to throw into the battlefield. Likewise for their soldiery. Every single soldier counts as cavalry, being who they are. On an open plain, their mobility is a huge advantage. Their bowmen are also quite gifted."

"Scary," I said. I could imagine a big group of them charging down a hill. That would be terrifying.

"Indeed. Unfortunately, I think any modern war will be fought in the skies. Which brings us to the sylphs."

"They have a big army," I said.

"It's not only big, it's modern," Amaryllis said. "I think only the Snowlands might have better equipped and trained soldiery. It's a mark of pride there to have served, as well as an obligation. They have . . . usable airships as well. They lack elegance, and I believe any harpy ship could outpace and fly circles around a sylph ship, but there's no denying that they make up for it in durability and numbers."

Nothing I didn't know, though I doubted some of Amaryllis's patriotic views about ship designs. She had some biases. Airships that looked like ships were nice, very romantic, but there was nothing wrong with big boxy ships too. It wasn't the size or the shape of the ship that mattered, but the way it handled and how much it was loved by its crew.

"So, that's the, ah, players? That's what my mother always called the people who were taking part in a big political event," Awen said.

"That's the players, yes. The big ones, at least. There's also the Snowlands to the north, who are likely to only defend their borders unless the cervids antagonize them, in which case they might expand southward a little. The independent cities are a mixed bag. No two of them are similar, except in their scope. For the most part, they're too small to really change things on an international scale."

"Those are places like Rosenbell, right?" The place where we'd first met Rhawrexdee and where I fought in that tournament.

"That's one of them, yes," Amaryllis said. "It's somewhere in the middle in terms of size, I think."

I nodded. Those cities likely had a lot of people in them, but they probably didn't care too much about other countries since they weren't part of any. "What about the desert?"

"The ostri? They'll be on both sides as mercenaries. Likely more of them on the harpy and grenoil side, if only because of geographical convenience. The only other big player on the continent is the Kingdom of Endless Swells, and that's only because they have a few colonies set up to the west, along the shores of the Moonstruck Sea."

"Are they nice?" I asked.

"They're very fixated on the sea and its surroundings. I can't say whether or not they'll fit whatever definition you have of nice," Amaryllis said.

Awen awa-ed, silently. "I've met some of their traders. They dressed strangely, but they were very kind."

I nodded. "That covers everyone, then?"

"We could go over the groups that make up these players," Amaryllis said. I think she noticed my pout because she rolled her eyes. "But we should move on. The current situation is somewhat precarious."

"Because of Rainnewt," I said. The no-good, mean . . . jerk who had tricked Amaryllis and I into almost getting kidnapped and who had blown up that ball.

She nodded. "In part, yes. Pointing out that he's likely an outside factor trying to aggravate the current political situation would be a good place to start. But there are a lot of tensions between all these nations. Right now, we need to navigate things toward a peaceful resolution."

"It's like trying to calm things down between angry neighbors," I said.

"And one of them is accusing the other's dog of pooping on their porches," Awen said with a barely restrained giggle.

"Immature, both of you," Amaryllis said. "But essentially yes. Even if this problem is solved, that doesn't mean the tension will disappear. Accusations are likely to be tossed around, and insults will follow right behind."

"So even after learning that it's a stray pooping on their porch, they'll still be mad at each other because they said mean things to each other before," I surmised.

Amaryllis glared. "Anyway. The situation is volatile, but I think we can keep ahead of it. First, though, we need to know what everyone thinks is going on and how they'll move. Which means either spying on everyone, which we don't have the equipment, people, or experience for, or we use the Broccoli method."

"What's the Broccoli method?" I asked. I *was* Broccoli. I should probably know what that was.

She grinned. "Aggressively befriend everyone."

I felt my cheeks puffing out. "I don't befriend people aggressively," I said. "And you can't just . . . weaponize friendship!"

"Not with that attitude you can't," Amaryllis replied. "We need to get information from each faction, in particular the diplomats who will be gathering here. There should be some from every nation, which means that Goldenalden will become the center from which a lot of important choices will be made. We need to learn what those diplomats know in order to know how to act ourselves."

I thumped my foot down. "I don't like any plans that involve pretending to be someone's friend just to use them. Friendship should be treasured, not commodified."

"I don't know," Awen said. "Forced friendship would be nicer than doing some of the things my mother encouraged me to learn. It's a lot more honest."

I thumped my foot harder. "Awen!"

Awen raised her hands in surrender. "It's like walking from house to house to see what everyone in the neighborhood thinks of the yard-poop situation before trying to fix things."

I considered it for a moment, then gave in with a nod. "Okay, fine. I wouldn't mind meeting more people anyway. Is that the whole plan?"

Amaryllis rolled up her map. "That's part of it. A lot of it will depend on what we discover. For the most part, if I can represent the Nesting Kingdom, then our goal becomes deflecting and discouraging open conflict. We want to avoid a war at any cost."

"I'm sure everyone can get over a few stains on their porch," I said.

My head stung, and it took me a moment to realize that Amaryllis had whapped me with her map. "Stop it with the dog-turd analogies!"

I rubbed the spot between my ears, then glanced at Awen, and we both giggled while Amaryllis fumed. She couldn't resist for long, though, and soon she chuckled before trying to hide her own amusement.

"So, what now?" I asked. A glance out the nearest window revealed that it was still midday.

"We have a week to get everything ready, which should afford us some time to reconnoiter between setting up appointments," Amaryllis said. "I also need an idea of where and when to meet everyone important."

"Oh! Then we have time for fun!"

· Chapter Two ·

Out Over the Town

Before you run off and find trouble," Amaryllis said, "we should decide whom to focus on first."

"You mean which group to go meet with first?" I asked. "Do we even know where we should go to meet with them?"

"We don't, but I suspect it won't be all that difficult to find out. There's a readily available source of information for us in this city."

"What's that?"

"The Exploration Guild."

I blinked. "Oh gosh, I almost forgot all about them. Is there a branch here?" I reached up to the bandoleer running across my chest. I still had the guild's pin attached to the front of it, just over my chest.

"There's a branch in nearly every country. Even in the Trenten Flats, though the organization is quite unpopular there. It's not all that influential in Sylphfree either," Amaryllis said.

"I'm not a member," Awen said. "Will that matter?"

"It shouldn't," Amaryllis said. "The guild often employs people outside itself to assist with certain things. I know some parties only have one or two members that are part of the guild, especially those made up of poorer members."

"To avoid the guild fees?" I asked.

"Exactly. The guild's missions pay relatively well for someone willing to risk talon and wing, but they're only available to members. It's a business, after all, though not one that's centered around profits first."

That sounded a little strange for a business, but I couldn't complain. "Right, so we visit the local branch for information first, then we . . . uh, scout out the city?"

"That's an interesting way of saying *sightsee*," Amaryllis said.

I grinned. "Isn't it?"

She bounced to her talons and started for the door. "We're wasting time, girls! We have a world to save, because it certainly won't save itself."

"Yes, ma'am," I replied before giggling and hopping after her. "Do you know where the local Exploration Guild building is?"

"I don't," Amaryllis said. She opened the door into the corridor and held it open for Awen and I to step out. "We can ask the innkeeper."

I took the lead heading up to the topmost floor. The Dewdrop Inn was getting busier. I guessed that being close to noon meant that many more people were coming out to grab lunch.

Mister Jared was at the counter, smiling at a customer while he set a plate before them, then filled a pitcher from a tap behind him. His eyes lit up when I bounced closer and leaned onto the countertop.

"Hello, Miss Bunch."

"Hello, Mister Jared," I replied with a big old grin. "You know the city well, right?"

"Like the back of my hand." He chuckled. "What are you looking for?"

"The Exploration Guild," I said. "I heard they had a branch in Golden-alden, and I thought I'd stop by to see. Plus, don't tell Amaryllis, but it's an excuse to walk around."

"That sounds like a great excuse to see the sights," Jared said. "Here, give me a moment." He reached under his counter and brought up a frame with a map within it. "This is a little old, but it's still good enough. We're in the Gold District now. The Yellow District here is where you'll find all the best shops in the capital. Just head north and west from here. The Green District bisects it, so don't worry if you end up there. If you find yourself at the big wall, then you've gone too far. Now, you're looking for the Exploration Guild. They're on the far side of this park here."

"Oh, I see," I said. "Which way is north from here?"

Jared laughed and pointed toward one corner of the inn. "That way, my dear."

I pointed north with one ear, then pointed northwest with the other. I had it pretty much figured out, I thought. "Thanks!"

"No problem. If you get lost, don't be afraid to ask a passing guardsman."

"I will! Do you think we can travel from above, or will we need to go to the ground level?"

"As long as you don't purposefully jump into people's way, you should be just fine," Jared said with a nod.

Laughing, I stepped back and ran over to my friends. "I know where to go!" I said. "We're going to need to jump a bunch, though."

"I can fly," Amaryllis said. It was a bit of a white lie. She could hover a little, and I think if she was aiming for something below, she could glide quite well, but she didn't quite have the whole "upward lift" thing handled well enough to call what she did *flight*.

"Awa, that might be hard for me. I can't jump like you do, and I don't have wings," Awen said. There was a gleam in her eyes, a dangerous one. "Though, I think I could make do. I took a good look at those rockets the cry used. With a small tank and some thrusters . . . I'd need a magic element to create the initial flame and some sort of control surface too. Oh, and directional thrust and some wings for lift."

"I think we can settle on Broccoli carrying you across any gaps for now," Amaryllis said. "I don't know what you're thinking, but the mere mutterings about it are giving me shivers."

"I could mount a repeating crossbow to it," Awen whispered.

"Come on!" I said. "Daylight's burning, and we have a whole heap of city to explore."

I led my friends out of the Dewdrop Inn. The top exit opened onto a wide platform that served as the building's roof. There were flowers next to the roof access and no railings on the edges, but there were nets just a step off the side to catch clumsy people.

I glanced up as a sylph in a blue courier outfit buzzed by. There was plenty more traffic in the air too. Sylphs zipped about, most in loose, flowing clothes that didn't hamper their wings.

Instead of backpacks or purses, a lot of the sylphs I saw had fanny packs dangling in front of them. That made sense. They didn't want anything catching on their wings, and most flew . . . not quite upright, but not horizontally either.

I looked toward what I hoped was the northwest—my ears had never stopped pointing that way, like a fluffy compass atop my head—and I judged the distance to the next building over. The space was a bit shorter than the width of a road, if only because both the Dewdrop Inn and the building across from it had balconies around their tops.

I could make that jump easily, and so could Amaryllis.

"All right, Awen, hop on my back," I said as I hunched down.

Awen stared at me, then at my back. "Are you sure?"

"Oh yeah, it's just a small hop. You don't need to worry!"

She hesitated a little more, then jumped onto my back, and I grabbed her knees while she wrapped her arms around my collar. It was like a back hug!

I bounced up and down a couple of times, to make sure Awen had a good grip on me, then I stepped back and away from the edge. I probably didn't need a running start, but it might help. Feet thumping on the balcony, I sprinted ahead until I was on the very edge, then shot some stamina into my legs and launched myself over the gap.

Awen screamed, a mixture of fear and delight that had all four of my ears ringing. The wind flapped around us, Awen's hair a streaming banner and my own a tangled mess, before I landed at a jog on the other rooftop.

"Awa! That was great!" Awen cheered.

I laughed and turned around, Awen still gripping onto me. "Come on, Amaryllis, you can do it!"

I couldn't hear her huff, not with the distance and the wind, but I'd know that facial expression anywhere. She backed up, pinched her tongue between her lips, then lowered her goggles over her eyes before she took a running leap over the chasm. Her arms flapped twice, catching the wind and giving her just enough lift to land right on the edge of the balcony.

"Easy," Amaryllis said as she walked to a stop.

"Uh-huh," I agreed. Still, I made a note to find shorter paths to jump next time. I didn't want any accidents, and a crosswind could come up at any time and cause some trouble.

The Exploration Guild headquarters was supposed to be to the west of a big park. It wasn't too hard to spot that part. A section of the mountainside had been built out with dirt, and big old trees were growing in clumps.

We jumped over to another building, and I couldn't help but notice all the strange looks we were getting from the sylphs passing us by. There weren't any other humans or buns or harpies up on top of these buildings— at least, none that I could see.

We crossed over to the Yellow District, then into the Green, then back into the Yellow. For all that the sylphs seemed to care a lot about being neat and orderly, they still had to work with a mountainside as the location for their city, which meant that they had to build around the bumps and inclines of the landscape. I imagined that not all the buildings around us were at the same height. There were clearly ramps below where carts had to be helped up to higher or lower levels. The entire city was built atop a whole heap of artificial plateaus.

Once we reached the edge of the park, Amaryllis found a building with a few shops in it. A bakery on the top floor, a butcher in the middle, and a grocer's at the bottom, all connected via stairwells. So I let Awen down, and we climbed down to street level, with only a quick pause to buy some pastries.

The sylphs, it seemed, preferred these small, supersweet pastries. They were little balls of bread, fried and dipped in a glaze and stuffed full of either jam or something the baker behind the counter called mountain-bee honey. They were so sweet my entire face puckered up, and I couldn't help but shiver after every bite.

I didn't dare eat more than six or seven of them, else they'd do terrible things to my tummy.

We went down and down until we reached the ground floor, then we headed outside and walked along the edge of the park. Lots of younger sylphs were within, with sylph moms looking after the teeny-tiny sylphs who were darting around and play fighting and learning how to fly. A few neat play forts were tucked away in the woods, and I saw more than one squealing group of sylphs running around with blunted wooden swords. Others were jumping off jungle gyms, playing something that was like extreme hopscotch by flying from suspended plate to suspended plate.

Amaryllis gave me a *look* which I interpreted as "No, you can't go play with the kids. You're a big girl." She was probably right—a lot of them were pointing at us already. I bet I was the first bun they'd ever seen!

We found the Exploration Guild right where Jared said it would be. It was a shorter building, but no less stately for its size. There was a big brass compass rose above the entrance, with the familiar bandoleer across it and the name of the guild beneath it.

The building was nice but also a little bit on the shabbier side. The plants next to its entrance looked like they could use some watering and maybe a bit of weeding, and the stones were water-stained in a few spots.

"I have the impression that I'm not going to get all the answers I want from here," Amaryllis said.

"Well, there's only one way to find out for sure," I said.

· **Chapter Three** ·

The Guild House

I pushed the front door open with a squeal of protesting hinges and peered inside. The interior wasn't all that well lit—the only light slipped in from the windows at the front, illuminating a lobby area filled with shadows and a thin film of dust.

"Hello?" I called out as I stepped in. My voice echoed across the room.

I had only ever been to two Exploration Guild houses before: the large one in Port Royal, which was a stately building, well maintained and richly decorated, and a smaller one in Awen's hometown, which had been clean and quite nice, though not as affluent. Maybe that clouded my impression of the guild, because I was expecting something similar here, especially in Goldenalden, where the city seemed much richer, and the people here had a greater focus on propriety than I was used to.

There were some decorations. The last two guilds had had dioramas of dungeons and hand-drawn maps made by members of the guild. This one had glass-covered plinths to the sides, with strange weapons and artifacts with little plaques next to them. They might have been impressive if a number of them weren't missing and the rest weren't currently being used as scaffolding by enterprising spiders.

"This place looks abandoned," Awen said as she glanced around.

"Yeah," I replied. I had that impression too. "But the door wasn't locked, and there's still some things here."

"Nothing of great value, but still enough that I suspect a common thief wouldn't just leave it lying around," Amaryllis said.

The clink of a door opening had all three of us looking up and to the end of the room. A desk was there, and a door behind it slowly swung open. A sylph stepped out.

I wasn't great at judging the age of people, but I guessed him to be in his thirties or so—a proper adult. He had a suit that was well cut but a bit rumpled, and he walked with the hunched back of someone who had given up.

"Hello!" I called out.

The sylph jumped, then spun to stare at us. His confusion quickly gave way to a shaky smile, and he scurried around the desk to come and address us properly. "Hello, hello," he said. "Welcome to the Goldenalden Exploration Guild. It's been some time since . . . Ah, never mind. I mean to say that you're all very welcome. Are you looking to hire someone to find something? A scout, a map-maker? Perhaps a dungeon diver?"

I shook my head. "We're not looking for anything like that," I said. "My name's Broccoli, and these are my friends Amaryllis and Awen. We—at least Amaryllis and I—are part of the Exploration Guild."

The sylph froze, his smile turning brittle. "An inspection team?"

"Huh? No, nothing like that," I said. "We're just normal members."

"Oh! That's wonderful. Are you looking for a mission? We don't have many, but there are a few outstanding ones that we could use an experienced team on."

Amaryllis raised a talon. "What's going on here? I'd suspect that the Goldenalden guild was just not as popular or as well off, but the location of this building and its size suggests otherwise. It looks, at a glance, as if this branch is falling apart."

"What? No, no, we're . . ." He tried to keep up his smile, then gave up. "All right, so you're not wrong. We're basically skirting failure here."

"What happened?" I asked. "It looks like this was a nice place." The decor was poorly maintained and dirty, but I could imagine it being quite fetching beneath all that.

"Happened?" he asked. "Ah! Where are my manners? My name is Reginald Leaflock. I'm the current guild master of the Goldenalden branch of the Exploration Guild, it's a pleasure to meet you." He bowed.

"Nice to meet you too!" I said. "Are you the only one here?"

"No, no, we still have some staff. Not many, though," he replied with a glance over his shoulder. "Mostly the older members who have been around for so long that they wouldn't know what to do with themselves." He laughed, but it lacked any humor.

Amaryllis shifted, and I could see the calculations flashing by in her eyes. "So, what happened here? The guild looks like it's underperforming."

"We're getting along," Reginald said, but he folded at Amaryllis's look. "Or we're trying to. It's a long story, and not one that I think anyone would want to hear. I'd much rather listen to your own. Are you members from the Harpy Mountains?"

"We both joined in Port Royal," I said.

Reginald's eyebrows rose. "Ah, a nice branch over there. The guild master is a woman of great repute. Did you have a mission that needed you around here? We might be able to provide some assistance."

"Mister Leaflock, could you tell us what happened here?" Amaryllis repeated. "We came because we were looking for some information, but the state of the guild is questionable at best."

Reginald winced. "Well, ah, perhaps we can have this discussion in my office? Though, I'm not sure if it's a discussion worth having at all."

"You seem worried," I said.

He shrugged a shoulder, a very careless gesture for a sylph. "I don't think the guild has much time left, at least not this branch."

"Well, now I want to know what happened too," I said. "But not if it'll hurt your feelings to repeat it."

Reginald stared at me, then took a deep breath and shored up his resolve. "No, no, I don't mind telling you what happened. Come, my office is at least a little more comfortable."

We followed Reginald to the back, and instead of going around the counter as he had, he led us to the side and headed toward a staircase at the rear. Once we were up a floor, we moved down a richly appointed corridor and finally reached an office.

Reginald's office was nice and big, with a stout desk in its middle and a few plush chairs for guests. Portraits were hanging on the walls, and from the plaques beneath them, I guessed that they were the former guild masters for this branch.

"Take a seat, please," Reginald said as he gestured to the free seats before his desk.

I looked to my friends before pulling one out and plopping myself down onto it. A small puff of dust rose around me that I quickly and quietly got rid of by pushing some magic into my Cleaning aura. I didn't want to interrupt anything, so I kept it subtle. His desk was less dusty due to regular use.

"So, what happened?" Amaryllis asked.

Reginald worked his jaw. "I don't know exactly where things started taking a turn for the worse. We were having a relatively difficult year. Securing government contracts was made more complicated by the army ramping things up and edging into the budget we're usually allocated, but otherwise we were doing well financially. You have to understand, the Exploration Guilds in Sylphfree are treated . . . in an interesting way."

"Interesting how?" I asked.

"In most countries, the Exploration Guild is primarily made up of two groups: well-off members of the gentry who can afford to mount expeditions and talented individuals looking for reliable work who can assist with those expeditions. There are always new dungeons to find, ancient ruins to explore, and new cultures to visit and exchange with."

I nodded—that was what had made me want to join, mostly.

"But in Sylphfree, there's a powerful pressure for most to join the armed forces. Most nobles will try to find a place in the military hierarchy, and it's not as common for one to wish to join our guild. We still have . . . *had* plenty of members, though."

"What was the appeal?" Amaryllis asked.

"Mostly the ability to move outside of the borders of the country. And we worked closely with paladins and others of the sort to scout out new dungeons and locations of interest across Sylphfree." Reginald seemed quite proud. "The Exploration Guild allowed its distinguished members to make a mark in a way that being part of the more traditional sylph culture wouldn't allow."

"You still haven't told us how everything turned out like this," Amaryllis said.

Reginald's proud look deflated. "It started with . . . I suppose we received a new member. He was very talented, a young human from somewhere. He never really said. He was a hard worker, and while he was rather antisocial, he worked well enough with the rest of the guild. He took quite a few missions, mostly mapping out dungeons. There are a few in the nation that aren't as popular, so they're not delved as often, and our maps of those have become dated."

"I imagine he did more than just that," Amaryllis said.

The sylph nodded. "We didn't know it at the time, but he . . . Well, he destroyed some of the dungeons he visited. Three of them, as far as we now know."

Amaryllis took in a deep breath, and I saw Awen raise her hands over her mouth. As I understood it, dungeon destruction was a big deal. It would probably be really wise of me not to mention the dungeons I'd destroyed.

"The Inquisition marched in here and started rooting around, looking for him, but he had disappeared. Worse, he took a lot of paperwork with him when he left. Gold as well. I think the only silver lining in the entire matter is that the Inquisition wanted the destruction to stay silent."

"Did they ever find him?" I asked.

Reginald shook his head. "No. We lost a few members then and there. Others left soon after. I scrambled to fulfill the missions we still had, but that meant sending less experienced members out to tackle more complicated missions. We had to deal with a big surge in injuries. Then the news broke out amongst the nobility, and a lot of our members who were part of the gentry parted ways with us."

"Oh no," I said. "They were the ones supplying the guild with money and stuff?"

"In part, yes," Reginald said. "We used to receive frequent donations from the nobility, often in lieu of donating to other organizations."

"Huh?" I asked.

Reginald blinked. "Ah, yes, you're not from Goldenalden. Ah, the nobility are legally obligated to pay a certain amount of their earnings back to the nation. They can get an exception from this if they donate some of those proceeds to certain organizations. Some are military, others are civil services."

"Ah, tax evasion," Awen said with a nod.

"It's . . . not technically that. Anyway, a lot of noble families would donate to the guild, especially those that enjoyed the banquets and meetings we held here. Which we can no longer hold here, not with the state the guild is in."

"And all of this was caused by a single human?" Amaryllis asked.

"One human, yes. At least, I think he was human." At our looks, Reginald shook his head. "Never mind, just a rumor."

"Wait," I said as I leaned forward. "You're not sure if he was human . . . Did he ever just change appearance? Like an illusion spell or something? Or shapeshifting?"

"It was just a rumor. We needed to track him down after all the crimes he committed. So I employed some of the guild's best to chase him down. They cornered him, but all they found was a scared and confused sylph who didn't know anything. I trusted those members to track someone down, so it was a strange occurrence. Then I heard that something similar happened to the Inquisition."

"What was his name?" I asked.

"Drizz. His name was Drizz L. Lizard."

I blinked. "No!" I said as I jumped to my feet. My palm slapped the table. "That's Rainnewt!"

· **Chapter Four** ·

Lost and Found in Translation

Rainnewt?" Reginald asked.

"How do you figure that?" Amaryllis asked.

I gestured vaguely through the air. "The name. It's obvious, isn't it?"

"No. No, it really isn't," Amaryllis said.

I huffed. "Come on. Drizz L. Lizard? It obviously means *drizzle lizard*, and that's just a terrible pun for *rain newt*."

Amaryllis blinked. "None of that made sense," she said.

I stared at my birdy friend. The clues and all were super obvious, and she was a smart girl. Then it clicked, and I felt silly. "It's a multilingual pun," I said with mounting horror. Puns were already a bit evil. Puns that required translation . . . That was a whole new level of terrible. Rainnewt really was a villain.

"How does it work?" Amaryllis asked. "I don't see the link between the names."

"It might be because of my autotranslation," I said. "But the name means *rain lizard*. A newt is a kind of lizard. That, and Reginald mentioned something that might have been shapeshifting."

"And there's a solid link with the Exploration Guild," Amaryllis added. "But then, for him to be able to make that kind of—dare I say—joke with his name, he would need to either have a gift for multiple languages or be a Riftwalker."

"That would make sense, wouldn't it?" I asked. "Him being a Riftwalker. He's been destroying dungeons. Reginald! Did the dungeons he destroyed have any Evil Roots in them?"

Reginald leaned back in his big office seat. "Evil Roots? Ah, I don't know? Actually, there was— Give me a moment." He slid his chair to the side and opened a drawer. "I only have these on hand because the Inquisition demanded copies of everything related to Drizz. They couldn't find him initially, so they started to investigate with more depth. That meant going over everything with a fine-tooth comb." He pulled out a stack of papers and set them on his desk, then he started flipping through them.

I watched as he paused on a page, frowned, then turned it around and slid it our way.

Awen, Amaryllis, and I all leaned over to inspect the paper. Reginald tapped a paragraph near the middle.

The Hidebank Dungeon was explored by a local delve team, who reported strange growths on the boss floor of the dungeon. The dungeon has not acquired any new floors since its last survey, but there have been some noted changes in its behavior.

"What's this report?" Amaryllis asked.

"It's the demand from Riverhide to send someone to explore one of the small dungeons in the region. It's not a very popular dungeon, so there wasn't a lot of local interest in uncovering the changes within it. It was one of the first missions that Drizz took. That dungeon was destroyed."

Amaryllis turned my way, a talon resting against her chin. "It's not much to go on. Circumstantial at best."

"But it's something," I said. "Did any of the other dungeons mention plant stuff? Big roots, the dungeon acting weird?"

"Not that I'm aware of. Drizz had a knack for tackling dungeons across the nation, but he only destroyed three as far as I'm aware." Reginald sighed. "Only three. As if that's not an enormous number of lost dungeons."

I looked at Amaryllis, and she nodded, though it was a little reluctant. "All right, I'll admit that you might be onto something."

"You know Drizz, then?" Reginald asked.

"Yeah, but not under that name," I said. "I'm not sure, not without seeing them, but it sounds like Drizz might be Rainnewt. He was a man that worked at the Port Royal Exploration Guild. He tried to get Amaryllis kidnapped at some point, and he might be responsible for a bunch of diplomatic problems in the area too."

"Not to mention what he did in the Nesting Kingdom. He set off an explosion that killed and injured members of a sylph diplomatic party," Amaryllis continued. "He got away with it, too, as far as I can tell."

Reginald paled. "He did what?"

"Yeah, it was really bad," I said. "I don't know if he destroyed more dungeons along the way, but I wouldn't be surprised if he had."

Amaryllis's eyes narrowed. "Why did you suspect he was linked to the Evil Roots, Broccoli?"

I shrugged. "The World told me to fix those. So if there's another Riftwalker, maybe they're here for the same reason. Trying to start a war doesn't make sense, though. If all he wanted was to destroy dungeons, he could be a lot sneakier about it."

"Awa, maybe he doesn't want to do it himself?" Awen asked. "If he could convince the nations to fight, then one of the first things they'd do is destroy each other's dungeons, right? I know that my dad had some procedures in place, if there was ever a war or something, to protect the dungeons closest to Greenshade."

That made some sense, but it was such an awful way to go about doing things. Why not just warn people? Or find another way to get rid of the Evil Roots. I'd proven that Cleaning magic could do it, so I bet there were other ways to get rid of the roots too.

"This is distressing," Reginald said. "But, at this point, I'm not sure what the guild can do about it. It's obvious that this is a problem that's much bigger than the guild."

"Humph, that's no reason not to try to do your part," Amaryllis said. "We've moved very much offtrack. I came here to ask the guild for help finding certain groups in the city. It would aid us a lot if we could track them down."

"We're trying to stop Rainnewt," I said. "Or at least the war he might be trying to start."

"I can try to help," Reginald said. "But I'm not sure if there's much I can do at all."

I shook my head to clear it. Too many thoughts were bouncing around in there at once, and I only had so much room for thinking about things. "Maybe we can help you while you help us!"

Reginald sat up a little straighter in his seat. "You think you can help the guild? At this point, we'd accept any help we can get."

"We might be able to help, a little, on the condition that the guild helps us in turn," Amaryllis said. "Notably, we're looking for the location of the diplomatic parties sent over for the summit. We have a little over a week to try and convince all the players here not to go to war with each other over the actions of one madman."

"Or madperson," I said. "Rainnewt can shapeshift. We have no way of knowing who they are."

Amaryllis nodded. "That's a fair point. I suspect that most nations will have ways of intercepting and preventing that kind of security breach, if only to counter skilled spies and assassins. Warning them of a potential issue wouldn't be amiss."

"The weakest point of any defense is the people behind it," Awen said. It sounded like a quote. "Even if everyone has things in place to catch spies, they might not be paying them all that much attention. Though I guess that wouldn't make sense now, not with everyone being on high alert."

"No, it's a fair point," Amaryllis said.

I nodded along. Spying and such wasn't my forte, but I imagined that my friends were probably right. "So, that's what we need: to know who and where the nice diplomats from everywhere will be."

"I think I can manage that," Reginald said. "I don't have many contacts left, but I still have some. The guild isn't lost, not yet. If I can help you with that, what can you do to help the guild?"

"We don't have much money," I said.

Amaryllis shook her head. "Certainly not enough to keep an entire guild afloat."

"Surprisingly," Reginald cut in, "we're still staying afloat financially. We had to cut off a lot of services and the like, but we had some gold saved up. It's our reputation that we need to salvage the most."

"Well, I don't know about that," I said. "But maybe if we cleaned the place up a little, that would help? Give me half a day and some gardening tools, and I can have the whole place looking like new."

Reginald smiled. "I think that would help, at least a little. I suppose we're not presenting the greatest image while looking so slovenly." He nodded, then eyed me and then my friends up and down. There was a calculating gleam in his eyes, and I couldn't help but feel that maybe Reginald was the guild master for a reason. "You've been on some interesting adventures, haven't you?"

"Oh yeah, plenty," I said.

"Any of those recent?"

I considered the trip from the Nesting Kingdom to here. "Yeah, I think a few of them are."

Reginald's eyes narrowed, and he leaned his elbows onto the table. "Would one of you mind telling the story of your voyage? Truthfully, that is. No need to exaggerate or anything of the sort, just a straight recounting of what occurred."

I glanced at my friends, then shrugged. "I can do that,"

"Awa, maybe I can do it?" Awen asked. "I have a good memory for that kind of thing, and Broccoli might be busy cleaning and doing gardening work."

"And in the meanwhile, I have a few small questions I'd like to ask," Amaryllis said. "Notably, what exactly are you thinking of doing with our story?"

Reginald nodded. "That's only fair. The guild needs a victory right now. Several, in fact. And spreading the story of a successful venture by some intrepid young members might just count as that victory. It's not much, but I'm sure we can find some mutual benefit from announcing to the nobility of the nation that you're a force to be respected and admired."

"Ah, I see," Amaryllis said.

It sounded to me like Reginald just wanted to use us to create a good image for the guild. I wasn't exactly against the idea. We hadn't done anything too amazing, I figured, but maybe stories about going around and making friends would attract more people who needed friends too.

After all, Amaryllis joined the guild because she secretly wanted to make friends, deep, deep, down inside.

I bet there were plenty of Amaryllises out in Goldenalden who needed a good friend too!

"I like it," I said. "But no lying or embellishing."

"He wouldn't be able to in any case," Amaryllis said. "We had Bastion with us for the entire trip. He would be able to fact-check any part of it, and to most sylphs, the word of a paladin is assumed to be truthful by default, and usually for good reason."

"Bastion?" Reginald asked.

"A paladin who accompanied us on our voyage," Amaryllis said.

Reginald's brows shot up, and he seemed genuinely impressed.

I clapped my hands. "So! Should we do all this stuff today?"

"Ah, well, as much as I would enjoy that, I'm afraid that I can't uphold my end of the bargain today. The information Miss Amaryllis wants isn't something I know offhand. Would it be possible for the three of you to return tomorrow?"

"Sure thing," I said. "Can you set out some gardening supplies? I'm hardly an expert, but I can fix up the front no problem. And I *am* an expert at all things cleaning."

"I look forward to seeing the results. In any case, yes, I think we have tools and cleaning supplies lying about."

Reginald stood, and so did we.

"You've given me a lot to think on. But I think this might be the start of the Exploration Guild's return to a proper level of decorum. Or at least I very much hope so. Thank you, girls."

"No problem," I said.

· Chapter Five ·

Taking a Friendtrip

The final summit thing was going to happen in one week, which was a very long time. Still, we'd spent half our first day in Goldenalden already, which left us with closer to six and a half days to have fun and also stop a war.

"I think we should put off any sort of preparations for the summit," Amaryllis said. "We don't know what the local fashions are like, and we don't want to accidentally imply something with the way we dress and prepare for it."

We stepped out into the full light of day, and I had to squint to protect my eyes. I hadn't noticed just how dark it was inside the Exploration Guild, at least not once my eyes had gotten used to the relative lack of light. "So, if we can't go shopping, should we play tourist? I bet there's all sorts of things to see. Didn't Jared mention a parade ground?"

"Broccoli." I turned toward Awen, then followed her gaze. She was looking to the side, where a sylph was walking toward us. He was the tallest sylph I'd seen so far, coming right up to my eyes in height, and he wore the same sort of dark armor as Bastion.

The paladin came to a smart stop a pace away from us and bowed at the waist. "Greetings, ladies," he said in a gruff, formal voice. "Are you Broccoli Bunch, Awen Bristlecone, and Amaryllis Albatross?"

"And if we are?" Amaryllis asked.

"Please just confirm your identities," he said.

"We are," I said. It would be rude to lie, and besides, there weren't exactly a wealth of bun-human-harpy threesomes on the street.

The paladin nodded and tugged a small scroll out from his belt. It had a wax seal on the front, with pretty yellow tassels hanging from beneath. "This is for you," he said.

Amaryllis took the scroll gingerly, as if it might explode at any moment. "And who exactly is it from? For that matter, what is it?"

The paladin obviously hesitated, but not for very long. "It's from Her Royal Highness Princess Caprica. As for the contents, that isn't something I'm aware of."

Amaryllis quirked an eyebrow. "Very well. Is it your professional opinion that this should be opened in private?"

"The princess isn't known for sending ultimatums, threats, or matters of intrigue in this fashion," the paladin replied.

"I wanna see what it says," I said as I crowded over Amaryllis's shoulder. Awen got onto her tippy-toes to peek over Amaryllis's other side.

Amaryllis sighed, but she edged a talon under the seal all the same and popped it open with a practiced flick. The scroll unrolled itself to reveal a letter written with very pretty calligraphy.

Dear Ladies Albatross and Bristlecone, and Captain Bunch,

I wish to cordially invite you for tea sometime this early evening or, if such isn't convenient to you, sometime tomorrow morning.

Please don't fret. This isn't a grave matter. I merely heard some very interesting stories and wished to speak with those responsible for them. We have at least one mutual friend already, and I'd consider it a wonderful idea if we could become friends ourselves.

If you're unable to attend, then please write back. I'm certain we can arrange something.

Sincerely,

Caprica

"Aww," I said.

"It could be a trap," Amaryllis said.

I scoffed. "It's an invitation for tea and to make friends!"

"Yes, which sounds like exactly the sort of bait I would use if I intended to lay a trap for you," Amaryllis said. "I would be attracted by the political machinations, and Awen . . . Well, honestly, I think she'd come along just because we're going."

"I like tea too," Awen said with just a hint of a pout.

Amaryllis nodded. "Yes, but bait specifically designed for you would involve the kind of machinery that wouldn't be present near a princess, or my sister."

"If it helps, the princess also isn't known for trapping people," the paladin said.

Amaryllis waved the comment off. "You could be on her side. For all we know, you're not even an actual paladin."

The sylph blinked. "Impersonating a paladin is illegal."

"Well, at least you have the right amount of stick up your—"

"I think we should go," I cut in before Amaryllis could say anything too rude. "This Princess Caprica sounds nice, and the friend she mentioned sounds like Bastion. He wouldn't lead us into a trap."

Amaryllis gave me a *look*.

I retaliated with a pout.

"Very well," Amaryllis said. "Sir Paladin, would it be possible for you to lead us over to the princess? The time given in the letter suggests that we should arrive this evening, but we have little else to do at the moment, and we aren't familiar with the quarters where the princess resides."

"Of course, Lady Albatross," the paladin said with another short bow. "Would you like to stop by your inn on the way? It isn't too far from our destination, and it would give you the opportunity to freshen up."

I let out a quick burst of Cleaning magic, then combed my fingers through my hair and straightened my ears. "I'm freshened."

Awen giggled and nodded. "I'm ready too. I don't really have the kind of dress that would be appropriate for tea with me. Ah, unless I wear the same outfit I wore at the ball?"

"Oh, that would be cute," I said. My own outfit was pretty cute too. It wouldn't hurt to get niced up for tea.

Amaryllis shrugged. "If you insist. I'm more comfortable in my current outfit. A dress would get in the way if fighting broke out."

The paladin cleared his throat. "I doubt that there would be any fighting at the palace."

I nodded. "Better to stay in armor, then, just in case."

I don't think he expected me to interpret his words that way, but I knew from experience that when someone said not to expect trouble, that was the ideal time to start expecting trouble.

Taunting fate to have more fun adventures was one of my favorite pastimes, after all. "Too bad we can't bring all of our gear with us," I said.

"I don't think I can bring a repeating crossbow into a palace," Awen said. "It might be seen as an insult—or as a threat."

I nodded. That sounded wise. "So, Mister Paladin, could you guide us over to the princess? Oh, should we tell her that we might be a bit early?"

"I'll dispatch a runner as soon as we arrive near the castle," the paladin said. "Follow me. We'll take the quieter route."

"That's fine by me," I said. A nice walk would be refreshing after the rather heavy conversation we'd had with Reginald. I had a bit of stuff to think about, mostly Rainnewt and his involvement in . . . in . . . Amaryllis's kidnapping, and . . . I couldn't help but remember Amaryllis, bound up by those cervids, disappearing into the swamps. I tried to put it out of my mind and think, but then all I could remember was crying on that bridge.

Rainnewt had caused that, hadn't he? Then the ball, with the explosion. There had been so many nice people screaming, so many innocents hurt.

How could someone just . . . be that way?

No, that wasn't a fair question to ask. Sometimes I wanted to do mean things, too, to be rude and to put others down because—even though I knew better—it felt good to do that. Not good-good, but still . . . a squicky-yucky kind of good. Did Rainnewt feel that when he blew up the ball?

I was probably not the best when it came to philosophy, I knew.

Usually, I only dealt with smaller problems of morality. How to be careful not to tease someone too hard, how to help a friend while still taking care of yourself. Little problems that a bun like me could handle just fine. What Rainnewt was doing was a whole order of magnitude more complicated than what I was used to thinking about.

Actually killing people, and not during some morally grayish thing, like self-defense. He was harming people because . . . I didn't know *why* and I really wanted to. Maybe there was some excuse out there for what he'd done. I didn't know if I'd accept it, but it would be nice to know that the violence and hurting wasn't just senseless.

I did have an inkling of what it might be, but it made me nervous to think about it.

The Evil Roots.

Rainnewt's trick with his false name.

Was it possible that he really was a Riftwalker, like me?

If so, I didn't know why the World picked him of all people.

I felt a bump against my shoulder, and when I looked up, I found Awen looking at me. She had a small smile on, but there was no mistaking the concern in her eyes. "Are you okay, Broc?"

"Oh, yeah, I'm fine," I said.

"Okay," she said. "It's just you're not looking around as much as you usually do, and your ears are all, you know." She brought her hands over her head and loosened her wrists so that they dangled before her.

I tilted my head, ears twitching up. "What did my ears do?"

"They were droopy," she said before she giggled. "They looked sad."

I sniffed. I loved my bun ears, but sometimes they came with quite the disadvantages, like bonking on doorframes and giving away how I was feeling when I didn't mean to worry my friends.

Reaching up, I tugged my ears up by the little tufts on their ends. "There, is that better?" I asked. When I let go, they both flopped right back down like a pair of wet rags.

Awen laughed, and I joined her a moment later. It was kind of funny. The look from the paladin ahead of us only made me laugh harder. After that, my ears actually did perk up.

We were getting a few looks, mostly because we were in a part of the city that had fewer tall homes. Most of the buildings around the walls of what I guessed was the palace were a fair bit smaller and wider. Homes that looked more like small mini-mansions than they did family homes, with gates and fences and small, well-tended gardens out front.

I didn't know enough about sylph fashion to say anything definitive, but I had the impression that the people we were passing were dressed a lot better than the average citizen. Nobles? Or just the upper crust of sylph society, out and about.

"If you don't mind," the paladin said, "we can use one of the more discreet side-gates to enter the palace."

"Certainly," Amaryllis said after I glanced her way. She knew this kind of thing better than I did, so of course I deferred to her.

We were technically still in the Yellow District, but there weren't any more shops or businesses around. I guessed that the area was too small to be worthy of having its own color name, so it was folded into the Yellow District, even though it was mostly residential.

We reached a small road that led right up to a wall. Unlike the much larger city walls, this one was maybe only a floor and a bit high. I could probably leap right over it if I spent a bit of stamina and had a running start.

A gatehouse sat in the wall, flanked by two soldiers in all-black uniforms. They had very strange hats on, part helmet, part fluff, with long crests of purple feathers sticking out the top. A third soldier stood above, protected by a small roof over the gate, and I imagined there were a few more around.

The paladin stepped up to the gate and spoke a few words to the guard next to it, who then turned smartly, stepped to the side, and pulled a cord.

The gate—a big wooden thing with iron bands across it—thunked before opening up from within.

The paladin saluted the guard, who saluted right back, then turned toward us. "Welcome to the Purple Palace."

· Chapter Six ·

Royaltea

The palace was a grand building, long and tall, with carefully laid stone walls and huge windows. Cleanly trimmed hedges encircled it, only broken up where there was an entrance into the mansion-like building. All along the exterior wall were small guard posts, not visible from the outside, where sylphs in uniform were standing at attention in the shade provided by their stations.

"This way," our paladin escort said. He took a sharp turn to the left and led us along a cobbled path around the estate. There were little rock gardens, some more normal flower gardens, and a couple of enclosed greenhouses. The paladin stiffened as we passed one such greenhouse.

I looked past the green glass walls and saw a young sylph girl, maybe a year or two younger than me, staring up from where she was trimming something that looked like a rosebush. I grinned and waved, and she eventually waved back, though she looked confused about it.

"That's Princess Gabriella," the paladin said. "She's the youngest member of the royal family."

"She likes gardening?" I asked.

"Her flower arrangements are admired and often treasured," he said. "Don't repeat it, but she's doted on by the staff and her guardians. She was frail when she was younger. Gardening was an attempt to get her outside to take in some fresh air, and she seems to have taken to it quite well."

"That's cute," I declared.

"This way," the paladin said.

He led us over to one of the side entrances, this one flanked by two more guards wearing plumed hats, halberds by their sides. After speaking with them, they opened the door and let us into a long corridor. There was a long carpet across the length of the room, with tiled floors visible along the edges. Every meter, there was a light sconce, with picture frames between each.

I noticed even more guards at the end of the hall. "There's a lot of guards here," I said.

"It's considered a great honor to be a guard at the royal estate," our guide said. "They receive additional training, as well as additional pay, though the real prize is the right to wear the uniform and crest of the royal family."

I didn't quite get it, but I nodded along and followed as we crossed the length of the corridor, turned at a junction, then came to a stop before a pair of double doors.

The paladin knocked twice. "Guests for Her Royal Highness Princess Caprica," he said.

"Enter!" someone called out from within.

The door opened, and we were ushered into a large, high-ceilinged room. There was a small shelf to one side with some few dozen books, and half the room was taken up by a small stage on which sat a grand piano. The other half was occupied by plump-looking sofas and seats, as well as a small table in the center.

"You're here, wonderful!"

The girl who I assumed was Princess Caprica stood with the grace I'd expect from a princess. She wasn't wearing a very princess-y outfit, though. Instead, she wore a uniform not too dissimilar from the one I'd seen soldiers wearing. It looked like it was made of a finer cut, and instead of being the same black as all the other uniforms I'd seen, this one was a deep, near-burgundy red.

"Hello!" I said with a cheery wave.

The princess approached us and paused a meter or so away from me. She stared at all three of us before chuckling. "It's a pleasure to meet you. I'm Princess Caprica, but please, just call me Caprica."

"In that case," I said. "I'm Broccoli. Let's be friends!"

```
Caprica Buttercup Sylph

Desired Quality: Someone who will accept her for who she
is—another romantic soul

  Dream: To marry her crush and live a long, happy life
```

"Hello," Awen said next. "I'm Awen."

"And I'm Amaryllis," Amaryllis said. "It's a pleasure."

Caprica nodded, almost a short bow. "It is! I hope you don't mind, but I suspect I know more about you than you do about me. Unless Bastion said anything?"

I shook my head. "Nope, he didn't speak too much about his work with the royal family." Actually, I could remember him telling me a story about one of the princesses breaking his foot, but that sounded a little embarrassing. "How come you know about us?"

"Oh, nothing sinister. Bastion handed in his report, and I had a quick peek at it. But come, let's sit down. There's tea being brewed as we speak, and the staff make excellent little pastries."

Caprica led us over to the seats, leaving a larger sofa for us while she sat primly on the edge of a seat opposite.

"So, what did the report say?" Amaryllis asked. "I have to admit to a certain level of curiosity."

"Oh, I can imagine," Caprica said. "I have never been exactly keen on gossip—that's the purview of some of my sisters more than myself—but I can't imagine not being curious about a document that mentions me."

I nodded along. Caprica seemed very nice so far. A bit excitable? She still had the poise and bearing of a noble lady, but it felt like she was brimming with excitement under the surface. She was bouncing on her seat, sitting right on the edge, and her wings were fluttering every so often. Quite the opposite of Awen, who was more of a born introvert, and certainly nothing like Amaryllis, who was all sharp and rough on the outside with a soft, squishy inside.

"I hope Bastion didn't exaggerate our adventures," I said.

"Oh! I hope he did. The report was a little light, owing to the limited time spent on it, I suppose, but it was positively terrifying to read. I can't imagine Bastion facing so many challengers, and you with him, of course," Caprica said.

I nodded. "He's a great friend. We were lucky that he was there with us."

"He is pretty great," Caprica said.

"Have you known him for long?" Amaryllis asked.

Caprica shifted on her seat. "Oh, for some time now. He was mostly attached to my older sister when I was a little younger. He's always been someone I admire, of course." She smiled demurely, but I didn't miss the faint blush touching her cheeks.

"You called us over for tea—are there any tea-drinking traditions in Goldenalden?" I asked. It would be nice to know, but I also wanted to shift the subject just a notch. It would be embarrassing to be caught bragging about our adventures.

"Oh, nothing too complicated, I don't think," Caprica said.

Tea arrived, served by a pair of sylph ladies in maid outfits who set a tray down on the table between us and then poured us four cups of fragrant tea. They left some honey on the table, next to cream and milk in little porcelain saucers.

"Thank you," I said as I took a cup and breathed it in.

Mountain berry and sweet leaf tea. Steeped overnight and served with aged honey. Professionally brewed. Provides a boost of energy and assists in stamina regeneration.

"Oh, this is great," I said as I took a sip. It was sweet, even without the honey. The honey did help, smoothing it. "Do you think I could buy some sweet leaves?"

"You recognized the tea leaves from just a taste?" Caprica asked. "That's impressive."

"Oh, I have a Tea Making skill," I said. "It's great for making good tea. A big part of my, ah, build is about buffing and helping make new friends."

Caprica laughed. "That's excellent. I don't think you'll find many people here who have skills like that. We tend to have a more martial focus, though you will find some excellent craftsylphs. My littlest sister is considering dipping her toes into potion making, for example."

"Oh, that does sound nice," I said. "What's your class? Mine's Cinnamon Bun Bun."

One of Caprica's eyebrows rose. "You didn't inspect me on entering?"

"Isn't that impolite?"

"Oh, it is, but that hardly stops people." Caprica said. "But if you want permission, then you have it."

I grinned and fired off my Insight skill at her.

An Indomitable Bastion, sylph level ??. Intrigued.

I blinked. "Your class is Bastion?"

"It is," she said quite demurely. "It's a respectable though uncommon class. Mostly, it means that I'm quite hard to move when I don't want to be moved. I think a few of my siblings have some unkind things to say about the hardness of my head, for example."

"That's a neat class!" I decided. "I bet you're tough in a fight."

"I can stand on my own, though there hasn't been too much fighting in my life. Being a princess doesn't lend itself to many life-or-death battles. Though, from what I understand, two of you are noble ladies in your own right, and you certainly haven't shied away from any fights."

"We've been in our share of scraps," Amaryllis said. "Though I wouldn't call any of us expert fighters or combatants."

"Yeah," I agreed. "Fighting isn't usually any fun. It's all scary, and you spend more time worrying about your friends and thinking you might get hurt rather than enjoying it. There's stuff that's fun around it, though. It's nice to be able to really trust your friends with your life, and exploring dungeons is super cool. I've seen places and things that I'd never have seen if I hadn't taken the risk."

"Interesting," Caprica said. "I never really had too many opportunities to go out and explore on my own, or in a small group, like that. I must admit to a certain amount of envy."

"Aw, I'm sorry. I didn't mean to bring things up that way," I said.

She waved the comment off. "It's entirely fine," she said. "So! Bastion's report didn't mention why your group flew all the way to Sylphfree. Though I imagine it has something to do with the summit coming up."

Amaryllis nodded. "Indeed. We're here to deliver a few letters. The usual political riffraff."

I blinked. That didn't sound entirely right. Was Amaryllis doing something?

"Speaking of, what do you know about the summit? We might attend, especially if there's still room for a few extra people to be present," Amaryllis continued.

"Honestly, not all that terribly much," Caprica said. "My interests tend to lie more on the military side of things, which I know has had some small changes as of late. But I can't say that I'm well versed with the political side. Some of my brothers care about that a lot more than I do."

"We're a bit worried," I said. "That's why we came."

"Worried?" Caprica asked.

I nodded. "Yeah. A lot of the nations on Dirt, or this part of it anyway, seem to maybe be thinking of fighting each other. A war would be terrible."

Caprica shook her head. "No one would be foolish enough to challenge Sylphfree in an open war."

Amaryllis snorted. "Some harpies would be eager to do just that, and the cervid outnumber any force Sylphfree could muster ten to one. Your nation has an impressive military, but only when viewed in a vacuum. I think a war on the scale now possible would be a disaster for everyone involved."

Caprica looked genuinely confused. She took a slow sip from her tea while considering it. "Maybe I have been a little naive," she said. "I suppose it's easy to believe stories about your own nation's greatness."

"I'm impressed you can look past that so easily," Amaryllis said.

"I happen to know that a lot of the stories that are spread around are quite inaccurate. You wouldn't believe what people think of the royal family. It's almost as if my siblings and I can do no wrong, according to some. They've never seen little Gabrielle sick or my father trip over a loose bit of rug."

I laughed at the mental image of a fancy king losing his crown to a crooked carpet. "I guess not. We should talk about nicer things, though! Being all sad isn't any fun."

· Chapter Seven ·

Okay-Authoritarian

Any plans now that you're in Goldenalden?" Caprica asked. She leaned forward and set her teacup down with a faint clink of porcelain on porcelain.

"We have a few," Amaryllis said. "Mostly, in order to see where everyone stands, we want to speak with the representatives of each nation attending the summit. Otherwise, I think Broccoli wants to play tourist a little."

"And we promised to clean up the local Exploration Guild!" I added. "Oh! Actually, that reminds me. Bastion told me something and I kinda forgot all about it."

"Oh?" Caprica asked.

I nodded. "Yeah, he mentioned that there was a library in the capital that could help with skill-related stuff."

"Do you have issues with that?" Caprica asked.

"A bit? I got a new skill called Proportion Distortion, and I don't exactly know what it does or how to train it. I'd like to know if it's useful at all before investing in it," I said. "I did receive some less than useful skills before, so I'm hoping that this one isn't like that. Actually, that's another thing I'd like to look into: how to get rid of terribly unfair, no-good skills." Like Adorable, but I wasn't about to admit to that skill aloud.

"Proportion Distortion. Can't say I've ever heard of that skill," Caprica said. "The library is open until decently late, and it's only barely noon. If you want, I could escort you over. Perhaps we can grab something to eat on the way? I rarely have an excuse to try food outside the palace."

"You'd do that?" I asked.

"Of course! As long as you tell me more stories about your adventures with Bastion," she said. "Besides, the library won't give you trouble if I'm there."

"Is it a private establishment?" Amaryllis asked.

Caprica shook her head. "Technically, it's entirely public. But the librarians are quite jealous of their books and institution. They tend to show ruffians the door if they're too noisy, and they might not offer to help some-one who they think looks . . . bizarre."

I glanced at my friends, then up to the ears hovering on the edge of my vision. "Yeah, we probably don't look like the most normal bunch, do we?"

Caprica giggled. "I'm sure Bastion didn't think of that. He's a great sylph, but on occasion, he forgets the impact that a paladin has on the citizenry."

"What kind of impact is that?" I asked.

"People tend to be on their best behavior around a paladin. Not just because of their abilities as law-enforcement, though I suppose that is a factor, but also because . . . there's a certain romanticism about paladins. Those like Bastion—who tend to embody every part of that ideal—most of all."

That made some sense. If he was a respected person, then people would treat him with respect, and he might not notice that those same people weren't treating others the same way.

I could remember people who were popular and had lots of friends fail-ing to notice those who had none, because to them, it was normal to have a lot of friends.

I glanced at Amaryllis and Awen and noted that they were both done with their tea. "Well then, maybe we should head out? We can talk on the way, and I bet you know all the best places to eat in Goldenalden."

"I know a few good spots," Caprica said. She stood and tugged her coat's lapels on tighter. "Do you ladies mind waiting? My station doesn't afford me the ability to leave on just a moment's notice."

"That's fine," I said.

Caprica smiled and walked off toward the room's exit. The guards there were so quiet and had moved so little that I only noticed them now that one reached out to open the door for Caprica.

"She's pretty nice," I said to my friends, voice low enough that we wouldn't be overheard. We weren't saying anything mean, but it was still a bit rude to talk about someone when they weren't around, even if it was mostly to compliment them.

"She's strange," Amaryllis said.

Awen stifled a giggle. "Strange? I think she's okay. She seems to, ah, really like Bastion."

"Yeah, to get a whole class with one of your friend's names in it, that's something," I said.

Awen's cheeks reddened and she nodded. "I think, ah, well, it's none of our business, I guess. Maybe she's being nice because she's jealous?"

"I don't think being jealous usually leads people toward people being nice," I said.

"No, no, she's, ah, is it envious? Right, she's envious that we spent a lot of time with Bastion, so now she's being nice to us so that she can find out what happened when we were with him," Awen said.

"That is strange," I said. "Then again, I'd love to make friends with my friend's friends, if they had any."

"Somehow, I feel insulted, but I'm not entirely sure why," Amaryllis said.

Caprica returned, now wearing a coat over her uniform-like outfit. "I'm ready to head out. I hope the presence of a guard doesn't distract you?"

"Of course not," I said as I bounced to my feet, then turned to help my friends up. "What kind of street food is there around here?"

"You won't find much in the Purple District," Caprica said. "But farther south, there should be a few places where we can grab a bite. Street vendors are considered a bit crass, but they need to submit to frequent inspections, so there's little to worry about."

"Huh. Yeah. So far, Sylphfree feels very . . . rule-heavy, and street food is, like, the opposite of that?"

"How is street food anti-authoritarian?" Amaryllis asked.

"Well, it's kind of messy but it tastes good," I said.

Amaryllis rolled her eyes. "You're entirely nonsensical at times, I swear."

Laughing, I wrapped an arm around her wing, then turned toward Caprica. "Let's go? You can tell us about the city on the way. We haven't had time to do all the tourist things yet."

"Certainly."

When Caprica mentioned that she would need an escort, I was thinking something along the lines of a chaperone. Maybe that paladin whose name I never caught who delivered her letter to us at the guild.

I wasn't expecting to follow Caprica—who was making small talk about the palace and its various additions over time—to the main entrance hall of the palace, where a squad of soldiers was waiting.

"Oh, you're here already," Caprica said to the soldier that looked like she was in charge.

"Ready when you are, ma'am," was her quick reply.

I didn't see that many girl soldiers around, but half of this little unit had girls in it. Maybe that made sense—if they were going overboard with the protection like this, then they'd probably insist on following Caprica to the washroom and such.

It was a bit much in my opinion, but maybe the streets of Goldenalden were a lot more dangerous than I expected them to be.

Caprica had to prepare a few things quickly, mostly involving instructions to serving staff while my friends and I and the soldiers waited around. At least the lobby was quite nice, with tile walls all delicately placed to create pretty patterns that rose up to the arched ceiling above. It was more artful decoration than I was used to seeing in Goldenalden.

"All done," Caprica said as she returned to us. She tugged on a coat around her shoulders, the fur inside looking nice and soft. "Shall we?"

"Sure!" I said. "Lead the way."

We stepped out into chilly weather. Big, lazy snowflakes fell from above, and the wind, though weak, had some bite to it.

"Snow!" I cheered. I bounced up and caught a flake on the tip of my tongue. "I haven't seen snow in forever."

The wind was carrying great white sheets across the mountainside, some of it rolling up and toward the peak of the mountain on which the capital hung.

"It's always a bit colder up here," Caprica said. "We're a ways to the north, and we're high off the ground as well."

"It's pleasant," Amaryllis said. "The Nesting Kingdom often has to deal with cooler winds and snow, though we have the warmer wind from out west to keep things mostly mild in the warmer seasons."

"It's c-cold," Awen said.

I spun toward her to find my friend hugging herself and looking even paler than usual. "Oh no," I said before I moved to her side and wrapped an arm around her back. "You poor thing."

"Is she well?" Caprica asked. "I can give you my coat. The staff will throw a snit over my being outside without a coat, but I'm quite used to the chill."

"A-ah, it's just, um, colder than I'm used to," Awen said. Her coat wasn't made of a material suited to the environment. It was more of a windbreaker in that way, and the little bit of armor she wore likely wasn't helping.

I nodded. "We should find you a blanket before we get too far. Caprica, I don't mean to impose, but do you think there's a spare blanket around?"

"I'd be quite surprised if there wasn't at least one in the entire palace," Caprica said. "Although, Lady Awen, do you know any Fire magic?"

"Ah, not really? Enough to light a candle?"

Amaryllis huffed a "I'll handle this" huff and walked over to Awen. "Give me your hands. Caprica's likely thinking of a simple warming spell. There are a few that we use in the Nesting Kingdom."

"Can you apply that on someone else?" I asked.

"There are some that are mostly used to keep little chicks warm," Amaryllis said. "They're perfectly safe, though the spell will wear off in a few hours."

Amaryllis took Awen's hands, and there was an exchange of magic that I could only barely feel. Awen let out a gasp, and her cheeks flushed. "Oh, that's nice."

"You'll have to teach me that spell." I said.

"You seem to be handling the cold well enough," Amaryllis said.

"Well, yeah, I'm from a cold place. This is nice and comfy weather, but I still want to learn that spell. Imagine getting a hug from someone, and then you feel all warm and cozy inside?" I clenched my fist, a new determination filling me. "It would bring me one step closer to perfecting the hug."

Caprica giggled demurely. "How determined. Are you an expert at hugging, then?"

I shook my head. I wasn't an expert. I was nowhere near as talented as someone like Momma. "Not yet. But I'll get there one day. Which means lots of practicing on my friends."

Awen laughed. "I don't mind. Hugs are nice."

Amaryllis sniffed, but she didn't deny the obvious truth.

We walked out of the front gate, a group of guards opening the path for us. "I hope you don't mind walking all the way to the library?" Caprica asked. "We could get a coach, but the fastest route is through a few narrow roads. And stretching my legs would be nice."

"Sure," I said. My friends didn't seem to mind either.

"So, your hugging, did you try that on Bastion?" Caprica asked. "I can't imagine his being, ah, willing to do that kind of thing."

"Huh? Of course I've hugged him. He's a bit stiff, but he's not too bad."

"You . . . you did?"

"A couple of times," I said. "He was a member of the *Beaver Cleaver*'s crew. We're all very close, you know."

Amaryllis shook her head, talon over her face in the way she did when I said something silly without realizing it. "So, which direction is this library in?" she asked.

"Oh? Ah, yes," Caprica said. She seemed a little bit flustered. "This way."

And so, with the princess in the lead, we took off toward the grand library, a trail of soldiers behind us like orderly ducklings.

· Chapter Eight ·

Fortress of Knowledge

T his is it," Caprica said. "It's not the most impressive of buildings from the exterior, but the library has been a part of Goldenalden since its very founding. It was actually the second building commissioned by my great-great-grandfather after the construction of the royal palace, not that the palace from back then would be at all recognizable today."

I gawked at the library—it seemed like the polite thing to do. The building was, unlike most of the other buildings in Goldenalden, still clearly part of the mountain. Stone rose up around it on all sides but the front, as if someone had turned the mountainside into wet clay and pressed an entire edifice out of it.

The front was different, made of large stone slabs stacked together and with a pair of colonnades next to a large doorway. There were windows, too, but they were the thin, slitted sort that I'd seen on castles before, not the wider windows you'd expect to see.

"It looks a bit strange," I said. Especially compared to the far more ordinary buildings surrounding it.

"The library was built at a time when Sylphfree was still very much plagued by dragons and their offspring," Caprica said. "It was designed to be a repository for crucial knowledge, books, maps, and scrolls. I think it served as a school once, too, for young nobles."

"Was it meant to be hidden?" Awen asked. "The rocks look like they were moved by a geomancer, maybe. I've seen places that look a little like that before. The ostri build huts out in the desert near Mattergrove the same way, though those aren't as big."

Caprica nodded. "The ostri are the desert folk, right? I imagine that this is somewhat similar. And yes, the building would be hard to see from above if it weren't placed in the middle of the city. Thick stone walls, decent natural camouflage. It was all designed so that a creature flying above wouldn't notice it. I do believe that, at the time, the paladins—the Order being much smaller four or five generations ago—were skilled with magics that allowed them to hide better as well."

"So the library was hidden in plain sight," I said.

"More or less. Come on, it should be open at this hour."

We followed Caprica into the library, some of her guards forming up next to the entrance both inside and out.

I was expecting the interior of the library to be fairly fancy. Maybe some big room, with plenty of lighting, but instead it was relatively cramped within. Thick walls and lots of small rooms except for a big stairwell right in the center, where stone steps led up and to the floors above.

A counter to the side had a nice librarian sylph behind it, perusing a big tome that looked like it was filled with names and addresses and the names of books. A system to tell who had taken out which book, maybe?

"Hello," Caprica said as she walked up to the counter.

The lady behind it stared with wide eyes. "P-princess," she said. "It's a pleasure to meet you. How can I help?"

Caprica smiled. "I have a few guests here, friends from . . . well, all over, really. We were looking for some information. Ah, Captain Bunch?"

"If you're a friend, you should really be calling me Broccoli," I chided softly. "Then I can keep calling you Caprica, because if I'm your friend, then you're my friend too."

Caprica's cheeks actually warmed a little, which I found very cute, but I wasn't about to tell her that because it was far too rude. "Thank you, Broccoli."

"Ah, very well then. What is the captain looking for?" the librarian asked.

I leaned on the counter, a big grin on. "I was told that the library here had a sort of record of all the classes and skills."

"We hardly know all of them," the librarian said. "But we do keep a record of both."

"Neat! I got a skill recently that I was wondering about. I don't really know what it does, or even what I did to get it. Could you help me?"

"Are you looking to merge it into something better, or do you just want to know what the skill does?" she asked.

"Uh," I said.

Caprica laughed demurely. "I think perhaps we can look at both options. What was the exact name of the skill again?"

"Proportion Distortion," I said. "The description only says that it can help me fit in and out, which is very vague."

"That is rather on the vague side," the librarian said. She pulled out a notepad and scribbled something on it. "I'm afraid that I'm not the most qualified to assist you. Forgive me. But there is an archivist on the second floor, the blue room. He should be able to assist you and is more familiar with the stacks, besides."

"Thank you!" I said.

"Awa, is there a section of the library with, um, blueprints and mechanical things?" Awen asked.

"Those would be in different sections," the librarian said. "But I can help you find both."

I turned toward Amaryllis. "Are you going to look for something too?"

"I don't have anything I need in particular here, though I wouldn't mind perusing, if that's permissible. Or perhaps I can look at whatever spells they have publicly available here." Amaryllis's eyebrows rose. "Actually, disregard that. I'll come with you, Broccoli. If this archivist knows anything about skills, they might know of some skills that I could merge to help me reach my goal."

"You mean your goal to turn people into meat puppets?"

"Please, please don't call it that," Amaryllis said.

We started up the stairs, only one of the guards following us from a slight distance. "Meat puppets?" Caprica asked with an amount of concern that was probably warranted.

"Amaryllis has a cool Puppeteer class," I explained. "She can control puppets really well."

"I'm still far from skilled enough to call anything I do with the art proficient," Amaryllis said.

"Puppetry is an interesting hobby," Caprica said. I had the impression that she really didn't care all that much but was being nice anyway.

"Anyway, Amaryllis's main class is electricity-based, and people's nerves use electrical currents to signal their muscles to move, so she's combining the two to make spells that allow her to puppet people's bodies with magic."

Caprica blinked, then stared at Amaryllis.

"It was an idea I had," Amaryllis dismissed. "It's still very experimental."

"That sounds quite terrifying," Caprica said.

"It's of limited use for now," Amaryllis admitted. "I think most strong combatants would be able to work around it. Some magics counter it entirely, and it doesn't prevent a spellcaster from casting spells, not unless they still need to gesture to cast. That's not counting adversaries with strange biology. We frequently run into bizarre creatures in dungeons where my skills would go to waste."

"Yeah, but then you can just blast them with lightning. That usually works too," I said.

"True," Amaryllis replied. "The Puppeteer class is meant to be used as more of a force multiplier. If I can control someone's body, then I can take them out of the fight with far less effort. Its greatest advantage, I imagine, is in subterfuge and from a more psychological perspective."

"I see," Caprica said. "Is everyone in your crew quite so fearsome?"

I laughed. "No, of course not! I only have Cleaning magic going for me, and some weird bun martial arts. Awen mostly uses her mechanic's skills to fix and use her crossbows. I think she's still working on her Glass magic. We're not actually all that focused on fighting and stuff."

"I suppose that's one of the advantages of being more exploration focused. Though from the reports Bastion filed, you were in quite a few high-risk adventures."

"Not that many," I dismissed. "We had entire days go past where nothing happened."

The archivist's room wasn't too hard to find. Not only did it have a colored door, there was also a plaque next to it that read The Archivist, which was very handy. Grinning, I stepped up to the door and knocked twice. "Hello!"

My ears twitched as I heard some shuffling on the other side before the door opened. A man stood there, a sylph who was on the shorter side, with rumpled robes and a big scowl on. He adjusted his glasses and fired off a glare at the three of us. "Yes?" he snapped.

"Hi! I'm Broccoli, and I was told that we could find the archivist here? For skill stuff?"

"'For skill stuff,'" he repeated before scoffing. "Let me guess: one of you three unlocked some skill you've never heard of in your short, poorly educated lives, and now you think to bother me about it?"

"I mean, essentially, yes," I said. "I got a new skill, and I have no idea what it is or does, and I was told that the people here could help?"

"Then search the stacks. That's assuming you're literate at all?"

This man was being very rude, but it wasn't nice to be rude back to someone, even if it might feel better in the moment. "I think all three of us are able to read, yes," I said. "But if we weren't, then we'd still ask you for help. It's not fair to discriminate against people like that."

"Ah yes, because why would I discriminate against a bun and a harpy of all things?" he asked.

A hand grabbed my shoulder, and I half turned to find Caprica smiling past me while carefully pushing me aside. "Hello, sir," she said. "As I understand it, you're unwilling to assist these two?"

The archivist frowned. "They hardly look like they belong here, do they?"

"I see. Thank you for your time, then," she said before turning. "Come on, the library is technically run off the royal coffers. I'm certain that the head librarian will make time for a quick visit."

The archivist snorted. "Are you done bothering me, then?"

"You wouldn't happen to know if the head librarian is in, would you?" Caprica asked.

"If he is, I doubt he'd want to speak with . . ." He paused to stare at Amaryllis and me. "Ruffians."

Caprica nodded, then she turned to the soldier waiting behind us on the top of the steps. Judging by the way the archivist blinked, he hadn't noticed them. "Could you inform the head librarian of my upcoming visit? A minute's warning is better than none."

"Yes, Princess," the soldier said before doing an about-face and running off.

"Princess?" the archivist asked, his voice losing some of its surety.

"Yes," Caprica said. "I was escorting these diplomats around, showing them the great luxuries of Goldenalden, when one had a question that we thought an archivist like yourself could answer."

"Oh," he said. "Well, I'm certain I can answer any question."

Caprica looked very unimpressed. "I think you've answered plenty of questions," she said. "Captain Broccoli, Lady Amaryllis, if you wouldn't mind following me, I'm certain we can get everything sorted out in no time at all. I'm very sorry for this entire thing. You don't deserve such treatment."

"It's okay?" I said as I followed after her. Had that entire thing been . . . speciesism? I reached up and tugged at one of my ears. I'd been told I couldn't do things because I was a girl before, but never because I had big ears and a tail. "He was very rude," I said, even though I knew that the archivist could probably still hear me. It felt very . . . vindictive.

"I'm sorry," Caprica said. "I wish people weren't like that. Once we find the head librarian, I'm sure we can sort everything out."

"It's fine," Amaryllis said. "I think we expected to run into this kind of treatment at some point while being here."

Caprica's frown suggested that she was very much not pleased with that answer.

· Chapter Nine ·

Chivalry Isn't Dead

The second archivist we met was a whole lot friendlier than the first. A bit too friendly, maybe?

Not that I believed that someone could be too friendly, but they were . . . nervously friendly. Like they knew they might get into trouble if they didn't act nice, so any niceness they did have didn't feel quite as genuine as it could have been. It reminded me of talking to a salesperson in a store. The smiles weren't fake, but they weren't entirely real either.

"Proportion Distortion," the archivist said as they walked through the stacks, their eyes roaming over the bindings of the books above them. The shelves were taller than I was used to, but then again, the sylphs could fly, so it made sense they'd build without worrying about height. "Ah." They reached up and tugged a book out from a high shelf and then opened it on the spot, pages flipping by as they skimmed through the tome. "Yes, this is it."

We returned to a quieter table in a corner of the library illuminated by a magical, flameless lamp and one of those tall slit-windows. Caprica, Amaryllis, and I squeezed in around the table while the archivist laid the book down in front of us.

"This section right over here, Captain," they said, a finger tapping at the page they'd opened to. "This is an older text. It hasn't been reformatted to the current standard. I can explain some of it, if you wish."

I leaned forward to read.

Proportion Distortion. A skill thus far associated with a few rare stealth, infiltration, and entertainment classes. At the lower ranks (Novice to Apprentice), the skill seems to lend a certain amount of flexibility to the user. This flexibility mostly functions when the skill holder is attempting to enter a small location or pass by a small obstruction.

This skill tends to be notably less useful than a skill like Enhanced Flexibility, especially as the conditions to trigger it are more specific.

Uniquely, the skill has a social component, assisting the user in appearing to be part of any group they are attempting to join or infiltrate or entertain. This is difficult to assess and test, but it is a noted, if minor, advantage of the skill and may be why more assassination-inclined classes have access to it.

At higher ranks (Disciple and above), the skill allows the user to enlarge or reduce themselves in size. The user's weight remains constant, but they literally become larger or smaller at the expense of a constant drain of magical energy. Useful for infiltration, and an ability that can be used in combat to some effect.

"Whoa," I said. That sounded really neat. I could do without the whole assassination stuff, but the . . . I guess it was a buff to social stuff was nice, and being able to make myself bigger or smaller sounded super neat.

"That's such a Broccoli skill," Amaryllis said.

"Well, it's from one of my classes."

"I meant more in the sense that it looks like a waste of a skill, but I'm certain you'll find a way to use it to its full potential," Amaryllis said.

I grinned over at her. "I can try," I said. Reaching down, I turned the page, but there didn't seem to be anything more about the skill except for a long list of what I guessed were references. "Huh, there's nothing on how to train the skill."

Caprica reached up and cupped her cheek, an elbow on the table. "Usually, that comes from using the skill. Though in this case, I can see how it would be a difficult skill to practice."

I nodded. "Well, I can always try squeezing into small places. That doesn't sound too hard."

```
Proportion Distortion
E - 29%
```

The skill had already gotten a bit of experience, though rank E was usually very easy to fill up. I guessed that it was more the social aspect of the skill that was getting me that experience. I couldn't recall squishing into anything, except maybe for a few shorter sylph-made doorways.

"If I may," the archivist said. "You might consider practicing in some dungeons that are known for having confined, tight spaces. It's been noted that training in a situation where the person is challenged tends to produce much greater results."

"Broccoli's leveling speed is genuinely incredible," Amaryllis said. "She went from basically nothing to catching up to me in a little over two months. I blame her lack of self-preservation."

"Hey now!" I said.

Amaryllis huffed an "I'm just tugging your tail" kind of huff.

"Are there any other skills that you have questions about?" the archivist asked.

"Well . . ." I trailed off.

The archivist gave me a smile that was clearly trying to be encouraging.

"Uh . . . since we're here, and you don't seem to mind answering, I . . ." I paused, glancing at Amaryllis, but she merely looked perplexed, so I turned back to the archivist and took a deep breath. "This is embarrassing, but do you know of any good skills that can combine with Adorable to get rid of it. Please?"

I noticed one of Caprica's eyebrows rising, but she didn't comment, which was great. My cheeks felt warm just from admitting I had that no-good skill.

"On the topic of unfortunate skills," Amaryllis added, "I have, of all things, Huffing." She huffed very nicely to prove it. "I don't imagine there's something that can combine neatly with that?"

The archivist stood and bowed quickly. "I'll be right back. We happen to have a lot of resources for combinable skills. Are there any others you want me to search for?"

I shook my head, and Amaryllis did the same.

"You two seem to have some fairly unique skill sets," Caprica said.

"Really? I think we mostly just have skills that we picked up along the way. I was never one for min-maxing or anything like that," I said.

"We have been in some relatively dangerous situations. I think we've faced, what was it, four dungeons in the last month?"

I frowned. Had it been that many? "We did some other stuff too."

"Ah yes, our other activities, such as visiting small, hostile dungeons, negotiating with dragons, beating up a gang, fighting pirates, and getting shot at with lasers."

I laughed, and then had to explain to a curious Caprica that our adventures really had been pretty tame so far. Amaryllis argued the opposite, but Amaryllis liked arguing.

"I've brought anything I could find," the archivist said as they returned, this time with a stack of tomes that they dropped onto the edge of the table with a heavy thump. "Forgive me, I didn't expect it to take quite so long, but both skills are rather uncommon, and it took a moment to draw up a list."

I blinked as the archivist set down two pages onto the table. One was labeled "Adorable," the other "Huffing."

"Did you write all of that while you were gone?" I asked as I picked the page up. A short list was on it.

"Library magic makes cross-referencing works relatively easy," they said.

I set the page down and leaned over it.

The Adorable skill has been noted to combine with the following skills to produce the following result:
Adorable merged with Romancing creates the Friendzone skill.

"What's the Friendzone skill do?" I asked.
Caprica choked.
"The Friendzone skill passively increases romantic attention, but also makes it actively easier for the skill holder to reject that kind of advance. It can also provide a buff in a zone around them to anyone who considers the holder a friend. It's a skill frequently held by courtesans. Did you want to read the full reports on the skill?"
I hummed. Not something I really needed, then. It wasn't like people were frequently attracted to me that way. Besides, I had a lot of buff skills already. "I think I'm okay, thanks."

Adorable merged with both an Unarmed Combat Proficiency or a martial art skill and a Homemaking skill creates the Wai-fu skill.

Another strange martial art? Well, I had Way of the Mystic Bun already, so I probably didn't need this one.

Adorable merged with Book Smart creates the Adorkable Skill.

"What's the Adorkable skill?" I asked.
"It makes the user seem more attractive, especially when they're working on something they're passionate about, usually an academic subject," the archivist said. "It's common enough with librarians and archivists who are more socially inclined."
Not what I was looking for either. Then again, I wasn't sure what I was looking for to begin with. Something better and more useful than Adorable. Something I could be properly proud of!

Adorable merged with intimidation-based skills creates the Ador-ifying skill.

Nope.

Adorable merged with Door Making Proficiency creates A-door-able.

Too silly.

Adorable merged with Persuasion creates Mystic Eyes of Puppy Dogs.

That was just weird.

Adorable merged with a chivalry-based skill and a leadership-based skill creates Dork Knight.

My hand slammed into the table, and I jumped to my feet. Everyone startled, but I could apologize later. "That's perfect," I said. "What's the Dork Knight skill do?"

"Ah," the archivist said. They shuffled through the books and opened one up before paging through it in a hurry. "Dork Knight. It's an uncommon skill—we only have two examples on record to pull from. The skill seems to focus mostly on assisting the user with chivalrous actions. They tend to be unaffiliated, and somewhat difficult to read."

"So it's like a dark and mysterious knight skill," I said.

"I'm quite certain that's exactly what it isn't," Amaryllis said.

I decided to ignore her. I was allowed to dream, darn it. "What's a chivalry-based skill?"

"Certain sets of skills are broadly folded into a wider category," the archivist said. "In this case, there are dozens of skills centered around chivalrous and knightly actions. Chivalry is one, Paladin's Chivalry is another, then there are knightly orders with their own unique skills. Chivalry of the Paladins of the World is a nearly unique skill that still shares most of its traits with the Chivalry skill."

"Oh, that makes sense. So it's like Swordplay Proficiency and Sword Fighting Proficiency."

The archivist nodded. "Two skills that are, for the most part, identical, but with slight differences in execution or use. Your example would both fit under the Sword Proficiency, for example. Some careers ask that a person have a skill that fits within a broader category. Librarians obviously need some sort of book-related skill, but whether that's Book Smart or Book Learning Proficiency doesn't truly matter."

I nodded along. It made sense, if only so that people didn't have to have big lists of applicable skills. "So how do I get a chivalry-based skill?"

The archivist shuffled through their books again, but they answered while searching. "Broadly speaking, such a skill will probably come from focused, continuous action."

"So I need to be real chivalrous for a while," I said.

"Exactly."

I grinned. "That sounds perfect."

"Oh, World," Amaryllis muttered.

"Now, what's chivalry?"

Caprica giggled, a hand pressed over her mouth to keep her mirth in. "Oh, you are wonderful, Captain Bunch. Chivalry is the way a knight or soldier should act. It's a code, basically. A promise to act with courtesy and kindness, to uphold justice, to help the weak, and to act with honor above all else."

I blinked. "But that's just being nice. How can being nice be a skill?"

"The skill presumably helps the skill holder act accordingly," Caprica said. "It helps knights pick the just option."

"But . . . I mean, some situations make it hard to know what the right thing is, but most of the time, it's just the right thing to do."

Amaryllis reached over and pat me on the head. "Not everyone has the same moral fiber as you, Broccoli."

"My morals aren't complicated. Just be nice to everyone and treat everybody fairly. It's not hard."

"Sure, sure," Amaryllis dismissed.

There had to be more to this chivalry thing than just being nice. "Does Bastion have a chivalry skill?" I asked.

"I would imagine that he does, yes," Caprica said.

"Well then, I'll just ask him how he got it, and then I'll do the same thing."

· Chapter Ten ·

Knight of the Feather Duster

After you, ma'am," I said as I opened the door before my friends.

Awen curtsied, as she had done at every other door I opened for her, and Amaryllis rolled her eyes, also as she had been doing all morning.

After leaving Caprica at the entrance of the library the day before, I had started practicing my chivalry. That meant opening doors for ladies, helping them sit down, and also fighting monsters. So far, I was two for three in the chivalry department, and I was sure we'd have to fight some sort of monster eventually.

"You know, this isn't going to work," Amaryllis said.

"It *probably* won't work," I said. "Which doesn't mean it will never work, just that it's somewhat unlikely to work. Unlikely isn't impossible . . . ma'am."

Amaryllis huffed a mighty huff. "Stop calling me ma'am."

"I think it's cute," Awen said. "Broccoli's not doing anything mean."

"Opening doors and being courteous isn't mean, no, but it's annoying when it's coming from Broccoli," Amaryllis said. "Besides, I can open my own doors, thank-you-very-much."

"I would never imply that you can't, ma'am," I replied.

Awen giggled while Amaryllis fumed quietly.

I'd started practicing chivalry the night before, and so far I hadn't gotten a skill for it. But I did get a lot of innocent fun teasing Amaryllis by being too nice to her, so that was a plus. I figured I could keep it up for a little bit. Being chivalrous was basically being nice with extra steps, and that sounded just peachy to me.

"Are you going to open the door to the guild too?" Amaryllis asked sometime later as we arrived at the front of the Goldenalden Exploration Guild. The place still looked as rough as it had the day before.

"I certainly will, my lady," I said before bowing at the waist to Amaryllis.

She crossed her arms and pouted while Awen laughed next to her. "You don't know how to bow," Awen said.

"I don't?"

She shook her head, then smiled as I opened the door for her. "I'll show you later."

"Please don't," Amaryllis said.

"Ah, hello!"

Reginald was standing in the lobby, along with a sylph that I didn't recognize but who was obviously some sort of journalist. He had a small cap on, with a feather sticking out of it, and he had a notepad tucked into one of the pockets of his ink-stained coat. A bag sat by his feet, big and lumpy, with the flashbulb of a camera sticking out of the top of it. The journalist nodded. "Hello," he said.

"Hello, Reginald," Amaryllis said. "And hello, Mister . . ."

"Yanick. I work for *World Watcher Weekly*," the journalist said.

We had a quick round of handshaking and introductions, Reginald standing to the side and smiling the entire time. "Yanick here will be running a small article on your journey all the way here. I was hoping that one of you could sit with him and recount the tale?"

"Ah, it can't be me," I said. "I promised I'd do some gardening and clean the place up, remember?"

"Yes, of course," Reginald said.

"Awen and I should be able to retell the story without issue," Amaryllis said. "Should we do that here, or is there a more comfortable place to have this kind of discussion?"

"There's a lounge room upstairs," Reginald said. "I'll guide you there in a moment. Captain Bunch, you'll find all the tools you need in the shed out back." He searched his pockets before handing me a key ring. And then, before I knew it, my friends were ushered up the stairs, and I was left in the guild's lobby with a key ring in hand.

"Uh, okay," I said to the empty room.

Shrugging, I wandered around. It didn't take long to find a broom closet under the stairs. I had Cleaning magic, of course, but that didn't mean I didn't want to swish a duster around as I worked. And I couldn't swish-swish a duster around if I didn't have a duster to swish-swish.

I started with the lobby, humming to myself even as I pushed Cleaning magic into the duster I wielded and into the air around me as an aura. That meant that the more time I spent around a corner, the more my magic ate away at the dust and grime and cobwebs. Swishing the duster against the glass display cases and spiderwebs only made it faster.

Of course, I made sure that there weren't any poor spiders on the webs I was cleaning away, and when I did find one, I'd carefully coax it onto my hand, then go outside, where I'd place the nice spider on the grass next to the guild.

Once the lobby was sparkly and clean and smelled fresh, I moved through the guild, mostly keeping to the corridors until I found an exit to the back.

The yard there was rough, with the grass having gotten too tall and filled with weeds.

The shed at the very back was a bit run down but still serviceable, though there was a small beehive clumped onto one side of it.

I made sure not to disturb any of them as I fetched a few tools. There was a reel mower, stuck in the back, and some trowels and rakes and other tools. Most of them had a patina of rust, but a quick inspection, and I figured they were perfectly usable, if in need of maintenance.

So I tugged out the tools I needed and got to work. The reel mower chewed through the grass with a whirl, especially after I pumped some magic into it to make it run smoother, and then, once the small lawn was all trimmed up, I dug out the weeds one by one.

I was actually having quite a bit of fun! Gardening was a nice, quiet way to spend some time. I wished I had a friend to share the quiet with, but being alone for a little bit wasn't so bad.

I moved around to the front and tended to the plants around the guild's entrance.

It was quiet out. People were at work, and those who weren't were usually older sylphs moving past in a hurry, clearly quite busy, or younger sylphs who seemed like they were scouring the city, looking for some fun trouble to get up to. I had a few gawkers—I guess a bun doing gardening work in an armored dress wasn't all that common a sight in Goldenalden. No one interrupted, though, except for some kids who ran off laughing when I made silly faces and wiggled my ears at them.

The flowers at the front of the guild were in dire need of some love. They were still strong, with good roots holding them in place, but they were being choked out by some meddling weeds.

I tugged the weeds out and set them to the side. They could be mulched up later and used as fertilizer, maybe.

```
Gardening
```
```
D - 34%
```

Not bad!

Once the flowers were given a bit of space and some water, they had a better chance of growing big and strong. I cleaned up the flower boxes, then got to cleaning the front of the guild. It was tricky to get to the higher parts. I could only jump so high, after all, and flinging cleanballs at the windows and facade was only so effective at taking off the grime and dirt caked onto the bricks.

I was trying to figure out a way to get to the very top of the building— maybe I could hang off the edge?—when the front door opened, and Awen stuck her head out. "Oh, there you are," she said.

"Heya," I said. "Is everything going well?"

She nodded. "Yes, for the most part. The journalist is done with the interview, I think. He wants to take a picture, and we want you to be there."

"Oh, sure," I said. I patted down my knees, a bit of Cleaning magic taking care of any dirt stuck to me and washing out the grime under my fingertips. "I'm ready!"

"Great," Awen said. "We're waiting upstairs, in the lounge."

"We're going to take a picture there?"

"I guess," Awen said. "Come on?"

I nodded and followed after her. It was nice seeing the lobby without any dust in it, the few loose items reorganized, and the room smelling much more fresh than it had before. There was just something very satisfying about a room that was entirely clean.

"It looks nice," Awen said. "Did you do everything?"

"No, just the lobby and a few of the little open spaces around. Mostly, I spent my time outside. I didn't get Reginald's permission to do all the other little rooms. Though I did blast a bunch of Cleaning magic into the washrooms, so those should be clean too."

"I think he'll be happy," Awen said with a nod.

I hoped so too! And maybe it would help the guild get a few more members if they saw that it was nice and neat inside and out.

We climbed up to the second floor, then moved over to the lounge where I darted ahead of Awen and opened the door for her. "M'lady."

Awen laughed. "That's awful. But thanks."

Reginald looked like he was in a much better mood, with a big grin on and enough energy pouring off him that he couldn't stay still. The journalist, meanwhile, just looked confused. He was staring at his notepad, as if not quite believing what was written there.

Amaryllis was seated, all prim and proper, on the biggest lounge chair in the room. One leg was carefully crossed over the other, and an aura of smugness so strong it was almost physical wafted off her.

"Uh-oh," I said.

"It's not . . . that bad?" Awen said, likely guessing at some of what I was thinking.

I cleared my throat. "Ah, I'm here."

"Oh! Wonderful!" Reginald said. "We just wanted a photo for the newspaper. I'm certain the article will be that much more impressive with an image to go with it."

"Sure," I said.

The journalist set aside his notebook and fiddled with his camera, something that seemed to require a lot of his attention. Meanwhile, Reginald got the three of us to stand closer together. I got to be in the middle, because I was the tallest, with Amaryllis to my right and Awen to my left.

"I kind of regret not bringing my captain's hat," I said.

"It would be a bit ostentatious," Amaryllis said. "Best to look somewhat humble, as a contrast to the story itself."

"That sounds surprisingly worrying, coming from you."

Amaryllis grinned. "Now, now, I said nothing but the truth."

"She didn't lie," Awen conceded. "But, ah, I think Amaryllis said the truth in an interesting way?"

"That sounds like something she would do," I said.

"I'm literally standing right next to you," Amaryllis said.

I grinned at her. "I know. I can feel you. Your feathers are nice and soft today. Have you been doing something special with them?"

She gave me an unamused look. "You're a moron. Also, no, but the temperature here is more agreeable than I expected. Feathers tend to be somewhat more temperamental than hair or fur, I think. At least when it comes to things like humidity and pressure."

That was interesting. "Neat."

"Ah, yes, could everyone squeeze in a little closer?" the journalist asked. "Mister Reginald, yourself as well."

Reginald stepped to the side so that he was next to Awen. Close, but not so close that he was actually touching her. "Like so?" he asked.

The journalist nodded. "That's great. Is this anyone's first photograph?"

Amaryllis was the only one to nod. She blinked then looked at me. "You've been in photos?"

"Plenty," I said.

"Oh. Well, I haven't."

"Just blink a lot after the flash," I said.

"All right, everyone," the journalist said. "Look into the lens here, that's right."

"And say *cheeeese!*" I said as the pan exploded with a bright burst of light.

· Chapter Eleven ·

Hot Springs Episode

Now what?" I asked as I stretched my arms way way up.

Amaryllis, Awen, and I were milling around the exit of the Exploration Guild. The journalist was long gone, and Reginald—after thanking us profusely for our time and for the cleaning—was back at work. I think he was out of whatever slump he'd been in before, or at least he seemed very enthusiastic about fixing the guild up again.

"We could walk around," Awen said. "Ah, explore a little? We haven't really tried any sylph food, except what was at the inn."

I nodded. That sounded like a nice way to spend the afternoon.

"I have a better idea," Amaryllis said. "Reginald wasn't able to tell me everything I wanted to know about the other delegations, but we do know where one of them is now."

"Oh?" I asked.

She nodded. "The grenoil delegation is in the Purple District, which I imagine isn't too surprising, but, notably, they have been visiting a bathhouse next to their embassy every day."

"How did Reginald learn that?" I asked.

"I think it's mostly the city's rumor mill," Amaryllis said. "The sylphs find it amusing that the grenoils are so ill-suited to the weather here." She gestured to the sky, which was a particularly drab gray. There was some sunshine, and it wasn't too cold. Not cold enough to snow, at least.

"That's not too kind of them," I said.

"The grenoils are from a much warmer area of Dirt. It's normal that they wouldn't handle the cold here well," Awen said. She was probably a bit biased there herself. She was wearing as many layers as she could get away with and had been applying warming spells to herself all morning.

"So, we know where to find the delegation, then?" I asked.

"Oh, finding their actual location isn't hard," Amaryllis brushed off. "The trick is finding a way to actually reach them. I don't think the three of us could walk up to their embassy and ask to speak with the delegate and expect a meeting. But a chance meeting at a bathhouse? That's far more manageable."

"All righty, then!" I said. "I've never been to one of those before. I also haven't taken a bath in a while."

"Please keep your strange hygiene issues to yourself," Amaryllis said.

"I'm clean," I protested, but it fell on deaf ears. "If I didn't have Cleaning magic, I'd take baths all the time, I swear."

It was Amaryllis who took the lead and guided Awen and I back toward the fancier districts of Goldenalden. We went up a stairwell, then hopped over a few easy rooftop gaps on a meandering path toward part of the city that seemed a little older. The plateau there was more pronounced, with buildings spaced out on a flat, rocky surface.

Most buildings were distinctly sylph-style, but one of them stood out like a sore thumb. It was made of stone, like the others, but instead of being all angular and brutalist, it was round, with the second floor and up made of carved wooden panels occasionally broken up by circular windows.

"That has to be the grenoil embassy," I said.

"Did you read the sign?" Amaryllis asked.

I blinked and only then noticed the swaying sign next to the building's lot. It very clearly had the address, and Deepmarsh Embassy, embossed on it. "Oh," I said.

"The bathhouse should be one street down," Amaryllis muttered.

We eventually found it. The bathhouse was rather squat and fairly large. Smoke poured out of a pair of chimneys at the back. Just inside the entrance was a large lobby area, with seats and a big counter before a trio of double doors. One was labeled Men, another Women, and the last Other.

I stared around as we slid in and Amaryllis moved to the counter. A few coins were paid to a young sylph woman, who then accompanied us into the women's section. The main area was filled with cubicles with little pads next to them. A push of mana into the pad would lock the cubicle, and only the same person's mana would unlock it.

"Right, this is where we store all of our equipment," Amaryllis said. "And if this is anything like the bird baths at home, then there should be showers that you can clean yourself off in before heading to the baths. Usually, you wash yourself with cooler water."

"Okay, wait," I said. "Two things. First, cold water?"

"Yes," Amaryllis said. "It wakes you up properly, and it's good for your feathers."

I nodded slowly. "Second, you call them bird baths?"

"Well, that's what they are, aren't they?" Amaryllis huffed.

I supposed that she was right. We took off all our stuff and stored it away. The air was a bit chilly, but the floors felt heated. Awen was shy about it at first, but I reassured her that there wasn't anything to worry about, and she seemed to get over it by the time we found the showers.

I made sure to lather up my ears nice and good. They were a bit strange, and I wasn't entirely sure how normal buns kept them clean, so I just did my best and hoped that was enough.

Maybe I could find a bun to tell me how to fix my hair up around my ears? They parted my hair in odd ways, and I was worried it looked a little off. The small fluffy bits just inside the ear were weird too. They weren't like normal head hair but were a lot softer and thicker. Also, I now had to make doubly sure to remember to wash behind my ears!

I had to ask around and find another bun settlement or group where I could ask some more questions.

Once we were all done showering, we followed a dripping wet Amaryllis over to the main bathhouse.

We had to climb down a spiral staircase to reach the bathing area. It was a cavern of sorts, though I suspected it wasn't entirely natural. The middle of the room had a large circular bath, filled with steaming-hot water. Smaller baths to the side, all of them recessed into the ground, seemed to be held at different temperatures by magical, rune-powered devices.

"Oh, it's so warm!" I said. The air was thick with warm humidity that seemed to seep right into my skin and hair.

"It's nice," Awen agreed.

Amaryllis hummed, then gestured to the largest of the pools. "It seems that we're either too early or too late." The room was empty save for a pair of sylph ladies, one helping the other clean her wings with a big, soft-looking sponge.

"So, if they're not here, what do we do?"

"Enjoy the warm water until they show up, obviously," Amaryllis said. She walked over to the largest of the pools, her talons click-clicking on the stony ground.

I skipped after her, then wobbled my arms around as my feet almost slid out from under me. I giggled as I caught my balance, the sound echoing strangely across the room.

Amaryllis lowered herself into the water, and I splashed down next to her, with Awen slipping in carefully, one toe at a time.

"This is nice," I said as I leaned against the side of the pool. It wasn't all that deep, the water stopping midwaist unless I leaned way back and let my head rest against one of the smoothed stones along the edge. I was sure they were designed to act as pillows.

"This really is nice, yes," Awen agreed.

Amaryllis raised a wing and sighed. "My pinions are a mess," she said. "And I'm certain it'll be a nightmare to find a proper wing groomer."

"I could help," I said, sitting up with a splash. "What do you need?"

Amaryllis huffed a "there's no way" huff, but then she huffed a smaller "well, maybe" huff. "Preening isn't as easy as it looks. But if you want to try . . ." She shifted closer, then spread a wing out before her. "There are many kinds of feathers. These little fluffy ones here are down feathers. Their barbules are softer and tend to warp and waver a lot."

I leaned in and stared at the smaller feathers that were at the base of her arms. "Those are like your hair feathers," I said.

"They're not hair," she said. "These need to be brushed straight when wet, otherwise they clump up, and when they dry out, they become a mess of tangles."

I nodded. That made sense.

Amaryllis reached up to her head and plucked a small feather. "These are contour feathers. They're shorter and fatter, to make you more aerodynamic in flight." I grabbed the little feather and twitched it this way and that.

"Does it hurt to pluck them out?" I asked.

"Only a little. It's a . . . relieving pain when you take an injured feather out. Like cracking your spine to work out a kink. Now, these are wing feathers." She ran her talons through the longer feathers in her arms. "These are the easiest to care for. They need to have all their barbs lined up properly. Those are the little arms sticking out of the main shaft of the feather. There are smaller feathers under the wing feathers, for insulation, and you need to make sure they're not curled up underneath."

I nodded, then gingerly grabbed her arm. It took a bit of focus, but it really wasn't all that hard. She stared at me, one eyebrow raised, as I lifted her wing feathers up and tugged the feathers under them straighter.

"You're actually not bad at this," Amaryllis said. She relaxed against the bath's side. "You could find work as a preener, what with your little human hands."

Awen giggled at that before asking a question, "Don't you use any tools? For preening, I mean."

"Of course we do, but some puritans only use their talons."

Awen nodded. "I can think of a few ways you might make hooks to grab the smaller feathers underneath. Or small brushes."

"Hmm," I agreed. I found a broken feather near Amaryllis's elbow joint. "What do I do with this?"

Amaryllis had to twist her head to see the feather near her elbow. It was no wonder harpies needed help preening if they couldn't see what they were doing. "Oh, that's broken. Just tug it out. It's probably best to pile the broken feathers together. We don't want to make a mess."

I pinched my tongue and tugged the feather out. Amaryllis hissed, but she didn't flinch. I placed the wet feather to the side and went back to playing with Amaryllis's feathers. "I wish I had feathers. They're neat."

"You've changed species once already—isn't that enough for you?" Amaryllis asked. "If you truly want, I'm sure you can become some monstrous multispecies chimera."

"Does that happen?" I asked.

"It does, actually. Much like how you evolved into a bun, some people will evolve into multiple other things. Usually, that requires three or four classes, though, which means, obviously, that those people are ridiculously strong."

"Huh," I said.

Amaryllis tensed, and I was afraid I'd done something wrong, but a glance at her face, and I noticed that she was staring at the entrance.

I shifted around and saw a group of people entering the baths. Frog people.

There were three of them, squat female grenoils with greenish skin that already glistened wetly with all the humidity in the room clinging to them. The three were moving closer to the bath.

"Is that them?" I asked Amaryllis.

"Possibly," Amaryllis said. "They're definitely from the embassy, judging by their classes."

I glanced over at the grenoils again. One was a Secretary, of all things, and the other two were a Ribbiting Conversationalist and a Cold-Blooded Politician.

It was actually hard to tell which one was the most important one when none of them were wearing anything. Still . . .

"Hi there!" I said with a wave. "Do you come here often?"

Chapter Twelve

Casus Antibelli

Hello," the grenoil Cold-Blooded Politician said. She was half a head taller than the other two, which meant that she reached about my nose in height. I imagined she was taking the lead because she was their leader, being a politician and all.

Not that I really knew enough about politics to comment.

"Hi," I said. "Come on in. The water's nice and warm and cozy."

Awen scooted over, even though there was plenty of room for everyone in the warm waters, and after hesitating, the three grenoils dipped into the bath. They sighed, obviously quite pleased. "I was not expecting to meet a harpy, a bun, and a human here," the grenoil lady said.

"There aren't that many grenoils in Goldenalden either," Amaryllis said. "I'm Amaryllis, Amaryllis Albatross. These are my friends, Awen Bristlecone and Broccoli Bunch."

I waved at the three grenoils, my hand splashing out of the water to do so.

"Hello, Lady Albatross," the grenoil lady said. "And Lady Bristlecone and Bunch as well. A pleasure. I'm Sylvie Robespierre, and zese are my companions: Chloe, who is a secretary at ze embassy, and Lucrece, one of my greatest friends in Goldenalden."

"It's good to have friends when you're so far from home," I said. "It makes it less lonely, and you know you have someone to rely on if you need the help."

"It does help," Sylvie said with an agreeing croak. "I must admit to a certain level of curiosity—it is not often zat we meet so many nonsylphs in Goldenalden."

Amaryllis leaned back against the smoothed stones around the edge of the bath. She slid her talons through her feathers, straightening them out where I'd been playing with them. "We're here for the summit. I presume that it's the same for you?"

Sylvie nodded. "It is. So, zis is a political meeting, zen?"

"All meetings are political, once you can exert a certain amount of power," Amaryllis said. "But I don't think this has to be anything like that. Though, I would love to chat about the summit. I do have an agenda to push, after all."

Sylvie chuckled, a raspy laugh that sent ripples across the water. "Of course. Well, I suppose I can't blame you for trying. What agenda are you trying to push, exactly?"

"We want to avoid war," Amaryllis said. "And we're trying to discover those responsible for spurring on the nations gathering here toward a war that no one sensible wants."

"Is zat ze opinion of all ze harpy?" Sylvie asked.

Amaryllis shook her head. "No. It wouldn't have been possible for Rainnewt to create this narrative if the foundations for it weren't laid out already."

"Rainnewt?" Sylvie asked.

I decided to pipe up to help Amaryllis since she was the only one talking. "He's this big meanie who's been trying to trick everyone into attacking each other. He started trouble here in Sylphfree, and in Port Royal, and even in the Harpy Mountains. He's very dangerous. We know that he's destroyed some dungeons already, and I think that maybe he's trying to cover for that by fermenting war."

"Fomenting," Awen corrected. "It's 'fomenting war.'"

I blinked. "Really?"

"Ze little lady has ze right of it," Sylvie said. "But zat is quite ze accusation . . . It stretches plausibility to its limit, and perhaps beyond." She turned to her friend, Lucrece, who nodded once. Sylvie's brow rose at the confirmation. Did Lucrece have a social skill?

"Is it truly that implausible?" Amaryllis asked. "My family is one of the largest producers of airships on Dirt. We stand to profit handsomely if widespread war breaks out, simply by launching new warships to bolster our navy and replenish any losses." She looked the grenoil square in the eye. "Since I am willing to throw all that away, it should give you some idea of how serious I consider the threat presented by Rainnewt to be."

"It would certainly indicate you consider zese accusations to have merit," Sylvie agreed. "Perhaps you would be willing to share why you are so convinced?"

"Of course," Amaryllis nodded. "Our first encounter with him was when he sent me on a cartographic mission that resulted in me nearly being kidnapped, which he tried to pin on the Trenten Flats. Then, at a ball in the Nesting Kingdom, Rainnewt caused an explosion that killed multiple members of a sylph delegation . . . Obviously, you can see how that might spark a war between our two nations. Lastly, we believe he likely killed multiple dungeons around the Kingdom of Sylphfree, which I suppose is not directly likely to cause a war but certainly speaks ill of his character."

Sylvie sat back in the water and regarded Amy for a long minute.

I started to fidget, despite myself. Awen looked a little nervous, herself.

"I'm not entirely sure I believe you," Sylvie said. "Are you really so altruistic zat you'd come all ze way to Goldenalden to stop a war zat would help your family profit?"

I nodded. "Of course Amaryllis would. Under all the meanness and huffing, she has a heart of gold. Besides, it would be wrong not to give it our all to stop something as awful as a war. So many innocent people would be hurt. If we don't do what we can to help, then we're, in a small way, responsible for them being hurt."

Amaryllis huffed most mightily. She really couldn't take a compliment.

"But let's presume zat I do believe you," Sylvie continued. "How are you trying to stop zis war from happening?"

"Well, we have a two-part plan," I said while raising my hand out of the water. My poor fingertips were getting all wrinkly. "First, we'll meet with the grenoil, cervid, sylph, and harpy delegations to ask them nicely not to go to war and to explain that it's not a very nice thing to do."

Sylvie stared, then giggled. "I zink I see. Do go on."

I only had my index left pointing up. "Well, the last part is to beg really, really hard for people not to fight. Maybe we can even find Rainnewt and, like, arrest him or something. A lot of the things he's done caused big misunderstandings, and he should at the very least apologize for those. He . . . he also caused people to die, which is . . . It's bad."

"I have ze impression zat you have a razer simple worldview."

I laughed. "I prefer to call it optimistic. I'm a small bun in a very big world, and there's a lot of scary things out there, things that are really complicated. So I just hope that the world is a nice place, filled with people that are friendly deep down and who aren't all that different from me. They just need a friend, someone to listen when things are hard and help them through the worst days they'll face. Seeing people actively trying to hurt each other because of things that aren't important? That hurts."

"You zink ze war would be over unimportant zings?" Sylvie asked.

"Wouldn't it? Nationalism, patriotism, a huge emphasis on the things that are different from the people around you instead of the things that are similar—I think they're all rather dumb things to fight over."

"Zose are what every war has been fought over."

I shrugged. "Then all those wars were dumb."

Sylvie croaked with suppressed laughter. "Oh, you're an opinionated young bun, aren't you? I zink a few of ze lords and ladies zat fought in zose wars and who promoted zem would disagree. Worse, zey might find insult in what you say."

"I'm not sure I can agree with someone who thinks that they should be proud of that kind of thing," I said.

Sylvie eyed us, then leaned forward. "Very well. Let's say zat I enjoy your optimism. It's certainly better zan ze way a lot of ze sylphs around here zink. What exactly is your plan to stop zis war?"

"As I said," Amaryllis began. "We mostly want to meet with all of the representatives from the groups attending the summit and convince them to take a more peaceful route out of this current political mess. It's in everyone's best interest, especially seeing as how this war is being incited by a third party."

"You know zat convincing some of ze delegations will be complicated. And while ze delegations have some political say from here, not all of zem are all zat powerful. While I can push ze Deepmarsh agenda here, and what I report back may have an impact on ze choices carried out by ze king, zat doesn't mean zat I could stop the king's choice if he decided to push for war."

"Maybe not, but your word might carry just enough weight to it to shift the balance," Amaryllis said. "I know that the harpies are looking to this summit with great interest. If things go poorly here, that would be enough for the war hawks to push for open conflict. And if things go well and end agreeably, then that will give those who want peace proof that peace can be found if everyone is willing to work for it."

Sylvie leaned back and let her eyes close a little so that her second eyelid could blink across her eyes. "I will ask you to do a favor for me," she said.

"What kind of favor?" I asked.

"Nothing too complicated. See, if I listen to you merely because we happened to be in the same bathhouse, then your words will mean little. But if you assist me in some small way, zen I have a reason to report back zat I find you trustworthy."

"Oh," I said. "That makes sense."

Sylvie nodded. "It's nothing too complicated, just a delicate matter zat would actually help the embassy anyway, which is part of what you want, isn't it?"

"Awa, that sounds a bit, ah, openly manipulative," Awen said. She'd been mostly quiet the entire time we were in the bath.

"Better openly zan hidden," Sylvie said. "Besides, it is a simple thing. A shipment destined for ze embassy arrived at ze port two days ago, but it never made it to ze embassy. We're only a hop away, and ze cargo was labeled as politically sensitive, so it's strange zat it has not made it to our doorstep yet."

"That is a little weird," I agreed. "You just want us to fetch it?"

"Or find out what happened to it, if it's truly lost. Chloe, would you mind fetching a copy of the details?"

The Secretary bobbed her head up and down and climbed out of the bath with a splash. I felt a little bad for her, having to leave the nice warm water so soon after arriving. Then again, we had been talking for a good long while. My fingers and toes were both going to be extra wrinkly.

"I'm sure we can manage that," I said with a glance at my friends to make sure they were okay with the idea too.

Awen and Amaryllis both nodded.

"Helping a new friend is perfectly fine," I said.

"As long as said new friend needs the help and isn't just using your innocence against you," Amaryllis added. She didn't need to. Someone who did something like that clearly wasn't a friend to begin with, though they might just be someone who *did* need help.

"I'm glad you're willing to assist us," Sylvie said. "Chloe will leave ze papers with ze sylph by ze exit. Paperwork shouldn't be brought into a bathhouse."

"When we've retrieved your cargo, where do you want us to bring it?" Amaryllis asked. "And how can we know that you'll actually help us?"

"You know because our goals align," Sylvie said. "Deepmarsh doesn't want a war any more zan you do. We've defeated ze cervids once before, but it was a near zing. Zeir own stupidity cost zem more zan our attempts to slow zem down did. If another war were to start with ze cervids, zen none of ze lords and ladies of Deepmarsh expect us to be able to win it, not if ze war goes on for long enough and not if ze cervid have an ounce of wisdom between ze lot of zem."

It sounded like they were more concerned because of their own safety than anything else, which . . . was fair, I supposed. "Okay," I said. As selfish as their reasoning was, it wasn't something I could blame them for feeling. Heck, it was quite the opposite. "I trust you."

Sylvie's brow rose. "For a group so steeped in ze darker side of politics, you truly are optimistic. I hope zat your optimism will be rewarded."

"I hope so too," I said. I sighed as I stood up, warm water dripping off me. "I guess we should get going."

Awen and Amaryllis rose, too, and then we said our goodbyes to Sylvie and her friend before leaving the bathhouse. It was hard, mostly because the air outside was so much chillier.

It was time to do some side quests!

· Chapter Thirteen ·

Have You Tried Asking?

So, how are we going to do this?" I asked.

"That depends," Amaryllis said. Her head feathers were still dripping a little, even though she'd patted her head down with a towel. I wasn't so dry myself. I strapped my breastplate on, and it felt a bit humid. Cleaning magic wasn't Drying magic—that was a whole other thing.

"Depends on what?"

Amaryllis closed her locket and turned toward me. "It depends on how seriously we want to take this little side mission of Sylvie's."

"Well," I said as I tilted my head and cleaned out my—human—ear with my pinkie, "I think she wasn't lying about the cargo thing. It doesn't sound all that complicated. Go to the port, ask around, discover why the cargo's missing, then ask the people there to send it back to the grenoils."

"I don't think it will be that simple," Amaryllis warned.

"Ah, it could be many things," Awen said. She seemed to be feeling a little better now that she was all dressed up and ready to go. The bathhouse might have strained her social skills a little—she was a bit of an introvert. "But, ah, we won't know what those things are until we go and look."

I bobbed my head up and down. "Awen has a good point. We'll never find out if we don't go and check things out on our own."

Amaryllis shrugged, "Then we go and find out. I feel like we're moving without much knowledge on our side, though. This doesn't tell us much." She waved the stack of papers that the secretary had given us. There were maybe four pages in all, most of them copies of forms and contracts that used a lot of words to say very little. They did have the cargo's information, though: dock numbers, manifests, and the supposed port of arrival.

"It's a start," I said. "Come on, it's still early in the day. Maybe once we're done, we can do a little bit of sightseeing? We keep getting sidetracked from playing tourist."

"It's hardly a priority to go around and gawk," Amaryllis said. "Besides, once you've seen one sylph building, you've seen them all. A box is a box."

I held back a giggle, because while it was funny and not entirely wrong—the sylph did like their straight angles—it wasn't terribly nice to mock an entire nation's architectural style like that. I was sure they had good reasons to build everything in such a square way.

We exited the bathhouse and, after a bit of chatting to figure out which way was which, headed toward the outer edge of Goldenalden.

The port that the cargo was supposed to be at wasn't the same one we had arrived at. There were a few ports around the edge of the city, and we were heading to one that was farther in, past the Red District to the south.

The farther we traveled, the more the city changed, especially as we moved past the first set of walls and into the next district. The buildings of Goldenalden were clearly all kept at a decent level of repair, but as we left the center of the city, there were still signs that maybe there wasn't as much maintenance going on.

There were also fewer and fewer nonsylphs the farther from the Purple District we moved. I started to feel a bit uncomfortable from all the strange looks we were getting from the sylphs we crossed.

It had to be worse for Amaryllis. While I got curious glances, she got outright glares and hostile glances. Some sylph kids would point to her and then run off screaming when we approached. It wasn't very nice to see, really. They didn't know Amaryllis except that she was a harpy, and they were being kind of rude. Then again, Amaryllis could be a bit rude right back, which probably wouldn't help things if they did actually try to talk to her.

We arrived at the edge of the port soon enough, a part of the city that was quite busy. Carts moved by, tugged along by big draft horses or smaller donkeys or even strange goats, of all things.

Because of the way that Goldenalden was placed right on the side of a mountain, it meant that large sections of the city were much lower than the parts above. The airship port used that to its full advantage, with the shear wall used as free space from which they could build big docks where ships were parked.

A few larger, boxier vessels were moving into the port even as we approached, one of them being guided in by a tugboat.

"That looks like the right spot," Amaryllis said. She gestured to a lighthouse sticking out of the side of the port, with a domed roof that had some complex assembly of mirrors and reflectors on gantries being worked by a pair of sylphs. A sort of longer-range signaling device, I guessed. The bottom half of the tower looked more like an office building, with brick walls and windows all over looking into older-style offices.

"It says 'Port Authority' on the side," Awen said.

"Good enough for me," I said.

We crossed a busy road—after looking both ways, of course—then moved across the equally busy yard to the port authority. There were a few dozen large warehouses not too far away, many of them with their doors open and cargo flowing in and out nearly constantly. I imagined that maybe the things we were looking for were in one of those.

We stepped into the port authority. The lobby was a tight little spot, with a counter at the end blocking off the rest of the room from the entrance. Sylphs in office-wear were moving about, shuffling papers over and generally looking quite busy.

"Broccoli, you might want to do the talking here," Amaryllis said.

"Are you sure?" I asked.

"I am," Amaryllis said. "I have the impression that the sylphs here aren't the well-bred and polite sort that we've been dealing with so far."

"Oh," I said. That was disheartening to hear. Then again, it was just a hunch on Amaryllis's part. Maybe things weren't nearly so bad.

I walked up to the counter at the front. Unfortunately, it wasn't occupied. That was, until I flagged down a passing office worker with a wave. "Hello?" he asked.

"Hi," I said. I decided that maybe things would be better if the office worker thought I was someone a little more important than just plain old Broccoli Bunch. People in general tended to be a little more responsive and respectful to people they thought were in charge of things. It wasn't great, but that's how a lot of people acted. "I'm Captain Bunch, of the *Beaver Cleaver*, and I'm here because I'm looking for some cargo that I think was misplaced."

"Huh," the office sylph said. "You'll want to take that up with Isaac. Second floor, near the back."

"Thanks," I said.

He darted off, continuing on with whatever work was on his plate. I glanced at my friends, got a few shrugs in response, then moved around the counter and toward a stairwell at the back. We didn't make it far before a sylph lady with a mean-looking scowl intercepted us. "Where are you going?" she asked.

"Uh, to the second floor?" I said. I probably didn't sound all that certain, which was fair seeing as I wasn't. "To see a Mister Isaac about some missing cargo."

"Do you have an appointment?"

"Do we need one?"

"Obviously," she snapped.

"Cool! Can I get an appointment, then?" I asked. I tried to smile to make sure she didn't feel slighted.

I don't think it worked. "Your sort are always barging in where you don't belong," she muttered. "You can get an appointment by mail. Do you know how to write?"

I worked my jaw. That hadn't been nice at all. "I think I'll just take my chances and go check to see if he's busy or not. It'll be faster that way."

"I'll call security," she said.

I blinked at her. "I thought you might be trying to help us at first, but you're really not. Don't you have better things to do?"

That was apparently not the right thing to say, because the sylph lady became extra snippy and stomped off. "I will be getting security," she snapped as a parting shot.

"Awa, we should probably go upstairs faster," Awen said.

"Good idea," I said. "I could probably have handled that better."

"I was about to use some magic to tie her beak shut and puppet her into a closet," Amaryllis said.

I considered it. "That would be a lot ruder than what I said, I think. Also, probably illegal."

"Yes, but it would have taught her an important lesson about the value of being polite to strangers. Did you see her level? She had no business being so rude to three people who outmatch her so completely."

"Amaryllis, you know that judging people based on their strength isn't nice."

"It's not about being nice, it's about having common sense."

The second floor was the same as the first, a big open-floor office broken up by pillars here and there. There were lots of filing cabinets and entire rooms filled with properly organized stacks of paper.

I stopped a younger sylph who was walking by and asked him to point us toward Isaac's office. That turned out to be an office way out on the other end of the floor. It had a door, but it was held open, probably because of all the sylphs slipping in and out of the room.

A bigger sylph was plopped behind a huge desk, imperiously looking over pages and pages of notes and manifests that others placed before him. He'd sign them, sometimes make a note, and occasionally he'd bark something to the sylph who'd given him the page before they ran off again.

"Maybe you two should wait out here," I said. It looked a little cramped in there.

"Sure," Amaryllis said. "We'll keep an eye out. Scream if you need some help."

I nodded and slid into the room. At a guess, Mister Isaac was the sylph in charge. The pages he was taking were cargo manifests. He seemed to be the equivalent of a living computer, though I'd never seen a computer dress someone down for making a mistake before.

When it was my turn, I stepped up to his desk, placed the papers with the information for our cargo down before him, then smiled as best I could. "We're looking for this," I said.

He stared at the page, then brought his head up. "Who in the world are you?" he snapped.

"Captain Bunch," I said. "I'm here on behalf of the grenoil embassy. Their cargo seems to have been misplaced, so I'm, ah, investigating."

"Are you even allowed to be here?"

"Would I be here if I wasn't allowed to be?" I asked. The answer was yes, yes I would be there if I wasn't allowed to be, because that was probably the case.

He stabbed a finger on the page. "Warehouse seventy-four. If it's not there, the Mitchhum family probably stole it—that's their area." He shoved the paper back. "Now go. People are working here."

"Thanks!" I said as I took the pages back. Warehouse seventy-four, that seemed easy enough to find.

"Broccoli," Amaryllis said as she barged in.

"More weirdos," Mister Isaac muttered.

"We have company, the security kind," Amaryllis said.

"Oh, shoot." I looked around the office. There was a window at the back. A glance down revealed that it was a two-floor drop to the ground below. I'd fallen from way higher. "Awen, come in my arms. Amaryllis, can you glide down?"

"Sure."

Isaac protested as we opened his window. I was apologizing the entire time.

Awen clung to me as we hopped out the window and made our escape. Now we just had to find the cargo. Easy-peasy!

· Chapter Fourteen ·

Haystack

"This is neither easy nor peasy," I complained.

The area with warehouses was way, way worse than I had imagined. I thought it would be a few rows of warehouses, with the interiors filled with all the cargo passing through the port. But I was wrong.

Instead, there were several rows of warehouses, with warehouses above them, and then some warehouses below them too. The sylphs had a whole system of elevators, cranes, and scaffolds so that they could use the limited space they had to maximum effect.

That meant that everything was a whole complex array of passages, ramps, and lifts, with carts being pushed around all over by sylphs who weren't usually in a good mood when we happened to step into their way.

The warehouses had nice big numbers next to their doors, which was helpful.

Less helpful was the way the warehouses started at forty-two, went to sixty-seven, then had single digits beyond that for a bit. Some even had letters at the end, for some inexplicable reason.

"And the sylphs claim to be sophisticated," Amaryllis muttered.

"Maybe there's some sort of logic to the system that we, ah, just don't get?" I tried.

"I think the warehouses were numbered as they were built," Awen said. She pointed across the street and down. The road, which was really more of a grated catwalk, ended at a set of rails, and we could see down a couple of floors across. "The bottom floors are all lower numbers, and they tend to go up."

She was right. The warehouse across from us went from thirteen, to fourteen, to sixteen, to twenty-one.

"So they're always rising in number, but they don't have odd or even sorting, and the numbers sometimes skip a few," I said.

That had nothing on the warehouses that had multiple numbers next to their doors, for some unfathomable reason.

"All right, enough of this." I walked away from my friends and flagged down a passing sylph. He had a hardhat on, and a sort of yellowish tabard over plain clothes. "Excuse me, sir. Could you point us toward warehouse number seventy-four, please?"

"Huh?" he asked. Then he pointed toward the far end of the street. "That way, left, then right at warehouse one-one-one."

"Thanks!" I called after him. That had been easier than I'd expected. "Come on!"

We navigated around the maze of warehouses, and I realized that I hadn't asked which level warehouse seventy-four was on. That was a bit of a mistake, but there wasn't anything I could do about it, not unless I flagged someone else down, and I really didn't want to interrupt another worker. None of the sylphs on the roads were idling either. It was impressive. Or maybe they just had their own little corners for relaxing?

We had to go down a level when we came upon a block in the road, then back up around the next intersection.

Warehouse one-one-one was easy enough to find, the three numbers being painted all up the side of the building.

"There it is!" Awen said as she pointed ahead and down.

We were a floor above the closed doors of warehouse seventy-four, which meant we had to backtrack to the nearest elevator, then go down a floor and back to where we'd been.

In the end, the three of us stood in front of a pair of wide doors, hanging in place on a set of coasters. A smaller door was next to the main entrance, so I walked over to it and knocked.

Nothing happened.

"Well, this isn't great," I said. "Maybe we can come back tomorrow? We know more or less where it is, now."

"And lose another half-day?" Amaryllis asked. "I bet I can blow that smaller door right off its hinges."

"That would be a crime," I said.

"And noisy," Awen said.

I nodded along with her.

"I could pick the lock, I think," she went on.

I stopped nodding. "Awen!"

Awen shrugged. "I don't want to have to come back either."

"You two are giving into the idea that crime solves problems way too easily."

"If we're not going to break in, then we can at least check things out inside, right?" Amaryllis said.

"I . . . guess, but it's locked up," I said.

"Just here. Look at the side—they have vents," Amaryllis said.

I moved to the side a little, and in the space between the two warehouses, where a lot of junk was collecting at the bottom, was a small alleyway. The warehouses did have vents on their sides. "That would still be breaking in," I said.

Amaryllis rolled her eyes. "Fine. The warehouse above isn't locked up. We'll see if there's a staircase or something."

I nodded. That would be better. That way we could at least say that we were just looking for the grenoil cargo, without breaking and entering. Just . . . entering. I was pretty sure that wasn't as bad of a thing to do. It wasn't like anyone lived in the warehouse.

So, we went all the way back to the elevator, then back up a floor, and then back to warehouse number seventy-seven, which was just above our target.

Amaryllis grabbed my arm and had us wait as a group of sylphs left the warehouse with a couple of empty carts.

"Are you stopping me from walking into a busy warehouse because you don't want to raise suspicions?" I asked.

"Yes," Amaryllis said. "That's exactly right."

"That doesn't sound all that nice of you, Amaryllis. If we were allowed to be there, we wouldn't need to be sneaky about it."

"Oh no, please don't act sneaky. There's nothing worse than looking suspicious to attract undue attention. Just walk as if you're allowed to be there."

"Implying that we're not," I said.

Amaryllis patted my head with her talons. "Just follow along and don't ask any difficult questions."

I pouted as I followed Amaryllis into the warehouse. She really was walking as if she owned the place. Awen didn't quite have that level of birdy swagger, but she did make an effort not to hunch her back as she walked and was looking around with open curiosity as we stepped into a wide room, filled with rows of shelves where boxes and crates were resting.

"They use tags," Awen said.

I followed her gaze and noticed a long tag stapled to the side of one of the crates. The paper was yellowish and looked pretty cheap, and the stamps on it were a bit faded, but they were still legible.

"Maybe the tags on the grenoil boxes fell off?" I asked. "It might explain why they got lost."

"Maybe," Amaryllis said. "But I'm loath to attribute to stupidity what could be attributed to maliciousness."

"Doesn't that expression usually go the other way around?"

Amaryllis didn't reply. We moved past the entrance and immediately turned right and away from the brightly lit entrance. The warehouse wasn't all that wide, really. It was more tall and deep, with three main rows of shelves and a lot of boxes stacked up on the ground between them.

Amaryllis snapped her talons and summoned a small ball of swirling mana that she used to light the path ahead. Awen did the same next to me.

I focused, nose scrunching up hard, and managed to make a small light of my own. It wasn't all that bright, but, combined with my friend's light, it was more than enough to see the stacks as we moved into them.

The floor was wooden planks, and a glance at the ceiling above revealed that they'd used entire tree trunks as joists. I figured the warehouses probably got pretty heavy when they were full, so they had to build in consequence of that.

"Here," Amaryllis said. She gestured ahead to a part of the floor at the very, very back, where there was a hatch.

"It looks a little dusty," Awen said as we came closer. She knelt down and grabbed a ring from off the ground before tugging it up. The hatch shifted, barely, then refused to budge. "Heavy."

"Maybe if the three of us worked on it?" I asked. Awen let go and backed up while Amaryllis and I both grabbed the ring and pulled.

"Pull harder," Amaryllis grunted.

I let go of my magical light and grabbed the ring in both hands.

I pushed stamina into my legs and lower back, then really gave it my all. Amaryllis groaned next to me, and together we got the hatch to lift, little by little, until it was nearly ten centimeters open.

Then my hands slipped and the whole thing crashed down with a whump.

Amaryllis coughed, and I pushed some Cleaning magic out to clear the dust we'd kicked up. "You know, Awen, maybe if *all* three of us lifted," Amaryllis said.

Awen stepped up between us, a large metal clasp in hand, and hooked it to the hatch's loop. A chain was on the clasp that ran up to the ceiling. I followed it with my gaze to a pulley block above, then back down to a large locking wheel on the far wall.

Awen began cranking the wheel with one hand, and the hatch started to rise.

"Or you could do that. That is also helpful," Amaryllis said, a bit sheepishly.

I glanced down the hole leading to the floor below. The hatch was obviously large enough to let some cargo pass down, probably using the pulley system that Awen had found. That meant that there wasn't a ladder or anything to get down by. The sylph workers probably just flew up if they needed to.

The bottom was only four meters or so down, so I sat on the edge of the hole, then scooted forward. "I'll check for a ladder," I said before dropping.

I landed with a heavy thump on the wooden floor below, then created a small light to see by. More shelves, with more crates, though a lot less than we'd found on the floor above.

There was also a distinct lack of ladders with which to help Awen and Amaryllis down.

A chain rattled from above and came to a stop at about head height. I looked up, hand raising to illuminate the ceiling and Awen's legs as she crawled backward down the hatch.

Amaryllis leapt down next to her, wings spread to catch the air and magic roiling below her to create a cushion just before she landed talon-first next to me.

Awen hopped down and sighed. "That was harder than I thought," she said.

"Sorry, I should have carried you down."

She shook her head. "It's okay. I like figuring out my own solutions now. It . . . it's good."

I laughed. "Okay then. But if you ever do need help, then you know you can ask, right?"

She nodded, very seriously.

As long as she knew that. I grabbed the manifest and hovered my light above it so that I could actually read it. "Ah, more numbers and letters," I said.

Amaryllis moved closer and peeked over my shoulder to read the list too. "Great, we'll have to walk all over to find that. If it's even actually here."

"If what is in here? Trespassers? Because there are plenty of those."

All three of us jumped, and I flashed my light toward the corner.

A rather scruffy pair of sylphs were standing there, looking mighty displeased about our presence.

"Who are you?" Amaryllis asked.

"We could ask the same!" the sylphs said.

Then the door at the very far end of the warehouse slid open so fast it banged against the wall. "This is warehouse security! Come out with your hands raised!" someone screamed from just outside.

"Oh no," said the sylphs partially obscured in the shadows.

"Oh no," I agreed.

· Chapter Fifteen ·

Disorder in the Port

I glanced back and forth between the entrance and the sylphs who had decided to confront us. The entrance had security, who I imagined would probably not be super pleased that we'd maybe done a bit of trespassing.

The other sylphs, though, they were about as suspicious as people hiding in the shadows to ambush a group of girls could be.

In the end, it was Amaryllis who made the choice. She swiped a talon though the ball of light I was still holding, then she grabbed me and Awen by the scruff and tugged us back and deeper into the warehouse.

"Come on," she said. "We're getting out of here."

"Right, right," I said as I turned around so that I wasn't running backward.

There was just enough light from the entrance that I wasn't totally blind as I followed after Amaryllis.

The two sylphs who had appeared were running to the end of a row of crates. They pulled one aside, revealing a hole in the wall partially covered by a piece of tarp to keep the light from the other side out.

They slipped through a moment before we arrived. Amaryllis dove in. Awen turned around and swung her arm out in a wide semicircle behind us. Glass glinted in the partial light as a dozen little caltrops made of magical glass clattered to the floor.

That was a neat, if very mean, trick.

"Go, go," I said as I pushed Awen toward the hole. She nodded and squeezed through.

Then it was my turn. My upper body fit in fine, but things got a little tricky when I was hip-deep in the hole. I grunted while pushing at the edges of the hole, tail squeezing down to try and pass.

I fell through with a plop and got a quick notification for my efforts.

Congratulations! Through repeated actions, your Proportion Distortion skill has improved and is now eligible for rank up!

Rank D is a free rank!

Well, that was one use for that, I thought as I rolled to my feet. We were in one of those thin alleyways behind the warehouses, old boxes against the walls and trash heaped up and rotting on the ground.

"There!" Amaryllis said while pointing down the alley. The two sylphs were flying off in the distance, the taller buildings around us and the multitude of rails and poles above stopping them from gaining too much height.

We took off after the pair. I didn't know why, exactly. If our goal was to get away, then it made a heap more sense to not run after them and go the other way instead—then the guard would have to pick between us and them.

We spun around a corner, then darted across to the front of the warehouse. The two sylphs gained some altitude and moved up a floor before flying through the alley between two warehouses across the street.

A carriage was in the middle of the road, white, with the words Dock Security written on its side in blocky letters.

"Faster!" I said before I scooped up Awen midrun. I saw some security guards spin around by the entrance as we shot by.

I jumped and landed on the floor above. Amaryllis followed me a moment later after she jumped onto the carriage, then used that to boost herself up to the second-level catwalk. I made sure she wasn't far behind as I continued after the two sylphs.

"I think they're thieves," Awen said.

"Huh?"

"Those two! They're thieves!" Awen reached out ahead of us, and a ball of magic shot from her open palm. It rocketed past the sylphs, who both ducked and shouted some rather rude things about us.

"What was that spell?" I asked.

"Spar Ball," Awen said. The one spell that wouldn't hurt anyone, even if it landed a direct hit. So it was a distraction.

The sylphs landed at the end of the alley and then turned left at the next intersection.

Amaryllis caught up just as I started to turn that way too. "The guards are after us," she gasped out.

"Oh no."

"Faster!" she called out.

I could hear the disorganized and confused calls of the guards trailing after us. The sylphs took a right, ran past a road just outside the warehouse district, then into another alley where I saw them take another right.

I kept after them.

"There!" Awen called out. She pointed to a small shack set up against a rocky cliff. It wasn't all that big, just a place where someone could store a few shovels and the like, maybe.

The sylphs disappeared through a window and then closed it behind them.

I slid to a stop in front of the window and tried to open it. It wasn't a glass window but a set of steel shutters, and it was completely refusing to budge even as I grunted and gave it my all.

"Back up," Amaryllis said.

I stepped back, especially when I saw electrical sparks racing across her feathers and hair.

A loud *crack-boom* later, and the window was blown off into the shack. "Amaryllis! You could hurt someone with that!"

"We don't have time!" Amaryllis said. She jumped forward, into and through the window just before Awen vaulted in too.

I glanced back down the alley. The guards weren't in sight, but I could hear them, and they were getting closer. So with a few last seconds of hesitation, I hopped through the window and into the poorly lit shack. Tools lay on the ground, along with bundles of tarp and broken shelves. There was a noticeable lack of sylph maybe-thieves too.

"Um," I said.

"They can't just have disappeared," Amaryllis said. "Quick, check the walls."

The shack's outer walls were all made of tin over a frame of wooden beams—there wasn't much to find there. But one wall, on the inside, was partially made of stone, the same rocky cliffside that the shack was pressed up against.

Part of the wall was covered by a shelf that, when Awen tugged back, swiveled out to reveal a square-cut tunnel cut right into the stone.

"Huh," I said.

"A smuggler's tunnel?"

"Doesn't matter," Awen said, shoving my birdy friend into the dark. "Go, go, go!"

"I'm going, I'm going!" Amaryllis squawked. "Broc, hurry up!"

I could hear the guard's feet hammering the alleyway but threw another glance down the tunnel. No telling what was down there, and I didn't want to be caught flat-footed again.

"Broc!" Amaryllis shouted.

"One sec, I need a weapon!" I called back as my eyes skipped over a scythe, some trowels, a few rakes, a hoe, wickedly sharp gardening spears atop a tin bucket—

I grabbed the bucket and lunged into the cave after my friends, dragging the door shut behind me. Instantly, we were plunged into darkness, so I summoned a lightball in my free hand and pushed some magic into the bucket itself until it glowed ever so slightly. The tunnel cut into the cliffside for a dozen or so meters before opening up into a bigger, wider tunnel. That meant that I only had to crouch for a bit, after which I could almost stand to my full height—my ears were squished down by the low ceiling.

"A mine tunnel?" Amaryllis guessed as she followed after me.

The tunnel continued to our left, but only for a little bit before ending at a rough wall. It went on to the right for quite a ways, at least as far as I could tell. Rails were on the ground, and I could imagine a cart using them to ferry stuff back and forth.

"Do you think tunnels like these are common under Goldenalden?" I asked.

"Maybe," Amaryllis said. "The city is said to have survived a few dragon attacks back in the day. Being partially underground might explain some of that."

"And now that it's abandoned, it's become a super-cool underground thieves' hideout," I said.

"I don't know if I would use some of those words to describe a grungy, poorly lit tunnel, but yes, essentially correct," Amaryllis said.

Awen looked up and down the walls, especially at the large wooden beams set every couple of meters. "I wonder if they build things above knowing that there are tunnels down here. It could be dangerous."

"Let's not look too deeply into it," Amaryllis said. "Knowing the sylphs, they'd accuse us of plotting to make their city fall apart."

"I'm sure they have inspections sometimes," I said.

We followed the rails. The lack of dust on them, and the bare, scratched metal on their surface, hinted that they had been in use recently, likely by the sylphs we were still chasing. It made sense—if their neat hideout had a system to carry stuff already in it, why not use it?

The tunnel curved, and we started down the intersection when I heard something thump behind us. I began to turn, when two sylphs stepped out of the shadows before us. A third was blocking the way back, long, shiny knife in hand.

"Who are you?" one of those in the lead asked.

"Hello!" I said with as much good cheer as I could manage, to put them at ease, of course. "My name's Captain Broccoli Bunch, and these are my friends. We were, ah, well, this is a bit awkward."

"What's a bun doing here? With one of those chickens and a human girl of all things?" the sylph asked.

"That's the thing. I'm not entirely sure. See, we were looking for some cargo in that place when two of you showed up, then the guards showed up and you ran, so we ran after you. I'm starting to think we might have made a mistake."

"Yeah," the other sylph said. "Your mistake was messing with the Mitchhum gang."

I blinked. "Oh! You're the Mitchhum family?"

"Who's asking?" he snapped.

"I just introduced myself, but I don't mind doing it again," I said.

"You mocking me?" he asked, his knife waving in the air before him. I inspected him real quick. It wasn't entirely polite to use Insight on someone without permission, but he was waving a knife in my general direction.

`Mitchie Mitchhum. Gutter Thief, sylph level 10. Agitated.`

The other two weren't much stronger than that. With our second classes, my friends and I had half a dozen levels more than them. "I'm not mocking you, mister."

Amaryllis sniffed. "Perhaps you could consider helping us, instead of being quite so hostile."

"And why would we help foreign scum like you, huh?" the first sylph to speak up said.

"Because the three of us are seasoned adventurers used to raiding dungeons far more dangerous than some old abandoned mine with a few scruffy thieves," Amaryllis said. There was a smell to the air, of ozone and danger, and it was very clearly radiating from my harpy friend. "Because it would be much better for you to work with us than against us, and because I have a notoriously short fuse and don't appreciate being called a chicken."

The thieves swallowed.

I grinned, even bigger and friendlier. "Come on, I'm sure working with us wouldn't be all that bad! We're nice people, I swear!"

· Chapter Sixteen ·

Ganging Up

So, are we going to relax, just talk things out?" I asked. I really hoped that they'd agree.

The sylphs glanced at each other. They shuffled their feet, and I felt a tingle in my ears that felt like bad news.

Mitchie, who seemed to be the one in charge, more or less, pointed toward Amaryllis. "Her first," he said.

"Me first what?" Amaryllis asked.

The nearest sylph's reply was to pick up a long piece of wood from the ground and run toward us while screaming.

"Are you all daft?" Amaryllis snapped. She flung a hand toward the sylph rushing her, and a *crack-bang* filled the mine as a bolt of lightning gripped the sylph midmotion and sent him convulsing to the ground.

"Don't kill them!" I said even as I sent more mana into my bucket and moved up between my friends and the remaining thieves. One of them threw a knife our way, but it wasn't the best or fastest toss. I smacked it out of the air with a swipe of my bucket.

"I won't kill them," Amaryllis said. "Just make them reconsider some of the mistakes they've made."

"Get her!" Mitchie shouted, and the sylph next to him took off running after me. Meanwhile, Mitchie himself spun around and ran in the opposite direction.

So much for honor among thieves.

The sylph charging me screamed.

I threw my bucket. It hit him in the face bottom-first with a heavy bonk before bouncing back into my arms. I grabbed it by the lip, and when the sylph came closer, stumbling and holding onto his nose, I brought the bucket down on his head with a heavy metallic clang.

"Oh, sorry," I said as he crumpled to the floor.

Awen sighed and stepped around me before kneeling on the sylph's back. She had a rope—somehow—that she tied around one of the sylph's wrists, then she looped it around an ankle and finally his other hand. "We don't want them getting away," she explained at my confused look.

"I'm more surprised you know how to hog-tie people," I said.

"Hog-tie?" She glanced down at her knots. "I'm just tying them so that they can't move."

"Girls, let's focus a little, shall we?" Amaryllis asked. "We should catch up to that moron that took off."

"Yeah, someone abandoning their friends like that, it's just wrong," I said.

"M-Mitchie would never abandon us!" the sylph on the ground said. "You'll regret this!"

I squatted down next to him. "Hey, you wouldn't happen to know what we're going to find deeper in that passage, right?"

He squirmed around so that he was looking the other way. "I'm not telling you nothing."

"That's a double negative," I pointed out. "It means that you will tell us something."

The sylph squirmed the other way to look up to me. He seemed pretty confused. "What are you talking about?" he asked.

"Oh, never mind." I bounced back to my feet, swept up my bucket, then pointed deeper into the tunnel. "Come on, let's go see what's down there."

We left the two sylphs—the one Amaryllis had zapped was waking up, though he was a little groggy—and started down the tunnel. It wasn't hard to follow the rails running down the center of the passage.

The rails curved into a large room and ended in a pile of sandbags, the cart sitting there all nice and quiet. Next to that was a wide entranceway, framed by wooden beams. I crept along the wall and leaned over to peer into the room, folding my ears back to keep them out of sight. Inside was a weird mirror of the interior of the warehouses we were just in a few minutes ago.

Shelves lined the walls, but the middle of the room had couches and chairs. A firepit in the middle was surrounded by a few sylphs, Mitchie among them. Stacks of pallet wood and broken crates nearby hinted at what they used to feed the fire.

A few tents were pitched at the far end of the room, and there was an improvised kitchen as well. Clearly, this camp had been lived in for a while.

Amaryllis tugged my sleeve, and I slunk after her until we were behind the cart. Awen only had the top of her head poking over the metal rim.

"I counted seven," Amaryllis whispered. "Two of them have gotten past their first evolution."

"What's the plan?" I asked. We weren't exactly great at stealth, so I figured we didn't have a lot of time to come up with something.

"I'm all for walking in there, spells flying," Amaryllis said. "They have knives and clubs, and only two of them are on our level. We can take them."

"That sounds dangerous."

"We've fought worse," Amaryllis said.

"I meant for them," I said.

She sniffed. "They're thieves."

"Ah, thieves don't usually get treated very well where I'm from," Awen said. "We're just here for the grenoils' stuff, right? Maybe Broccoli can negotiate and convince them to give us all of that, then we leave?"

"After we smash them, we can negotiate from a position of strength," Amaryllis pointed out.

I felt my nose scrunching up as I considered it. On the one hand, taking things that weren't yours was wrong. Thieves should at the very least be punished. On the other hand, I didn't want to see anyone get hurt. Then again . . . "I'd rather not fight if we can avoid it," I said.

"Fair enough," Amaryllis said. "But if that's the case, then you'd better be ready to be extra persuasive this afternoon. I don't think they'll be keen on just giving us what we want."

"They might be," I said. "It's not like it belongs to them in the first place."

"They currently possess it, so I think they will argue that it does belong to them, by default," Amaryllis said.

I shrugged, then stood up and walked around the cart. I didn't want to spook anyone, so I didn't make any effort to be quiet as I walked to the entrance of the hideout. "Hello there!" I called. "My name's Broccoli, and I'm here to, ah, make you an offer you shouldn't refuse."

Mitchie spun around and pointed right at me. "That's one of them!"

"Hello," I said again. This time I added a happy little wave with the hand not holding onto a bucket. Was there blood on the bottom of my bucket? That was nasty. I made sure to clean it off before anyone could notice.

One sylph in the group seemed different to the others. While most of the sylphs in the hideout wore simple clothes, often on the dirtier, threadbare side, he had full leather armor, darkened and covered in little pouches and pockets. He looked like a proper rogue. His hair was peppered with gray, and he seemed a lot more dangerous than the others.

"Who are you?" he asked.

"I-I just said, my name's Broccoli." Maybe he was going hard of hearing in his old age? "Look, mister, my friends and I are looking for something, and we think you might have it. We were wondering if maybe you could let us take that thing back?"

"Oh?" the older sylph asked. He stalked forward, the other sylph parting to let him through. He only paused next to Mitchie to pat him on the shoulder. "You think you can steal from the Mitchhum family?"

"Of course not, stealing is wrong," I said.

He looked baffled. "What?"

"I'm sorry, but it's true. Taking things that aren't yours isn't nice. It makes people very upset. Ah, I'm sorry, but I didn't ask you what your name was?"

"I'm Marvin, Marvin Mitchhum," he said. He stood tall and proud before me, which meant he came up to about my chin. "I'm the patriarch of the Mitchhum family, a family on whose ground you're standing now."

"Oh, really? Gosh, we kind of broke into your house, didn't we? I'm sorry."

Mister Marvin stepped a few paces ahead of me and squinted at me, then at my friends standing behind me. "Who are you? No, not your name, you've said that twice already. I mean who *are* you. Weird foreigners don't just follow my boys down mine shafts for fun."

"We're just some explorers," I said. "We come from here and there, and now we're in Goldenalden trying to stop a war. To do that, we need the contents of a crate that you might, maybe, have taken without permission. So if you could give it to us, that would be awfully nice of you."

"We don't just *give* people anything," he said.

"Come now," Amaryllis said sweetly. "You're thieves. You don't just gather things and let them collect dust. You have to be reselling them to someone. All we want are the crates you stole."

"And maybe for you to reconsider a life of crime," I added. I couldn't see Amaryllis, because she was mostly behind me, but I knew she was rolling her eyes.

"Well, well, you want to buy right from the source, huh?"

I glanced back to Amaryllis, and she nodded once. It was probably a better idea to just buy things outright than to fight for them, even if the things we were buying didn't belong to the people we were buying them from. They'd still end up in the hands of the right people in the end.

Marvin glanced back to Mitchie, then to us. "Fine. Mitchie, go check on your brothers. We'll see how roughed up they are. There might be an additional fee, for damages, you understand?"

"I guess," I said. "But your, uh, friends attacked us first. So it was all self-defense."

"I'm hardly one who's well versed in such lawful matters. I couldn't tell ya what is or isn't self-defense. But I know that I'm not fond of folk that hurt me and mine," Marvin said.

I crossed my arms. Mister Marvin was really quite rude.

"So, what're the goods you're looking for?" he asked.

"We know the name of the cargo, and probably the numbers on the crate, but we don't know what's in it," I said.

"You don't know? You're going through an awful lot of trouble to fetch something that isn't yours," Marvin said.

"We're doing this as a favor," I explained. "And, you know, to stop a war. I'm not too sure, but I think wars are bad for people in your line of work too."

He sniffed. "Wouldn't know."

Footsteps sounded out behind us, and Mitchie burst into the room, breathing hard. "The guard," he said.

"What?" Marvin asked.

He pointed down the tunnel behind him, then to us. "They brought the guards with them!"

There was a split second of calm before everything went to heck in a bucket. Marvin shouted a few orders, and sylphs scrambled across the room. There were more than we had guessed, sleeping in the tents at the back or hanging around quietly and minding their own. They seemed to know what they were doing as they rushed to pick up a few items and ran toward the back, where a part of the shelves covering one wall was moved aside. A second exit?

"Kill the three of them," Marvin said while pointing right at us.

"Oh no," I said.

I stepped back as a sylph swooped down from above with a long staff that smacked into the ground, right where I was standing. Another two ran toward us, long knives poised to attack.

"Guys!" I shouted before I had to use my bucket to block a stabbing strike from a knife. The knife planted itself hilt-deep into the bucket and lodged there.

I kicked at the shin of the sylph trying to turn me into a bun skewer, then backed up some more. Lightning cracked, and a pair of sylphs fell before a third summoned a thick dark fog. Magic!

Of course a few of them would have sneaky magic. It made sense.

I countered the fog with some Cleaning magic, just in time to see a sylph, running around to flank us, step onto a glass caltrop, and crash to the floor with a piercing scream.

And then the rattle of armor and weapons sounded out and a dozen guards, with short swords and square shields, formed a barrier behind us. There was a paladin at their head, one who looked very unamused at what they saw.

"Drop your weapons!" the paladin ordered, a shouted bark so loud it made my ears snap back. My hands went numb, and my bucket thumped to the ground before I raised my arms in surrender.

"Oh no, I've never been arrested before," I said.

· Chapter Seventeen ·

Jailbirds

Wow," I said as I leaned back onto the very uncomfortable mattress and stared up at the bare rock ceiling. "Being in jail sucks."

"Oh, really?" Amaryllis asked. She was in a cell right next to mine. "I thought that being in jail would be great fun."

"Don't be sarcastic," I said.

"Don't be dumb," she shot back.

Obviously, Amaryllis wasn't in the best of moods. It probably had something to do with our current incarceration. We were all placed in little cells in a large, semicircular room, with doors facing a small desk where a bored sylph guardsman was reading the newspaper while occasionally looking up to make sure we weren't up to anything.

Awen had the cell on Amaryllis's other side. She was pacing in little circles, her hands sometimes wiggling around with nervous energy.

I didn't have much else to do but complain. They'd poked at us and taken away all of our armor and gear. We couldn't fit in any of the sylph-made jail uniforms they had, so we were left in our normal clothes, which was nice. Then they put strange cuffs on our hands that glowed while burning off our mana about as fast as we generated it.

That meant that when I cleaned my cell, I had to do it the old-fashioned way.

But that was twenty minutes ago, and now I had nothing to do.

"This is really boring," I said. "Want to play a game?"

"Shut up!" one of the other prisoners shouted over at me.

"I'm sorry for bothering you, mister, but I'd really rather not. Talking with my friends is the only thing I can do right now," I called back. "Did you want to play too? We can do twenty questions maybe? Oh! We could sing some songs!"

"I don't want to sing any songs!"

"That's okay too. I'd never make someone participate in sing-along time if they're shy and don't want to."

Amaryllis sighed. "Broccoli, do you have any concept of how much trouble we could be in?"

"A bit," I said. "But really, if the sylphs are as fair and just as they claim to be, then we should be fine. We weren't doing anything wrong."

"Maybe we weren't doing anything wrong, but we were certainly doing something illegal. The sylphs have so many laws, many of which contradict each other, that no matter what you do, you're doing something that's breaking one obscure law or another." She crossed her wings. "I don't want to end up in some labor camp smashing rocks."

"We'll be fine," I said, this time trying to reassure her.

We . . . might not be fine. I didn't actually know that. But I hadn't gotten as far as I had in life by being a pessimist. I'd just have to hope for the best and work through the worst.

The door at the end of the prison building rattled, and the guard behind the desk sat up straighter while stashing his newspaper in a drawer. The door opened, and a warden walked in, then held the door open for a pair of guards who stationed themselves on either side of the entrance.

Then a familiar face walked in.

"Oh hey, Princess Caprica," I said. "Were you arrested too?"

The princess in question perked an eyebrow even as the guard on duty jumped to his feet so fast his chair clattered to the floor while he saluted.

"Hello, Broccoli. And no, I was not arrested. You three, on the other hand, were." She walked across the room and stopped near our cells.

"Are you here to visit, then?" I asked. "I didn't even know they had visitation hours here."

She chuckled, then shook her head. "Not quite, no." Her smile grew a lot more genuine, and I detected a faint note of blushing on her cheeks. "I was asked to do a favor by a mutual friend of ours."

Well, that had to be Bastion. "Really? What's the favor?"

"To look into why his three most troublesome companions found themselves behind bars within three days of arriving at the capital. He said that it was entirely expected that you'd all eventually get arrested, but he expected it to at least take five days."

"We're always pleased to defy expectations," I said. "And it wasn't our fault. We were chasing after stolen stuff and were caught up in the kerfuffle."

"And the accusations of breaking and entering in the warehouses, refusing arrest, and . . . autodefenestration?" the princess asked.

"Uh."

Caprica laughed. "Yes, I thought so. Fortunately, you did assist in the arrest of a known band of thieves. The Mitchhum family have been something of a thorn in the side of the guard for a while, and they'd recently stolen some goods from some rather prominent and important people."

"Oh, the grenoil cargo," I said. "What was in that in the end?"

"Insect jerky," Caprica said.

"You mean to tell me we went through all that trouble and were arrested just to free up some dried bug meat?" Amaryllis asked.

Caprica nodded. "It seems so. Now, Bastion asked me to look after you, and after a small talk with the chief of the guard, we decided to let you out on bond."

"That's a thing here?" I asked.

"It is," she confirmed. "Though, I had to pay for it myself."

Amaryllis huffed. It was a very "of course you did" sort of huff. "Which means that now we owe you."

"Just a little," Caprica said. "I've also lost an afternoon coming down here. It's not exactly next door from the palace, you know?" She placed her hands on her hips and looked quite pleased with herself.

"Thanks, Caprica," I said. "We really do appreciate it. We'll pay you back, of course. We have some money lying around."

"Oh, I don't need *money*, my dear Captain Bunch. Money is wonderful, but I have plenty of that. I'd be much more interested in obtaining . . . let's call it a favor or three?"

"Helping a friend out isn't a favor, silly," I said. "You know we'd help you with stuff without expecting anything in return."

"Broccoli, you moron, don't go around telling people that, or they'll start abusing your . . . niceness," Amaryllis grumped.

"If they're abusing my niceness because they need help, then it's perfectly fine," I retorted.

Caprica giggled, then cut herself off with a cough to clear her throat. "I think I really do see why Bastion reported that you were mostly harmless."

"Only mostly?"

"Only mostly," Caprica agreed. "You have caused your fair share of problems, you know."

"That wasn't on purpose."

One of the princess's eyebrows rose. "So you're telling me you wouldn't have broken into a warehouse and chased after a known band of thieves if you could have avoided it?"

"Ah, well, there were a lot of circumstantial things going on," I said.

Caprica laughed. "I'm sure. You three cool your heels for just a moment longer. I'll get the warden to get you out of there. Then you can meet me outside. I have a carriage waiting."

Caprica went off, and soon enough, a warden came and opened our cells. A few of the people in the other cells whined about it, but it was mostly the really drunk sylph that smelled like beer who complained the loudest.

We were escorted to a room where we were given back our stuff. I was quick to tie Orange's collar back on, then I summoned the spirit kitty, just to make sure.

I think I might have yoinked her away mid kitty-nap, because she was entirely displeased at being summoned in the middle of a jailhouse. I tried to make it up to her with chin rubs as I followed a guard out of the prison and back onto the streets of Goldenalden.

As promised, a carriage was waiting for us, a big one, with lots of gilding and nice paint trying to disguise the fact that it looked so square. Another guard, this one with the whole ornate getup of a royal guard, opened the carriage door for us.

We found Caprica sitting on the front side of the carriage, so the four of us—myself, Awen, Amaryllis, and Orange—bundled ourselves into the rear seats, facing Caprica.

"Did you find all of your things?" Caprica asked.

"Yup," I said, and my friends nodded.

"Good. Well, now that we're here, I wanted to talk about . . . What is that?" She stared at my arms, where Orange was grumpily settling in for a nap.

"This is Orange."

"Is that a spirit cat?"

I nodded. "Yup. Orange is the Grand Admiral of Mouse-Catching aboard the *Beaver Cleaver*," I said. I let go of Orange, who sat on my lap and puffed her little chest out. Though . . . she wasn't quite as little as she'd been when I first found her.

"May I touch her?" Caprica asked.

"Oh, sure," I said.

Orange shot me a *look* as I picked her up and placed her onto Caprica's lap. The little sylph princess seemed entirely uncertain of how to treat Orange. Carefully, she ran a hand down Orange's back, and Orange stood up with the gesture, pressing into the petting. "Oh, she's majestic," Caprica said.

Orange's smugness grew.

The carriage took off with a rumble, bouncing over the cobbled roads of Goldenalden while Caprica seemed to completely forget that we were there and made little cooing noises at Orange. She rubbed Orange on the head with her forefingers, then when Orange looked up, Caprica started squishy-squishing Orange's cheeks.

I think Caprica nearly fainted when Orange flipped over and let her touch her belly exactly twice before batting her hand away.

Amaryllis cleared her throat, and Caprica looked up, then blushed. She continued petting Orange, but with a more dignified air to her, as if she hadn't been making baby voices at the cat. "Yes, well, as I was saying earlier. I have something of a request for the three of you."

"Sure," I said.

"Broccoli, for just once, can we listen to the request before accepting it?" Amaryllis asked. Awen giggled next to her.

"Fine, fine."

"What I'm looking for isn't anything too complicated," Caprica said. "It is, in fact, something you want as well. The cervid delegation is stationed at their embassy in the Purple District. They're more or less closed off from the rest of the city, focused as they are on minding their own business."

I nodded. "You want us to befriend them."

"Essentially, yes. That would be nice. The delegation has a few younger members that expressed a wish to explore the city. We offered them an escort, but they don't like the idea of having a military escort, especially one that's from a nation with which they have some ongoing tension."

"Oh, you want us to take the place of a military escort," I said.

Caprica nodded. "And I want you to put your friend-making skills to the test. Try to befriend them. They might be younger members, but they still have a little bit of power, and perhaps the ability to sway their parents toward a less violent course."

"Yeah, that sounds easy!" I said.

"Um, Broccoli," Awen spoke up. "Do you remember Emmanuel?"

"Yeah."

"What if, ah, the other cervids are like that?"

I considered it. "Nah, don't worry Awen, there's no way any of the cervids we meet will be that bad."

"I would certainly hope not," Amaryllis said. "If only for the sake of the country's diplomatic ability."

"Should I know what you three are talking about?" Caprica asked.

I shook my head. "It's fine. So, when do you want us to meet these new potential friends?"

The carriage rumbled to a stop. Caprica smiled. "Why, right now."

"Oh, shoot," I said. "Whelp, you keep an eye on Orange for us, okay?"

"Gladly! And good luck."

· Chapter Eighteen ·

How to Win Friends and Influence People

The cervid guards before the embassy seemed to know that we were coming, because as soon as my friends and I were close, they opened the doors for us and let us into an expansive lobby.

The cervids—according to what Amaryllis had told me before—liked open spaces and had something of a dislike of stairs. Which I figured was perfectly understandable. If I were part centaur, I'd probably not like tight spaces and stairs either.

The lobby was sparsely decorated, with a few tall, chairless tables, and some beautiful banners hanging from the walls. The tapestries were all finely woven, often depicting cervids in armor and pretty plains, with patterns woven all around.

While I was gawking, a cervid in a butler's uniform clopped over to us and bowed. His antlers looked like they'd been trimmed to keep them short, or maybe he was another sort of cervid? I really didn't know much about them. "Greetings. Are you the escorts and local cultural experts?"

I was about to say that we were one but not the other when I felt a talon poke my foot. "Yes. Yes, we are," Amaryllis said.

"Wonderful," the cervid butler replied. "The young sirs and lady you will be escorting will be arriving shortly. Do you wish for any refreshments while you wait?"

I shook my head, and my friends did the same.

"Ah, what's the plan?" Awen asked as soon as we were alone again.

"The two of us will be on the lookout for danger," Amaryllis said. "While Broccoli here does her thing and befriends the cervids."

"You know, making friends is supposed to be a natural kind of process," I said.

"There's nothing natural about how you make friends, Broccoli," Amaryllis said.

"Hey!"

Awen giggled. "It's okay. So, where do we bring them?"

"Maybe they have somewhere they want to visit already?" I asked.

Amaryllis nodded. "If that's the case, then fine. Otherwise, there's the parade in the Orange District that we've heard about, and I suppose some of the airship docks might be impressive."

"And that park we walked next to, the one in front of the Exploration Guild," I said. "That might be a nice place for a quick picnic."

"Where would we get picnic foods?" Awen asked. "Ah, what do cervids even eat? There aren't many of them in Mattergrove."

I didn't know. I hadn't spent all that much time with any cervids, and when I had, it was never while sharing a proper meal. Maybe they ate hay or something. I noticed the butler cervid walking by, so I jogged over to him and flagged him down. "Heya," I said. "We were thinking it might be nice to eat outside today. But we don't know what, uh, cervids of a certain standing . . . uh, eat?"

Awen made a noise, like a giggle that was trying to squeak past but was cut off.

"I see. A picnic basket of sorts? Yes, that's a reasonable thing to ask for, especially as so many of the foods the sylphs eat don't sit well with most who have a more delicate palate. I can ask the kitchens to prepare a travel pannier, if you wish."

"That would be great! Maybe an old blanket or two as well?"

He nodded and even cracked a smile. "I'll certainly see what I can do."

"Thank you," I said before I raced back to my friends. "We have something of an itinerary now. Picnic in the park, a few nice places to visit and gawk at. It'll be a lot of fun, I'm sure."

"That will depend entirely on the people we're escorting, I would think."

"Um, speaking of," Awen said. She gestured to the end of the room where a pair of double doors were being pushed open. Three cervids stepped in. The first was a tall, muscular guy, with a mean-looking face covered in little scars. He had a jacket on and no shirt underneath, though he was wearing barding over his flanks and lower body.

Next to him was a smaller guy, with a smile on his lips that wasn't matched by his eyes. He glanced around until he saw us, then he continued to stare as he approached with the other two.

The third was by far the smallest. A cervid girl, the first I'd ever seen. She was just tall enough that her nose was level with my eyes, and unlike the other two, she seemed a lot more lithe and thin and bouncy. I supposed that came with being part deer. She had a nice summer dress on, one with little embroidery on the edges, and a few flowers were tucked in her hair.

"Hello!" I called out to them with a big happy wave. "Are you the ones who wanted a big tour of the city?"

The big guy stopped not too far ahead of me and crossed his arms while nodding. "Yeah, we are."

"Wonderful," I said. "What're your names?"

"Isn't it customary for you to introduce yourself first?" the other boy-cervid asked.

"Oh, right," I said. "I'm Captain Broccoli Bunch, and these are my best friends, Amaryllis Albatross and Awen Bristlecone."

"Hello," the cervid girl said. "I'm Ellie."

"I'm Nathan," the big one said with another serious nod.

"And I'm Rowan."

I grinned. "I'm pleased to meet you all. We're just waiting for the butler to come back,. We thought it might be nice to make a picnic of it. I don't know if you like the food they have around here or not."

"It's not that bad," Ellie said.

"You say that, but I think half the staff here have had indigestion since they arrived," Rowan said.

I laughed. "Oh no. Well, let's try to avoid that, then. I really hope that the three of you can become fast friends with the three of us!"

```
Ellie Lennart
Desired Quality: Someone who knows all the good gossip
Dream: To marry into one of the great families and have a
big family of her own
Rowan Nellis
Desired Quality: Someone who will fight by his side
Dream: To become a proud warrior
Nathan Oriam
Desired Quality: Someone who will share his love of
horticulture
Dream: To become the world's greatest gardener
```

I grinned. All three of them seemed like perfectly nice people. "I don't think we'll have to wait a very long time, but while we are waiting, I was wondering if you three had any places in particular you'd like to visit?"

Rowan shrugged. "I don't really care. I'm just glad we'll be able to get outside without a whole squadron of sylphs tailing after us."

"It will be nice to see the city up close instead of through a window," Ellie added.

I nodded along. "I bet! We've only been here for a few days ourselves. We're here for that big summit coming up soon. It's a nice place so far."

"Oh? Where did you travel from?" Ellie asked.

"All over! Amaryllis is from the Harpy Mountains, Awen here's from Mattergrove, and I'm from Canada."

"I'm not familiar with that last one," Nathan said.

"It's not exactly next door," I said. "Where are you three from?"

Ellie pointed to herself. "I'm from Manamere, the capital, and so is Nathan here." the bigger cervid nodded. "Rowan is from Cinderlock."

"At the foot of the Golden Peak," Amaryllis said.

"That's the one," Rowan said. "It's growing into its own little city now. A lot of folk who think that Manamere's getting a little too cramped are moving to the smaller cities around the capital."

"Or they're taking the trek to the new settlements on the other end of the continent," Ellie said.

"Oh, that's so neat. I barely know anything about cervids, I'm afraid. We only ever spent time with one, and it wasn't for much longer than an afternoon. I hope you don't mind teaching me a little," I said.

"Part of our mission here is to spread the glories of the Republic to the unknowing," Nathan rumbled. "I'm sure we can make an effort to teach you what you want to know."

"I'll return the favor," I said. "I don't know much, but what I do know, I'd love to share with my new friends."

The butler returned then, with two panniers tucked under his arms. "Lords and gentledoes," he said as he lowered the panniers to the ground. I noted that there were blankets rolled up and cinched to the sides of them. "Packed lunches, for your convenience."

"Thank you," I said. I tried to lift one of the panniers, and I did manage, but it was quite a bit heavier than I expected.

Nathan rumbled a laugh and took the pannier from my hand. "Let Rowan and I handle it, Captain Bunch," he said.

"Thank you!"

The cervids were a lot nicer than I had expected, which was a terrible thing for me to think. I shouldn't have expected them to be anything less— that sort of prejudice was just plain mean. I decided not to be too hard on myself. As long as I was kind enough to these three to make up for any notions I had, it would probably be okay.

"All right! My friends and I were talking just before you showed up, and we thought that maybe we could start by visiting the Orange District first?"

"That's where they have those parades?" Rowan asked. He tossed the remaining pannier on his back. "Yeah, I'd like that."

"Great!" I said. "After that, there's a nice park in the Yellow District that we could stop by for a bit of a picnic, if the weather holds up. It gets snowy here sometimes."

"We can handle a bit of snow," Rowan said.

"Speak for yourself," Ellie said. "I'd really rather not have to have my coat brushed again."

I gestured to the doors with my arms and ears. "Shall we? It's a bit of a walk, I think."

"Good, walking keeps you healthy," Nathan said. He took the lead, pushing the double doors at the entrance open with ease and holding one open for us to follow him out into the early afternoon air.

I flounced ahead of the group. I had a lot of energy, and I guess that being out of prison really made me feel bouncy and free. I think some of that energy infected the others, because even Rowan, who seemed a little gloomy, cracked a smile.

Ellie cornered Amaryllis and Awen and asked them about our trip to Goldenalden, and Rowan walked a bit to the side, idly looking at the building we were walking past. Which left me next to Nathan.

"So, Nathan, uh, I don't know if it's rude or not, but I have a neat skill that tells me what people like, and I might maybe have used it on you."

Nathan snorted. "All right," he said. "I think a few merchants have similar skills."

"Huh. Yeah, I imagine that would be useful. Anyway, you like gardening?"

"So what if I do?" he asked, a bit guarded.

"That's great! I have the Gardening skill too! Mine's not very high ranked, though. I never put any points into it."

"You have Gardening?" he asked.

"Yup. Although it doesn't come in handy all that often. We spend most of our time on our airship, and there's not that much room on a ship for a garden. I guess I could make a bit of room for one."

"All you would need are a few planter boxes," Nathan said. "And a way to cover them up, I suppose."

"Cover them? Oh, the wind. Yeah, when we're really moving, the wind might be strong enough to tear a plant right out of the ground. Or at least erode the topsoil away. The temperature changes a lot too."

"Then it depends on what you're looking to plant. A few flowering plants are pretty hardy. Especially here. The sylphs need strong plants to endure the cold this high up. And the lack of air too."

"Right," I said. I was glad I was getting him to talk. "I'm not sure if I really need flowers, though. They're pretty, but it would be a bit sad if I had to grow them in a box to keep them safe and no one got to see them. Maybe some sort of food?"

"Carrots or potatoes," Nathan proposed. "Both are fairly hardy, especially if you look after them."

"Oh, we could have a proper vegetable garden," I said. "That's a great idea! Free produce, and fresh too."

"Handy in a pinch," Nathan said.

I grinned. This whole thing was going just swimmingly.

· Chapter Nineteen ·

Finally Playing Tourist

Crossing the city with a bunch of cervids was a bit strange.

For one, talking to them was hard on the neck. I kept having to look up since they were all pretty tall. If ears counted for height, then I figured it was only fair that antlers counted, too, and that made Rowan and Nathan very tall indeed.

For another, we couldn't exactly go roof-hopping, so that meant that all of our traveling was done on the ground. We walked past a lot of sylphs who'd stop to stare, and the roads, while well-labeled, didn't exactly tell us where we were. There were some helpful signs that pointed people toward clinics and some that pointed toward dragon shelters, but otherwise, we had to guess our way across Goldenalden.

I did try to stop a few sylphs to ask for directions, but they tended to ignore me or walk away faster.

Still, we did eventually make it all the way over to the parade grounds.

The street was long and wide, made of something that felt a lot like cement underfoot, but that was a bit darker. The sidewalks were elevated a step, and there were a few stalls setting themselves up along the road.

I glanced around, but I couldn't see any armies walking in formation, though some sylphs were in uniform here and there. "Well, this isn't what I expected," I said.

"They can hardly be parading around all day," Amaryllis said.

Ellie giggled. "Are you sure? That sounds like a very sylph thing to do."

Amaryllis squawked a laugh. "Oh, it does, doesn't it? Well, in either case, they're not here parading now, so it's a moot point."

"Ah," Awen said. It was that particular sort of *ah* that someone shy said when they wanted people to listen to them but didn't want to raise a fuss. I turned her way and smiled encouragingly. "The stalls are still set up. I think if it were all over and there were nothing else happening, they'd be packing up."

"You've got good eyes," Rowan said. He scanned the area, then trotted over to one of the nearby stands. He had to lean in carefully to make sure his antlers didn't poke holes into the canopy hanging above the stall.

I ran over, just in case he needed some help. I wasn't even sure if the sylphs here spoke some other language than . . . whatever language the cervid spoke.

"Excuse me, sir," Rowan said to the lady behind the stall's counter. One of her eyebrows curled up, and she beat her wings once. "Do you know when the next parade is going to start?"

"There's one in the morning, one in the afternoon, and another in the early evening. You have about an hour to wait."

"Oh, shoot," I said. "That's a while. Thanks, miss," I said with my biggest, most apologetic grin.

"Ah, that's a woman sylph," Rowan said as he backed out and headed over to the others. I stayed by his side and hoped the stall-lady didn't hear. "It's always hard to tell with sylphs."

"Really?" I asked.

"Well, they mostly look the same. There's the facial hair, of course, but not all men have that. And none of the men have antlers," Rowan explained.

"Uh," I said.

"We don't spend too much time talking to them," he added, a little defensively.

"Ah, that's a shame. They've been pretty nice so far. For the most part. Actually, I think most people are nice by default, regardless of their species. It's all about being nice if you expect others to be nice in return."

"If you say so," Rowan replied. I don't think he really believed me.

"The show's not for another hour or so," I said to everyone as we returned. "What should we do until then?"

"Eat?" Amaryllis asked. "The park isn't far, and those of us who are feeling a little more adventurous can try some of the foods they're serving here." She gestured a talon toward one of the nearby stalls, where a sylph was dipping balls of batter into a deep fryer being kept warm by a magical element on its bottom. The smell wafting around was enough to make my tummy plead for a taste.

"That's a fine idea," Nathan said. "I've been meaning to try some of the local cuisine."

"They told us not to at the embassy," Ellie objected. "In case the food was tampered with."

Rowan laughed. "I doubt a street vendor would be equipped to tamper with anything. And besides, half the reason we left the embassy today was to see and try new things. Come on, Ellie, it can't hurt. It'll even give you something to buy. We all know how much you like spending your family's gold."

Ellie sniffed, but she didn't complain as we went from stall to stall, picking out whatever food looked tastiest. The sylphs, for all that they seemed to mostly be in good shape and have a fixation on military readiness, did seem to have quite the sweet tooth.

Most of the things we grabbed were pastries, usually of the sweet and gooey variety. A few stalls had some meat skewers, which Amaryllis zeroed in on, and one had something like a blender, which was serving up smoothies with ice and some green stuff. They were the healthy, unfun kind of smoothies.

Once we had enough junk food to last six teenagers exactly one afternoon, we walked off with our bounties to the park in the next district over. A few other people were around, but we found a park table large enough for all of us. The cervids stood next to it, though, since they weren't built for the sort of seats the sylphs had.

I frowned. "Do cervids have chairs?" I asked.

Ellie laughed. "No one asks that! And no, we don't have chairs. What we do have are these big cushions to lie down on. They're filled with soft stuff. It's nice. Though we can just lie down on the grass too."

"Oh, neat," I said.

It was strange, but I'd never quite appreciated the ability to just . . . sit before. I was happy I'd turned into a bun, which meant that I still had two legs and a butt for sitting.

"Broccoli," Amaryllis said.

"Yes?"

"You're thinking stupid things again," she said. "I can feel it in my feathers. They itch."

I pouted, then comforted myself with another bite from some of the street food we'd grabbed.

Nathan dropped his panniers, opening them and setting down some foods onto the table. I stared at the little glass jars and paper-wrapped contents. There were strange sandwich-like things, and jars filled with plump berries.

"What's that?" I asked as I pointed to one of the sandwiches. The bread looked really strange.

"Oh, that's a great snack is what it is," Ellie said. "It's a mushroom and ivy sandwich." She opened the wrapper and revealed the sandwich within. It was two large mushrooms with some green leaves stuck between them, as well as some sort of sauce. "There are crushed acorns in there too. Want a bite?"

"Can I?" I asked.

Nathan sighed and pushed Ellie's offering down. "No, you can't. No offense, but you literally don't have the stomach for it."

"I don't?" I asked.

Nathan shook his head. "No. Your teeth aren't quite right for it either. Cervids have flatter, blunter teeth for crushing, and we have more than one stomach that's specialized in digesting plants and the like."

"Oh," I said. "So you're all vegetarians?"

"No, we can eat meat," Ellie said. "But it needs to be prepared specially. Mushrooms and nuts and berries keep better."

Nathan pushed a box of berries my way. "Here, these are blueberries. You can eat those."

"Thanks," I said. We talked about food some more, because talking about food was easy. Most everyone liked eating, and nearly everyone liked complaining, so it wasn't hard to steer the conversation to keep everyone talking.

Once we'd scarfed everything down, and Nathan repacked his things, we all stood and stretched, and the boys roughhoused a bit before we took off again. It had been nearly an hour since we'd left the road where the parade was supposed to take place, and in that time, a few more stalls had appeared, and there were more people milling around the road.

"Come on," Rowan said. He gestured to the other side of the road, where the homes and businesses stopped, and the area was left open next to what I figured was the actual military academy. "Let's get a closer view."

We did a bit of jaywalking—after looking both ways—then installed ourselves to see the show.

We didn't have to wait long. Soon, sylphs in neat uniforms were walking out of the academy and forming up into neat rows under the screamed instructions of a very angry instructor. A marching band grouped up as well, and the entire formation marched out, with a second group forming up behind the first.

I clapped and cheered along with some of the civilians, though I refrained from making faces or silly noises at the stoic soldiers as they moved past.

A tug at my sleeve had me turning toward Awen. "Hey, where's Rowan?"

I spun, counted two cervids, then felt a deep sinking feeling in my tummy.

· Chapter Twenty ·

Are You Trying to Get Arrested?

Where's Rowan?" I asked.

Amaryllis, Nathan, and Ellie didn't seem to hear me and kept watching the parade. There had to be a few thousand sylphs out on the road, all resplendent and marching with perfect synchronization under the watchful eyes of drill sergeants.

I glanced at Awen, who shrugged. "I didn't see when he left," she said. "I turned, and he was just gone."

I chewed on the inside of my lip as I searched the crowds lining the street. I didn't want to scream out Rowan's name. Not that my screaming would help much. A marching band was stomping along in the middle of the formation of soldiers, brass horns and drums and cymbals hooting and banging in time to a marching beat. I wouldn't be heard over that.

"Guys!" I said as I ran up to Amaryllis and the others. I tugged on Nathan's arm to get his attention. "Rowan's missing."

Nathan looked at me, then glanced around to look for his friend. He had a height advantage. I was sure he'd see Rowan, and we'd all discover that the cervid had wandered over to a street vendor, or maybe the washroom, and everything would be fine.

"I can't see him," Nathan said, poking a hole right through my hopes.

"Probably just taking a walk," Ellie said dismissively. "Look, they're doing aerial parades too."

I glanced at the sylphs zipping through the air in tight formations, but that was all the attention I spared them. "I'm still worried," I said. "We're responsible for keeping you three safe, you know?"

"Just relax," Ellie said.

Nathan made a deep, growly noise. "Ellie, you're hiding something," he said. "I've known you long enough to tell. Where's Rowan gone?"

Ellie stepped to the side slightly, her arms crossing. "How would I know?" she said. It did sound rather defensive.

"You're all morons," Amaryllis snapped. She gestured with a wing, pointing toward the large military base right next to us. "Rowan's the one that wanted to stand so close to the base, and now he's missing. He's probably snooping in there right now. Right, Ellie?"

Ellie pouted before she glared at Amaryllis. "We're not spies," she said.

"I didn't accuse you of anything of the sort," Amaryllis said. "But I sure did think it."

"Amaryllis. We're trying to be friends here," I said with a warning look. "Nathan, Ellie, where did Rowan go?"

"If he did go to the base," Nathan said with a rather pointed glance at Ellie, "then it'll be against the orders of the embassy. Which means that he'd be under a different set of orders."

"I don't really know much about Trenten Flats politics," I said.

"I mean that it's likely that if he is trying to see what can be seen in that base, then he's doing so under the polite suggestion from a superior in the army. Rowan's always been ambitious. It wouldn't surprise me to hear of him taking this kind of risk to earn a bit of favor."

"Are there any cervid military types here in Goldenalden?" Amaryllis asked.

Nathan shook his head. "No. Well, yes. There's an escort and guards, who are under the orders of a commissar, but the summit is meant to be a peace talk, and the sylphs discouraged the presence of nondiplomatic military personnel. Which is all the military personnel in the Trenten Flats. We keep the army and politics far apart, as a rule."

"So, assuming we believe you, if Rowan is being a moron, then he's being a moron under either the orders of someone that's nowhere near here or he's doing it of his own free will to score points," Amaryllis summarized.

"Rowan's not a moron," Ellie said.

I butted in before Amaryllis could say anything else, because I knew that her next words weren't going to be all that polite. It took some time for people to get used to Amaryllis's Amaryllis-ness, and the cervids weren't quite ready for that. "Let's look for him," I said. "Just a poke around the base. *Around it.* We can't get into trouble for taking an enthusiastic walk, I don't think."

"What if he comes back?" Ellie asked.

I hesitated. "What if we split up, then? Some of us stay here, the rest go looking for Rowan?"

"I'll go with you," Awen said. "Amaryllis can stay with Ellie."

Amaryllis squawked. "Why should I stay?"

"Because you're a harpy. They'll think you're more suspicious than Broccoli and I, and if we get into big trouble, you're better backup than I would be."

Amaryllis sufficiently placated, I turned to Nathan and nodded. I tried my best to make it one of those serious boy-nods that guys sometimes gave each other, but I wasn't too sure if I pulled it off. Still, when I started walking toward the base, he followed right along with me.

The base itself had a yard all around it, probably something of a luxury in a place like Goldenalden, where space was such a premium. There were plain buildings on either side, though, homes, or maybe discrete offices. And behind the base was a sheer wall of stone, part of the mountain that had been carved out so that the base could be laid on even ground.

All that meant that there was really no reason for someone to cross the base to try to get to the other side, nor was there much room to move in next to the base without being right out in the open.

Despite all that, I couldn't see Rowan anywhere. "Do you think he really went toward the base?" I asked.

"It's possible," Nathan said.

I chewed on my bottom lip. I couldn't just walk up to the base. I'd be spotted, and someone would tell me off. But maybe we could circle around it? If he wasn't there, then we'd widen our search.

"Look, there's a passage there," Awen said. She pointed toward the back of the buildings next to the base. There was a gap between them and the stone wall. An alleyway?

"And I bet the alley between any two buildings leads right up to that one," I said. "Well spotted, Awen."

"It will be that much less suspicious, I hope," Nathan said as we ducked into the nearest alleyway. It did, indeed, meet up with the passage at the back.

"How did Rowan get around sneakily if he didn't come through here?" I asked.

Nathan sighed. I didn't know if it was a big sigh because he was a big guy or if he really just felt like sighing big. "Rowan has a few stealth-based skills. Part of his great ambitions."

"You need those to become a military person?" I asked.

"The Trenten Flats army has always put a lot of stock in stealth. For every brash soldier who thinks that the grand charge is the finest act of heroism, there's another who has invested years in learning the great bow and who can hide in the middle of an empty field."

"Oh," I said. That was rather impressive. "Rowan's that sort?"

"He thinks that charging at a line of spears and shields is a very dumb thing to do. So yes, he's the sort who dreams of becoming another . . . Ah, you probably wouldn't know the names of our folk heroes."

"Sorry," I said.

Nathan shook his head. "It's no matter."

We reached the end of the surprisingly clean alley—of all the dark alleys I'd been in, this was the cleanest so far—and stuck our heads out to look both ways. Nothing but cleared space. Some of the homes farther out clearly had some private backyards, with little fences around them, but otherwise, it was a boring old alleyway.

We moved toward the base, then stared out at it again, this time from the rear. The base had a few buildings, basically a complex of what looked like dorms and gymnasiums and classrooms. Really, I could only tell that much because they had large signs above the doors. Otherwise, the buildings didn't have much decoration. They were just tall but still squat buildings made of dark stone, with windows here and there and a bunch of entrances on the ground floor. Rowan was at one of those windows, peeking in.

"Oh no," I muttered.

"Well, nothing for it," Nathan said as he walked out of the alley.

I jogged after him, Awen by my side. "What are you going to do?" I asked.

"Give him an earful, after I drag him back to the street," Nathan said. "Just ditching us like that, it's not the kind of behavior anyone should exhibit. Especially when we're meant to be acting at our best."

"Right, but maybe we can be a little more subtle?" I asked.

"Too late for that," Awen said.

I turned in time to see a pair of sylphs jogging our way. They both wore armbands with an eyelike symbol, and they carried batons instead of swords by their hips. "Hey, you three," the smaller of the two sylphs said. "What are you doing out here?"

"Uh," I said. I had to come up with something other than "We're here to stop our buddy from spying on you." That would have been way too suspicious!

Before I could say the first lie that I thought up, Awen stepped before me and smiled. "Hi there! We're lost."

"You're lost," the officer repeated.

Awen nodded. "Yup! The two of us girls needed to use the little ladies' room, and then we wanted to see the parade, but now we can't find it at all."

"There aren't any 'little ladies' rooms' around here," the officer said.

"Well, I didn't say that we had used one, just that we *needed* to use one," Awen pointed out. "Do you know where there's a little ladies' room?"

The officer didn't look amused. "Really?" he asked.

"We could use a boy's room in a pinch," Awen said. She shrugged. "You know us, us humans and buns, we just need to wash up a lot."

"And what about the cervid?" the officer asked.

Awen glanced back at Nathan, then at me. "Uh."

"They're our chaperones," I said hurriedly.

"That's right," Awen said. "Nathan here's our chaperone."

"One of them," I added. "We have two."

The officer looked at Nathan, who stood a little taller. "You have two?"

I nodded, then pointed at Rowan. "See. There's our other one. Hey! Rowan!" I called. "Did you find a bathroom yet?"

The officer blinked, turning his head to follow the imaginary line of my finger, and saw Rowan with his face smooshed against a window. "Hey!" he shouted, reaching for his club. "This is a restricted area! You can't be looking in there!"

Rowan jumped, spun, then stared at us all wide-eyed. When the officer moved toward him, we followed, Awen and I making "calm down" gestures at him. Rowan looked like he wanted to run away, but Nathan shook his head, and he stayed on the spot.

"Did you find a little ladies' room?" Awen asked before the officer could start grilling Rowan.

"No?" Rowan tried.

The officer glared at Rowan, then at us. "Okay, I don't know what kind of funny business is going on here, but I don't like it."

"We don't like bathroom business, either, sir," Awen said. "But it's a necessary evil."

The taller officer snickered until his partner leveled his glare on him. He looked at us again, and I tried extra hard to look innocent. "Get out of here. Find a washroom elsewhere. Not . . . not here."

The nice officer escorted the four of us for a while until we could walk off on our own.

"Damned tourists," he muttered before walking off.

Nathan waited until we were back on the sidewalk and heading toward the others before he rounded on Rowan. "What in the World's own sacred Dirt did you think you were doing back there?" he asked.

"I . . . got lost," Rowan said.

"Oh, were you looking for a washroom?" Nathan asked with biting sarcasm. "You idiot. You could have gotten us all in a heap of trouble."

"I needed to," Rowan said.

"Needed to what? Get arrested? I don't entirely disagree," Nathan said. "But you getting in trouble would put me and these girls in trouble too."

"The sylphs are a threat to our nation," Rowan hissed.

"And you're a threat to my sanity," Nathan bit back.

I cleared my throat. "Um. Can we . . . not do this? Friends shouldn't argue. Come on, Rowan will tell us everything, I'm sure, but it would be nicer if we didn't have a big argument right on the sidewalk. Also, arguing when tempers are high already isn't great. I'm sure we can make an effort to be nice to each other."

The boys were silent until we reached Ellie and Amaryllis, who were both waiting with their arms crossed. "So, where did you find the moron?" Amaryllis asked.

I smacked myself in the face.

· Chapter Twenty-One ·

The Honorable Judge Bunch Presiding

We needed a quiet place to chat, so we looked around for one. I made sure to strongly suggest to the others—with finger-waggled threats—not to snipe at each other until we found a place where we could talk.

As it turned out, the first place we found was a bar not too far from the parade grounds. It wasn't too busy, probably owing to it being fairly early in the day still, and while the interior wasn't well lit, it was rather cozy, with a hearth in the corner providing some warmth and a sylph musician plucking away at a lute in a different corner. The barmaid gave us a table to ourselves in the far corner, away from most of the other patrons, who gave us strange looks. We definitely stood out, but as long as no one was snooping, it was fine.

Amaryllis and Nathan ordered a bunch of drinks so that we wouldn't be freeloading, and then we all sat or stood around the table.

"Okay," I said. I put on my—figurative—Judge Broccoli wig, then glanced at everyone around the table. "Who wants to go first?"

"How about Rowan goes first?" Amaryllis asked. "He's the one that nearly got us all arrested."

"Amaryllis, try to keep the accusations to a minimum. We haven't heard from Rowan himself about why he, ah, walked off to explore that sylph base."

"I was looking for a washroom," Rowan said.

We all stared.

"Mister Rowan," I said patiently. "That's, uh, not true, I don't think, and we all know it."

Rowan crossed his arms. "You're not my superiors. I don't have to endure this whole . . . charade. For all I know, you'll just spill to the sylphs."

"If they wanted to do that, they could have left you with the sylph guards back there," Nathan pointed out. "But they didn't. Broccoli here wanted to save you despite the risk to herself."

"Yeah, we might have gotten arrested again," I said.

"What?" Ellie asked.

"Anyway," I said. "You can tell us, Rowan. I'm sure you had good reasons. It takes a lot of bravery to sneak into a place like that. I'm sure you didn't do it just for fun."

Rowan glared at me, then at Nathan, and finally at the wood grain of the table. If time spent glaring was any measure of a person's anger, then he really loathed the table. "Fine," he said.

The cervid uncrossed his arms and placed them, hands balled into fists, on the surface. We had to wait a little before he really seemed ready to speak up.

"The sylphs are gearing up for war," he said. "They've always been very militaristic, but this is different. It started maybe a year ago. They have spies, too, you know, and those started to poke around a lot in Manamere and elsewhere. They were looking for something. I think they were checking to see the nation's readiness."

"Go on," Amaryllis said.

"Well, that's all there is to it," he said. "They're going to go to war, and this time it'll be big. Sylphfree, the Nesting Kingdom, the Republic. Maybe the grenoils and those humans too. They're a ways off, but with airships, it shouldn't be hard to drop a whole army on the Republic's lap."

"Wait, you think they're all going to go to war with us?" Ellie asked.

"Sylphfree and the Nesting Kingdom becoming allies is pretty far-fetched," Amaryllis said.

"It's not that implausible," Rowan argued. "Look, the grenoils want the bit of the Trenten Flats next to their home. The harpies want all that land that we took around the base of their mountains. The sylphs probably want the capital itself."

"All that from discovering a few spies?" Amaryllis asked.

Rowan looked up to her. "And discovering what they were spying on. That's not all. Dungeons all across the Trenten Flats have become unusable. The government is locking them up and refusing anyone entry."

"Evil Roots," I said.

Rowan snapped his attention onto me. "What did you say?"

"Evil Roots. They're these big root things that grab onto a dungeon's core and corrupt it."

"They're a sylph weapon," Rowan pushed.

"Uh. No? We've seen them everywhere. In Mattergrove, in Deepmarsh, even on the other side of the Grey Wall. That's where the infection was worst, actually. We know that there's been an outbreak here too. The sylphs lost a few dungeons."

Amaryllis and Awen both nodded to confirm what I said.

"It's not a sylph weapon, I don't think. If it is, they're losing dungeons to it too. Or at least, Rainnewt destroyed some of their dungeons because they were infected," I said.

Rowan was frowning, I wasn't sure if he believed us or not, but he was listening.

"Who?" Ellie asked.

I pouted. "Rainnewt. Or Drizz L. Lizard. Or . . . maybe other reptile nicknames. He knows a lot of languages and has been attacking and destroying dungeons here and elsewhere too. He was part of the Exploration Guild in Goldenalden for a bit, then he moved to Deepmarsh to make trouble there."

"Did you hear anything about a cervid diplomat getting into trouble in Deepmarsh?" Amaryllis asked.

"There was one that was killed there," Ellie said. "Everyone was talking about it."

"That's Rainnewt," Amaryllis said. "He's the one that bombed that gala, with the sylph representatives in Fort Sylphrot too."

Nathan raised a hand, stalling us. "You're saying that this one person has been to three countries and done all that?"

"Yeah. He's scary," I said. "I met him once and fought him once. He can shapeshift."

"It's very likely that he's not working alone," Amaryllis said. "But Broccoli's essentially correct. He's working to start a war."

"Why?" Nathan asked.

Amaryllis and Awen and I looked at each other.

Nathan leaned forward. "If you know, and you expect us to trust you, then tell us."

"Well," I said. "Um."

"It's your secret to tell," Awen said.

I nodded. It was. "That's true. Rainnewt is probably a Riftwalker."

"That's ridiculous," Ellie said.

"If he is a Riftwalker," I continued, "then he probably has a quest from the World to destroy all the Evil Roots. The World really, really doesn't like them. I think . . . We think that Rainnewt's solution to that is to get all the nations to fight each other. That'll mean a lot of dungeons being destroyed all over, which might stop the Evil Roots. They don't just make a dungeon more dangerous, they corrupt the mana around them, too, and they can spread. So every nation will have to start working to stop them."

"And how would you know any of that?" Nathan asked. His eyes were narrowed, as if he were holding back a suspicion.

"Well, I'm a Riftwalker, too, and that's what the World asked me to do. The dungeon fixing and Evil Root pruning, not the whole . . . war thing. I'm very antiwar."

"You want us to believe that you're a Riftwalker?" Ellie said. She sniffed. "You can't be."

"Why not?" I asked.

"Well, for one, Riftwalkers are special," she said.

Awen and Amaryllis both giggled. I felt my ears wilting. "I'm special," I mumbled.

"Miss Broccoli," Nathan said. Everyone turned to him. "How long have you been on Dirt?"

"Uh, about two months, I think? Maybe a bit less than that. I really should have gotten something to count the days," I said.

Nathan nodded and turned to the others. "Well, she speaks Lavaleigh Pastiche as if she were born to it."

"There are skills that could allow her to do that," Ellie said. "And for someone to arrive on Dirt and be here, with her own ship and . . . two people of some import in the space of a month and a bit is entirely too silly."

"Wouldn't that be good evidence in favor that she's a Riftwalker, then?" Amaryllis asked. "The stories about them frequently feature their far-fetched exploits. The World chooses them for a reason, after all."

"I'm not lying," I added.

Rowan sighed. "It doesn't matter," he said, cutting past the argument. "If what you're saying is true—and I'm not saying that I believe you—then Sylphfree isn't planning to go to war?"

"Oh, they probably are," Amaryllis said. "But their preparations are based on Rainnewt's machinations and possibly the dungeon infections. They're drawing the same conclusions you did—except they probably think it's all a plot by you to invade. They're being played for fools just as hard as your precious Republic is."

"And you elected not to tell them?" Nathan asked.

"That's what we're in this miserable country for. To show them the truth and convince them not to start a war on the global stage," Amaryllis said. "Do you have any idea how many would die in a war between all these countries? Not just sylphs, but harpies and cervids."

"The Republic would win," Ellie said with utmost confidence.

"The Republic is about a decade behind in weapons and airship manu-facturing, and you're ill-suited to fighting in mountains," Amaryllis said.

Nathan cleared his throat very pointedly. "We are not going to do a nationalistic girth-measuring contest now," he said.

"Yeah," I agreed. I didn't know what a nation's girth was, but that didn't matter. We were talking about more important things. "I don't think any of us want a war. But we've moved past our original subject. Uh, Rowan, what you did wasn't very nice, and it might have put your friends in danger. I think saying sorry would be an easy solution to everything. And if you really want information to give to your superiors or whatever, then you have all this stuff about Rainnewt."

Rowan sniffed. "I'm not going to—" Nathan's chest shifted, as if he had just moved one of his legs very quickly under the table, and Rowan winced. "Ah . . . I mean, yes, I'm very sorry. But that information, about Rainnewt or whomever, it's not going to be enough. If they even believe it."

"They can look into it too," I said. "It's the truth. It has to be easier to verify than . . . the not-truth."

"You're an optimist," Ellie said.

"The biggest," I agreed.

Amaryllis waved the discussion off. "We're not going to get anywhere with this. We don't have concrete proof to provide to you, and you have a bias toward whatever you were taught about how the World works."

"We all have biases," I said before I sighed. The conversation was over, more or less. There was no point in dragging it out. "So now what? We just continue being tourists for the rest of the day?"

"While the news is rather distressing," Nathan said, "I don't see the harm in doing just that. People might get suspicious if we don't do what we set out to do. And besides, I do want to see the city for myself, not just this little part of it either."

"All right, then," I said as I stood up. "Let's go out there and have as much fun as we can while we still can. And then . . . and then I guess we'll see what we can do. The whole reason we're going to the summit is to try and convince everyone not to start this whole war thing."

"A noble cause," Nathan agreed.

We got up just as the barmaid returned with all of our drinks and such. Amaryllis sheepishly paid for them all, then told the barmaid to hand them out to other customers. It was rather awkward.

"So, where to next?" I asked as we stepped out onto the street.

"I do still want to visit the shopping district," Ellie said.

"The docks," Rowan replied.

I nodded. "Great! To the shopping district and the docks! Amaryllis, which is closer?"

"How would I know?" Amaryllis asked. "I never made a point of learning where the best shops are in Goldenalden, of all places."

"Oh, don't be a wet duck," I said.

Amaryllis squawked, much like a duck would.

· Chapter Twenty-Two ·

Into Thin Air

Bye-bye!" I called out from the entrance, an arm waving above me.
Our new cervid friends weren't so enthusiastic in their goodbyes, but then again, there were other cervids around, guards and servants, so maybe they were embarrassed by such a public show of friendliness. A lot of people were like that.

I did my best to fight against such boring attitudes by being as loud and friendly as I could.

Once the three of them were back into the cervid embassy, we turned around and headed back to our inn. The evening was chilly. The lowering sun and a few gray clouds above darkened the streets even as lamps were being lit to fight off the gloom. The extra light didn't help against the creeping cold, though.

We hurried back, sometimes breaking out into little bits of jogging, both to keep warm and because it was fun to laugh and bounce around.

Big snowflakes drifted down from above, and I found myself laughing as I danced around on the sidewalk. It attracted plenty of strange looks from the sylphs, but this time, those looks were often accompanied by knowing smiles.

It took a good fifteen minutes to arrive at the base of the Dewdrop Inn, mostly because we took a wrong turn at some point. But a friendly city guard pointed us in the right direction.

The inn welcomed us with warmth and the aroma of freshly cooked food. We raced up to the top floor, where the inn's dining room was packed full of strangers digging into an early supper. I think we weren't all that hungry, but the assault from so many tasty fragrances broke down our resistance, and we ended up ordering a couple of meals to be sent up to our shared rooms before we retired for the night.

As soon as we were in our rooms, Amaryllis changed into a loose nightgown and sat down on the nearest couch, and I tossed off the more restrictive bits of my armor so that I was only in the gambeson beneath. I chucked off my shoes, then flopped back-first onto the sofa and placed my feet onto Amaryllis's lap.

"Disgusting," Amaryllis said. "You humans have such weird feet."

I wiggled my toes at her. It was nice to relax my feet. It had been a busy day, and my toes deserved a good wiggle. "Technically, these are bun feet. I think? Huh, I got a tail and ears, but I never really looked to see if my feet had changed."

"Well, don't ask me," Amaryllis said. "I have proper talons."

"What's wrong with my feet?" I asked.

"Your nails could do with some trimming," Awen said with a giggle.

"Another reason why talons are so much better than your fleshy little feet," Amaryllis said. "Long talons are a sign that you're healthy. They're also a far superior weapon."

"Compared to feet?" I asked. "But I can kick people with my feet. And stomp with them too."

Amaryllis raised a leg, stretched it straight out, and flexed her talons. The sharpened bits were about as long as a hand, and they ended in a wicked point. "I can gut someone with one of these. And who's to say that a harpy can't kick? Though, we are lighter, so perhaps you have the advantage with stomping."

"Hmm, I wonder if I could get a class evolution that would give me talons," I muttered.

Awen giggled. "We don't need you to have talons and ears and a tail all at the same time," she said. "You'd start to look like a chimera."

"A bunmera," I said.

Amaryllis huffed the unamused huff of someone who had just heard an excellent pun but was too snooty to admit that it was a great pun.

Someone knocked at the door, and I swung my legs around and bounced to my feet. "Food!" I cried. I still wasn't hungry, but I knew that would change as soon as I had a plate or two set out before me.

I skipped over to the door and threw it open. "Uh. You're not food."

"I would sincerely hope not," Princess Caprica said from the other side.

She stood flanked by two soldiers, both of them seeming rather unimpressed by my greeting. I cleared my throat and stood taller. "Sorry about that! We were just, ah, expecting dinner. Wait, do you call it supper here? Anyway, come on in!"

Caprica chuckled and stepped in. Her guards scanned the room from outside, then shuffled off to either side of the door and stood there at attention.

"Hello, Amaryllis, Awen," Caprica said. "I hope I'm not intruding?"

"Of course not," I said. "We were just relaxing. We had a busy day today, and this is the first time we can just sit back and chill out."

"I'm glad that you're able to find some time for that," Caprica said. "It's important to balance work and relaxation. Do you mind if I sit?" She gestured to a loveseat across from the bigger sofa.

Awen sat where I'd been earlier, which left me a big spot between her and Amaryllis. I sat back down, then flopped onto my side so that I was resting my head on Awen and my feet were back on Amaryllis's lap.

"Again? Do I look like a footstool?"

"You're the prettiest footstool," I said.

Caprica grinned. "I hope that your good mood means that everything went well?"

"Ah, so you're here to see what we learned?" Amaryllis asked. She nodded, then rubbed at her chin. "How familiar are you with the three cervids we met?"

"I've never met them. I've read a few reports that mention them, but they weren't exactly illuminating."

"They were pretty nice," I said. "Nathan's quiet but very dependable, and he feels like he's aware of how strong he is and is a big softie because of it. He's good friend material. And Ellie is good at reading people. And she knows a lot about fashion, and I think politics too. She's fun. Also good friend material. Rowan . . . wasn't quite as nice as he could have been. He put himself first. But he's clever and not mean, so he could be good friend material if you're willing to be a good friend first."

Amaryllis sighed. "You're such a Broccoli."

"What's that even mean?"

"It means that you have the weirdest perception about the World that I have ever encountered," Amaryllis said.

I rolled my eyes. I couldn't do much to change that, and I wasn't sure I wanted to, besides. "Well, whatever. We have important things to tell Caprica. Like how Rowan was kinda-sorta a cervid spy." One of Caprica's eyebrows rose sharply. "A really bad one."

"He's a spy?" Caprica repeated.

"No, not a state-sanctioned spy," Amaryllis said.

"States will rarely sanction spies," Caprica said with obvious humor. "At least, I know that the spies we hire in Sylphfree are definitely not hired by us."

"Didn't you just . . . say that you hire them?" I asked.

Amaryllis sighed. "She means that no nation would admit to hiring anyone to spy on anyone else. Admitting it would be the fastest, and stupidest, way to get into diplomatic trouble with another nation."

I groaned and pushed into Awen some more. "Awen, save me from all these political things. I just want to go on adventures and see new things and make friends."

Awen patted me between the ears. "I'm sorry, Broc, but I think we need to take care of all this stuff first. We can go on adventures after. Promise."

Caprica chuckled. "I envy your ability to get away from it all. Maybe, one day . . . Ah, but we should go over everything first. Miss Amaryllis, you seem the most . . . sensible when it comes to recounting events. Would you mind describing the day?"

I didn't protest her calling Amaryllis better than me at storytelling. She was probably right. Amaryllis went over the day's events, from meeting the cervids in their embassy, all the way to leaving them at the front of the embassy some hours later. She glossed over a lot of stuff, but spent a lot more time on things that I didn't think were as important.

Caprica spent the entire time nodding, only asking a few small questions for clarity or to make sure she understood. She was a good listener and asked a few good questions, especially about the Evil Roots once we explained those. "I see," she said when Amaryllis was done at last. "Well, I . . . don't think that Rowan is a proper spy. Just, perhaps, a misguided young man. I'll make sure that no one overreacts if they learn of his little escapade. I'll want to hear this stuff about Rainnewt myself, you know. I have the impression that I only have small bits of the story there."

I nodded along. I had to blink a few times. Awen running her hand through my hair was making me sleepy. "He's a mean person, and I don't like him."

"Strong words," Caprica said. "Now, I didn't come here just to bother you about your day spent with the cervids. Though I'm quite pleased with the results so far. I have some news that might interest you."

"Go on," Amaryllis said.

"A harpy ship arrived in port this afternoon, with some delegates for the summit," Caprica said. Amaryllis leaned forward at the news. "Not the official ship, mind, just a smaller vessel with some nobles aboard. It apparently left *after* the primary diplomatic ship, which officially makes the absence of the primary diplomats . . . suspect."

"Could it have been destroyed?" Amaryllis asked. "Or waylaid? I haven't had time to look at any weather reports from the past weeks."

"We don't know," Caprica said. "But because of who was onboard, the navy is sending out a taskforce to search along the route the ship was meant to take. Some are claiming pirates did it, but . . ."

"But that's ridiculous. The ship had an escort. And it wasn't unarmed either. The nobles onboard would have bodyguards. Some of them would be skilled enough to put up a good fight—not just the bodyguards but even the nobles. Quite a few of them would have second-tier combat classes."

I frowned. "Maybe there were a lot of pirates?"

"I don't think the sylphs allow large groups of pirates to control the skies so close to their lands," Amaryllis said. "There are few pirates that would be foolish enough to stay near the Harpy Mountains."

"So there would need to be pirates over the Trenten Flats, then," Awen said.

"Which is possible. The Trenten Flats have an abysmal air force," Amaryllis said. "But it's still unlikely. No, I think we're chasing the wrong rodent if we're looking for pirates to explain things. Sabotage is far more likely."

"How would you orchestrate it?" Caprica asked.

Amaryllis sniffed. "First, I wouldn't. I'm a loyal citizen of the Harpy Mountains. Second, I would ensure that I have at least one subordinate on each ship. There are explosives that can be triggered with chemical timers. One onboard each vessel, next to their main gravity engine, and that would be it."

Awen shook her head. "It wouldn't be that easy. Some of those ships were military, right? They'd have backups. And they can still float with their balloons for a while. Maybe a large fire in each ship's hold? With the right fuel, it could grow faster than even a fire mage could control."

Caprica hummed while touching her chin. "I suppose that would do it. A fire would leave less evidence as well. Though, with harpies on board, I can't imagine none of them making it to the ground."

"The sylphs might be more accomplished flyers, but we can glide well enough," Amaryllis agreed. "There should be lifeboats as well. And magic too." She leaned back, eyes narrowing.

"You have an idea?" Caprica asked.

"Something of one, yes. If you were to leave a large group of nobles—with few supplies and no ships—stranded between here and the Harpy Mountains, where would you leave them?"

"That's not something I can answer without looking at a map. And even then, I don't know the region intimately, so I'm not sure I could give an accurate assessment," Caprica said. "But, I can see the point you're trying to make, and I think it's a good one."

"Well, in any case, that's where I would start looking first," Amaryllis said.

· Chapter Twenty-Three ·

Warhawk

I stretched big, which meant that my arms reached as high as they could and my toes were stretched out until all of my limbs shook with tension. It was a nice thing to do just after waking up, though it did highlight an issue: I really missed pajama pants. Nice, thick flannel pajama pants. The sort that were all nice and warm and soft.

There had to be someone selling that kind of thing in Goldenalden.

Or maybe they hadn't been invented yet?

Would it be morally wrong of me to pretend to invent the pajama bottom in another world? What would I even call them? Broccoli Bottoms? That sounded too silly.

I trudged into the living room of our little corner of the inn and found Awen reading on the couch, already dressed for the day, and Amaryllis slumped across the table as if she had run out of energy. "Good morning!"

"Hey, Broc," Awen said without looking away from the page she was reading. "Did you sleep well?"

"Yup!" I declared. "How about you?"

"The beds here are nice, but I kind of miss the *Beaver Cleaver*," Awen said. "The noise helped me sleep at night."

"The noise?"

Awen nodded. "The engines, mostly. I could hear them running from my room. It's very quiet in here. You can barely tell that we're in a city if you don't look out the window."

"Enchantments," Amaryllis said. She pushed herself off the table. "To keep things quiet. So, you're finally awake?"

I giggled. "You don't look all that awake yourself, Amaryllis. What happened?"

"Too many thoughts in my head, all at once," Amaryllis said. "All competing for attention at the same time. It's a burden, being this smart."

"I'm sure," I agreed. "So what has your burdensomely smart brain figured out? What's the plan for today?"

"First," Amaryllis said with imperious decorum, "you dress in something other than a nightgown. Second, we obtain breakfast. That should take care of all our temporary needs. Then, once that's done and we've all cleaned up . . . I'm thinking of finding those harpies who arrived yesterday. They might know more about the diplomatic team sent for the summit, or they might have their own plans and reasons for being here, in which case it would be best to speak with them sooner rather than later."

"That sounds like a decent plan," I said.

Amaryllis nodded. "Of course it does. I came up with it."

"Well then, shall we enact the first stage of your glorious plan?"

I ran back to my room and got dressed and ready for the day. Armor shined up, dress cleaned, and hair combed until it was more or less straight. When I rejoined my friends I found them just as ready as I was.

We climbed up to the main inn floor and grabbed a quick bite to eat while Amaryllis detailed the next part of her master plan.

"The harpies are staying at an inn nearby. I trust Caprica's information that far, but it wouldn't surprise me if they changed locations if they're worried about trouble," Amaryllis said.

"Do you think they need to be worried?" I asked.

"I think the three of us have discovered ample evidence that Goldenalden isn't as safe as some sylphs would have you believe it is," Amaryllis said. "Also, the actual diplomatic mission did mysteriously vanish."

I shoved down a couple of spoonfuls of oatmeal with some sweet, fruity syrup on it—it wasn't maple syrup, but it was an acceptable, if inferior, substitute—then swallowed the glop down with a glass of juice. "Okay! Let's head out, then. The sooner we meet your harpy friends, the sooner we can see how we can help."

"I just hope that they'll see things the way we do," Amaryllis said.

"What do you mean?" I asked as I got up.

"Not all harpies will be as against the idea of a war as we are."

"It sounds like that's the case with most places," Awen said. "Sylphfree, the Trenten Flats, even the Harpy Mountains."

Amaryllis sniffed. "There will always be people who put their own good before that of others. Coincidentally, they're never the ones who will be doing any of the dirty work if things go wrong."

We descended back to the ground floor, then out onto the busy streets. There were plenty of sylphs out, pulling carts and hustling about despite the early hour.

Amaryllis took the lead, walking as if she wanted everyone in front of her to see up her nostrils. Still, even with her head tilted back, it didn't take long for her to guide us over to an inn a block away. It seemed, from outside, to be just a little bit less reputable than the Dewdrop Inn, though maybe I was being unfair by judging it from the street like that.

We stepped into a teeny-tiny lobby area, where a flustered sylph showed us into an elevator that creaked its way up to the topmost floor.

The inn's owner, a nice sylph by the name of Jordi, admitted that he had some harpy clients, but he seemed reluctant to tell us who they were. "Can you at least tell us if you've served them breakfast yet?" I asked.

"Huh? Well, I suppose there's no harm in telling you that I haven't yet. They came in just yesterday. I imagine they'll be a bit weary from the flight over."

"Thanks!" I said. I made a point of ordering more juice and a small helping of second breakfast so that Jordi wouldn't be insulted by us loitering around.

It didn't take long for the harpies to show up. Three young men, all a couple of years older than me, if I were to guess. They wore fine clothes and walked with their beaks up and a bit of a strut.

I recognized them. Or at least, I recognized the one in the middle of the flock.

"Francis?" Amaryllis asked.

The harpy stopped and turned to stare at Amaryllis, the surprise on his face masked under an ugly sneer. "Amaryllis Albatross," he said as if the name were a curse. "How terribly unfortunate to find you here."

Francis's buddies looked between him and Amaryllis, but it seemed like they weren't going to stick their beaks into what was brewing.

"What are you doing here?" Amaryllis asked.

"Didn't I ask you first?" he asked. He glanced past Amaryllis and at Awen and me. "You're here with your pet bun and some wayward human, of all things. What auspicious company the Albatross keep."

"Hi, Francis!" I said with a wave.

He glared. "It's Francisco," he said. "Francisco Hawk of the Hawk clan."

"Oh, sorry. It's been a bit, and we only met for a few minutes," I said. "My bad. Do you remember my name at all?"

"I don't care to remember the names of rabble," he said.

Amaryllis's feathers puffed. "What are you doing here, Francis?"

"You'd do well to call me by my name, too, honorless Albatross," he snapped.

"Honorless?" Amaryllis boggled.

I felt Awen lean close behind me. "Who is that?"

"That's Francisco Hawk," I said. "He's Amaryllis's ex-fiancé. They don't get along." Awen's eyes widened.

"Yes!" Francisco said. He stomped his way closer to Amaryllis. "Honorless. Don't you remember the last time we met? You said you would duel me, but you never showed."

"I . . . there was an attack on the ball! People died!" Amaryllis rebutted.

"A few sylphs," Francisco said with a dismissive wave. He spoke lower, tone pitched so that only those of us nearest to him would hear. "They're the sort that are all likely to die in the coming war, anyway."

I gasped, and Francisco looked at me with obvious pleasure. How could someone say something like that?

"So, you're one of the fools who want to drag the whole continent into a war?" Amaryllis hissed. "I should have figured you would be an advocate for the stupidest option. You are as brain-dead as I feared, Hawk."

"Don't pretend to be any brighter, Albatross," he said. "You and yours will profit from this just as much as any other harpy clan will. Moreso, maybe. There are only women left in your clan, right? Hardly good for war. You'll be left toiling back home while my comrades and I win honor and glory for our proud nation."

"You will do no such thing," Amaryllis said. "We're going to set things right at the summit. Put an end to this farce."

The harpy glared at Amaryllis, then his glare melted into a smile. "You can't attend," he said.

"Pardon?"

"I rescind your right to attend the summit," he said, his nose tilting up.

"Keep talking, and I might rescind your right to breathe," Amaryllis growled.

I stepped between them, mostly to restrain Amaryllis. The air around her smelled like ozone, which wasn't a good sign. "What do you mean, Mister Hawk?"

"I'm the senior diplomat here, aren't I?" he asked.

"Hardly," Amaryllis said. "Our clans are equal."

"Ah, but I'm older, he said. "And I'm the first son of my clan. You're just . . . the spare."

There was a *snap-crack*, and Francisco stumbled back, hand brushing at the front of his very nice coat where a burnt streak now traced itself across the lapels. "That is it," Amaryllis seethed. "I'm going to fry you like a rotisserie chicken!"

"Hey, hey, wait," I said.

"No, there's no need for waiting," Amaryllis said. She twisted her arm, and I just knew she was going to pull out her knife.

"A duel!" I said, loud enough that it made everyone pause. "You were promised a duel, right?" I asked Francisco. "Then why don't we provide you with one? The winner gets to represent the harpies at the summit. It'll be nice and, uh, official."

"To the death?" Francisco asked.

"To yours, maybe," Amaryllis said.

"No, no," I said. "I'm sure the sylphs have, uh, arenas or something for this kind of thing. They've got to have rules too. I'm sure it's all very civilized. I hope."

Francisco glared at Amaryllis past my shoulder, then nodded. "This afternoon," he said. "That should be long enough for you to prepare yourself. You certainly seemed ready to claw at my throat just now."

"Fine, then," Amaryllis said. "This afternoon. I'll send someone to you with the time and address."

Francisco's eyes narrowed. "How about we make it more interesting, then? My two companions here will want in on the fight too. You have two sycophants. It would be a shame if you lost them." Francisco's friends glanced at each other. They'd been very quiet so far, and I wasn't sure they actually wanted anything to do with the fight.

"Wow," I said. "Did you rehearse how to sound like a cheap villain in front of the mirror?"

Francisco sniffed. "Is that a no? Your animal half is showing, cowardly little bunny."

"We'll do it," Awen said. "I really don't mind."

Francisco glared some more, but then he snapped his talons and walked off with his friends, leaving us behind without so much as a word.

"Rude," I muttered under my breath. Then I turned to my friends, specifically Amaryllis. "What was that?"

She huffed the huff of someone who didn't want to talk about it. "He gets under my feathers."

"You almost attacked him. You *did* attack him. Amaryllis, that could have led to a fight!"

"I wanted it to, obviously," she said.

I pouted at her. "We could have gotten hurt. That wasn't very smart, I don't think. And you're supposed to be the one that's clever about these things."

Amaryllis crossed her arms. "Like I said. I dislike him."

I shook my head. "And Awen, why did you escalate?"

Awen hesitated a moment before answering. "Ah, well, it was to our advantage?"

"Our advantage?" I asked.

"They're weaker than we are. Their levels are the same, but their classes aren't as good, and they don't carry themselves like people who know how to fight. And if we do fight with them and win, then I think the sylphs here might respect us a bit more? They're very martial, you know, so that kind of thing probably impresses them a lot."

"That's . . . fine," I said. "How are we going to find a place for a duel on such short notice?"

"Oh, that part is easy," Amaryllis said. "We go and bother Caprica. She'll want us to win anyway, so I can't foresee her not stacking the deck in our favor."

"We're not going to cheat," I said.

"No, no, not cheating, just . . . ensuring an even playing field," Amaryllis said. "Francisco doesn't know how to fight fairly. Trust me?"

I crossed my own arms. "Fine," I said. "But I still very much don't like any of this."

"I know," Amaryllis said. "You can pout about it for the rest of the day, as long as we win."

"I think I need a hug."

· Chapter Twenty-Four ·

Political Ramblings and Rumblings

Our first step—if we really were going to duel Francisco and his bud-dies—was to find Caprica.

The princess would know a lot more about the local dueling scene and all the laws surrounding that kind of thing. Amaryllis probably knew her fair share, too, but we didn't know if the rules from the Harpy Mountains would apply in Sylphfree, and Amaryllis insisted on making sure that it was a proper duel, not just a brawl.

I . . . wasn't sure what to think about things as they were.

On the one hand, Francisco was about as rude as a person could be. On the other, that wasn't enough to make me want to fight him.

Awen caught on to my current mood. She bumped shoulders with me as we walked over to the palace. "Isn't this the same as that tournament you participated in, the one in Rosenbell?" she asked.

I shrugged. "I guess it's not all that different. Will it be all three of us against all three of them?"

"I hope not," Amaryllis said. "I want to face off against Francisco on my own."

She sounded just a pinch too bloodthirsty there. I patted her on the back. "I know you're angry at him, but I think you might be, ah, overreact-ing just a little, teeny tiny bit? He's rude, sure, but rudeness shouldn't be answered with violence."

"And how would you respond to rudeness that might very well end with thousands of lives lost to bolster a puffed-up Hawk's ego?" Amaryllis asked.

"Well, first I'd write a very strongly worded letter to Francisco's mom."

Awen choked on nothing, then giggled between coughs. "Broccoli! You can't!"

"Why not?" I asked. "He's not that old, so maybe his parents still have time to teach him some manners. And besides, if I were Francisco's mom, I'd want to know if my son was about to start a war just to make himself feel more important. Obviously, he didn't get enough hugs growing up, but there's always time to rectify that kind of misstep."

"That's . . . actually a fantastic idea," Amaryllis said.

I blinked. "It is?" I'd been pretty much positive she was going to dismiss the idea out of hand.

"Oh, yes. A public letter, sent to the capital and to Fort Sylphrot, denouncing Francisco's behavior and childish actions and the threat they both pose to the nation as a whole. Maybe a few public criers to read it aloud on street corners."

"That's sounding a lot more like blackmail than what I had in mind," I said.

"Yes. I took your idea and improved it."

"I don't know if I'd call that an improvement at all."

Awen giggled some more. "But can you imagine his face when he finds out?"

I pouted at her too. "You have a mean streak in you too."

Awen shook her head, but she didn't quite deny it. "I just think that . . . Ah, I guess there's more than one way to fight someone. If we lose here, Broccoli, then a lot of others will be losing too. We're having fun, and it's another big adventure, but the stakes are pretty high. Whether you want it or not, Francisco is on the other side." She crossed her arms, smile dying off as we walked into the shadow cast by a tall mansion-like home right next to the road. "My mom . . . wasn't a very nice person, but she did make sure that I learned a few things."

"What sorts of things?" I asked.

"I didn't like the lessons," she said. "So I can't say I took them to heart. But I did listen. Mostly, she talked a lot about how a woman should defeat her opponents. I think I like shooting people with a crossbow more than using the methods she spoke about. It's more honest."

Amaryllis snorted. "Yes, some people do prefer intrigue and rumors over a proper talon-on-talon fight. The Albatrosses aren't like that, though."

I didn't say it aloud, because I think I'd made my point clear often enough already, but I preferred it when people talked through all their problems and acted in a way that would mean that everyone would be happy or at least satisfied by the end of the day. That wasn't something that was easy to do, though.

"Well, whatever," I finally said. There wasn't much to say, really. We just had to do our best and hope that it was enough and that maybe we set an example.

I didn't have much time to ponder that, since we'd arrived at the palace. Amaryllis stepped up to the guards by the front gate, bowed shallowly, then asked them to send a message to Princess Caprica on our behalf.

The guard bowed back, the big feathery thing atop his helm bobbing with the motion before he spun around sharp-like and walked into the nearby gatehouse. I saw a young sylph fly off toward the palace, no doubt a messenger.

It only took a minute or two before the messenger sylph returned and relayed whatever news he had to the guard.

"The princess is willing to entertain you," the guard said. "She is waiting in the west garden." The sylph flagged down a pair of guards who were within the palace walls, and they quickly flashed a few gestures at each other. Mostly, the guard just asked them to keep an eye on us while guiding us to the garden where Caprica was waiting.

The garden turned out to be one of those glass-walled greenhouses along the outer perimeter of the palace. A gazebo was built into the side of the enclosure, where Caprica and another young woman were sitting down.

The princess was in her usual dress-uniform-like outfit, though she had added a sash today and had a few ribbons in her hair. The girl next to her was half a head shorter and wore a more princess-y outfit—a dress with bows on the hips and front, colored a soft lavender and covered in embroidered flowers that let her blend in with the wall of greenery behind her.

Two guards stood by the entrance of the greenhouse. They opened the door for us, and we stepped in eagerly.

I hadn't realized how chilly it was outside until I was smacked in the face by the warmth inside the greenhouse. It was a humid, muggy sort of warmth, filled with a whole host of pleasant, flowery fragrances that changed as we headed over to the gazebo.

"Captain Bunch, Lady Amaryllis, Lady Bristlecone," Caprica said without standing. The princess next to her bounced to her feet and curtsied.

The reason Caprica didn't rise became obvious when a big pile of orange fluff jumped off her lap and onto the table in the center of the gazebo.

"Orange!" I cheered. "This is where you were hiding?"

Orange sat, her chest puffed out with obvious pride. She had a few ghostly ribbons tied next to her head, and her fur looked extra soft. By the looks of her, she had been properly pampered recently.

I scratched her on the head, then under the chin for good measure.

"Yes, Orange has been a wonderful guest overnight," Caprica said.

"She's very handsome," the other princess replied.

"Ah, where are my manners," Caprica said as she stood and brushed her lap clean of ghostly kitty hair. Or she tried. Her hands just moved right through the fur, which refused to leave her pants. "Everyone, this is my little sister Gabrielle. Gabrielle, these are the . . . explorers and emissaries I spoke of."

Gabrielle curtsied again, and my friends and I did the same in return, though maybe with less grace. "It's a pleasure," she said. "Capri rarely makes new friends, so it's really nice of you to spend time with her."

"Gabby!" Caprica hissed. "Don't spread such vile lies."

Gabrielle apologized, but it was evident that she wasn't being sincere with her apology.

Caprica rolled her eyes, then gestured to the table. "Sit? I'm sure you're not just here to pick up Lady Orange."

"Lady Orange?" I asked as I took a seat. Orange looked at me as if to say "Are you going to question that?"

Caprica blushed, but faintly. "She seems quite ladylike," she said. "And a spirit cat is a rare being in these parts."

"I guess. Technically, she's an admiral, but I don't know if that makes her a lady. Maybe it should be Sir Orange?" I asked. "How did you get those bows on her, by the way?" I poked at the bows, but my fingers slid right through them.

"Oh, that was the court wizard," Gabrielle said. "He's a master illusionist. They're not real bows. I think they're cute."

I nodded, in full agreement.

"So, what brings you here?" Caprica asked. "And would you like some tea while we talk, or is it a little more urgent?"

"It's certainly delicate, and not something we can afford to wait on for too long," Amaryllis said. "But I don't think it's quite urgent."

"Do tell," Caprica said. She gestured, and I almost jumped when a maid bowed back and hurried off. I hadn't seen the maid at all. Did they have a skill that made them sneaky?

Amaryllis shifted in her seat. "We met with the harpies that arrived last night. The meeting . . . could have gone better. Though, honestly, with the quality of the harpy in question, I doubt it."

"They're adversarial?" Caprica asked.

"You could say that," Amaryllis said. "Though that would make it an understatement. Francisco Hawk, of the illustrious, boisterous, and full-of-itself Hawk clan. They're very much on the prowar side of things. They want to try and match arms with the sylphs, despite all common sense saying that it's a poor idea."

Caprica frowned. "That's unfortunate. Who has more seniority between yourself and this Francisco and his companions?"

"He does, though only barely," Amaryllis said. "I managed to maneuver things so that we would duel for the right to represent the Harpy Mountains."

"Truly?" Caprica asked.

I glanced at Amaryllis. *Maneuver* was a big word to describe what had happened.

"Yes. Which is why we're here. We want this to be a proper duel, not some street brawl. Francisco is the sort who would easily ignore a deal made. Even one that was won in a duel. I think the only way to make him keep his word is to put too much pressure on him for him to weasel his way out."

Caprica considered it for a moment, then nodded. "We'll arrange something, then. When is this duel supposed to take place?"

"This afternoon," Amaryllis said.

"You're certainly not giving us much time to prepare," Caprica said. "Still, I think we can figure something out."

"Can I come? To watch," Gabrielle said.

Caprica glanced at her sister, considered it, then nodded. "Sure."

Gabrielle blinked. "Wait, really?"

"Oh yes. You being present will attract all sorts of attention," Caprica said. "Half the available suitors in the city will rush to attend as well. It'll make up for the lack of time to set up something proper. And have rumors spread."

"Capri!" Gabrielle said, her cheeks glowing. "You can't just use me like that."

"You're the one who wanted to attend," Caprica said. "You'll be able to enjoy yourself, leave the palace, and I won't have to work as hard to get a crowd of nobles to oversee the happenings. Two harpies with one stone. Ah . . . forgive the expression."

Amaryllis waved it off. "It's fine. We have a few similarly uncouth expressions ourselves."

"I can imagine," Caprica said. "So, do you think you'll win this duel? I would hardly appreciate backing a loser."

"Oh, don't worry on our account," Amaryllis said. "In fact, this will be a lot of fun, I think."

· Chapter Twenty-Five ·

You've Got a Right to Your Fights

I was expecting it to take a few hours to set up an arena and have someone send an invitation to Francisco. My expectations didn't account for Caprica being really good at leveraging her princess-ness to get others to do the work for us. A few guards and messengers were dispatched across the city, zipping away on fleet wings to prepare things for our savagery.

We, in the meantime, finished our tea. It was a very nice flowery tea that tasted a bit like green tea but significantly sweeter. "I can't believe you're going to be in a duel," Gabrielle said. She was right on the edge of her seat, feet swinging with barely restrained energy under the table. "That's so cool!"

"It's less amusing when the person you have to fight is as loathsome as Francisco," Amaryllis said.

"You don't like him?" Gabrielle asked.

Amaryllis sniffed. "I dare say few people do."

That was a bit mean, but I didn't think I'd be changing Amaryllis's way of seeing people between then and the time the duel started.

"What did he do?" Gabrielle asked. She was genuinely curious and only stopped leaning forward when Orange decided that Gabrielle—being the current center of attention—had the nicest lap to sit upon.

"He's an uncouth, poorly educated, rude fool who likes sticking his beak where no one wants it stuck," Amaryllis said.

"He's her ex-fiancé," I whispered across the table. "They don't get along."

Gabrielle raised the hand that wasn't petting Orange to her mouth to stifle a gasp. "An arranged marriage."

"Deranged, more like," Amaryllis muttered.

"We're quite fortunate in that regard," Caprica said. "While I suppose Father could technically arrange something, I don't think he'd dare."

"The king wouldn't dare arrange a marriage?" Awen asked.

Caprica grinned and Gabrielle giggled. "Mother would skin him. Besides, Father broke with tradition when he married Mother."

"How's that?" I asked.

"She was a paladin. A nonnoble paladin. Better than a commoner, in the eyes of the nobility, but not by much," Caprica said.

Gabrielle nodded, entirely enthusiastic. "They married for love—it's *super* romantic. Apparently, Father tried really hard to impress her by becoming a good fighter, and she just kept beating him in every spar. Mother's very proud of her win record against him, and Father's face turns very red whenever she talks about it."

"That's really cute," I said.

Caprica chuckled. "I suppose it is. In any case, I think if Father tried to arrange a marriage for any one of his children, he'd have to deal with an entire cohort of angry princesses and a very irate queen."

A maid slid into the room and bowed next to Caprica to whisper something into her ear. She nodded, then patted down the front of her pants as she stood. "I think it's time for us to get going. There's a carriage waiting for us out front."

"Already?" I asked.

"It would be best to arrive early, I think," Caprica said. "That way you can have more time to inspect the grounds and perhaps stretch before you have to exert yourselves."

We gathered up our things and left the greenhouse. The cold outside stung my face. I hadn't expected it to get colder while we were inside. The temperature around Goldenalden seemed to vary a lot, but it was always hovering between cool and chilly. It probably had something to do with the altitude and all the mountains around us messing with the wind.

We boarded a nice carriage, Gabrielle, Orange and Caprica to one side, my friends and I on the other. Then we were off.

"The Calcifer Spood Memorial Arena isn't far from here," Caprica said. "It's not the most prestigious location for a duel, but it's a respectable one. The arena is open at all reasonable hours, and there are quite a few young nobles who hang around either to watch others fight or to spar."

"Is dueling a big thing?" I asked.

"More or less. It's one of the less civilized ways of resolving a conflict, but with stringent rules in place and healers on site, it's uncommon for someone to die, and it is a much faster way to resolve some petty arguments than any legal proceedings."

"Also, it's more fun," Gabrielle gushed. "I imagine a lot of dashing lords go there to fight for their honor when they are insulted or if a lady they're fond of has been insulted."

Caprica rolled her eyes. "Yes, I suppose there's that. Bastion always said that it was less about honor and more about hormones and shortsightedness. I never spent any time around dueling clubs or the like."

"I think the situation is similar in the Harpy Mountains," Amaryllis said. "It's a way for younger lords to blow off steam, impress each other, and not cause a ruckus in less appropriate venues."

It didn't take long before the carriage rattled to a stop, and a sylph guardsman opened the door for us.

There were a lot more guards around than when Caprica had headed out. Was it because two princesses were out at the same time, or was it because Gabrielle was different? I had the impression that she didn't leave the house as much.

When Gabrielle sniffled, a maid sylph was instantly by her side, wrapping a thick woolly shawl over her shoulders.

The Calcifer Spood Memorial Arena was a grand building. It squatted amidst buildings that rose above it, an impressively broad edifice of sculpted, weatherworn stone, whose wide entrance beckoned anyone to enter and beat people up.

There were other carriages, but the sylphs around the arena mostly seemed to be on foot. They were noble lords and ladies, young ones. They were also all staring our way.

"We're the center of attention." I said.

"That's hardly something unusual for you," Amaryllis said.

"I'm not an attention-seeker . . . am I?"

Amaryllis huffed, but she did bump into my shoulder as if to say she was just joking. "It's likely the carriage. And maybe they recognize the princesses."

"The crest does lack some subtlety," Caprica said with a tilt of her head toward the carriage. There was a big crest on the door that I hadn't really paid much attention to. The two or three squads of guards were likely not helping much either.

We walked into the building. The entranceway didn't have a door. Instead, it was a wide opening under an arch. A large brazier sat within, crackling with fire that warmed us up as we approached.

I glanced over my shoulder as we moved in and couldn't help but notice all the whispering from the people outside. A number of nobles were moving from restaurants and shops across the street toward the arena. There was a growing sense of excitement filling the air, as if everyone suddenly expected something grand to happen.

A sylph stood on the other side of the brazier, looking as though he was trying very hard to *not* look as though he'd just run over in a hurry. He bowed at the waist. "Princess Caprica, Princess Gabrielle, and of course your lovely companions. My name is Augustus Spood. I welcome you to my grandfather's arena. Anything you desire, I shall do my best to provide for you."

Caprica bowed back, a much shallower bow, but one that had the sylph standing straighter. "Hello, Lord Spood. I was hoping I could borrow one of your arenas? My companions here were issued a challenge, and we intend to see it through."

"I would be honored," he said. "We have one of the safest arenas in all of Goldenalden, as you likely well know. I can assure that we will keep your friends healthy and hale, regardless of the outcome of any spar or duel. Did you wish to use one of the smaller, more private arenas? I can have the area cleared of everyone but the judge and medical staff."

Caprica glanced our way. "How certain are you of being able to defeat Hawk?"

"Very," Amaryllis said. "He might have a decent class, but he has no real experience, and I suspect we at the very least match his level, if we don't surpass it outright."

Caprica nodded as she turned back to Augustus Spood. "In that case, having more witnesses wouldn't go amiss."

"We can certainly arrange that," Lord Spood said with a genial smile. "Might I have the details of this duel?"

They spoke quietly as we made our way down one of the corridors that seemed to bisect the building, then up a wide staircase. Soon we were crossing spaces where we could see little arenas below, sand-filled squares with a row or two of seats far above, none bigger than a wrestling ring.

I didn't pay much attention to the conversation, instead turning my focus inward. I was about to get into a fight. It didn't feel like it would be a very challenging one, but . . . still. I asked Mister Menu to display my skills, just in case.

Name	Broccoli Bunch
Race	Bun (Riftwalker)
First Class	Cinnamon Bun Bun
First Class Level	12
Second Class	Wonderlander
Second Class Level	4
Age	16
Health	145
Stamina	150
Mana	145
Resilience	55

Flexibility	70
Magic	35
Skills	Rank
Cinnamon Bun Bun Skills	
Cleaning	S - 04%
Way of the Mystic Bun	D - 100%
Gardening	D - 37%
Adorable	D - 100%
Dancing	D - 100%
Wonderlander Skills	
Tea Making	D - 100%
Mad Millinery	D - 89%
Proportion Distortion	D - 14%
General Skills	
Insight	C - 100%
Makeshift Weapons Proficiency	C - 17%
Archeology	D - 00%
Friendmaking	C - 75%
Matchmaking	D - 64%
Hugging Proficiency	E - 48%
Captaining	E - 49%
Cinnamon Bun Bun Skill Points	1
Wonderlander Skill Points	3
General Skill Points	3
First Class Skill Slots	0
Second Class Skill Slots	0
General Skill Slots	3

I had improved, but it felt like it wasn't all that much. There was a natural slowdown as my skills took longer to improve, of course, but also I hadn't done any really focused practice in a while. At the rate I was going, it was going to take a long time before I hit any big milestone again.

I still had some free skill slots for my general skills too. Those weren't, surprisingly, filling up with random skills. I'd have to ask Amaryllis to see if that was normal or not. I really, really had to find a chivalry-based skill so that I could turn Adorable into Dork Knight.

"This is the main arena, ladies," Augustus Spood said with a grand gesture.

The main arena was about the size of a badminton court, with a floor covered in fine sand and lit by hanging chandeliers with glowing crystals that filled the room with blue and yellow and orange light.

Three rows of seats circled the room about a meter off the ground, a shimmering barrier between the crowds and the floor. Likely, that was in case some spell went off and flew toward the witnesses.

"I suspect this will do just fine," Caprica said. "Lord Spood, do you have a way to inform people of an upcoming . . . small event? Ah, and a place where my companions can be filled in on the rules of a proper gentleperson's duel?"

"Certainly," he said. Then he glanced past our group and guards and to the end of the corridor.

We followed his gaze.

I hadn't expected Francisco to show up so soon. Did he know we'd be here?

For that matter, I hadn't expected him to show up with new friends. Two sylphs and a human, all in nice but well-worn armor and all looking very much out of place amongst so many nobles.

I had a sinking feeling in my tummy as I saw the grin Francisco wore.

· Chapter Twenty-Six ·

Say Hello to My Little Friends

Who are your friends?" Amaryllis asked. She was eyeing the three new figures a step behind Francisco and his two buddies.

The human walked with a hunch, hands in his pockets. The sylph to his left had his head up high, as if daring anyone to look down on him, and the other sylph was glancing all over the place, as if he was expecting something to jump out from the shadows at any moment.

"Hello, Lady Amaryllis," Francisco said with dripping meanness in his tone. "It seems that you really have forgotten every last aspect of decorum and etiquette. Did no one ever teach you to greet people when you meet them?"

"People, yes," Amaryllis. "So will you answer the question?"

The harpy's face reddened at the cheeks and his feathers puffed out, just a little, before he gathered himself. "These three new friends of mine are some very kind fellows I met at a tavern. They heard of my plight, having to fight someone of your repute, and bravely decided to step up so that I might avoid soiling my feathers with your presence."

"You mean to say that you were too cowardly to fight me and my friends head on, so you hired three mercenaries to fight in your place?" Amaryllis asked.

I glanced back at Caprica and Augustus. "Can he do that?" I whispered.

Augustus Spood bowed his head. "If the gentleman, ah, wishes to have someone fight in his stead, then he can elect someone to do so. It isn't entirely uncommon. It's more often than not used by a lady of the court who doesn't have skills as a fighter. She might employ a champion to fight in her stead. On occasion, an older noble, past their prime, might also elect a champion. Usually, these would be a member of their family, but there are no laws against merely hiring an outsider."

"But a young fighter designating a champion in their stead is seen as cowardice," Caprica said. "Or, at least, as very distasteful."

Augustus stepped up, placing himself between Amaryllis and Francisco. "Greetings everyone," he said with practiced geniality. "My name is Augustus. I'll be the person in charge of today's duel. Lord Hawk, from what I overheard, you will be having these three gentlemen fight in your stead?"

"Yes. Yes, I will," Francisco said. "What about you, Amaryllis—will you be fighting yourself? You always did like to brag and strut with your chest puffed out. Or maybe you'll send someone else in? That little sylph girl behind you, maybe?" he chuckled, and his friends joined in.

I followed his gaze and saw that Gabrielle was blinking back at him, completely confused.

Augustus cleared his throat. He was still smiling, but a vein was visible along the line of his neck. "Lord Hawk, I believe I speak for every sylph when I say that if you could avoid involving Her Royal Highness in your affairs, it would be appreciated."

"Ah," Francisco said. I think he noticed all the guards nearby, many of whom were giving him *looks*, and decided to backpedal. "A pleasure to meet you, Your Royal Highness. Please forgive my earlier impertinence. The presence of this barbarian brings out the worst in me."

"Um." Gabrielle hesitated before dropping into a quick, shallow curtsy. "It's fine? I wasn't really paying you much attention. I'm just here to see my sister's friends fight."

"Your sister's friends?" Francisco mused. "Ah, perhaps after our bout, I will remain here to observe that fight."

"But . . . but that's the fight you were supposed to be in?" Gabrielle asked.

I eyed Gabrielle. She sounded innocent. A bit *too* innocent.

"Right, big sister Caprica?" Gabrielle asked. She blinked at Caprica with big, wet eyes, and I could imagine her lower lip trembling even if it wasn't.

Gabrielle was a very tricky little sister, it seemed.

"That's right, Gabby," Caprica said. "We're here to watch Lady Amaryllis, Lady Bristlecone, and Captain Bunch put up a good fight."

"On that note," Augustus said, "Lady Amaryllis, did you intend to fight yourself?"

"We have some royal guardsmen here who I am certain would be honored to be your champions," Caprica added. "We even have a paladin or two. Some are in their fourth tier."

Francisco was looking a bit pale.

"I appreciate the gesture," Amaryllis said. "But I am no coward. I intend to win based on my own merits. As for my companions, they can decide for themselves. Besides, if we use the sylph military to win this battle, then anyone at the summit could turn around and accuse us of being supported directly by Sylphfree. It would discredit us."

I glanced over to the three guys we'd have to fight.

Jacob Hayer. Bladesinger, sylph level 15. Distracted.

That was the sylph who had been looking all over the place earlier. Now his attention was mostly split between staring at the back of Francisco's head and the two princesses.

Malter Roggen. Frozen Batterer, human level 14. Apathetic.

That was the human. He was staring past everyone, looking like he was entirely bored with everything.

Next to him, the last of the sylph mercenaries looked pretty darned conflicted. I had the impression he didn't want to be there anymore, but he didn't have a choice about it.

Flein Bocking. Hardened, sylph level 16. Worried.

All three were a few levels above my friends and I, and that was just what I could see from their primary classes. It was possible that all three had a second class that was at max level. I'd have to see if Amaryllis could tell me more about them.

I snapped my attention back on the conversation as Augustus called someone over from the sides, a young aide who moved over to the mercenaries and guided them away. Meanwhile, Augustus turned toward my friends and me. "Please, allow me to escort you to the preparation area."

I waved Caprica and Gabrielle goodbye, the younger of the two giving us a quick wave in return as she called out, "Good luck!"

"Have any of you participated in this sort of duel before?" Augustus asked as we headed down a corridor, then through a side door and down a flight of stairs. The decorations stopped at the door, and everything became a lot more functional and austere.

He glanced back and took in our shaking heads.

"Well then, let me explain the basics. In order to keep things somewhat fair, the fights—all one-on-one competitions of prowess—will be chosen based on drawn lots. The fight will start when the arena glows red. The moment the arena glows red again, you must stop."

"Glows red?" Awen asked.

He nodded. "You'll understand when you see it. The referee will demonstrate regardless. There are enchantments that light up if anyone in their vicinity is gravely injured, knocked unconscious, or otherwise incapacitated. The referee should be treated as a god of their domain. What they say is sacrosanct and should not be defied."

"Ah, all right," I said. This was starting to sound pretty serious.

"The weapons you pick must be chosen from our armory. These will be enchanted to make them nonlethal. That does not mean that they cannot cause harm, only that they will blunt any great impact and will not pierce or cut into flesh the way a normal weapon would," Augustus said.

The stairs ended, and we started down a long corridor that ended at a sharp angle. Augustus pointed to a door to our left before he opened it. He didn't step in, though. "This is the waiting room. You can see the arena through the glass there. There are barriers in place to prevent magics from harming the room and the rest of the arena as well."

"The weapons are all enchanted not to hurt people, right? What about magic?" I asked. I didn't really have much in terms of offensive magic, but Awen had her Glass magic, and Amaryllis had electricity and puppeteering and probably a few other magical tricks hidden away in her sleeves too.

Augustus sighed. "Unfortunately, stopping someone from using magic isn't as simple as blunting a weapon. We ask that anyone fighting a duel keep in mind that there's no honor in killing an opponent in this arena. If we see that a mage is going too far, there are enchantments in place that can disrupt the flow of mana. We leave those off unless they are absolutely needed, though."

"All right," I said.

Augustus nodded. "Don't worry. The referee will go over the rules again before the duel starts."

"Thanks, Mister Augustus," Awen said. "You're very kind."

"Merely doing my job, Lady Bristlecone," he said. We continued down the corridor, around the bend, and stopped before a door that was closed. It had a small lightbulb-like thing above it that was currently off. Reaching up, Augustus flicked a switch next to the door, and the light glowed a magical bluish hue. "And this is the armory. Take whatever you need. There are pieces of armor at the back as well. I will be waiting out here for your return."

"Thanks," I said.

The room was well lit, a few hanging lanterns casting an orange-yellow glow across rows of racks and shelves laden with hundreds of weapons. The next room over, past an archway in the room we were in, had armor on dummies and on more shelves—enough to equip three dozen warriors and then some.

"Whoa," I said as I reached over and picked up a sword larger than I was. Or I tried to. It was way, way too heavy.

At least the edges on it weren't sharpened. I couldn't imagine that helping too much if someone took a swing at me with it, though.

"All right," Amaryllis said. "We . . . don't exactly have an advantageous situation here. Three opponents with abilities we can only guess at, all above our levels, and on an even playing field."

"It's going to be a tough fight," I said. "But we'll do our best, right?"

"Awa, we don't need to do our best," Awen said. "We need to win. This is important, Broccoli. We need, um, strategy more than we need optimism, I think."

"Oh, right."

Awen turned to Amaryllis. "What's our strategy?"

Amaryllis rolled her eyes. "Of course. With great intelligence comes great responsibility." I chose not to comment. "Let's see. The Frozen Batterer is likely an ice mage. His armor was lighter than most frontline combatant sorts. If I'm against him, I'll try to overwhelm him. Ice magic tends to be slow to act. Awen . . . I'm afraid you're not in the best position in any fight here."

"I need equipment and time," Awen said. "I'm not really much of a fighter at all, really."

"You're great," I said.

She shook her head. "I'm a mechanic first. It's okay not to be good at fighting, I think. You don't need to worry about me, though. I have a few tricks that might work." She reached over to one of the racks, then pulled a heavy shield from it.

"Right," Amaryllis said. "The Bladesinger is a somewhat common sylph class. High mobility, focused on swords. He's going to be fast, and he's going to have a lot of tricks. Keep your distance and pelt him with magic. Broccoli, I'm sure you could manage to keep away and fling some fire at him."

"Uh, all right," I said.

"The last is a mystery, and the highest leveled opponent we have to face. I'd guess he's more of a defensive expert, but I can't say for certain. Just . . . try to hit hard."

Amaryllis glanced around, then nodded to herself before moving to a wall-mounted rack covered in knives and daggers and other short, pointy things.

I looked around myself. There were so many weapons, but I didn't have a knack for any of them. I slid over to the next side and grinned at a wall covered in helmets. I swept one right off the topmost rack. A big gladiator's helmet, with a metal lion's face on the front, and it had a furry ruff on the top and back, with a few holes that my ears could poke through.

That didn't leave me with any weapons, though.

That was, until I spotted something in the corner. "Perfect!"

"What's perf— Oh please, Broccoli, no."

"Broccoli, yes!" I said.

When we left the room, all kitted out, Augustus was waiting for us, as promised. He stared at the weapon I had slung over a shoulder and the dustpan I held in my other hand. "Captain, is that our broom?"

· Chapter Twenty-Seven ·

Don't Cut Yourself on All These Edges

The worst part of getting into any sort of tournament-y fight, I was discovering, was the waiting.

Sure, this was only my second time experiencing this, but still. Having to wait in a little room while watching sylphs fill the stadium seats above wasn't all that fun, not while waiting for stuff that was out of our control.

I was mostly waiting for Augustus to return with my broom and dustpan. He applauded my choice in nonstandard weapons, then refused to allow me to take anything unenchanted into the arena because that would infringe upon his honor or something.

"They've arrived," Amaryllis said. She was staring out the window and across the arena, eyes narrowed to see into the darkened room just like ours on the other side.

I shifted over to her and looked across too. I could just make out the three mercenaries we'd have to fight milling around. "Looks like it," I said. "Any last-minute strategies?"

"None that I can think of," Amaryllis said. "I know you have a tendency to hoard points on occasion, and that's fine, but now would be a good time for even a small boost in your combat ability. This one fight might very well determine the entire war."

"Right," I said.

I only had one Cinnamon Bun skill point to spend. It was meant to get my Cleaning magic up a rank, but Amaryllis was right.

Congratulations! Way of the Mystic Bun is now Rank C!

Way of the Mystic Bun

Rank C - 00%

You have taken your first big hop on the path of the Mystic Bun, combining devastating magic-laced physical attacks with incredible mobility. You may now expend your own mana to manipulate an enemy's own.

I blinked. What did that even mean?

"I've upgraded the only skill I really can," I said. "I, uh, don't know if it'll help all that much."

"Which one?" Amaryllis asked.

But before I could get her to give me some advice, the door at the back of the room opened, and Augustus stepped in. He had my broom and dustpan! "Ladies, Captain," he said before placing the broom and dustpan to the side. "The hour is upon us now. The referee will be calling out your name as it is picked out of a hat. The hat is enchanted to prevent tampering, so no worries."

"Someone tampered with the hat before?" Amaryllis asked.

"We used to use a goblet," Augustus said. "Very dramatic but, alas, not tamperproof. Now, there are quite a few faces out there, but, as I always suggest, just don't pay them any mind. Do your best, and I'm sure you'll come out on top!"

I nodded, then slapped the lion-faced helmet I'd picked up onto my head. It took some wiggling to get my ears to poke out from the right spots, but I managed.

New skill acquired: Pit Fighting

Rank: E

"How do I look?" I asked.

"Like some sort of hideous lion-rabbit crossbreed," Amaryllis said.

I turned my head this way and that. The helmet was acceptably snug, tight without being too much so. It did limit my range of vision a little bit, but not enough that I thought it would really impact me midfight.

Augustus left us while I was getting my helmet on. I sighed, picked up my weapons, then put them back down. "Okay, no, before we head out, we should do buffs."

"Do you have a tea set?" Amaryllis asked.

"No, but I have arms," I said. I raised them. "Hugs?"

Amaryllis made a show of being huffy, but we were among friends, so there was no heat in the protests. Awen, on the other hand, giggled and wrapped her arms around us both to make it an even better hug.

I did my best to snuggle my friends, which was hard, given the helmet. Maybe if I had practiced more, my hugging skill would be a bit better. I regretted not hugging people more. But that regret wouldn't stop me from making the change I needed to become a better hugger.

Augustus's voice snapped us out of the hug, and we all glanced over to the arena where the sylph was talking up to the crowd, his voice amplified by a microphone-like device hanging from the ceiling by a long wire.

"—And our first combatants for the day will be . . . Representing Lord Francisco Hawk . . . Jacob Hayer."

The door to the far room opened, and one of the sylphs stepped out. He held six swords by their middles, three in each hand. He shifted his shoulders as he took in the crowd, then let his wings buzz behind him. One of them wasn't moving as much as the other. An injury?

"Representing Lady Amaryllis Albatross . . . Lady Awen Bristlecone."

Awen eeped and jumped on the spot. So I gave her a bonus squeeze to help with her nerves. "Kick his butt, Awen."

Awen nodded. "I'll do my best," she said. She looked really determined as she picked up her big shield and moved toward the door. "Ah, I kind of regret not practicing a bit more," she said.

"I think I regret that too," I said. "But we can't worry about that now. Do your best, Awen!"

Awen smiled back. "I will," she said before stepping out into the arena. Awen glanced up for just a moment before refocusing on her opponent.

Augustus gestured to either end of the arena, and Awen and Jacob moved into two squares marked out on the sandy ground. A sylph referee in a padded leather outfit stepped into the middle of the arena and raised a bright red kerchief. "Once this hits the ground, you begin. No moves that are meant to kill outright. This is a gentleman's and gentlewoman's duel. I'll have no barbarism in my arena. If I call a stop, you stop, if I tell you to back off, you back off, and if I tell you to jump on one leg and sing lullabies, you'll do that too. Am I understood?"

Awen and her opponent both nodded.

"Good." The referee made a show of looking around. "The arena is cleared. There is no magic in the air. Testing the magelights now."

The entire arena turned red as the lights above shut off and a bunch of red lights came on. It was bright enough that it didn't really interfere with anyone's vision.

"If you see those lights come on again, you stop," the referee said. He turned to Jacob. "Repeat my instructions about the lights," he said.

Jacob cleared his throat, then repeated them. The referee turned to Awen next.

"Awa? Oh, um, if the lights turn red, I have to stop."

"That's right," the referee said. "I take my job seriously, and I expect you both to do the same. This will be an honorable fight, or I'll make it one, and no one wants that. Now, are both combatants ready?"

Awen and Jacob nodded, and they both shifted in their squares. Awen brought her shield up before her. It was big enough that she was almost entirely hidden behind it. I didn't know what her plan was, but I hoped that it was good.

"Dropping the kerchief now," the referee said.

The red piece of cloth fluttered in the air before touching down on the sand.

There wasn't quite an explosive start to the fight. Awen just stepped forward slowly and carefully, her right hand held close to her side.

Jacob stepped to the side, then flung all six of the swords he was carrying into the air.

Then he started to sing.

It was just a single pure note at first, but it slowly turned into another, more like a dirge than a proper song, really. The interesting thing was the way the song interacted with his swords. They hung suspended in midair, shivering as if they were bells that had been struck.

"Oh, that's neat. Neat and really not great for Awen," I said.

The song stopped as Jacob let out a piercing whistle.

Two of the swords shot forward.

Awen bent her shield, and the first sword struck it and ricocheted off to the side, stabbing into the sandy ground behind her. The second looked like it was going to smack her, but at the last moment she reached out with a bare hand, and . . . and the sword scraped against her hand with a crystalline ringing.

It sounded as if someone had pressed a finger along the rim of a wineglass, a humming note that only stopped once the sword slid past Awen and bounced off the ground behind her. The sword flipped and rose back up as Jacob returned to humming.

"She has a gauntlet," Amaryllis observed.

I squinted at Awen and could make out a glove covering her entire hand all the way down her elbow. It was glass, shaped and curved, and growing to cover her more and more every moment, with what looked like complicated joints around the fingers and the bend of her elbow.

Was she making magical glass armor for herself on the spot? That was so cool!

"Go Awen! You're awesome!" I cheered.

Awen moved forward again while Jacob walked in a wide circle to reposition himself. His first two blows had been more like testing attacks than anything else, it seemed.

Then Awen swung her arm around her shield, and a dozen little things caught the air as they scattered on the ground before Jacob.

The mercenary paused, eyes narrowing. He continued to sing even as he knelt down and pinched something off the ground: a caltrop, made of four bits of twisted glass.

"Well, she's not holding back," Amaryllis said.

Awen flung more caltrops around her shield, then even more of them, most disappearing into the sand so that they were nearly impossible to make out.

Jacob whistled, and a sword shot toward Awen. She carefully stepped to the side and batted it out of the way with her shield, but a second whistle sent another sword flying toward her, then a third. Soon, Awen had to twist and crouch behind her shield while three of Jacob's swords spun around her. They'd dart in, then back out, cutting at her shield and trying to poke her from behind.

I winced. Awen was having to dodge and block a lot, while all Jacob was doing was humming his constant dirge. I was starting to make out very faint changes in pitch and tone that seemed to help the swords move, but there was no way I could figure out the pattern without a whole lot more studying. It was a neat set of skills.

Awen ducked under her shield, then she flung her arm out.

Instead of more caltrops, a foot-long scintillating crystal dagger shot toward Jacob's chest.

His song shifted as he took a quick step back, and one of the swords near him swung around and placed itself between him and the dagger.

Awen twisted her hand, and the dagger's flight path changed in midair. It arced around the sword and stabbed into Jacob's armor.

The blade burst into shards on impact, and it left a stub of broken glass jutting out of his armor. Not deep, but it was first blood.

Jacob's song deepened and sped up ominously. He jumped up as one of his swords swept down and landed on the flat of the blade.

"Damn," I heard Awen say as he surfed over the ground she'd trapped.

Jacob plucked a sword out of the air and landed next to Awen already swinging.

She staggered back, shield imposed between herself and the mercenary to parry the swing. It was a lot heavier than the blows from the flying swords, though, and it smacked her arm out wide.

Jacob moved in, still singing and still with his other swords flying circles around himself and Awen.

One of the blades nicked her in the back, and I winced as Awen squeaked. They were circling in closer.

I think we all sensed the moment that Awen started to lose steam.

So, she went out with a bang.

Thrusting her shield forward, Awen rammed it into Jacob. But the mercenary was quick on his feet, and he rolled with the blow, stepping to the side as she moved past. Then he let out a long hiss, and I noticed that the shiny glass on the ground had been moving.

Awen had pulled the glass closer? Maybe, since he'd moved out of her trap, she'd moved her trap to him!

It didn't help much.

Awen's shield was shoved aside, and she only just caught his sword mid-length with her gauntleted hand.

Jacob let go of it, grabbed Awen by the shirt, and with a shove and a flip, threw her up and around to crash into the sandy ground with a hard *oomph*.

One of the flying swords came around and rested a handspan over Awen's neck.

In a flash, Awen had a gorget over her throat, then the glass continued to grow until her head was encased in a crystalline helmet. It was a bit crooked and was obviously rushed, but it was enough that Awen was able to roll around and back to her feet even as Jacob's swords hounded her every move.

Awen was incredible, but her fight wasn't turning out well. The more armor she added, the slower she moved and the harder Jacob hit her.

He was twisting his blades to only strike with the flat side, but it was still tossing Awen around, and after the third time she landed on her back and had a sword stop above her, she stopped fighting back.

Awen' reached up and tore off her helmet. She glared up at the sword, then let her head fall back. "Fine, I yield," she said.

· Chapter Twenty-Eight ·

I'm Not Touching You!

Awen returned to our little waiting room after a sylph in white robes fussed over her at the edge of the ring. Some magic was used, but Amaryllis assured me it was nothing but Healing magic. Members of the Healing Sentinels swore an oath to only heal, so there was nothing to worry about.

"Are you okay?" I asked anyway as soon as she was close. Then, when she slipped into hugging range, I pounced and squeezed her tight.

Awen giggled and wrapped her arms around me to return the hug. "I'm fine, Broc. Well, mostly fine."

"Mostly?" I asked as I pulled back a little.

She narrowed her eyes. "Yes, mostly. I had a few more tricks I could have used in there. I shouldn't have held back as much as I did. He was a much better fighter than I am, but I think I could have made him bleed a lot more if I'd just pushed myself a little harder."

"But you did great out there," I said.

Awen pulled out of the hug entirely while shaking her head. "I lost, Broccoli. I'm not going to beat myself up over it. You don't need to worry about that." She glanced back at the arena. "But I could have done better. I should have. I . . . I think I need to think a little bit about it."

I sighed but let her pass. Amaryllis hesitated next to her, then carefully gave Awen a hug too. I couldn't help but smile at that. It was nice seeing Amaryllis opening up, at least.

"When I next write to Rose, I'll tell her that you were spectacular out there," Amaryllis said.

"Awa! N-no!"

Maybe Awen was right too. I'd been thinking of the fights as games more than anything else.

"Representing Lord Francisco Hawk . . ." Augustus was already in the center of the arena. "Flein Bocking!"

That was the other sylph, the Hardened. I didn't know what that class could do, and that was pretty worrisome. Plus, he was level sixteen. That was a good chunk ahead of me.

The sylph stepped into the arena and glanced over to our side of it. He didn't have any weapons on him that I noticed. Did that mean he was a magic user? Or something else?

"Representing Lady Amaryllis Albatross . . . Captain Broccoli Bunch!"

I paused for a moment, only moving when I felt talons and a hand touching my back. "You can do it," Amaryllis said.

"Kick his butt," Awen suggested quite seriously.

I nodded, my resolve made up, then I grabbed my broom and dustpan and moved into the arena.

I came to stand across from Flein. "Heya," I said.

He nodded to me. "Greetings."

I took only one moment to glance up and around. The stadium seating was full. Nobles and a few more modestly dressed sylphs, all packing in as close as they could. The only exception was a small box where I saw the princesses and Francisco looking down on us.

Looking up was a distraction I couldn't afford, so I refocused on Flein again. "Usually, I'd try to make friends, Mister Flein, but I really, really have to win this, okay? So, ah, maybe we can chat after the fight? No hard feelings?"

The sylph smiled. "No hard feelings, Captain Bunch."

The referee glanced at us both, then started an abridged version of the speech he'd given before the last fight.

"Uh, I have a question," I said when he was nearing the end.

"Yes?" the referee asked.

"Is there an out of bounds?"

He nodded. "Going too far up, above the level of the first row of seats, will activate a barrier. Leaving the arena through the side doors is forbidden as well, though those will remain closed for the duration of the fight."

"All right, thank you," I said.

"Good." The referee made a show of looking around. "The arena is cleared. There is no magic in the air. Testing the magelights now."

I blinked as the arena turned red. It made the open space a whole lot more sinister for a moment.

"If you see those lights come on again, you stop," the referee said. He turned to me. "Repeat my instructions about the lights."

"If the lights turn red, I have to stop."

He nodded, then turned to Flein, who repeated the instructions without looking away from me.

I bounced on the spot. I should have stretched more, I realized.

"Are both combatants ready?"

We nodded. I shifted my grip on my broom and turned so that I was side-on to Flein in case he launched a spell at me. I had a plan forming in the back of my head already. I adjusted my gladiator's helmet one last time.

"Dropping the kerchief now," the referee said.

The handkerchief fluttered down and landed gently onto the sand.

That sand instantly shifted up and moved of its own volition.

Cleaning magic gathered on my broom as I stepped to the side and flicked it out, firing a bright cleansing bolt toward Flein.

Could I negate his sand control? If so, this would be an easy win!

I wasn't so lucky.

Flein ducked to the side, then spun around on the spot.

The sand around him leapt up from the ground and clung to him, two long tendrils forming past his arms and snapping toward me with twin cracks.

I hopped to the side, narrowly avoiding the two sandy whips. They rammed into the arena wall behind where I had been standing with two echoing thumps. That . . . would have hurt.

Flein wasn't going to give me any time to come up with a plan. He spun around, and two more whips swung out at me, one slicing the air horizontally, the other snaking out right at my face.

I jumped, ears back to keep them safe, and rolled over the horizontal strike while the other cracked at empty air.

I landed in a roll and bounced back to my feet. I needed to react! Pushing my mana out, I created a burst of Cleaning magic as another pair of whips approached.

They kept coming, only a small portion shimmering away. The sand itself wasn't something that was dirty, it was just plain sand.

One of the whips slashed past my side, and I hissed as it grated open a thin streak on my arm.

I couldn't stand still.

Flein walked toward the middle of the arena, arms still spinning around to form new whips. He was going to cut the distance and give me no time to react.

I flung a large fireball at him while backing up, then, in the pause where he ducked out of the way, I brought my foot back and kicked forward. The end of my shoes met my dustpan in midair, and Flein cursed as he redirected his whips to bat it out of the air.

The dustpan went sailing far out of reach, and before he could reset, I darted toward the wall, sprinting all out with stamina coursing through my legs. A whip snapped behind me a moment before I leapt up and landed feet-first on the wall.

My legs sprung out, and I shot across the arena on a straight path for Flein, broom held wooden-end out toward the sylph.

Flein flung his arm at me, a fresh whip forming in the air.

So I kicked out with one leg, a fireball streaking from the tip of my foot on a straight path for his arm.

He rolled to the side, but in doing so, his newest whips fell apart into plain sand.

I was close!

I landed, rolled, scraped across the ground, then shot in the opposite direction right toward Flein, who was recovering from his own dodge.

He swung his arm out at me, and half a dozen ropy tendrils of sand formed in the air between us. They weren't moving whip-fast, but there would be no dodging them.

So I swung my broom at them. The haft glowed with Cleaning magic as I put my Makeshift Weapons Proficiency to work. The thin wood smacked though the sand, and the magic glue on it wrapped around Flein's, disrupting the shapes where it hit them and turning the ropes into loose sand in the air.

Flein didn't shy away from my charge. He ran right up to me and, abandoning his ranged strikes, threw a punch at my head.

I ducked out of the way of his punch, then smacked him in the side with my broom.

The broom made a nice *thwap* sound and little else.

His clothes and skin were covered in a layer of caked-on sand.

I sidestepped another punch, then backed away as Flein kept swinging at me. He had a simple stance, legs apart, arms cocked before him, hips swaying to give his punches more force, like a boxer. But boxers didn't have fists enclosed in rocky lumps of hard-packed sand.

I blasted him with fireballs, but that didn't seem to do anything at all.

Flein ducked in toward me and swung an uppercut at my chin. It was only the fact that I was taller than him that let me bend back and out of the way of the blow, but then he was right up in front of me, and he brought a knee up to smack me in the thigh.

I stumbled back, making some space between us.

I was losing.

He had the advantage at range. He was tougher up close and hit harder too. All I had was speed and a broom. I was faster, more agile, too, but no amount of cartwheels would help here.

I had to try something else. Fire didn't work. It wasn't hot or hard-hitting enough. Cleaning wasn't doing anything other than washing his sand out. My broom with Makeshift Weapons Proficiency could disrupt his whips and sand but not much else.

Way of the Mystic Bun . . .

I nodded to myself. That could be a solution, maybe, but I'd need to get in close.

I spun my broom around, holding it by the haft while the bristles were interposed between Flein and me.

When he took his next swing, I pushed it aside with the broom. I didn't just push my mana though my broom, though, I pushed it into him.

There was a weird moment, like touching a carpet a moment after shuffling on it with big woolly slippers—not a shock, but the impression that a shock was due.

Nothing happened except that I shoved the punch aside enough to dodge it. But I had felt something.

My new rank in Way of the Mystic Bun allowed me to control an opponent's mana, but it didn't come with an instruction manual.

Flein swung his free hand, and I squeaked as a rope of sand snaked out and almost caught me around the throat. My face almost met his rising knee eye-first as he jumped up into a kick.

Acting on reflex, I placed a hand on his knee and pushed it back. At the moment the contact was made, I felt his magic moving. It wasn't like my own, all friendly and clean. His was coarse and rough, and it felt like it wanted to pack itself in tight.

Pushing off his knee strike was enough to launch me into a backflip. The sense of his magic vanished as I broke contact, but despite the distraction, I still stuck the landing.

I didn't pause, circling around him close enough that I could move in if he tried to make another whip and far enough that he couldn't punch my lights out.

Only two dozen seconds had passed since the fight started, and I think we each had a measure of the other.

I was in so much trouble.

But I had a really bad idea, and sometimes bad ideas were a great way to get out of a bind.

It was a reckless idea, too, but that's how I fought most of the time anyway.

Flein was the first to move. Sliding toward me on a wave of sand, his fist punched out and released a big poof of loose sand that filled the air before me.

I countered with a blast of Cleaning magic that didn't do much. Some of that sand splashed through the front of my helmet and against my face. I had to blink fast to keep it out of my eyes.

Flein's quick motion ended with a heavy punch toward my middle. His fist had gained a long narrow bar at the end of it, giving him more reach.

I stepped back, grabbed his wrist, and pulled. At the same time, I grabbed onto his magic and cast a spell.

It wasn't anything fancy. It was the sort of thing I'd done a thousand times before—a wave of pure Cleaning magic.

The wave burst out of him and washed over me to no effect.

I grinned.

I'd just cast a spell with *his* magic!

Better yet, the sandy construct around his fist fell apart.

Flein pulled his arm back in a hurry, and I hopped forward and followed.

I saw his eyes filled with confusion behind a sandy mask as I jumped toward him. "This might tickle!" I shouted.

I darted in and poked at him with my free hand while shoving my broom between his legs and behind his knee. Every poke turned his Sand-aspect mana into more Clean-aspect mana, and with the change, his armor fell apart in big clumps.

Flein wasn't going to let me off so easily, though. He reached out and grabbed my broom handle. I lost my grip on it as he tugged it away and immediately let it fall to the side.

I might have been out of a weapon, but I had just gained a second hand to poke him with!

"Annoying," he said.

"Thanks, I'm trying really hard," I said.

And then Flein exploded, a burst of sand shoving off him hard enough to send me reeling.

I guessed that it wouldn't be so easy to win here.

· Chapter Twenty-Nine ·

Sandblasting

The fight was . . . I wasn't sure if it was going well for me or not. In terms of stats, I was fine—barely any stamina or mana spent. My health was a couple of points shy of full. In terms of everything else, the gap between us was still wide.

Flein had the advantage. Close up, he was much slower than me, but he moved as if he knew what he was doing. Maybe it was a skill, maybe it was a martial art, maybe he just practiced fighting a whole bunch. I don't think it mattered how, as long as I kept in mind that he was the better fighter up close, despite my reach and speed advantage.

From afar, Flein had whips of sand and likely a few other ways to make my life difficult. I couldn't just keep dodging him forever. Eventually, my stamina would run out, or I'd get tired, or one of his whips would hit me hard enough to disable me. There was a chance that he'd run out of mana first, but that was a lot to hope for.

I bounced on the balls of my feet, hands raised defensively before me and ears laid back against my head. Flein took a moment to loosen his shoulders and carefully rebuild the armor covering his hand.

So far, the only trick that had worked was getting in real close, touching him, and disrupting his mana. Turning it into Cleaning mana was easy, and it did a number on his sand armor.

My eyes darted around the arena—where was my broom anyway? Oh! It was a few steps to his right.

My eyes shifted back to Flein, and I saw a blur of sand already halfway to my face.

Yelping, I tossed myself out of the way of a sandy tendril that . . . flopped onto the ground harmlessly where I'd been standing.

A feint!

My little bun heart was clawing its way out of my chest as I watched

Flein draw up more sand into a fresh whip. It spun around the air above him, then darted at me faster than I could blink.

I was on my feet and running already, but not fast enough.

The whip cracked against the back of my thigh, and I hissed at the fresh line of pain it left there. The crowd above, almost entirely forgotten, gasped.

Flein wasn't going to be swayed that easily. He pulled the whip back, then cracked it out again.

I ducked under it this time, the snap going off just above my head, louder than a gunshot.

Staying at range wasn't going to work.

I planted my foot down and flung myself toward Flein. At least when I was close, I had a chance to take him out, maybe land a lucky blow. From far away, all I was doing was letting him bully me around the arena.

Flein was ready for my move. It was a rather predictable thing to do, I guess, and he had to know that I was nearly out of options.

The arena's sandy floor burst upward, turning into a hip-high barrier of long spikes. Running into that would be like headbutting the back end of a hedgehog. I squished myself down sideways, and somehow, barely, I managed to slip between two of the spikes, then dropped into a roll.

A roll which ended right where Flein wanted me.

I screamed as his whip caught me right across the face. I was wearing a helmet, but that blow crossed right through it, and the padding within the helmet shoved against my face and sent me reeling back. I coughed and blinked hard as sand grit into my eyes and cheeks.

I only barely caught sight of the whip returning to circle above its master's head. He was going to hit me again!

I'd never formed a fireball so quickly. My mana spun into shape and launched a burning dart across the arena with a whistling shriek.

Flein aborted his attack and tore his sandy spikes apart to form a barrier between him and me. It caught the fireball with a dull thump.

Planting my feet, I squatted, then shot myself up and into the air as hard and fast as I could so that I was launched over Flein. Humans didn't tend to look up, but sylphs were able to fly. It was only natural that he would glance up and catch sight of me zipping above him.

He twisted around, tracking my arc as I flung fireballs and cleanballs at him as fast as I could make them.

Depleting my mana supply wasn't an issue. The fight would be ending soon either way, and if I lost it while I still had mana left, that just meant that I didn't give it my all.

Flein swatted my magic out of the air with a twisting mass of sand. It burst apart at every impact but reformed just as quickly.

I landed across from him, spun around so that I was facing his direction, then charged toward him, fists raised before me and body low to the ground.

Flein swung his arm out wide between us, and a second wall of sand spikes formed.

Good!

I hadn't jumped this way for nothing. As I ran, I ducked low and picked up my broom, both hands gripping onto the very end of the handle and mana flooding through the shaft.

I swung with a grunt of effort, more and more magic pouring out of the mop until it glowed.

A broom was a tool for sweeping, and right then, all I wanted was to sweep the sand away.

Something about Cleaning magic made it . . . strange. It would only clean out impurities, but the sand wasn't an impurity. When I tried to clean it away, all I was getting was clean sand.

What if I didn't target the sand so much as the mana holding it together?

It was a weird idea, and one that I really, really hoped would work out as I charged right into the teeth of his barrier.

My mop tore into the spikes . . . and right through them. Where it passed, the sandy construct burst apart into a cloud of dust.

I was through the barrier and right up against Flein faster than either of us could think.

Turning just a little, I rammed into the sylph shoulder first.

I was a lot heavier than he was, even with his sandy armor, and I was moving pretty darned fast. It still hurt. His chest had a thick layer of hardened sand over it, rough and coarse and not something I'd normally want to run into at a full sprint.

We crashed into each other, then I drove him to the ground. I heard him grunt beneath me before he swung a fist and hit me in the ribs. My armor took some of the sting out of the blow. Some of it.

Flein twisted, trying to throw me off him, but I pinned one end of my broom under a knee and pressed down on the other with one hand. With the other, I tried to reach for his face.

Sand twirled around us and shot toward my face. Was he going to try to suffocate me?

I let out a powerful burst of Cleaning magic, wiping his mana out of the air.

Then, finally, I placed a hand over his face. "Stop!" I screamed.

He grunted and shifted under me.

"Stop, or I'll turn your mana into fireballs inside you," I said.

He froze.

I froze too. That was a very mean thing to say to someone. Worse . . . I wasn't sure if I meant the threat or not.

He sighed and let his head fall back. "I'm not being paid enough to test that."

The referee was suddenly right next to us. "Winner, by forfeit, is Captain Broccoli Bunch," he declared.

I carefully shifted off from on top of Flein, then sat down on the ground. I hadn't noticed earlier, but all of the sand of the arena was bunched up around us, forming a slight hill. That . . . had been close, very close, *way too close*.

"Ma'am, are you well?"

I blinked and looked up into the eyes of a white-robed sylph. A young man, maybe five or six years my senior. "Uh? Oh, yeah."

"I'm going to touch your shoulder and hand," the sylph said. He was very gentle as he grabbed hold of me.

I felt his magic coiling under his skin, then it shot into me, and I flinched. My own mana twitched and his dispersed.

The sylph blinked. "Oh, you have very fine mana control, Captain. I assure you, on my name and oath, that I mean you no harm. I'm just going to run a diagnostic to make sure you're in good health."

"Oh, sorry," I said. I glanced to the side and noticed another sylph doing the same to Flein, though they were just finishing up.

This time I let the mana move in without touching it. I couldn't even begin to guess what he was doing. My senses weren't anywhere keen enough to figure it out. It felt warm, though.

"Two small cuts, arm and upper thigh near the buttocks, one forming bruise on the left side of the chest near the short ribs. Some light scraping of the skin around the shins . . . A lot of tension in your muscles and bones, especially around your legs. You might want to consider switching to a day-on-day-off workout schedule and adding some more protein to your diet. Otherwise, I validate you as being in good health."

"Oh, thanks," I said. He helped me to my feet, and out of curiosity, I checked my arm. The fabric of my gambeson had been cut, and . . . that was it. No blood, of course, not with all the Cleaning magic around, and no cut under that, either, just smooth, pale skin. "Healing magic's pretty neat."

"I must agree," the healer said. "You should rejoin your friends now, before the referee's patience runs dry."

I nodded and headed toward my friends, but not before trading a nod with Flein and taking off the lion-headed helmet I wore.

The moment I stepped into the room with my friends, I was swept up into a big, big hug. "You did great!"

"Well done!"

I laughed as the tension bled out of me. It took a bit of wiggling to free my arms, but as soon as I could, I squeezed Awen and Amaryllis right back. "Thanks," I said. "I wasn't sure I'd win that."

"I didn't doubt it at all," Awen said.

"Well, I certainly did. That was a tough opponent for you," Amaryllis said. "Which only makes it all the more impressive that you managed to pull off a victory."

"Yeah," I said. I wasn't sure what I was agreeing to. Maybe it was just the hug speaking. It was nice and warm and made all the tension in my shoulders bleed away. It also ended all too soon, though I knew I could always get more hugs if I asked.

"Are you well?" Amaryllis asked in a hushed voice that only we could hear.

I bobbed my head up and down. "I'm fine. That really was a tough fight. But we won."

"You won," Amaryllis said. "And you deserved it too."

"You were great out there," Awen added.

I was going to deny that, but then Augustus's voice cut me off. "Our final contestants. Representing Lord Francisco . . . Malter Roggen! And representing Lady Amaryllis Albatross is the lady herself."

Amaryllis took a deep breath. "My turn."

"Be careful out there," I said.

"Show him why you're so scary," Awen added.

"Oh, don't worry," Amaryllis said. She was almost purring. "With things at a tie, I have no choice but to win. I'm going to put the fear of me into that mercenary and maybe show Francis what'll happen to him if he crosses me enough."

Contrary to Amaryllis's wishes, I was worrying a lot.

· Chapter Thirty ·

BlitzKrieg

The last of the people we had to fight was Malter Roggen, the only human in the trio and, according to Insight, someone who had the Frozen Batterer class.

The height difference between Amaryllis and Malter was kind of obvious. Malter was a tallish human, and Amaryllis was maybe a tiny bit taller than average for a girl harpy. That meant that Malter had a good head of height over her.

Not that Amaryllis seemed to care. She stood at the end of the arena, oozing such a powerful aura of malice that I could feel it despite being behind a window. Was that what killing intent felt like? I thought it was just a thing in cartoons.

"I bet he's nervous now," Awen said.

Malter did look a pinch uncomfortable. He was level fourteen, the lowest-leveled person on the opposite team, and the only one equal to Amaryllis. He had light armor on, a padded outfit with a sort of hardened leather carapace atop it. He was armed, but he kept fiddling with his strange weapon.

"What is that thing?" I asked.

"It's a meteor hammer," Awen said. "The ostri like to use those. They can be pretty dangerous, but usually, if you're using one, you need a lot of space to maneuver, so you can't stick close to your allies."

"All right," I said. Hopefully, Amaryllis would be able to counter it properly.

The referee stepped back into the ring and glanced at both Amaryllis and Malter before he started his usual spiel. He must have said those exact same lines hundreds of times by now. It was impressive that he still put so much energy into it. Though, maybe there was a Referee skill out there?

He had Amaryllis and Malter each repeat his instructions before finally pulling out a handkerchief and raising it above his head.

Amaryllis brought her knife around so that it was before her, and she crouched into more of a fighter's stance.

Malter shifted as well. His meteor hammer was a lump at the end of a thick ribbon. He gave it some slack, then automatically started to spin it around.

The handkerchief dropped.

I held my breath as it fluttered through the air, gently making its way down until . . .

The arena exploded with sound and light as Amaryllis fired a spell across the space between her and Malter.

There was no dodging something that fast, even if the air around Malter seemed to fill with icy crystals. He grunted and stumbled back as Amaryllis's electrical discharge wracked his body.

Still, he managed to get his arm moving to spin his hammer around some more. His free hand, still holding on to the coil of rope for his weapon, rose, and he formed a sort of hexagonal shield in the air, like a giant, hovering snowflake.

Amaryllis didn't sit idle, though. She jogged around the edge of the arena, a careful spiral that would bring her around to Malter's position soon enough. He had to turn to keep his shield interposed between them.

As she circled him, Amaryllis fired three more quick spells, little zaps of magic that snapped through the air. Malter hopped on the spot to avoid one that went for his exposed feet, another missed him entirely, and the last tested the strength of his shield. It held, though it steamed from the heat where the magic hit.

Then Malter started to dance. He spun, arm shifting out, and the twirling ball at the end of the ribbon he held flung itself out and came around in a big loop.

Amaryllis paused her run to let it swing by her. She eyed it, eyes narrowed as the hammer came back around in a deceptively slow arc.

Malter shifted a leg out, caught the ribbon behind the hammer, then spun and kicked. The hammer flew in a straight path, right toward Amaryllis.

The distance was great enough that Amaryllis was able to duck out of the way, but it was a close thing.

Unfortunately for Malter, it left him open, and his weapon required a specific set of motions to reset itself.

Amaryllis flung little zappy spells at him. Nothing that would take him out on their own but enough of them that he had to move fast to duck and weave so that they'd miss. His shield came around and took a few hits, but it was just small enough that some part of Malter was always sticking out.

Amaryllis started jogging again, one hand flinging lightning toward Malter, the other . . . trailing down next to her, just over the sand.

"Oh!" Awen said.

"What?" I asked.

"I just caught on to what she's doing."

I glanced back at the fight. Malter and Amaryllis were now circling around each other. Soon, they'd have traded places from where they started the fight. "I don't see it."

"She's herding him."

I watched a bit more as Malter finally reached the spot where Amaryllis had been earlier. He was putting up a decent fight now that he'd gotten used to Amaryllis's style of fighting. His weapon afforded him good range, and judging by the heavy thumps that sounded out when it hit the ground, it hit hard too.

Amaryllis was using the fact that he had to shield himself from her constant barrage of little spells to make dodging easier. After all, he couldn't exactly go all out while also working so hard to keep safe.

And then it happened. Amaryllis grinned the sort of grin she only deployed when she'd caught someone flatfooted. Her free hand rose up, and then she turned her talons down and tensed.

Malter stumbled out of nowhere, feet planting themselves onto the ground even as he scurried to wrap his hammer around his arm. He tilted back, foot kicking out to hit the back of his shield hard enough that I winced. Judging by the confused and pained look that crossed his face, he hadn't meant to do that.

I think Malter realized just how much trouble he was in, because he suddenly threw caution to the wind. He flung his hammer out with a grunt, and where it flew, the air filled with shimmering fog.

Amaryllis jumped to the side, and the hammer sailed past where she was to impact the wall behind her. A huge burst of icy spikes exploded out of the wall, almost skewering my friend from behind.

I gasped, hands covering my mouth. That had been close!

Amaryllis seemed to think so, because she raised her hand, and for a moment I was able to make out the wires she held. They trailed along the ground all the way over to where Malter was.

He saw them, too, and clawed at his legs and sides, but it was too late.

Amaryllis smiled, and the air, even in the room we were in, started to smell like ozone.

There was a great big bang and a bright light. For a moment, I swore I saw the outline of Malter's skeleton before I had to blink away from the light. Sand was kicked up around the mage, and his hammer's ribbon trailed to the ground.

Then Malter flopped to the floor, completely out of the fight.

I held my breath as a medic sylph, the same one who had helped me, ran out to Malter and checked on him. The man sat up soon enough, looking rather groggy but alive.

He was fine, which meant . . . "Woo! Well done, Amaryllis!" I cheered.

Awen and I slipped out of the room in a quick sprint. Awen stopped before Amaryllis and shook her talons with a big smile on.

I, being less reserved, tackled Amaryllis off her feet with a flying hug. "You won!"

"Get off me, you clingy bun," Amaryllis protested. "People are watching, you know!"

I laughed, squeezed her extra tight, then hopped to my feet and helped her back up so that I could give her a second, standing hug. Awen joined in that one, despite Amaryllis's continued protests that it would make her look improper or whatever.

The referee cleared his throat, and we backed off. A medic came to check on Amaryllis, but she'd been unscathed throughout the entire fight, so she was given a clean bill of health.

I didn't quite know what to expect then, but I didn't have to worry much.

Augustus stepped into the arena and carefully directed my friends and I to stand on one side while a team of sylphs swept in. A big carpet was unrolled across the ground while another swept up the sand with a spell.

Caprica descended, accompanied by a couple of guards who stood watch by the doorway, and soon the three mercenaries we'd fought were standing at attention across from us.

Then Francisco entered the arena.

Judging by the way he glanced up at the crowd, he was very aware of all the eyes taking us in. I had the impression that, to some people, this was the best part of the show.

Francisco was directed to stand in front of his team, and Amaryllis took a half step forward as well. There was only a meter between them—a very tense one.

"Fighters, spectators, noble lords and ladies," Augustus said with his most boisterous voice. "We have gathered here to watch a duel, declared between the noble houses of Hawk and Albatross over the right of participation in the upcoming International Summit. This duel is now complete."

There was a long pause, and I only just managed to catch myself before I clapped.

"Lord Hawk, do you concede your loss, as witnessed?" Augustus asked.

Francisco's nose rose right up, and he glared at Amaryllis. Still, the pressure must have been pretty hard on him. "I suppose it was a well-fought duel. I think it's tradition in these parts to shake talons when two opponents meet honorably."

Augustus nodded, but slowly. "Yes. Though that is the choice of the victor."

Amaryllis huffed, a very mighty and powerful huff that carried much pride with it. "I won't shake the talon of a bully nor the talon of a coward. To shake with someone who has demonstrated that he is both would abase me and my family."

"A coward?" Francisco snapped.

Oh, things were going off-script. Augustus seemed ready to step in, and I was sure that he'd be able to calm everyone down. He had to have some public-speaking skills of some sort. But then Caprica reached out and very subtly touched his side, and the speaker kept mum.

"You would call me a coward?" Francisco snapped. "You're the one who's terrified of a little scuffle."

"A war is not a scuffle," Amaryllis shot back. "And I think I've proven amply that I'm not afraid to put my claws where my beak is. You, on the other hand, are proving to not only be a coward and a bully but an idiot too. I think it's well-known that I have little tolerance for birds who replace their brains with festering worms."

Francisco choked, his face turning red and his feathers puffing out.

"I ought to gut you for insulting me so."

"Do you want another duel?" Amaryllis asked. "Will you actually participate yourself this time? Or will you cower behind the back of more hired goons?"

"I-I don't need to prove myself to you."

"Oh, shut up, Francis," Amaryllis said. "You're giving our entire race a poor name when you put your idiocy on such public display."

Augustus cleared his throat. "It is the opinion, as witnessed, of the Calcifer Spood Memorial Arena that the victory goes to Lady Amaryllis Albatross!"

Now the clapping started for real, though it was the demure, careful clap of proper people.

I didn't bother with that—those nobles could use a bit more enthusiasm—so I clapped loud and hard, and then I tossed in a few whoops for good measure. Judging by the barely restrained smile on Caprica's face, I was doing just fine.

· Chapter Thirty-One ·

To the Victor, the Spoils

I didn't know why, but I'd sorta expected there to be something after the fight—maybe not like a party or anything, but at least an opportunity to chat and relax. The nobles in the stands above dispersed to talk in clumps, Francisco left after giving Amaryllis a downright mean glare, and then Augustus escorted Caprica out of the arena.

My friends and I followed after her because there wasn't much else to do, really.

Caprica waited for us in the corridor outside the arena proper, her guards standing at either end, as attentive as ever. "I suppose that was a grand success," she said.

"I hope so," Amaryllis said. "It'll mean that, unless the main harpy delegation shows up between now and the summit, I'll be representing the Harpy Mountains."

"You'll need to do more than just show up," Caprica said. "Do you have a dress for the occasion?"

"I have something suitable."

"And do you have anyone that can assist you at the event itself? A secretary, at the very least. You'll want to study the reports on the other delegations, and you need to submit your text, prepare a speech for the opening, a main argument speech, and a closing. The closing speech will be tricky—you want different versions of it to respond to different likely possibilities."

Amaryllis huffed. "I know that it won't be as simple as showing up."

"It will certainly not be that simple," Caprica said. "This summit is supposed to be a grand diplomatic event. Especially between Sylphfree and the Harpy Mountains. The . . . failure of the diplomatic meeting at Fort Sylphrot is putting even more pressure on this event to be a success. And I think that your Lord Francis isn't the only one who wishes for war. We have more than a few generals and nobles who would be eager to do more than parade around."

I puffed my cheeks out as I let out a big breath. "We'll have to convince everyone not to start anything."

"It won't be easy," Caprica said.

"Nothing's ever easy," Amaryllis said.

"Huh?" I asked. "A bunch of things are easy. I guess this might not be one of them, but I'm sure if we share the work, it'll get done!"

Caprica chuckled. "Well, I suppose at least you won't have to do all the work on your own. I should have some free time in the coming days. Maybe I can stop by your inn and assist you."

I clapped. "That would be super! We could have tea and a study session. I'll have to ask the innkeeper if we can have more cushions."

"Cushions?" Caprica asked.

"Don't encourage her," Amaryllis said. She gestured to Caprica. "What about the rest of the day? I can't imagine it's much later than noon."

Caprica glanced up, toward where I imagined the stage was. "I should rejoin Gabrielle. She mentioned wanting to tour the city a little. She very rarely leaves the palace, and while I'm worried that it might put her health at risk, I don't want my sister to be raised entirely in isolation."

We started for the nearest staircase, back up to the parts of the arena that were better decorated. Amaryllis and Awen surrendered their borrowed gear along the way. I had sort of left my bucket and mop behind at some point.

"You mentioned that Gabrielle is a little sick a few times," I said. "Is it bad?"

"It's not great," Caprica said. "But it's under control. Sylphfree has unmatched medical facilities and the best doctors on Dirt. Our medical and healing arts are second to none, and that's in large part thanks to the same affliction that Gabrielle has."

"Huh?" I asked.

Caprica nodded. "It's not a secret. Quite a few members of the royal family grow up feeble, with fainting sicknesses or ill health. In the past, a few have passed away far too young. I have a great-uncle who poured a considerable amount of wealth into shoring up our medical facilities and building great schools to study and experiment with the healing arts."

"That seems nice," I said.

"He was moved when his sibling passed away from a wasting sickness," she said somberly. "When the schools started paying dividends in the form of a healthier populace, the military saw the potential as well. It became . . . Well, suffice to say that in Sylphfree, the most honored sylphs after the royal family are the paladins, followed by the brass, and swiftly followed by those who dedicate themselves to medicine and healing. It's seen as a very acceptable alternative to military service, though a costlier one."

We made it up to the floor above and found Gabrielle and the rest of Caprica's guards waiting there. The girl grinned wide and stepped closer. "You did so well!" she said.

"We did what we had to do," Amaryllis demurred. There was no denying the smug aura around her, though.

"Would it be insulting if I said that I didn't expect Caprica's new friends to be such talented warriors? All three of you."

I shook my head. "We only barely won, I think. That was tough. If we were actually warriors, then we would probably have done much better."

"I'm not so sure of that," Caprica said. "You all fought in rather strange ways. I'm particularly impressed with Awen's Glass magic. It seems tremendously useful."

"Awa? Oh, it's nothing special. I hope I'll be able to improve it as we continue to level and grow stronger."

"So you three really do intend to keep growing?" Caprica asked.

I blinked. "Should we stop?"

She chuckled. "Most civilians will make it past their first tier if they find something they truly love and focus on it. I think most of our forces reach the top of their second tier eventually. But you all sound like you want to go far beyond that."

"I don't see why more people don't," I said. "It's not hard, is it?"

"It's time-consuming," Caprica said. "And more importantly, requires that one travels and reaches more and more dungeons, not to mention increasingly dangerous challenges to level efficiently."

"I guess it's not something for a complacent person to do," I said.

She shrugged. "It's admirable that you want to grow more personally powerful. Don't let anyone tell you otherwise. Now, we could stand here and chat, or we could be more efficient with our time. Gabrielle, I don't recall eating out with you in a long time. Would you rather return home or stay with us for a meal?"

Gabrielle sniffed, eyes rolling even as she placed her hands on her hips. "Obviously, I want to go with you. I'm not twelve, Caprica."

Caprica eyed Gabrielle. "I don't know. The way you were jumping up and down and cheering earlier, I think I could be convinced to believe that you were."

The little sister's cheeks reddened, and her wings flapped furiously behind her. "Capri!"

Caprica grinned back at us. "We should all go. My treat, to celebrate your grand victory today."

"Thank you!" I said.

Augustus greeted us by the exit. He made sure to shake everyone's hands and welcomed us to fight at his arena whenever we wanted to. Judging by the number of nobles still milling around, our little fight had attracted a lot of attention. I imagined that in a place like Goldenalden, where royalty was honored, having two princesses visit someone's establishment and come out looking pleased would be great for business.

Caprica's guards ran ahead and formed something of a wedge leading to the carriage, that was, until Caprica waved over one of the guards who had more feathers on his helmet. "We'll walk down the street a little. Take in the air, window shop, then likely find something to eat along the way," she said. "Could you do a wide formation, please?"

The guard bowed, then spun and made a few quick gestures that had the other guards dispersing into an even wider net.

Gabrielle didn't even seem to notice all the motion. She was too busy taking in the street.

It was a bit weird, hanging out with some new friends while being aware from the periphery that we were constantly surrounded. The worst thing was that it felt rude not to speak to the guards. Some seemed really nice, and when I smiled at them, they smiled or nodded back. They were people, too, and they obviously deserved to be befriended just as much as anyone else, but their job got in the way of that.

"Broccoli?" Awen asked.

I snapped out of my thoughts and gave her a quick side-hug to tell her I was fine. "So, are we going to get fancy food, or are we going to get fun food?"

"Fun food?" Gabrielle asked.

"You mean food we . . . like?" Caprica asked right after.

"Nothing so simple," I sniffed very haughtily and as fancily as I could. "Well, you see, dear princesses, normal food is just food that's meant to be eaten, as all food is. It can be tasty or not. Fancy food is all about the presentation, being all nice and prettiful. But fun food, now that's food that's meant to be fun to eat!"

"Sometimes I wonder how I became friends with you," Amaryllis muttered.

Ignoring Amaryllis's interruption, I went on: "I don't think they have hot dogs or hamburgers here."

"You eat dogs?" Gabrielle gasped, hands over her mouth.

I shook my head so hard my ears whipped together. "No, no, I'm a vegetarian. Hot dogs are like . . . sausages placed in this piece of bread, usually with condiments on top."

"Eating sausages doesn't sound very vegetarian," Gabrielle pointed out.

"No, they're not for me. I just like them. I wasn't always vegetarian."

"Oh." Gabrielle gave me a weird look. "So, these hot dogs are basically sandwiches?"

I held back a pout. "Never mind that. I'm sure there's some sort of junk food sold around here. There has to be."

"I don't know. The sylphs are notoriously prudish. It's possible that they don't like the idea of such frivolous food," Amaryllis said.

"We're not prudish," Caprica said . . . prudishly. "I'm sure we have plenty of fun food." She waved the same guard captain over and asked him if he knew where we could find fun food. He looked completely stumped for a moment, that was, until one of the younger guards cleared his throat and said that there were a few places some blocks over.

So off we went, chatting about this and that and nothing at all while pausing in front of windows to stare at the stuff within. I don't think any of us failed to notice the small entourage of nobles snooping about some distance away, coincidentally always going the same way we were. I'm pretty sure that most of my friends didn't notice that the city guard patrolled the same street six times in the space of half an hour. I think they were pretty much just going around the block in a big circle by the end.

The next blocks over had more shops, though they catered toward a less distinguished crowd. The clothes were more utilitarian and clean, and the things behind the windows had less silver and gold trim on them.

At long last, we found a restaurant where a very flustered young sylph lady made space for us, then shyly presented us with a menu. All sorts of wraps and sandwiches were for sale, usually with goat meat prepared with sweet sauces, and a few salads that had more bread and cheese and sauce in them than veggies.

We ate, we laughed, and we teased each other over every little thing.

It was nice to unwind after such a stressful day. And we'd need all the relaxation we could get. Things had reached a maximum level of complication, and I had a feeling deep in my tummy that things wouldn't get any easier for a while.

· Chapter Thirty-Two ·

In This Solemn Hour

Everything is terrible, and I hate my life."

I glanced up from the paper I was reading to stare across the room.

Amaryllis was standing over her desk. It was a desk that Mister Jared, the innkeeper, had brought in with the help of a few manservants.

Mister Jared had been nothing but nice since we arrived at the Dewdrop Inn. I think having Bastion escort us over had helped a lot, though he had seemed like a good and friendly person from the start.

Having two princesses show up at his door, though? That had really made him pepped up and excited. I was pretty sure that any one of us could ask him to draw twelve baths in a row, and he'd do it all himself with a smile and a spring in his step. Asking him for a desk or two so that Amaryllis's paperwork could stop crowding the dining table had been easy.

"Are you okay?" I asked, setting aside mental tangents about nice innkeepers.

Amaryllis wiggled her wings at the desk. "This," she said. She groaned, then started pacing.

"Uh, yeah, that," I agreed.

She nodded her head, and I was pretty sure that we had communicated something that I hadn't meant to.

"But besides . . . that, are you okay?" I asked again.

She huffed an irritated, tired huff of frustration. I wasn't sure if it was aimed at me or the papers. "This is a lot more complicated than I thought it would be," she finally said.

I was happy that she was back to using words. "It's all political stuff. Aren't those usually pretty complicated?"

"Yes, of course. But . . . well, as loath as I am to admit it, I suspected that I would have a much easier time with all of this. I grew up in the Harpy Mountains, I studied Sylphfree's politics as a hatchling! This should all be stuff I know!"

I nodded. "You're doing just great."

She puffed out her chest and placed talons on hips. "Oh don't patronize me, Broccoli. You don't have a clue what's going on here."

It was my turn to huff. "Well, I'm trying to help, that's all," I said. I took a deep breath. I didn't want to start arguing with her. We didn't need that, and it wouldn't be productive at all. "I'm sorry I can't help you more. But that doesn't mean I can't help you at all. What's the matter right now?"

"It's," she started, then waved her wings at all the papers again. "All this. It's too much."

"Exponential complication," Awen said. She was sitting on a big poofy chair next to a bay window at the end of the room, a large tome on her lap that nearly hid her entirely.

"What's that?" I asked.

She glanced up from her book. "Suppose you start with a small, simple problem. It has one variable, only one thing to keep track of. If you add a second variable, however, you must track not only the two variables, but also the relationship between them—three things you must keep in mind. If the variables increase to three, then the number of things to track increases to seven—"

"Wait," Amaryllis interjected before I could wrap my head around that. "I only counted six. Three variables and three unique pairings that each yield another interaction."

"There's a seventh interaction because all three variables could have a trinary interaction." Awen paused. "I think."

"Hm." Amaryllis leaned back in her chair and crossed her arms. "Now that I think of it, couldn't interactions also trigger more interactions that don't otherwise occur? Some kind of cascade?"

Awen frowned. "It might depend on how you philosophically model the concepts of variables and interactions. I haven't studied this that much."

"Uh . . ." I trailed off.

She shifted back in her seat. "All right, imagine . . . imagine fuel for an airship."

I nodded for her to go on.

"If you're the quartermaster in charge of fuel for one ship, then all you need to know is how much fuel that ship needs every time it comes to port. You also need to know how long the ship's trips are so that you have enough fuel waiting for it when it arrives. That's one factor—the ship's fuel—and two variables—how much it needs and how much it used."

"All right," I said. "That sounds pretty easy."

"Yes, because it's just one ship. Now, add in oil consumption as well. That's a bit trickier, but you can probably guess how much it needs every trip, so it's just one more little thing to keep track of." Awen licked her lips. "Now, let's say that you also need to keep track of rations onboard the ship. And it's a ship that has passengers. It doesn't always have them both ways. Now that's three things to keep track of, right?"

"I guess so, yeah," I said.

"Now add another ship. You're not just keeping track of fuel and oil and food for one ship but two. Plus, maybe those ships can trade those things on the go, or the number of passengers and how far they travel changes depending on which of the two ships arrives at port first."

"Uh."

"Now instead of two ships, make it thirty. Also, you need to keep track of crews now. And the ships can trade crewmates between each other. Oh, and there's another small port that they can use sometimes, but they won't tell you if they do or not, because visiting that port is technically illegal. Also, you need to keep track of repairs and maintenance schedules, but you only have a limited number of mechanics, and they all need to work on each ship for a different amount of time. Your goal is to make it so that each ship is ready to leave port as quickly as possible with the right amount of fuel, oil, food, enough crew onboard to work the ship, a good load of passengers and cargo, and that the ships are in tip-top shape before they leave."

My head was spinning and my ears were wilting like unwatered flowers. "Huh?"

"Exactly. It's a lot of stuff to keep track of, and every added factor makes it exponentially more complicated. That's Amaryllis's problem right now."

I glanced at Amaryllis. She was staring at Awen, a little shocked. "That's . . . yes. Exactly right, and succinctly put."

"That was succinct?" I asked.

"It would have been if you didn't need a whole analogy to make sense of it," Amaryllis said.

I closed the book I'd been reading. It was a history book, something that I didn't often read back home, but this one was about harpy clans, and it had talks about magic and politics and romance and all sorts of neat things. Learning about world history back home would have been way more engaging if there were more dragons involved. "All right, so everything's getting too complicated."

"It's not *getting* too complicated, Broccoli. It was complicated all along. I just didn't know how complicated it was."

"Right, a 'good old days' problem," I said. At her confused look, I explained. "People often say that things were easier in the good old days, but things were just as complicated back then, it's just that we don't know all the things that made it complicated."

"Strange, but all right," Amaryllis said. "I need a good speech for the summit, something that will make sure that everyone there takes me seriously."

"Isn't the fact that you're the representative enough?"

She shook her head. "Not after rumors of the fight with Francisco circulate. The sylphs might come to believe that whoever fights better can gain the spot as representative. I need to make it clear that I'm not just there because I'm personally powerful and somewhat well connected. I need to make it clear from the onset that I have political acumen."

I nodded. That made lots of sense. "And that's why you're trying to cram every last bit of political stuff you can get your talons on into your head all at once."

". . . An oversimplification of what I'm attempting, but not entirely wrong," Amaryllis said.

"You know that knowing stuff won't make it easier to talk about the right stuff."

"I'm aware," Amaryllis said. "This is all just preparatory. There will be questions asked, and the representatives will have the opportunity to ask their own questions in return. I should at least know enough about the desires and fears of the various harpy factions that I can make a point of bringing them up."

"And you need to sound fancy while doing it," I said.

"I'll be going up against people who have entire classes dedicated to politics and diplomacy, not to mention entire skillsets that revolve around charisma. In that regard, your own skills might trump mine once behind the podium."

I considered it for a moment, then slowly nodded. "If we're just counting skills, then yeah, I guess. You can't use puppetry or lightning to get your way in a debate. Well, not fairly at least. But those are just skills. You're pretty great at this kind of stuff, even if you don't have skills around it."

"Those skills I don't have are a huge force multiplier," Amaryllis said.

"Then I guess we'll have to work real hard to make up for it."

She sighed. "Which is exactly what I'm doing. And why I think my feathers will fall right off me. This is a lot to take in. I'm dipping into sylph history, too, there are plenty of books around here that touch on that. A few reports on the cervids, some on the grenoils, though not as many there. This is . . . a mess."

I bounced to my feet, walked over to Amaryllis, then gave her a good hug. She really needed it. "It'll be fine," I said. "Maybe we can start on the speech instead? Just a first draft, we can overhaul it once you learn more. Besides, how much do you want to say?"

She frowned, then nodded. "You're right. Less might be more here. A shorter, more concise speech. I can touch on the wants of the larger harpy populace, maybe mention our fears of what a war would mean."

"Not all the harpies want to avoid a war," I mentioned. It wasn't a nice thought, but it was true.

"You're right . . . Maybe I can mention as much? Acknowledge that a lot of harpy are reveling in the possibilities brought on by new technologies, but insist that they shouldn't be turned toward slaughter?"

I nodded along. "That sounds like a good start."

Amaryllis rushed over to a desk, muttered something rude as she brushed aside some papers to find an inkwell, then returned to the dining table and pulled out a seat for herself. She looked around, then said something very rude to no one in particular before plucking a feather out of her wing to use as a quill. She scribbled a bullet list on a piece of loose leaf.

"All right, that's a very rough outline," she said. "I also need to flatter the others, though not too much."

"That would take up too much time," I said.

"No, the time isn't the issue—well, not the only one. If I spend even a word too much flattering the cervids, they might think that we're in a weaker position relative to them. They'll confuse humility for weakness. At the same time, I need to praise and compliment the others. But I can't single out any one of them. Well, perhaps the grenoils—they're ostensibly allies in this."

"Don't," Awen said. "Try to keep it even. Favoring the grenoils would insult the cervids. There's still some old animosity between the two, I'll bet."

"Right," Amaryllis said. "You're pretty keen with all of this, Awen."

"My mom made me take lessons about this kind of stuff," Awen said. "I thought I'd forgotten a lot of it, but I guess it's all still in the back of my head."

"That's handy," I said. I didn't think I had any awesome secret knowledge to rely on.

Awen shrugged. "It doesn't come up very often, but it's not bad to know."

Amaryllis scribbled a few more things. "What else," she muttered. "Oh, right." She bent down and added a few more lines to her list. "And a bit of . . . of course . . ."

"Uh, you all right?" I asked.

"Yes. Now give me about eight hours to write this, then we can start the revisions and rewrites," she said.

I held back a sigh. This was very important, to the world and for Amaryllis, so I wasn't going to tell anyone that I found it a little bit boring.

Sometimes it was hard to be there for a friend, but that was okay too!

· Chapter Thirty-Three ·

Dawn of a New Day

Wake up!"

I blinked as I sat up in a vaguely familiar bed. "Huh?"

Amaryllis was above me, talons on hips and frame bent so that her face was close to mine. "I said wake up. We need to get ready."

"Huh?" I glanced around. My inn room was still dark, the only light coming in from some lanterns in the main room. The world outside the window was that blue-black that the sky took on when the sun was considering coming up. "Wha' time's it?"

"It's time for you to get up and get ready," Amaryllis said. "The summit is today."

"But it's still dark out?" The confusion of sleep was wearing off, only to be replaced by other, new confusions.

She sniffed. "Obviously. Come on, we don't have all day!" With that, she stomped out of the room. A moment later, I heard her telling Awen to wake up from the next room over.

Yawning so hard my jaw ached, I stretched my arms over my head, then shifted so that I was sitting on the edge of my bed. I was very much not bright-eyed and bushy-tailed. I was more . . . blurry-eyed, and my tail was sleep-squished.

I stood up, ran my hand through my hair, which was getting pretty long—I'd need to see about cutting it—then I stumbled out of the room and into the main lounge area. The desks covered in Amaryllis's papers had moved. So had all of the papers stacked on them.

Amaryllis stepped out of Awen's room looking like she was caught somewhere between smug and nervous. "Hey, Amaryllis," I started. "When did you go to sleep?"

"Sleep?" she asked.

"Amaryllis, you did sleep, right?"

She huffed at me. "As if I had time for something like that. Do you have any idea how much work there is left to do still?"

"But you need sleep," I said.

"I can sleep once the summit is over. And it will be over soon," she said. "Why aren't you dressed yet?"

I glanced out of the nearest window. "Because it's still nighttime?"

"Hmm, yes, you might get your dress dirty. No, wait, you could just clean it off! That's no excuse! Go get dressed, Broccoli." Amaryllis scurried off to her own room, the door clicking shut behind her.

I turned to find Awen leaning against the doorframe of her own room. "She's lost her mind," Awen said.

"Maybe the stress is getting to her," I said. It wasn't quite an agreement, but it wasn't far from one. "I'll ambush her with a hug once she's out of her room."

"I think she needs more than a hug," Awen said. "More like a vacation, and maybe a few days of sleep." She yawned, and I suspected that she wanted that for herself too. "This is way too early to be awake."

"It's fine," I said. "I think you can go back to bed for a few minutes. Get a few more winks in before we really do need to get ready. I'll talk to Amaryllis."

Awen hesitated. "I should probably be there too," she finally said with a sigh. I could tell she'd really rather go back to bed, but Awen was a good friend, and good friends could put sleep aside for each other sometimes.

I knocked on Amaryllis's door twice. "Amy?"

"Are you dressed already?" Amaryllis asked. She opened the door, then stared at me and Awen. Both of us were in our usual sleeping clothes. "Did you forget where you put your outfits?" she asked.

I shook my head, then stepped into the room. "No, we're, uh, staging an intervention."

"Can you do that tomorrow?"

"I don't think so," I said. I walked up to Amaryllis and caught her in a hug, one that Awen joined in on a moment later. It didn't last all that long— Amaryllis was too nervous to appreciate a good hug. "Are you okay?"

"I'd be better if you were dressed and ready," Amaryllis said with a huff.

"I know. I promise I'll get dressed right after this. But, uh, we're a bit worried."

"Well, so am I," Amaryllis said. "This is big. Really big, Broccoli."

"And it's a lot of pressure on your shoulders," I said. "But, uh, I think you're taking on a bit too much of that weight all on your own."

She glowered. "Well, then take some of it for yourself. I wouldn't be this stressed if you were up and ready already."

"Uh," I said. "Amaryllis, it's very, very early still. Like super-very early. Even if we were all dressed and ready to go, we wouldn't have anywhere to go to, not for a few hours. I think that maybe you're trying to overprepare."

Awen nodded. "My uncle used to tell me a lot of stories about his adventures. And sometimes he'd tell me stories of other adventurers and explorers. Some of them used to be super meticulous. They'd scout ahead a lot, bring lots of equipment, and tackle every challenge very carefully. Uncle said that they were some of the very best explorers out there. You remind me a bit of those."

"Thank you, I suppose," Amaryllis said.

"Uncle also said that they tend to get in over their heads as soon as things don't go according to plan, and things never go according to plan. We both live with Broccoli—we both know that plans don't work out the way they should."

"Uh," I said.

Amaryllis sighed. "Fine," she said. "Maybe I'm slightly—very slightly—too nervous about today for my own good. You can give me another hug, if you want."

I laughed as I gave her another, even better hug. Amaryllis saying that meant that she really wanted the hug, I figured. "So, can we go back to sleep now?"

"Oh, it's probably too late for that," Awen said. "Besides, the sun is coming up."

I glanced out of the nearest window and saw that Awen was right. The darkness outside was lightening up. Not quickly, but it was undeniably getting brighter. In a few more minutes, I bet the sky would be all blue, and then the sun would be properly on the horizon, and everything would come awake.

"When does the summit start?" I asked.

"Technically, at noon," Amaryllis said. "There's the opening statements, then a luncheon before the main event begins. So we need to be there at least an hour before noon."

"That's plenty of time to get dressed. What else do you need to prepare?"

Amaryllis gestured vaguely in the direction of the living room. "I should practice my speech some more. Also, getting a refresher on all the things I need to know wouldn't hurt."

"Fine, then," I said. "Awen and I will get dressed, then we'll go have breakfast together, then we'll head over to the summit, and you can practice your speech on the way."

Amaryllis nodded. "Fine, fine." She took a deep breath and let it all out at once. I made sure to give her a last squeeze to help get the last of the stress out, like toothpaste at the end of a tube. I would make tea in a moment. Something to calm her down and keep her awake.

I let go, then rushed back to my room. We hadn't brought a lot of luggage with us from the *Beaver Cleaver* but I did have a few things. I really had to get around to buying more outfits. As it was, I had exactly two things to wear: my armor and the one nice outfit I'd gotten for that ball in Fort Sylphrot. A girl ought to have more than two things she could wear.

Cleaning magic was making it too easy not to bother having any changes of clothes.

My dress was less a dress and more of a suit, with flowy pants and a nice blouse and a well-tailored jacket. It made me look very adult and serious. It even had a hole over the bum for my tail!

A knock at my door had me bouncing over to open it. Awen was standing there, with a platter in one hand. "I've got some makeup stuff," she said. "Did you want me to help you with yours?"

"Uh, sure," I said.

I didn't have anything like that. Then again, adventuring didn't usually require much by way of makeup, and besides, I was never great at using that kind of thing. At most, I liked using lip balms because the flavored ones were tasty, and they were nice in the cold.

I sat down in front of a little vanity in the corner of the room, and Awen went to work attacking my face with powders and creams. She didn't say anything, so I figured she knew what she was doing. The end result, some ten minutes later, was quite nice. "It looks like I'm blushing a little," I said, peering into the mirror.

Awen nodded. "Putting makeup on you is just so easy. You have the Adorable skill, right?"

"N— Yes?"

She shook her head. "And you don't even want it. You know, you're very silly, Broc."

I pouted. No. I pouted *prettily*.

Awen rolled her eyes, then gestured out into the living room. "Amaryllis is probably ready by now. I still need to get into my own dress. Want to go distract her while I get ready?"

"Sure," I said. It was better than talking about Adorable. I really had to get my hands on one of those chivalry skills so that I could transform it into something more useful.

I helped Amaryllis—who had changed into her own ball gown, which was quite pretty—pack up her notes in a satchel. Then I spent a couple of minutes convincing her that we didn't need to bring every history book and all of the notes she'd made, especially since they'd fill up three or four luggage bags and be hard to carry with us.

"I'm ready," Awen said as she stepped out of her room. She'd done something with her hair, sticking it up in a ring of braids around the crown of her head.

"Oh, you both look very pretty," I said.

"Awa, don't say that," Awen said. "Do we know how we're getting to the summit?"

"Of course we do," Amaryllis said. "I had the innkeeper reserve a carriage for us. We're not going to walk across the city dressed like this."

"It wouldn't be too bad, I don't think," I said. "I could keep things clean."

"Sure, but think of the message it sends. Besides, I'm stressed about this enough. I don't need to be stressed and exhausted at the same time."

I gave her another hug, because hugs were free to give, and then grabbed her by the talon. "Breakfast first."

"I'm not hungry," Amaryllis said.

"Then it'll be a light breakfast for you. But you don't want to be hungry on stage, and you don't want your tummy rumbling during the summit. Oh, and you'll want to use the bathroom before you start your speech."

"I can take care of myself, Broccoli."

"Sure."

Awen and I still dragged her over to the inn's dining room, where we got a quick breakfast. Mostly, it was fluffy pancakes and a bunch of fresh fruit, with some sugary sauces to dip them in—light but sweet stuff.

Once everything was eaten up—we made sure Amaryllis had a few bites—and I'd sprinkled some Cleaning magic around to keep hands and talons clean, we headed all the way downstairs, where a member of the inn's staff had us wait for the carriage to be prepared.

Amaryllis paced back and forth, of course. Eventually, she started to mutter her way through her speech, with Awen and I listening and telling her that she'd do just fine.

Soon enough, we were led up onto a neat carriage behind a pair of big horses, and we were off to the summit.

Everything was going to be just fine. At least, that's what I kept telling my nervous bird friend.

· Chapter Thirty-Four ·

Hugs and Wishes

Whoa," I said as I leaned out of the carriage's window. I had to shake my head because one of my ears stayed stuck inside. "That's so pretty!"

The building hosting the summit was just past the Purple District, near the northernmost end of Goldenalden and pressed right up against the rising side of the mountain. It stuck out of the mountainside, the very back of the edifice merging into the sheer wall of stone.

It was like a cathedral, cavernous, with a peaked roof and a facade covered in careful stonework and colorful windows that were warped and shaped to produce great images. I didn't know that the sylph used stained glass. I hadn't noticed any anywhere else.

Two narrow towers stood out at the front, each on a corner and rising to be half again the height of the palace itself.

"I think that's the old palace," Amaryllis said. She didn't sound entirely sure about that, though.

"It's very nice," Awen agreed.

Our carriage moved off the main road and onto a rounded pathway made of inlaid bricks that circled around the front of the summit building. The wheels clacked and clattered over the cobbles, announcing our approach. We weren't the only ones there, of course. A few other carriages were waiting by the front, and we had to settle in behind them to wait.

I was about to stick my head back into the carriage when I saw a familiar face step out of her own. "Caprica!" I shouted.

The princess turned our way, noticed me dangling out of the side of our carriage, then placed a gloved hand over her mouth to hide a smile. She gestured to her guards, then walked over. "Hello, Broccoli," she said.

"Hey! How are you doing?"

"I'm very well, thank you. Are you going to come out, or will you wait until you're at the front of the line?"

I glanced ahead. Whoever was in the next carriage was taking their sweet time. "I guess we can get out here just fine," I said.

Amaryllis sighed. "I didn't expect decorum to last, but I didn't expect it to fall apart so soon," she said. "Come on, let's all get out here. Might as well roll with it and make a scene."

Laughing, I shoved myself back into the carriage, then opened the door properly. I landed next to it, then reached up to help Amaryllis and Awen down. They had big skirts, which made using the tiny steps on the side of the carriage a bit tricky.

"You all look very fine this morning," Caprica said.

"Thank you!" I said. "I have fancy pants. I like your dress, by the way."

Caprica had changed from her usual militaryish uniform into a deep red dress with a bit of black lacework along the hems. It was a very tight dress, with big pads at the shoulders and a bow on her lower back that made it look like her wings were longer. I gasped as I realized that her skirts were actually two loose pant legs.

"Why, thank you," Caprica said. "I don't prefer this kind of dress, but it is the sort of occasion where it's appropriate. Father's here, and while he doesn't care what we wear in our day-to-day, he might whine if I showed up to this kind of thing in pants."

"The king is here?" Amaryllis asked.

"The king is whiny?" Awen asked right after.

"Yes, to both," Caprica said with a poorly stifled laugh. "Come on, maybe I can have you meet him before all the speeches start and your image of him is ruined. He's a good public speaker, but his talks get a little long-winded."

"If everyone here is quite done speaking ill of the king," Amaryllis said, "we should head in."

"Certainly," Caprica said. "Have you seen the old palace before?"

"No," I said as I bounced up next to her. "It's really nice, though, and it looks different from all the other buildings I've seen here."

Caprica nodded along. "It predates a lot of the city. Once, when Goldenalden was but a tiny town, the entirety of the city was partially underground, and the old palace served as something of an entrance to that. When things expanded, the style of construction changed significantly. The old palace was almost entirely built by a legendary stone mage, who sculpted it out of the mountain."

"Whoa," I said.

"The art isn't lost, but it's not as common as it once was. Sylph talents tend to lie in areas other than earth and stone," Caprica said.

We chatted about nothing while heading up to the front of the old palace. More paladins were here than I'd ever seen before. One on either side of the entranceway and a third just inside, all stoic and motionless, as if they were deadly statues.

I noticed that the others entering—mostly sylphs, but there were some grenoils, too, and a small group of cervids were standing just past the entrance—were pausing before an armored figure, who would touch them on their shoulders or forearms before they could move on. It was only when I was a bit closer that I noticed that the figure doing the checks was familiar.

"Is that Bastion?" I asked. His armor was a little bit fancier and a lot shinier than when I'd last seen him.

"Bastion?" Caprica asked. "Oh."

It didn't take long for the line ahead of us to thin enough that we were next. "Forgive me for the intrusion, but because of the heightened security of this event, I will have to touch you lightly," Bastion said. Then his eyes scanned over our group, and the seriousness in them faded a little.

"Hey!" I said.

"Hello, Broccoli," he said. "Amaryllis, Awen." He nodded to both, then bowed at the hip. "Princess Caprica."

"So, you need to touch us?" I asked. "Do hugs count?"

He chuckled. "That wouldn't exactly fit the protocol, but then, when did you ever care for that?"

"That's true," I said before I stepped up and pulled Bastion into a big, tight, tight hug. I had to squeeze extra hard so that he'd feel it through all that armor.

"It's nice to see you again, Bastion," Amaryllis said. "Did you get promoted? The armor's new."

Bastion patted my back while he answered. "It's a more formal set, for events such as these. Not quite as practical, I'm afraid."

"It looks nice," Awen said. "How are you?"

"I'm quite well. It really is nice to see you three. And you, of course, Princess Caprica."

I ended my hug—there were people in line, and it wasn't nice to keep them waiting, even if hugs were important—and stepped back from Bastion. I glanced at the others, then blinked as I noticed Caprica.

She was standing stiff, face a strange shade of red. "H-hi," she squeaked.

"Hello, Your Royal Highness. Please forgive my lack of professionalism. Though from what I've heard, you have spent some time with these three already."

"Don't bunch me in with Broccoli," Amaryllis said.

"You don't mind being bunched in with me?" Awen asked.

Amaryllis huffed. "You're strange but not nearly as bad as Broccoli."

"T-that's fine," Caprica said. It sounded like she was trying not to choke.

I glanced back at Bastion, then back to Caprica. "Wow," I muttered. "So, uh, maybe we should all head in? After Bastion hugs everyone, of course."

Caprica's face reddened even more, somehow.

"I think I'll reserve my hugs for you, Broccoli," Bastion said with a chuckle. He reached out a hand toward Amaryllis, who touched it lightly before walking past. Awen did the same, then Caprica slipped by Bastion. He didn't seem to care that she hadn't paused to let him touch her. I guess that was normal for a royal.

"We'll see you again, right?" I asked.

"I'll be at the summit all day," he said.

"Good! You promised me a ride with the air guard you know. I didn't forget."

He patted me on the shoulder, then nodded into the building. "I'll make some time for you, no worries. The main hall's accessible from the left. There's a break room to the right if you need to freshen up."

I laughed as I reached back and grabbed Caprica's hand and led her into the old palace. The entrance hall was a bit cramped, with a corridor that led around what looked like a wide-open room in the center of the building. We moved to the side, next to one of the entrances that was quieter.

"Are you okay?" I asked Caprica as I let go of her.

She rubbed at her hand, took a deep breath, stuck her nose up as high as it would go, then said, "I'm perfectly fine, thank you."

"Are you sure?" Amaryllis asked. "I was almost convinced that you were going to faint back there."

"I would hardly faint," Caprica said.

Awen took a small step closer to the princess and placed a hand on her shoulder. "It's okay," she said.

Caprica's cheeks reddened again. "It's not what you think."

"So you don't have a hopeless crush on Bastion?" I asked.

"It's not hopeless!"

One of Amaryllis's eyebrows rose up. "How old is Bastion?"

"There's only two and a half years between us," Caprica said. "There's nothing inappropriate there."

"Except that you're a princess, and he's merely a paladin," Amaryllis added.

Caprica crossed her arms. "Mother was a paladin before she married Father. There's a clear and obvious precedent. B-besides, I don't have to explain anything to you."

I walked over to Caprica, then gave her a hug. It looked like she really needed it. "It's okay. We're your friends, so we were just a bit surprised and worried is all."

Caprica was a bit of a stiff hugger. Actually, that did give her one thing in common with Bastion. "Thank you, Captain Bunch."

"No, no," I said. "Don't call me Captain Bunch, that's just you trying to put some distance between us, but I've already decided that you're my friend, and there's no distance between us because we're literally hugging right now."

". . . What?" Caprica said.

"Give up," Awen said. "You've been chosen to be Broccoli's friend. There's no escaping it now."

Amaryllis reached over and tugged the back of my collar so that I had to let go of Caprica. "Jokes aside, Caprica, I don't think you need to worry about what we think. Nor are we likely to blackmail you. If anything, you should worry more about Broccoli's fumbling matchmaking attempts."

"Hey, my Matchmaking skill is only at Rank D. It could use more practice."

Amaryllis clapped her wings. "Let's focus a little, shall we? We didn't come here to save Caprica's doomed love life."

"Doomed?"

"We're here," Amaryllis continued, "to attend the summit and convince the world not to go to war. I think that takes priority over Caprica doing whatever disgusting things you mammals do when you love each other."

"You're right," I said.

"She is not!"

I nodded. "We need to put on our serious faces. Caprica, we'll arrange a date between you and Bastion later. For now, it's time to save the world."

"Do you want to go over your speech one last time?" Awen asked.

"I wouldn't mind that, but I think the pre-event is important too. It's one of the only chances I'll have to meet all the speakers. They might leave as soon as it's over, and this way I can make a better impression," Amaryllis said.

"Cool! So, we stick together, find our targets, then ambush them with friendliness."

"Yes, that, but more diplomatically. In fact, let me handle most of the talking. We'll use you like a sort of social battering ram if they're too obstinate," Amaryllis said. "Oh, Caprica, did you want to help us too?"

Caprica's mouth opened and closed a few times. Then she frowned and glared at us.

"Fine," she finally settled on.

· Chapter Thirty-Five ·

Free Action

This is my father," Caprica said. She smiled as she gestured toward an older sylph man. He was a bit shorter than Caprica herself, with graying hair and a thin, almost emaciated visage. He wore a militaryesque uniform, though unlike those of the high-ranking officers around him, there were few embellishments on his. He could have passed for a new lieutenant if it weren't for the grave look in his eyes and the crown atop his head.

"Ah, so these are the new friends Gabby has been going on and on about," the king said. He smiled, and with that one gesture, his entire personality seemed to change, from gruff and no-nonsense to . . . well, to a proud dad.

"That's right," Caprica said. "This is Amaryllis Albatross. She'll be representing the Harpy Mountains today."

"So young! I imagine you're quite the talent, to be in such a position already," he said.

Amaryllis bowed with a flourish of her wings. "It's a pleasure to meet you," she said. "I've heard a lot about you and your family back home."

"None of it good, I imagine," he said with a chuckle. I could tell that some of his guards and . . . flunkies bristled at the implication.

"I'm afraid not," Amaryllis admitted. "But so far, I think I've found that what's said and what's true isn't quite the same. Caprica has become a good friend, and we spent a lot of time with Paladin Bastion on the trip over. He proved a very capable and agreeable traveling companion."

"Ah yes, Bastion. I think I might have heard a thing or two about him," the king said. His lips twitched as he glanced at Caprica. She blushed up to her roots, but it left almost as soon as it appeared.

"These are my other new friends," Caprica continued. "Awen Bristlecone, from Mattergrove, and Captain Broccoli Bunch from the, ah, *Beaver Cleaver*."

"Oh, I never did say where I was from, did I?" I asked. "I'm from Canada."

"I've never heard of Canada. Is it a small village?" the king asked.

I nodded. "That's what it means, yeah."

"Interesting. You seem to be a diverse-enough group, good folk from all over," he said. "That's a great way to have a healthy exchange of ideas."

"And making all sorts of friends is important," I said. "You can't just make the one sort, or else that would hardly be any fun."

The king eyed me for a moment, then shrugged. "I suppose you're not entirely wrong. I'm afraid that Sylphfree hasn't been graced with as much diversity as you might prefer."

"That's okay!" I said. "This whole summit is about listening to each other, isn't it? I can't think of a better time to start considering things from other people's points of view than when they're literally going to tell you what those are."

The king laughed, a single bark of good humor that had his shoulder shaking. "I suppose there's some worth in bluntness. Interesting companions you've found, Caprica."

"Yes, Father," Caprica said. "They're very much interesting."

"I'd love to talk more, but my life has never not been busy, and today is no exception to that. Good day, Ladies Albatross, Bristlecone, and to you, Captain Bunch."

The king gave us a nod, then turned toward his daughter. He unfolded his hands from the small of his back, then brought them up before him. I knew an invitation for a hug when I saw one.

"Father, not in front of all the guards," Caprica said.

"Come now, not even before my big speech?" he asked with a gesture to the room around him. There had to be a couple of hundred people gathered in the grand hall already.

"Oh, fine," Caprica said. She gave her father a very quick and very reserved hug. I giggled in spite of myself, and she glared at me as she stepped back from her dad.

Once the king and his retinue were off, Caprica turned back to us. "Has anyone indicated where you should go?" she asked Amaryllis.

"No, not so far," Amaryllis said.

Caprica walked past. "In that case, follow me."

The grand hall of the old palace was arranged so that there were three big rows of seats all pointing toward a big stage at the back of the room. Little boxes on the floors above also allowed people to look down onto the stage from a position of some safety. A few sylphs were flapping their way up to those upper-floor . . .

"Hey, what are those boxes called?" I pointed to the nooks above.

"Boxes," Amaryllis said.

"Huh, all right," I said. "I've never been to one of those. They're fancy."

"Well, you have one all to yourselves," Caprica said. "Each delegation has one near the front. Mostly as a position of pride but also so that the speakers have easier, more discreet access to the stage."

"I thought this would be less a presentation and more of an open forum kind of thing," I said.

"Oh, that will be later," Amaryllis said. "I imagine they'll rearrange things for that part of the summit."

"Tables will be brought in, yes," Caprica said. "And we have sound mages that can ensure that everything spoken at the table will be heard by everyone in the room."

I nodded along, then glanced at Amaryllis. "You don't have stage fright, right?"

"Of course I don't," she said.

"Oh, good," I said.

Caprica led us across the very front of the room, just under the lip of the stage. It was a bit emptier up at the front, and there were fewer nobles.

At the sides of the room were large doors—guarded by a pair of sylphs, of course, because the sylphs seem to have as many guards as they did citizens—which we passed through into a luxuriously appointed corridor. There was a stairway at one end, and the corridor continued on in the same direction as the stage in the other.

"What's that door?" I asked, pointing to one door that seemed different. It didn't have the same pretty decorations as all the rest.

"I think that's access to the basement," Caprica said. She didn't sound entirely sure.

We climbed up the stairs to the second floor, where entrances to the boxes were set a few meters apart from each other. Ours had a little placard in front of it with Harpy Delegation written on it in a nice cursive font that was so fancy it was barely legible.

The box had comfy-looking sofas along the edges, as well as some rather tall seats in the middle that allowed us to see over the rails on the edge and into the main room.

I clambered onto one of the cushioned seats, then leaned way forward so that I could take in the entire hall below. Even though the summit wasn't going to properly start for another little while, the room was already filling up quite nicely. Some people were in their seats, but it looked like most were just milling around and talking.

I noticed a group of cervids, with Rowan and Nathan standing tall enough that I could make them out from the rest. No sign of Ellie, but she would be a bit harder to spot.

The grenoils were there too. Even if their delegation was a bit smaller, they still made a good showing. Grenoil gentlefrogs in nice suits talking—or rather *conversing*, since this was a fancy sort of event—with interested sylphs while hanging onto goblets of wine or some such.

"Whoa, I didn't realize how high these boxes were from down there."

"You really make yourself sound like such a competent captain," Amaryllis said.

I giggled as I leaned back into the seat and away from the edge. "Fine, fine. I'll just have to be careful not to fall. So, when does it all start?"

Amaryllis glanced up, and following her gaze, I noticed a big clock above the stage for the first time. "We have another ten minutes. I imagine that's why the king left. He needs to prepare his own parts for all this."

"Oh, I doubt it," Caprica said. "He puts on airs of being prepared, but most of the time, he leaves whatever speech was written for him behind and just wings the entire thing. Fortunately, he's fairly good at coming up with convincing arguments and riling people up."

"I suppose he would have to be, being king and all," Awen said.

Caprica shrugged. "He might be king, but he will always be my rather embarrassing father to me."

"Sounds like there's a story or two there," I said. I was about to tease Caprica some more, but the loud blaring of a horn had my head snapping around toward the stage. The horn was soon joined by strings and flutes as a band started to play a big bombastic piece. "Whoa!"

The music was so loud I almost had to fold my ears back not to be deafened, but even so, it made me grin. I'd never been to an orchestra before.

"I should head out," Caprica said. "My seat is with my family. Amaryllis, I can show you to the staging area right now. I imagine you'll be able to find your way back up here?"

"I should be able to manage," Amaryllis said.

"Wait!" I said. I got up and ran around. "Hug for good luck."

She rolled her eyes but raised her arms all the same. I'd trained her well! I gave her a good squeeze, then stepped back and let Awen give her a hug too.

"Kick butt out there, all right?" I asked.

"I'll do my best to impress," Amaryllis said.

I waved to Caprica, and we promised that we'd meet again during the intermission in an hour or so. Caprica said that she knew where to find the nonalcoholic drinks.

And then they left, leaving the box with just me and Awen.

"Whelp," I said as I sat back down, "now we wait, I guess."

"I suppose so," Awen said. She didn't sit down just yet, though. "I think I need to use the ladies' room. I don't want to miss Amaryllis's part."

"That's not a bad idea," I said. I stood back up, again, then gestured to the door. "I'll go with you. That way if we get lost, we'll be lost together."

Awen giggled, but she didn't protest.

We slipped back into the corridor, then looked around for signs pointing to the washrooms. Finding none, we started down the corridor and down the steps to the level below. A ladies' room was there, one with barely any line at all. Awen and I stepped up behind an older sylph lady and waited while talking about nothing much.

It was probably because I was both bored and anxious that I noticed the musician. The sylph had the same uniform as the sylphs on stage. A large bag hung by his side, seemingly some sort of heavy instrument case.

My eyes skipped over him, then back. Something about his face was familiar.

I saw him glance our way, and our eyes met.

I smiled and waved, and I saw him glare before he slipped past, walking fast. A bit too fast?

What was he doing here? And where had I seen him?

"Broc?"

I turned to Awen. She pointed to the washroom door, which didn't have a line in front of it anymore.

"Oh, right," I said. "Sorry, it's just . . . Awen, I have a weird feeling."

"Like a stomachache?" Awen asked. "I have things for that." She touched her little purse.

"No, not that, I . . ." I glanced back down the corridor.

I had seen that sylph once before. I was sure of it.

"I think I'm going to go do something illegal," I said. "Want to come with?"

"Can I use the washroom first?" Awen asked.

"Sure!"

· Chapter Thirty-Six ·

My Bunny Sense Is Tingling

Tracking down the strange musician wasn't as easy as I'd expected it to be. It wasn't like we were outside, where he might have left footprints on the ground or anything. This was a nicely appointed building, and while there might have been a scuff or two on the carpet that would give someone with a tracking skill enough to go on, I wasn't that person.

"Dang," I said.

"He can't have gone too far," Awen said. She looked up and down the corridor.

It seemed unlikely that he'd backtrack, so I ruled that out. It wasn't impossible, but it was less likely, I thought. That left . . . every other direction, which was a lot of directions.

He could have gone into the main hall, but that would mean bumping into politicians and diplomats and important people. That felt unlikely—he would stick out like a sore thumb. So, that left the back rooms behind the stage and maybe the basement.

The stage was a more obvious choice. If the maybe-mysterious musician was just an ordinary, unmysterious musician, then it made sense that he'd head for the stage where all the other musicians were currently playing for the crowd. Maybe he was part of another act?

"Come on," I said. "We'll look backstage, and then if he's not there, we can start looking elsewhere."

Awen nodded as she stepped up next to me, skirts swirling around in a pretty way. "Broccoli?"

"Yeah?"

"Are you sure that the person you saw was weird? It could just be someone who works here."

I considered it. "You might be right," I said. "You're probably right, even."

"Then why are we chasing after them?"

"Because . . . I don't know," I said. "I know I've seen them before. It's like a word on the tip of my tongue, but a person's face instead. Uh, not a face on the tip of my tongue, that'd be weird."

Awen giggled. "Let's not start licking people, please. I think the sylphs think we're strange enough without us doing anything like that."

I nodded. "I promise I won't lick anyone."

"Good," Awen said. "Now, where did you see them last?"

"Uh, I don't know. I think that's part of not remembering."

"Was it in Goldenalden?"

I frowned. "No, I don't think so. Before that, maybe?"

"We didn't see that many sylphs before arriving in Sylphfree. You did head out at that one town, uh, the one near the coast."

"Granite Springs. Yeah, maybe I saw him there?" That didn't sound quite right. It was really starting to bother me. How could I forget a potential friend I'd met? It was just wrong. I had to set aside my mental search as Awen and I arrived behind the stage. There was an open doorway, the other side of which wasn't nearly as well decorated, and the corridor there had racks and heaps of ropes and the sorts of things I guess were normal to find behind a stage.

If I were Rainnewt and I were up to no good, where would I go?

I didn't *know* that it was Rainnewt, of course. I only suspected it, a lot. So much that my tail felt twitchier than usual.

There were also two guards at the doors, both of them looking mighty serious. "Hello, ma'am, can we assist you?"

"Yes!" I said. "In two ways. First, did you see a musician come past here? A sylph, about this tall." I brought my hand to around the sylph's height. "Dark hair. Like brownish-black. I guess about your age? Um, was wearing the same uniform as the people in the orchestra."

"Are they a friend of yours?" the guard asked. "Did they accost you?"

"Huh? They might be a friend? They didn't accost me or anything, and I'm not sure I've ever seen them before," I said. "But I'm looking for them now."

The guards glanced at each other. "Why?"

"Well, he was a bit suspicious, maybe. Did you see him?"

"We didn't see anyone of the sort, no," the guard said. "The orchestra all came in from the back."

"All right, thanks," I said. "Uh, my other thing! I was wondering if you could get someone for me? Either Princess Caprica or Amaryllis Albatross. She's a harpy. You can't miss her."

"Ma'am," the guard said, "the summit speech is about to begin. Perhaps you should return to your seats?"

I pouted, but Awen's hand on my shoulder reminded me that I was maybe being a little bit weird about this. "Fine. Thank you," I said before turning around.

"It's okay," Awen said. "You did what you could?"

"Yeah, I guess," I said. "At least we learned one thing: he didn't come over here."

"Which is a bit weird," Awen said. "He had a big case with him, right? I think it would be hard to forget someone like that, maybe."

"It would be extra weird if he returned to the main hall," I said. I paused as we arrived in front of one set of doors—the plain doorway that Caprica had said led into the basement.

Awen glanced at it. "You don't think . . ."

"Maybe," I said.

"I don't think we're supposed to go down there."

"Just a peek. It's probably locked anyway." I reached over and tugged on the door. It opened, the hinge a bit rough, but it was definitely not locked.

The room beyond was dark, only lit by the cracked-open doorway and little else. There was a staircase, made of wooden planks and lined on all sides by rough-hewn stone walls, as if the entire passage was melted through the rock of the mountain.

"I guess he might have gone down there," Awen said.

"I guess."

"Should we go back? Maybe tell the guards?"

"I kind of want to go exploring down there," I said. It looked creepy and dark and fun.

Awen sighed. "I knew you'd say that. Let me tie my skirts up a little. I don't want to trip down the stairs."

"Oh, you could stay up here," I said. "Watch Amaryllis's bit to make sure it all goes well."

"Amaryllis will be fine," Awen said. "But you're likely to get into a heap of trouble. Someone needs to be there to save you from it."

"I don't get into that much trouble."

She gave me a look.

"No, really. I get into a little bit of trouble here and there, but so far, we've always gotten out of it just fine."

"I'm still coming with you. Unless you really don't want me to come?"

I crossed my arms. "Don't be silly, Awen, you're one of my best friends. Of course I want you to get into trouble with me . . . a little bit of trouble. Probably less than an inconvenience, really."

"Sure," Awen said. It didn't sound all that sincere, but she did step ahead of me, one hand rising a moment before it started to glow faintly as a ball of light appeared.

I slipped in next to her, my own hand rising while I tried to copy the same spell. I was a bit out of practice with that one, but it was a simple enough spell that I got it before I was more than a couple of steps down.

"Someone's been here recently," I said.

"The dust on the steps," Awen said.

I nodded, then realized she couldn't see it. "Yeah, you're right," I muttered, almost in a whisper. There were footsteps imprinted onto the steps, leather soles marking a path down and down.

The steps went down much lower than just one floor, and by the time we were at the bottom, the door we'd entered from was barely visible.

The stairs bottomed out into a large room. It was almost a cavern, with sleek stone floors and distant walls. Pillars stood out at even intervals, turning the shadows we cast into choppy lines across the near-emptiness.

The basement wasn't empty-empty, just near-empty. Crates lined the sides, some in big piles, others stacked up in neat rows closer to the center of the room. There were no signs of our strange musician except for a few faint marks on the dusty ground and maybe a few broken spiderwebs.

"He went this way," Awen said. She knelt next to some of the tracks, then looked up in the direction they flowed in. "This really is getting suspicious."

The ceiling was low enough that the little floof hairs on the tips of my ears brushed against it. It made me want to hunch down subconsciously. "Why is the basement here so big?" I whispered.

"I think they might have used it as a shelter or something," Awen whispered back.

We followed the path our mysterious friend left in the dust. It led around some boxes that looked like they were filled with big cloth banners. I heard a faint ticking sound. It wasn't just one—there were a few that were echoing across the room—but I figured it was just water dropping or maybe some old abandoned clock ticking away.

I really hoped it was someone's collection of antique clocks.

As we came around the boxes, the sound grew much louder.

"Oh no," Awen said.

A case was left on the ground, the same case that our musician friend had been carrying earlier. It was pressed up against one of the pillars. The case was open, revealing an intricate little machine made of brass and steel. It was like a clock, but next to it was a big barrel that filled most of the case.

"I've played a lot of musical instruments," Awen said. "And I've seen more. But that's a new one."

"That looks a bit like a bomb," I said.

"It does look like that, yeah."

We both glanced around, but there were no signs of the musician, just a few tracks leading off deeper into the darkness.

Awen's light dimmed. "We might want to be a little less obvious," she whispered as she moved over to the probably-a-bomb. She knelt next to it, then carefully leaned over the clocklike device on the side.

"What is it?" I asked.

"A timer. See, there's a mainspring there, and those gears are turning with its push . . . And look at that part there, and there. They look like primer rods. See, they're under tension, and I bet those little plates there are strikers."

"So, definitely a bomb."

"Probably," Awen said. "It's pretty complicated, but it looks like it's set up to be a big timer that goes off at a specific time."

"Do you know when?"

She looked at the mechanism again. "Maybe two hours? It doesn't exactly have a clockface, so I'm guessing."

"Huh . . . Well, I think we should probably tell the guards," I said.

"That sounds reasonable," Awen said. "I can disarm this too. It's got two antitampering things, but that's all I see."

"There could be more."

"I can be careful," Awen said. "Even if we get the guards, and they believe us, it might take a while to disarm this."

I licked my lips while looking around some more. "Awen, what are the chances that this is the only one?"

Awen glanced up at me, then stared at the other pillars. "Low. Just one of these pillars breaking might shake the building, but I don't think it'll bring the whole palace down."

"So you'd need more than one?"

She scanned the area. "If it were me, I'd blow up as many of these pillars as I could. All at the same time. I'm not sure what's in that box, but it might not be enough to destroy the pillar, so you'd want enough of them going off at once to make sure you took out at least a few of them. Plus the explosion might be contained in the room. It looks pretty solid in here."

"Right," I said. I didn't quite know enough about explosions to follow, but I was clever enough to remember that more bombs made for more boom. "Oh."

"What?" Awen asked.

I shivered. "I remember where I saw him before," I said. "In Fort Sylphrot. The ball. The explosion there. We saw a harpy running away, then he transformed into a sylph." I spun as I heard a scuff, a shoe scraping on stone. "It's Rainnewt."

Rainnewt clapped slowly, the sound echoing out into the empty space. His face was set in a sardonic grin. "You are one persistent bun, you know that?"

· Chapter Thirty-Seven ·

The World is Diseased, and I Alone Can Cure It

Rainnewt," I said.

The man across from me was recognizably Rainnewt—a tallish human man, in a well-cut suit and long coat. He clearly had some sort of breastplate under the coat, and he had greaves fixed to his legs, too, painted some dark, light-absorbing black that matched the rest of his outfit.

I could only make out so many details. He had a small light hovering around him, but it wasn't very bright, and the basement's darkness cast deep shadows on everything.

"Hello, Miss Bunch," he said.

I glanced back at Awen, who shared a look with me. She tilted her head subtly toward the bomb, then nodded.

I nodded back. I'd take care of Rainnewt, she could work on making sure the entire building didn't fall down on our heads.

"Are you done planning with your little friend?" he asked.

"Not yet, no," I said truthfully. "But I don't think you're going to be giving us a lot of time to chitchat."

One of Rainnewt's eyebrows rose. He reached into his jacket, and I tensed a little until he pulled out a timepiece that he flicked open. "No, we still have a good ten minutes to talk. I do intend to be gone long before that, of course."

I balled my hands into fists by my sides. I didn't have anything like a weapon on hand, just . . . crates and the bomb and pieces of crates and maybe Awen. "So, did you stop to gloat?" I asked.

"Nothing quite so crass, no," he said with a shake of his head. "I had a few questions, actually. Perhaps even an explanation. I suspect that we're working on the same side, and . . . Well, maybe I was a little wrong in how I acted toward you before. So I wanted to apologize too. Sincerely."

I blinked, then narrowed my eyes while I inspected him.

Bright Clearnote. Musician, level 10. Nervous and late.

"Bright Clearnote?" I asked, confused.

"Oh," Rainnewt said. He chuckled, then made a gesture as if brushing off some dust from his suit. "Try again?"

Quincy Rainnewt. Manyfaced Hero, level ???. Curious.

"Do you have a skill that hides your name?"

"I wouldn't be able to infiltrate places very well if the first person with an Inspect-like skill could reveal me," he said. "This is my real name and class, for what it's worth. Tell me, did the system allow you to change your name?"

"What?" I asked. "No, this is my name. I didn't have ears before, but you met me before I got those, didn't you?"

"Huh," he said. "So your name is *actually* Broccoli?"

"Since I was born, yeah."

He rubbed at his chin. "Wow. Is that a common name where you're from? Because I'm thinking that maybe we're not from the same world."

"Oh, no, Broccoli's a pretty unique name," I said. "My parents were hippies."

"That could explain it," he said. "Perhaps we are from the same Earth. The World seems to be more than willing to take whoever is willing to accomplish its goals."

I peeked back again. Awen was sweating as she toyed with the bomb. I noted that Rainnewt was still a good ways away. Was he standing outside the range of the explosive? "Why are you doing all of this?" I asked.

"I imagine you're referring to both the destruction of this summit and the war overall?"

I nodded, then watched carefully as he stepped to the side, then hopped backward to sit on the edge of a crate. He was very casual about it all.

"It's rather simple, Broccoli. Well, no, in actuality, it's a complex mess of deep-rooted political issues, long-standing rivalries, and a nice helping of prejudice. But I think I've worked out a solution to it all."

"Did—" I swallowed. "Did the World ask you to start a war?" I asked, horror coloring my tone.

"Oh, no, no. The war is just one part of a much greater plan. A phase that I'm hoping will go well. This summit is one of the last steps toward ensuring that all involved nations are primed for what might be Dirt's first truly massive war."

"Why?" I asked. "You know that a lot of people will die. Why are you doing it?"

"Hmm? Oh, I won't go into all of the details," he said. "If you leave here knowing everything, you might ruin some parts of the plan. No, I think I'll be playing most of these cards close to the chest."

I shook my head. "I don't get it. The World asked me to get rid of those Evil Roots. Didn't it ask you the same thing?"

"Oh, it did," he said. "I'm just being effective about it."

"You don't need to start a war!" I cried out. "You can destroy the roots without breaking the dungeons."

Rainnewt blinked. "Really?"

"Yes!" I shouted. "Cleaning magic! You need it at a high rank, and then you can just wipe the root away. It's worked so far."

"Oh, that's fascinating to know," he said. "Well, too late to back out of my plan now. Still, thank you. I'll be sure to have the information distributed around—it could save us some trouble in the future. It would be unfortunate to see some of the infected dungeons be destroyed."

"So you'll stop the war?" I tried. "Turn off the bombs?" I was practically pleading. If he could just stop all of this, then . . .

He snorted. "No."

"We could be friends if you did," I said. "I guess. I . . . Please?"

```
Quincy Rainnewt
Desired Quality: Someone who will assist him in taking
over the world
   Dream: To save the world in his image
```

"I'm certain we could be great friends," Rainnewt said. "Or maybe not. Honestly, it seems our methodologies are far too different for a partnership to work out."

"Broccoli," Awen whispered. "It's disarmed."

I didn't say anything to Awen. I didn't want Rainnewt to know that this bomb was off. I imagined other bombs were hidden around the room. "Why are you talking to me, then?" I asked. "Instead of fighting us?"

Rainnewt looked like he was actually considering the question. "You might have been foiling a few of my plans, in small ways, but for the most part, I can't really fault you for that. I'm not entirely unable to put myself in your shoes, you know? Besides, our end goals are the same. You've discovered a new way to take care of the Evil Roots, which . . . Well, I would never have tried, so clearly you've proven your worth. Besides, I think some parts of our philosophy match up quite well."

"I'm not trying to start a big war," I said.

"No, not that part," Rainnewt said. "Your level. When we first met you were . . . Oh, I can't actually remember. That was a while ago, in Port Royal. You still only had one class, you were weak, even compared to the average person on Dirt, but you know what made you different?"

"What?" I asked. Maybe if I could keep him talking, help would arrive? But no, we hadn't exactly told anyone we'd be sneaking into the basement.

"You were trying to improve. You must feel it, too, right? People here can grow! It's a tangible thing—effort is actually rewarded directly." He raised his arms, like a priest at the pulpit. "And yet the people of Dirt, with few exceptions, refuse to excel! Do you know what the average level is? I've looked into it, both here and in Port Royal. It's thirteen. Thirteen!"

"Is that bad?" I asked. That was a little bit higher than my own level, wasn't it?

"Broccoli, it means that most people never bother pushing themselves past their tenth level. A few exceptions exist, but then they tend to stop at the very next tier. Dirt affords people the possibility of infinite growth, and instead, most people grasp for the bare minimum and just . . . stop. It's infuriating!"

"Uh."

Rainnewt lowered his arms with a sigh. "I'm being a little melodramatic, aren't I? Forgive me, this work leaves me with no one to talk to for long stretches, so I have a good number of pent-up rants."

"You know, I always give my friends all the time they need to rant," I said. "I . . . I don't know if I can forgive you for everything you've done, but I've never said no to a potential friend before . . . before. If you want, we could . . . could work to set things right? Find another way to fix things?"

He smiled. For a moment, I had hope. "You're not a bad person, maybe," he said. "Manipulative, but innocently so. Maybe if we had met a month earlier, I'd be tempted by your offer." He bounced off the crate and onto his feet. Then he pulled out his timepiece again. "I'd love to stay and chat, but if I don't leave soon, I'll become collateral to my own plan, and that would be a disappointing way to go."

"You're leaving?" I asked.

"I wasn't going to stay in the room with all the explosives," he said. "You should consider running too. There's plenty of time to make it out of the old palace before it collapses."

"Wait!" I called out.

"I don't think I will, no," he said. "Good luck! Do keep up the good work. I'll appreciate it, even if the World doesn't."

Rainnewt took off at a walk, but his long legs meant he was out of sight past some pillars and crates, the darkness of the room swallowing him whole.

I spun toward Awen. "The bombs, do you think you can take them out?"

"Awa! I'll try," Awen said.

"If you can't, just run. Tell the guards, tell Caprica and Amaryllis and . . . and everyone else!"

"Broccoli, where are you going?" Awen asked, even if it was obvious.

I grinned at her. "I'm going to kick Rainnewt's butt."

I bounced off after Rainnewt, a bit of extra mana shoved into my light-ball to illuminate the room around me. I flew past a second bomb, tucked up against another pillar, before I spotted him at the far end of the room. He casually slid aside a heavy metal door before disappearing beyond it.

Pushing myself to move faster, I bounced after Rainnewt.

It was probably not the smartest thing to do. Catching him wouldn't unexplode the bombs if they went off. But then, if I didn't catch him, he could try something like this again. And if what he said about being disappointed that the people on Dirt didn't work hard enough was true, then the next time I saw him, he'd be that much stronger. I couldn't let him get away.

I burst through the door and into a long, narrow corridor. It was all stone, carefully smoothed and worked with little patterns. At the end of the corridor was another doorway.

I slid to a stop next to it, then twisted the latch around. It wasn't locked, but it was really heavy. I had to plant my feet against the ground to push it open. When it finally swung aside, I stepped into another room, then stopped.

My light could only reach so far into the massive, engulfing darkness, but it was enough to make out some of the details of what I was seeing.

It was a city or maybe a town—dozens of homes, all short and squat, along a main road with alleys and sideroads branching off to the sides. Pillars rose, holding up the uneven ceiling.

An entire town, hidden inside the mountain, and obviously long abandoned.

I locked onto Rainnewt, who was a good ways down the main street of the town.

I could wonder about what I'd found later. For now, I had to catch up to him!

"Rainnewt! Wait! I promised that I would kick your butt!"

· Chapter Thirty-Eight ·

True Colors

I glanced around the old city, peering through the darkness while search-ing for something I could use as a makeshift weapon. There wasn't much, unfortunately. Some of the homes had gutters, which I imagined I could rip off. (Why did they have gutters? They were underground. It couldn't rain here right?) Some had windows on their fronts, with sharpened jaws of bro-ken glass opening into the deeper darkness in the abandoned homes. A cart or two was left to decay along the roadsides.

Nothing easy to grab, no obvious gardening tools, no street lamps, or a handy pile of buckets and spades.

I grit my teeth and gave up on the search. If I stumbled on something, then that'd be great, but I couldn't lose sight of what I was here for just for that.

Rainnewt was maybe halfway down the street, walking at a brisk pace toward the far end of the little city.

I grunted as I shot after him, pouring a bit of stamina into my legs to give me an edge. I'd need it.

Rainnewt was a lot stronger than I was, at least with raw levels. The only person I'd fought who was that far ahead of me was Bastion, and he'd kicked my butt in every spar while also clearly holding back.

Hopefully, Rainnewt's abilities weren't combat oriented. He seemed focused on deception, so it was a possibility that I could gamble on.

I hopped up and onto the flat roof of one of the nearby homes, feet thump-thumping on rusty old tin as I ran for all I was worth.

Rainnewt turned and looked up just as I jumped off the roof and came flying toward him. I put my heels together and kicked down.

My feet passed right through Rainnewt, as if he were made of smoke.

His body dissolved, leaving me to crash feet-first into the ground.

I turned the rough landing into a roll and bounced back onto my feet.

"You're pretty fast," Rainnewt said. He was standing a few feet to the right of where I'd tried to kick him. "But you're a little . . . What would be a polite way of putting this? Loud? Unstealthy? Obvious?"

"Was that a clone?" I asked.

"What? Oh, no, that was just an illusion. Do you have any idea how many dungeons I've cleared?"

"Uh," I said. "A dozen, maybe?"

"A few more than that," he said. "Most of them solo. Now, to be fair, I try not to overestimate myself. I do know the value of preparing for a fight, but still, perhaps underestimate me a little less?"

I swallowed back a pout. "I wasn't underestimating you. I'm fighting you knowing that you're probably way stronger than me."

"Ah, so it's . . . bravery, then, not stupidity. Though I guess there's a little bit of that as well." He nodded as if he understood something that was obvious. "That's entirely fair. In either case, I don't intend to fight you, so perhaps you could just move along? I'm almost certain that this part of the old city won't be destroyed by those bombs, and there are a few tunnels leading back to the surface here. You could be safe."

"I don't want to be safe," I said. "I want to . . . I don't know." I shook my head, ears bending back while I brought my hands up in two little fists. I didn't know how to box or anything, but I'd figure it out. "I think you're wrong. Super wrong, and I don't want you to continue."

"So, what's your plan exactly, Broccoli? I do think I'm stronger than you, I'm definitely more experienced, time is on my side, and even if you do beat me, then what? You'll unexplode the king?"

I frowned at him, then whipped a spray of Cleaning magic at him.

It sliced right through whatever mana he was using to make his illusion.

"So, you're not a shapeshifter," I said as I started to look around for Rainnewt. He had to be close . . . I hoped.

"Oh, I am a shapeshifter," the illusory Rainnewt said.

I jumped to the side and flung out a big wave of Cleaning magic. It spread out, washing across the ground and walls and finally over the real Rainnewt, who looked like he was just standing there next to one of the homes along the street.

"That's interesting magic," he said, this time in person. "Cleaning, right? You mentioned it being good against Evil Roots. I can believe it. What rank did you take it to?"

"Rank S," I said.

"Oh, your ranks are letters too? Interesting!" He smiled genially. "Well, that's pretty impressive. Most of the locals don't bother investing everything into one skill. It's too much of a pain to wait for so long to invest all of your points later. I think our rapid growth kind of negates that disadvantage."

I spun toward him, then knelt down to pick up a pebble off the street.

Rainnewt blinked as I flung it at him and he casually batted it aside. "What was that for?"

"To see if you're solid," I said.

"Oh, clever." He nodded along, then glanced back down the road. "I think I really will be heading off now. It was fun chatting. I don't get to talk to too many people, at least not honestly."

"So you're lonely?" I asked. "Is that why you're being so mean? Because, well, you did a lot of bad things, but I guess I might not be so nice if I was very lonely too."

"Oh no, I doubt that's the case," Rainnewt dismissed, but I felt like it was a bit too easy of a dismissal. "I'm pursuing my goals. I don't have time for people. I've always considered myself a nice guy, but, well, people get in the way."

I nodded, then, midnod, I lunged for Rainnewt. I tried to hit him with my shoulder, but he stepped to the side.

Planting my foot, I slid to a stop, spun around, and launched myself back toward him. My right arm fired a punch straight at his face while I hid my left behind me and formed fireballs around it.

Rainnewt ducked under my swing, then when I tried to elbow him, he shoved my arm aside with a hard smack.

I gritted my teeth, brought my other hand around, and fired the six fireballs I'd made.

Rainnewt hissed as all six blasted him in the chest. He stumbled back a step, his hand rubbing at the burning spots on his suit. "That was expensive, you know!"

"So's the building you're trying to bomb!" I shouted back.

Rainnewt huffed as he bounced back and moved out of the way of a swift kick toward his knee.

I bounced forward and, with a quick smack, finally managed to touch him. It was only a moment, but I did what I could to scramble his magic.

Rainnewt's eyes widened as raw mana poured out from his chest. It was a bit strange, not smoke or a stream but a flickering mass of colors and reflective surfaces and strange textures. It was almost like a visual glitch.

I didn't have much time to inspect it before he ducked to one side, and also the other.

I was confused as two Rainnewts moved in two directions, but a pair of flung cleanballs revealed that both were illusions as the Cleaning magic disrupted the images.

"Dang it!" I cursed before shoving a big heap of my mana into a burst of Cleaning magic that exploded out of me and raced across the street.

It revealed that Rainnewt was a good ways away, quietly jogging off toward the far end of the city.

I grunted as I sprinted after him. I was vaguely aware that I had used up a lot of mana in that short tussle, and some stamina too. My heart was pitter-pattering in my chest.

I jumped at Rainnewt, hand wrapping around the fabric of his suit. "Got you!"

Then the floor skipped beneath us.

A loud *bang* roared across the room, and long-settled dust came pouring down from the ceiling.

I was so surprised that, for a blink, my lightball faded, leaving us both in the trembling dark.

"What?" I asked.

Rainnewt spun out of my grasp and shoved me back. "Seems like your friend wasn't all that skilled at disarming things."

"No!" I said.

"That was very premature. There's not much else it could be. For what it's worth, I'm sorry."

"No!" I said, louder. Awen was fine. She had to be.

I blinked hard, then jumped toward Rainnewt.

He weaved around my grasp, then slapped me across the face.

I squeaked as I crashed to my knees, the world spinning and a sharp, burning pain across my face. It hurt. Thinking that Awen might be . . . No, I couldn't be distracted.

"All right, now you're just annoying," Rainnewt said.

I got up, a hand cradling my cheek and the side of my face. It still hurt, the pain only ebbing away slowly. "You're not a very nice person, are you?" He'd hurt Awen, maybe. Probably not. Awen was good. She was a great mechanic. She knew what she was doing.

"You were literally attacking me," he said. "Besides, what I do, I do for a reason. I'm a nice guy, I swear."

I glared at him as hard as I could. "No, I don't think you are," I said. "I . . . I don't like fighting people. I don't even like fighting things. But you're just mean enough that I think fighting you is the right thing to do."

He rolled his eyes at me, and that was when I spun and kicked his chest.

Rainnewt caught my leg, a hand gripping tight around my shin with a meaty *thwack*. He pulled me forward, then, when I struggled to regain my balance, he punched me. I coughed as the air was blown out of my lungs. His fist stayed buried just below my ribs. I tried to disrupt his mana, but I couldn't think straight. I was too slow. He let go of my leg and shoved me back.

"Shut up, Broccoli," he said. "You're such a self-righteous little child. Going on about . . . friendship and whatever. Grow up."

"No," I said, then I kicked him in the shin.

He was wearing greaves, though, and other than a wince, it didn't look like I'd done much to stop him at all.

"I'm done here. If you survive the blast, then maybe we'll see each other again. Honestly, I'm not sure if I want you to or not, but I don't have it in me to kill a fellow Riftwalker."

"What? What makes me so special? You're going to kill a ton of people with your bombs. You're going to start a war!"

He shrugged. "Maybe. But they're the products of the World. They're . . . I suppose less people."

"That's not true," I said. I spun over onto my stomach and coughed a few times, then, with a wipe of my nose, I climbed to my feet. I felt a little nauseous still, and the world was wobblier than I'd like, but I wasn't going to let him insult everyone everywhere like that. Those people were my friends. "You're a liar, you know?"

"Yes, obviously," Rainnewt said.

His voice sounded faint, and it took me a moment to realize that it hadn't come from his mouth.

A weak splash of Cleaning magic washed over him, disrupting whatever illusion magic he was using enough to reveal the trick. The jerk! Another fake!

I groaned as I fired off another big blast of Cleaning magic, revealing Rainnewt, on the edge of an alleyway a dozen meters away.

My mana was almost spent.

"You're persistent," he said.

"She is."

Rainnewt and I both glanced down the street to see a very familiar face. Bastion, in his ceremonial armor, cape fluttering behind him like someone out of a poster. Behind him, and still much closer to the doorway, was Awen and a few guards, who were working on creating balls of light to illuminate the dead city.

"But she's got a good heart," Bastion continued. "Which is more than I could say about you. I'm supposed to formally ask that you surrender, but I would much rather you resist."

· Chapter Thirty-Nine ·

Someone Set Up Us the Bomb

Seeing Bastion was like having a weight lifted off my shoulders. Seeing Awen, healthy and unexploded, was like replacing that weight with a warm blanket.

My friends—some of them—were safe, and they were here to help me when I could really use the help.

"I don't actually know you," Rainnewt said. "Are you that paladin that's been following Miss Bunch around?"

Bastion nodded. He reached to his hip, hand gripping around the hilt of his ornate sword. "I am. Would you do us both a favor and drop to your knees. Place your hands flat on the ground. Surrender. It's the only logical option you have left."

"You do seem terribly confident in yourself," Rainnewt said. He glanced around the darkened city. The place was becoming lighter and easier to see as the five guards that followed Bastion raised lights above their heads and moved closer to us. "But I'm afraid that I'm nearly gone already."

Bastion's eyes narrowed, and I think it clicked for me at the same time. "He's an illusion!" I shouted. If the Rainnewt we were looking at was a fake, then where was the real one?

"There," Bastion said. He whipped his sword out of its scabbard and pointed to his right with the tip of it.

I spun and searched the near-dark for Rainnewt, but I couldn't see him. Still, if Bastion said he was that way, then I'd trust my friend. My mana and stamina had been refilling during that little break. I could still fight for a while! I jumped up and onto one of the nearest rooftops, then sprinted in the direction Bastion was pointing. I almost stumbled over some loose debris on one flat rooftop, but I managed to keep my footing.

I needed light. My tiny ball of light was only strong enough to push the dark back in a little circle around me. I did have one other option when it came to magics that made light.

"Rainnewt, you'd better duck!" I shouted as I jumped up, then flung my arm out in a wide arc. A brace of fireballs rushed ahead of me in a rough semicircle. As the balls wooshed ahead, they cast orangey light over the pale, shadow-dusted walls of the dead city.

No signs of Rainnewt. But then I saw a curtain shift in a window just before I landed on the edge of a rooftop. I spun and shot a huge gush of Cleaning magic that way, the magic moving faster than most people would be able to avoid. It washed away dust and grime, and Rainnewt's illusion magic too.

"Found him!" I said.

"Engaging!" Bastion called out as he buzzed past me. He had discarded his cape at some point, freeing his wings so that he could fly with no impediments.

He landed in a roll, then sliced out with his sword, snake-quick.

The blade met metal as Rainnewt pulled a long dagger from the small of his back and parried the assault. "Really, Broccoli, you had to send one of these dogs of the king after me?"

". . . Is that an insult?" I frowned, leaping closer to the fight. "I like dogs!"

Bastion stepped back, then ducked to the side and lunged in from an entirely new direction. The motion was so smooth it almost looked like a dance.

Rainnewt wasn't much slower, though, and he was pretty strong, his own level likely very close to Bastion's own. Dagger met sword again. Bastion had the advantage in length, and he used it right away.

I paused, not sure what to do and entirely captivated as Bastion danced around Rainnewt, his sword plunging in and out just long enough for Rainnewt to bat it aside. He was looking for an opening, and judging by how Rainnewt was scrambling to push aside every strike, he'd find one eventually.

And then, as Bastion was lunging in again, Rainnewt flung his free hand out toward the blade. There was a clink, and a second long dagger wavered into being in Rainnewt's offhand. He slipped past Bastion's guard and sliced at the sylph.

I gasped, but Bastion had the experience and skill not to lose his head. He weaved around the knife, brought his sword back, then flapped his wings once to regain some small amount of distance before he changed stances and resumed his strikes toward Rainnewt. He was being a lot more cautious now.

Bastion spun and slashed at empty air, only for his sword to meet something where nothing was visible. A second Rainnewt appeared there, smiling confidently while the first faded away like dust caught in a strong wind. "You're a decent fighter," he said.

"And you are one of the most infuriating," Bastion said. "You know that I will win this."

"If my goal was to defeat you, then yes. But time, as you well know, is on my side."

Bastion glared at him. He never took his eyes off Rainnewt as he addressed me. "Broccoli, make sure the guards know where we are. I believe I might require their assistance soon."

"All right!" I said. "Just be careful, okay?"

I spun and ran to the other end of the roof, away from the *clink-clink* of sword and dagger meeting behind me as Bastion and Rainnewt continued to test each other.

On arriving at the other end of the roof, I waved an arm over my head, signaling the guards making their way across the city closer. "This way! They're over here! Fast!"

The guards put on some extra speed, dashing over even more of a hurry. Some took to the air and skipped from rooftop to rooftop, magical lights trailing behind them and brightening the world around us.

"Awen!" I called out as I saw my friend running after the guards. She had a cloth bundle held close to her chest and was huffing and puffing as she tried to keep up with the others.

I bounced off the roof, skipped off another building, then landed with a huff next to Awen. "Awa!" she said as she jumped in fright. "Oh, Broccoli."

"Yeah! Did you get all the bombs?"

She shook her head. "I couldn't, there were too many. But I did manage to take one apart, and I detonated another. Ah, in a controlled manner. Bastion was one of the first guards to show up, so I explained things as quickly as I could."

"And the rest of the bombs? How many are there?"

"I don't know. A lot." She puffed out a breath. "More than enough to take down the entire building, but I think the guards might be able to handle it. I hope they're evacuating."

"Good," I said. At least Rainnewt's plan was foiled in the end. Or maybe now, if he wanted to anger the sylphs, the threat of a bomb might be as good as the bomb itself. "What's that?" I asked with a gesture to the thing she was hugging close.

Awen grinned. "A gift for Rainnewt. I thought, maybe, you could throw it at him?"

"Is that a bomb?"

"More like half a bomb?" Awen tried. "The arming mechanism is still there. There's a five-second delay."

"Uh, that seems dangerous."

She shrugged. "It'll work!"

Maybe we could bluff him?

Awen and I rounded a corner onto the road where Bastion and Rain-newt had been fighting. The guards had arrived before us, but it didn't look like they'd tipped the balance all that much. Two of them were injured, being tended to by a third as they leaned against the front of an abandoned home.

The other guards were holding back, keeping a good few meters away from Rainnewt and Bastion, who were still carefully trading blows.

At some point, they'd turned to using magic. Rainnewt was swinging around sharp beams of light that cut through everything they touched. Bastion countered with glowing shields and arcing balls of fire that hissed as they burned the air.

Every time Rainnewt moved, a new image of him would split off and attack or dodge in a new direction. Sometimes those images turned out to be the real thing, and Bastion had to constantly block attacks that weren't entirely real. He was ignoring some of the feints, but I had no idea how he could tell that those weren't real while others were.

"We need to do something," I said.

"Bomb?"

Well, it was an idea.

"Can you make it explode at a certain time?"

"I can make it explode when your Cleaning magic hits it," Awen offered.

"Okay, do it."

Awen grinned and unwrapped the cloth she held to reveal a mechanical contraption of clockwork gears around what looked like a mason jar filled with something brown. She broke off a brass tine on part of it, then pinched her tongue between her teeth as she summoned a thin piece of glass in its place. "Okay. One good blast of Cleaning magic, and it will go off," she said.

"Perfect," I said as I took the bomb away from her. "Get to cover. I'll be right back!"

Awen didn't have time to protest that as I leaped up and onto the nearest rooftop. I started running again, glad that the sylphs liked using such easy roofs to travel on.

Bastion and Rainnewt were traveling a little as they fought, Rainnewt backpedaling and losing ground with every exchange. That was good. I didn't want anyone caught in the splash of the bomb.

"Hey!" I called out from above the two fighters. They both glanced my way, but it was barely more than a peek. I raised the bomb over my head. "I'm going to drop this behind Rainnewt now. Uh, it's one of his bombs."

The constant back and forth between the two stopped. Neither looked up at me, but I could feel their attention. "That sounds like a rather terrible idea," Bastion said.

The two remaining guards started to back away, little by little.

"I agree with the paladin," Rainnewt said.

"It's just half a bomb," I added.

"That's still a lot of bomb!" Rainnewt shouted.

"Well, in that case, you should surrender," I said.

"Broccoli, I'll hardly surrender when you might well be bluffing."

"She doesn't bluff," Bastion said.

"Come on, Rainnewt, last chance," I said. I raised the bomb over my head until even my ears could brush against it. "This thing is pretty heavy, you know."

"You won't do it," he said.

Bastion lunged at him, but Rainnewt ducked back and smacked Bastion's sword aside.

"Fine then," I said. I stretched way back, then with a heavy grunt, I flung the bomb up and into the air in their general direction.

"You're mad!"

"Sorry! Try not to get too hurt!" I spun on my heel, then darted away as quick as I could.

I heard Bastion say something that was very unpaladin-like, then a glowing barrier appeared in front of him. He didn't stay behind that, though, and instead flew to the guards nearest him and tackled them off their feet.

Rainnewt jumped through a window, glass shattering with a loud *crack*.

And then the bomb hit the ground. I sent a wash of Cleaning magic after it, then spun away.

I eeped as a wave of sound and warmth and wind picked me up from behind and sent me tumbling tail over teakettle.

Glass shattered, at least one wall crumbled apart, and the constant echo of the explosion rang back and forth throughout the entire old city.

I coughed as a wave of dust settled down around me, then I pulsed out a bit of Cleaning magic to clear enough air to breathe.

I really, really hoped that everyone was still alive, and that the idea hadn't been as bad as I feared.

· Chapter Forty ·

Out of the Dark

I shook my head and wiggled my ears. They were ringing a bit, which I supposed was normal after hearing such a loud noise.

Standing up, I dusted myself off, then glanced back.

Smoke and dust were still rising from the spot where I'd flung the bomb, and a couple of the nearby homes had had their walls knocked down into big piles of rubble.

I stumbled toward the explosion, a finger digging into one of my human ears to get it to pop back. The ringing faded as I arrived close to the edge of the roof where I'd tossed the bomb from. I didn't want to stand on the very edge, since there were a few big cracks running across the stone wall.

"Bastion?" I called down. "Are you okay?"

The shield he'd put up was gone, and I was worried that I might have hurt my friend.

A few wooshes burst from the smoke, clearing it away to reveal Bastion on his feet, sword by his side and wings flapping even though he wasn't flying. "Broccoli?" he called out. "You're still alive?"

"Yeah!" I said. "I'm fine!"

He glanced up and spotted me, then he waved me over. "Come over here, please."

I jumped down, landing with a crunch on the road that was now covered in little bits of rock. "Are you okay? You're not hurt, are you? What about the guards that were with you?"

Bastion shook his head. "I'm fine," he said before glancing over his shoulder. "These two look all right as well."

I pushed some Cleaning magic out to clear the area, revealing the two guards getting to their feet. They were covered in dust and grime, but they didn't look injured.

"I'm happy that everyone made it out okay," I said.

Bastion nodded, then he beckoned me closer. "Come here."

I stepped up to him. Did he need me to carry something? I watched as his arm stretched out above my head, then he turned his hand so that its side was facing down. "What are—" I began.

Bastion chopped down, clunking me right between the ears.

"Ow!" I yelped as I brought my hands up to rub at my head. "That hurt!"

"So did being blown up," Bastion said. "Broccoli, it's . . . it's not good form to drop explosives next to allies, especially not when they're within the blast radius."

"I . . . I'm sorry!"

"I really hope you are. Friends don't bomb friends."

I pouted, but Bastion was probably right. That hadn't been very nice of me at all. "I'm sorry. Really. Uh, but we should go check on Rainnewt. He was closer to the explosion."

Bastion nodded, then half turned to address the guards. He barked a few orders, sending one out to fetch reinforcements while the other gathered the nearby guards who could help once we found Rainnewt again.

Bastion and I took the lead in checking the area of the explosion. There was a black scorch on the ground, and a big circle where all the long-accumulated dust and debris had been pushed back. No signs of Rainnewt, though.

"There," Bastion said. He pointed to one of the nearest houses. I couldn't see what hinted that Rainnewt had gone that way, but I trusted Bastion's intuition on the matter.

He kicked open a door and I tossed a lightball into the room, filling it with pale white light that shoved aside the old shadows occupying the home. Rainnewt was there, lying on the ground with his back against the wall.

I gasped.

He was clutching at his tummy. Blood seeped out from between his clenched fingers, running down over his legs and pooling on the floor. His head was turned to the side and pressed against the wall, eyes squeezed shut and teeth gritted.

"Oh no," I said. "I'm so, so sorry." I started to run in, but Bastion held an arm out, stopping me.

"Illusion," he said.

We stepped into the room and I pushed a bit of Cleaning magic toward Rainnewt, and his body faded away into motes of light. "Oh, it really was just an—"

I was cut off as Bastion spun, grabbed me by the scruff, and shoved me aside.

It was such a brusque, sudden motion that I barely had time to wonder why Bastion was being so mean before his sword came up and caught something out of the air with a metallic clink.

A new Rainnewt appeared, holding onto a dagger midparry.

He looked rough, his suit covered in dust and grime, with a few tears in it that hadn't been there before. A long cut along his forehead was bleeding across his face, and he was grimacing as he moved back, as though the motion hurt him.

"Came back to finish me off?" he rasped. "You know, Broccoli, your whole facade, pretending to be so innocent, so harmless—you're not, are you?"

"Hey! I'm as harmless as I want to be!" I said.

"You tossed a bomb at me!" Rainnewt shouted right back.

I stood up properly as Bastion let go, and crossed my arms. "You're the one that brought the bombs. You can't blame me for using your own weapon against you."

Bastion must have been tired of our argument, because his arm blurred toward Rainnewt.

Rainnewt's eyes widened a moment before the paladin's knuckles met his chin with a hard crack. I saw his face go through a few strange expressions as he was spun halfway around. His eyes rolled up, and he crashed to the floor like a sackful of potatoes.

Bastion was on him a moment later, pinning his arms to the small of his back and tossing the two daggers he had to the corner of the room. "I need restraints."

I slid to the side as a guard ran in with a short length of rope which Bastion immediately used to tie Rainnewt's hands together. Rainnewt didn't stay unconscious for long. He came to and started to squirm to fight Bastion off, but it was no use, not with more guards stepping into the room and surrounding him.

"I believe it goes without saying that you're under arrest," Bastion said to Rainnewt. Looking up, he addressed the guards. "I want three pairs of eyes on him at all times. No exceptions. He's capable of shapeshifting, and it's possible that he has bribed some members of the guard. Do not trust anything he says. In fact, gag him. I'm certain someone can spare a sock."

The guards nodded, and soon they helped drag Rainnewt out of the home and into the street. They never actually let him get to his feet, though, preferring to drag him around by the armpits.

I followed the guards out of the building but paused when I saw that Bastion wasn't following. "Are you okay?" I asked.

Bastion looked up, then smiled. "I'm well. A little disappointed—I've scuffed my armor in a few places. It will take hours to buff it back to a shine."

"Oh," I said. "I could help?" I raised a hand, manifesting the barest glow of Cleaning magic.

He shook his head. "It's a paladin's responsibility to keep his gear in tip-top shape. Ceremonial equipment more so. Though I believe I will be forgiven for having become somewhat unkempt today. While traditions are important, lives are more so." He bent down and plucked Rainnewt's two daggers off the ground.

"As long as you don't get a talking-to for it. You were awesome earlier, fighting against Rainnewt like that."

"I'm more concerned over how difficult the battle was," Bastion said. He raised one of the knives, inspecting it in the faint light.

"Are the knives special?"

He shook his head and looked at the other. "No. Quite the opposite. They're perfectly ordinary. Well made but not mastercraft. No markings, nothing to make them special. I'm a little disappointed."

"How so?"

He smiled. "I was hoping the reason I had to work hard to keep up was because he had superior equipment, perhaps enchanted. This knocks that theory out of the air. That Rainnewt man is dangerous. Most paladins would defeat him in a straight contest, I think, but he doesn't fight fairly. Tricks and illusions and deception at every turn. He's dangerous."

I glanced back to where he was being held by the guards. A few more had joined the group, and I saw Awen loitering by the edge. Unless he pulled off some great trick, he wasn't going to get away. "What's going to happen to him?" I asked.

Bastion took a while to answer. "He will be judged. Likely in a more private venue. Then he will pay for his crimes, depending on the judgment handed down to him."

"So, jail?" I asked.

Bastion patted me on the shoulder. "Come on. Let's go see how your friends are doing."

"Oh, okay," I said. Bastion wasn't that great at distractions, but I didn't mind. I stuck close to him until I was close enough to Awen that I could run over and pull her into a tight hug. "You're all right?"

"I'm fine," Awen said with a giggle. "I heard an explosion. That was you?"

"I didn't explode. But I might have caused one, yeah. Your bomb worked, by the way."

"I figured as much," Awen said. "Fortunately, that's the only explosion I heard. I think that they cleared out the others."

"They had someone that could disable them?"

Awen shook her head. "I think they had some guards that could jam up the traps on the bombs, but they mostly just carried them out of the building. I guess they'll let them all explode where it's safe."

"Uh, is that safe at all?"

"An explosion outside, with nothing to redirect the force of it? I think it should be safe," Awen said. "The blast will just disperse in every direction. If it's far enough from any homes or anything important, then it shouldn't actually cause any harm."

I nodded firmly. "Good."

Bastion walked up next to us. "We'll be escorting the prisoner out. You should follow us. I'm certain there will be many questions."

"Questions?"

"Oh yes, plenty," Bastion said. "The fact that you both acted to help, that things might have been worse without your assistance, will help a lot."

"Why do you say that as if we'll need the help?"

"Because you might. With situations like these, there are some people who will immediately look for ways to put the blame on someone that isn't themselves. That means that they might see your involvement in the situation as an easy way to claim that you're somehow responsible."

"That doesn't make any sense," I said.

Bastion shrugged. "One of the first things the fearful and cowardly toss away is common sense and decency." He patted me on the shoulder. "Don't worry. I'll do what I can to allay suspicions. And besides, you have friends in good places, and something of a reputation."

I snorted. "Come on, we've only been here for a few days. We can hardly have a reputation already."

"Ah, if you say so," Bastion said.

The guards kept a formation around Rainnewt as they escorted him through the old city. Bastion, Awen, and I stayed at the back of the group, walking along at a decent pace through the ancient ruins until we reentered the basement of the old palace. The room was a hive of activity, with what must have been half the city's guards and paladins scouring the basement for anything out of place.

We got lots of looks, but Bastion being there probably saved us from some scrutiny.

A couple of paladins joined us, sharing quick signs with Bastion before they nodded and formed up on our flanks.

The halls above, unlike the basement, were eerily empty. Where dignitaries and diplomats and nosy people of all sorts had been gathering before, there was now a whole lot of nothing, only a few guards moving around in quick patrols.

It was only when we were outside that we found everyone again. "Broccoli Bunch!"

I flinched at the snap in Amaryllis's voice.

"I prepared all night for that speech. I should have known that I didn't need to bother, what with you around to cause a ruckus!"

· Chapter Forty-One ·

Royal Expositioner

I couldn't help but grin from ear to ear as Amaryllis pulled me into a hug of her own volition. "You moron," she muttered into my hair before letting me go. She pulled Awen into a hug, too, but didn't have any insults for her. "Thanks for keeping Broccoli safe."

"Hey!" I protested. "I can keep myself safe."

"Yes, yes, I'm sure," Amaryllis dismissed.

We were making something of a scene. An entire heap of nobles and dignitaries were congregating around, most looking like they didn't know what to do. Which was fair. I imagined that the plans for the summit had been upended pretty hard.

Caprica slid out from the crowd and walked over. "Captain Broccoli, Lady Bristlecone, you're back," she said. "Do you have any idea what happened?"

I nodded. "Yeah, we were involved with the mess. Not making it, but, uh, we were there."

"And what did happen?" Caprica asked. "I saw Bastion running off against the orders of Inquisitor Storm. Then the guards were thrown into a frenzy."

"I saw someone suspicious, so I followed him down to the basement with Awen," I said. "Then it turned out to be a shapeshifted Rainnewt, and the basement was filled with time bombs."

Caprica blinked, then glanced over to the old palace. "What happened after that?"

"Well, we fought. Awen disarmed some bombs. Bastion showed up. Uh, I might have set off one bomb, and then we captured Rainnewt." I looked to Awen. "Am I missing any parts?"

"I think you're missing a few little details," Awen said.

Caprica glanced over at Amaryllis. "Is this normal? I read Bastion's reports, but I didn't expect to see your group at work."

"Our group?" Amaryllis asked. She flinched back. "Please don't group me in with these two. I'm perfectly sane."

"I never questioned your sanity aloud," Caprica said.

"Aloud?" Amaryllis repeated.

Caprica cleared her throat. "I think your group might have the best first-hand information here. Come on, follow me. I think Father will want to hear all of this—he's with the delegates from Deepmarsh and the Trenten Flats. They might want to know what happened as well. This debacle is tarnishing Sylphfree's promise of safety."

"No one was hurt, right?" I asked. "I think that should matter a lot."

"No one was hurt, but they could have been," Caprica said. "It's an important distinction to some more politically inclined people."

Caprica led us through a small crowd of sylph nobles. Everyone was mostly gathered on the lawns across the street from the old palace. A few local shops had opened their doors and were serving drinks and food, and I suspected that the staff were working overtime to keep everyone happy.

Meanwhile, carriages were racing down the cobbled streets, with teams of guards on their backs. A cordon was forming on either end of the road, and I suspected that they were there to keep people out as much as to keep people in.

The king was sitting in a pavilion tent someone had set up in record time, halfway on the sidewalk and on the road. I counted six paladins encircling the tent, and more of them were within, hands on the hilts of their swords and their eyes peeled for any threats.

Caprica paused before the tent and spoke to one of the paladins in hushed tones. That gave me some time to peek over her head and into the tent.

I didn't recognize the cervid delegates from the Trenten Flats, but the grenoils were more familiar. Sylvie Robespierre was there, with her secretary friend and a couple of other grenoil representatives. No harpies, though. No humans or buns, either, for that matter, not until we walked in.

The king glanced up briefly while talking with a sylph, spotted Caprica, then smiled at her. She nodded back, then made a quick gesture with her hand. I didn't quite see it all, being behind her, but I had the impression it was asking for permission for something. Their own little sign language? That was neat!

The king frowned, leaned to the side to say something to his buddy, then waved us over.

There were even more paladins inside the tent than outside, a ring of them around the edges, barely noticeable because of how little they moved. One standing close to the king wasn't as subtle, though. Inquisitor Storm. The same paladin I'd met way back in Fort Sylphrot, the day I met Bastion.

"Hello, Caprica," the king said. "I see all of your friends made it out all right. Did you have anything to share? News, perhaps?"

The nobles around the king backed up, all except for Inquisitor Storm, who eyed us all very carefully.

"News and more," Caprica said. "Captain Bunch and Lady Bristlecone here were the ones who discovered the plot to destroy the old palace. They also fought and apprehended the culprit. I believe with the aid of Paladin Bastion?"

I nodded. "Yup! Though there were a bunch of guards too."

The king leaned forward. "Really now? Captain Bunch, Lady Bristlecone, would you mind sharing the story with the rest of us?"

"Your Majesty, are you certain you want to interrogate them publicly?" Inquisitor Storm asked in a low whisper.

The king nodded. "I think I have a good measure of their character. They're good kids."

I blinked, then realized that they didn't seem to be speaking the usual sylph language. That was a clever trick, though I imagined that a lot of diplomats probably had skills that would help them understand. "We didn't do anything bad, I swear," I muttered in the same language.

The king grinned. "See," he said. "Captain, Lady, please, tell us what happened."

I glanced to Awen, but she shook her head quickly. "You speak, you're better at it," she said.

Well, that made sense. Awen was a bit shy, and a lot of eyes were on us. I think the people gathered here really wanted to know what had happened. Either because it would be great gossip or because they were curious busybodies.

So I told them.

I started from the top. How I'd seen someone suspicious, then followed them down to the basement with Awen. Then finding the bombs, learning that the suspicious person was Rainnewt, arguing with him, running after him while Awen did her thing, and finally confronting Rainnewt in the old city under the mountain.

"And then Awen gave me a bomb, and I tossed it on Rainnewt and a little bit on Bastion"—Caprica gasped at that—"and that knocked him around really good. Bastion bapped me on the head after that, for kinda blowing him up, and then we captured Rainnewt, and that's the entire thing."

The king turned toward Inquisitor Storm. "Do you think you can confirm the story?" he asked.

"I can try," she said. "I will have to ask Paladin Bastion and perhaps some of the early investigators. This may take a few minutes."

I waved at her as she ran off in a hurry after bowing to the king. There were a lot of murmurs in the tent, but then, there had been murmurs from the start of my story.

"Caprica, my dear," the king said. "You know the captain and these two ladies better than I do. Perhaps you could help me a little. What are your opinions on their characters?"

Caprica glanced at us, then back to her dad. "They're insane. All three of them," she said without hesitation.

"Pardon me?" Amaryllis squawked.

"But," Caprica continued, "they genuinely do mean well. And I think we only see them as insane because all three of them refuse to believe in the sorts of common sense that lead to things like bomb threats and potential wars. They really do think that the three of them, on their own, can make Dirt a better place for everyone. It's mad, impossible, and somewhat inspiring."

The king chuckled. "Well, perhaps they're not entirely wrong. I believe Lady Albatross intended to speak on behalf of the harpies today. I imagine you were going to petition in the name of your nation to pull back from the brink of hostility?"

"What? No, that would be dumb," Amaryllis said. "Any half-bit politician can crow about what they want for their country. I'm here to tell you all that this war is stupid, and if you participate in it, you're stupid too."

The whispers from before turned into indignant mutters.

"Oh, don't mumble at me," Amaryllis grumped. "Half of you were champing at the bit to start a war entirely orchestrated by a single madman. Do you have any idea how many lives would be lost because of your lack of forethought? Don't you realize how close you came to dying in the last hour just because of this war? If it weren't for Broccoli and Awen, you'd all be buried in rubble right now." She sniffed disdainfully. "Idiots."

I patted Amaryllis on the shoulder to calm her down a little. It seemed that not everyone took to being called an idiot by Amaryllis as well as I did.

The king clapped his hands together. "Very well then," he said. "As far as I can tell, it seems as though two of these young women, at least, saved all of our lives. I think, as the host of today's event, the matter of a reward falls upon my shoulders."

I saw Caprica nodding slowly. It seemed like a good move on the king's part. I imagined that maybe there was some honor-stuff at play here, and the king was shouldering the responsibility for that instead of leaving it to each individual. At least, that's how I thought it would work out with the sylphs. The others I wasn't as certain of.

He regarded me and Awen in turn. "How about this," he said to us. "I will grant each of you a boon of your choosing. If it is within my ability to grant, then it shall be so."

"Father!" Caprica gasped. Judging from the reaction of the other sylphs in the room, and the heightened attention of the cervids and grenoils, the boon was a pretty big deal.

"Uh, that sounds nice," I said.

"I would hope so," the king said. "Sylphfree is undoubtedly one of the most powerful nations on Dirt. And a boon on my behalf shouldn't be taken lightly. Do you want some time to think on it? It would allow Inquisitor Storm time to return."

"Nah, that's fine," I said with a nod. "This one's easy. Can I ask that Sylphfree not get involved in this war business?"

The king laughed. "You can ask that. Though if the war comes to our doorstep, you understand that we won't fail to react."

I nodded. That was reasonable. "Deal, then!" I said while extending my hand. The king grinned and shook. I had the impression that was a faux pas, too, judging by the looks I was getting, but if the king wasn't insulted, then what did it matter?

"And what about you, Lady Bristlecone? Any favors you would like to ask?"

"Awa," Awen said. "I don't know what I'd even ask for. Can I wait?"

"Of course," the king said gently.

Inquisitor Storm walked into the room like her namesake, followed by Bastion and two guards, who paused by the entrance. She bowed next to the king and whispered into his ear.

"Well then," the king said. "I think that today has been very exciting, but, seeing as how the summit will have to be put off for some hours, I believe that the wisest course of action would be to pause everything for the day and continue on in the morning. I thank you all very much for coming and especially for keeping your calm. It's good to see the continent's nobility act in such a self-assured fashion."

The king gestured, and soon enough, a few nobles departed the tent. Others milled around, though, and I had the impression they all wanted to chat some more.

"Caprica," the king said, "do invite your friends over for dinner tonight. I'm certain we have a lot to discuss."

· Chapter Forty-Two ·

Alea Iacta Quest

Instead of heading to the palace in the carriage we had ridden over from the inn, Caprica insisted that we use her carriage.

It was probably for the best. The big royal seal on the side meant that we didn't have to wait around in traffic quite as much.

Amaryllis, Awen, and I crammed ourselves in on one side, while Caprica sat next to Bastion across from us.

"So," I said to break the ice. "How did you get roped into all of this?" I asked Bastion.

The paladin raised one eyebrow, then glanced subtly to the side. "In times of heightened alert, it's normal that all members of the royal family be escorted by a greater number of paladins. There should be two more stationed with this carriage. One next to the driver and one flying above. Having a third within the carriage itself only makes sense."

"Yeah, but there's a bunch of paladins around," I said. "I'm happy that you're the one with us, though."

"Yes. I'm certain it's all entirely a coincidence," Bastion said. His tone was as even and serious as always, but I couldn't help but feel a hint of something else was there.

"Indeed," Caprica said dismissively. "Now, let's go over the important things. Tonight was already going to be a night charged with political import, but I don't think anyone expected it to be as . . . complicated."

"How will Sylphfree react to the bomb threat?" Amaryllis asked. "For that matter, to Broccoli's request?"

Caprica shook her head. "Hard to tell. I think the population has been primed to expect conflict. I don't keep up to date with all of the journals, but there was a lot of rising tension in the city. Recruitment has been up for a few weeks as well. If the truth comes out, and it definitely should, then I don't know how the average sylph will react to a new adversary being discovered."

"Some will accuse the kingdom of using a scapegoat," Amaryllis said. "Others will be angry that something is interfering with a potential war that they want to see realized. I think most will just want to know more. You might have to inform people about Rainnewt's motivations, otherwise the story won't make sense."

"Which raises the question," Bastion said, "what are his motivations? I didn't have time to have a good discussion with the man while we fought. Though there is some truth in the saying that combat is a conversation, it's unfortunately not a terribly verbose kind of conversation."

I nodded along. "He mostly wanted to start the war because he thinks it's one way to accomplish his quest," I said.

"A quest?" Caprica asked. She really perked up at that. "As in a World-given quest?"

"Yup, same as mine, I think," I said. "The World's worried about the Evil Roots, and it's pulling in Riftwalkers to take care of them. I, uh, mostly ignored my quest because exploring and making friends is more fun, but I guess Rainnewt didn't."

Amaryllis rubbed her face. "You're not supposed to admit to ignoring a quest, Broccoli."

"But it's true?"

"Yes, which just makes it worse," Amaryllis chastised.

"Awa, I don't think it's so bad. Broccoli found a way to destroy the roots without destroying the dungeon the roots are strangling. It's a good step forward."

Caprica raised a hand. "Give me a moment, I need to dissect this. I knew you were a Riftwalker, which is impressive. But to have a quest . . . Did you know?" she turned to Bastion.

The paladin didn't meet her eyes. "I may have omitted a few minor facts from my report," he said. "An issue that arose from the lack of time to create a fully detailed report."

"I see," Caprica said. For some reason that seemed to make her pretty smug. "Well then, Rainnewt has a World-given quest. I'm not sure if that should be made public."

"Why not?" I asked. "It'll explain why he did what he did."

"Yes, but some people, across all countries, will place the will of the World far ahead of the will of a nation. Someone who communicates with the World is given great weight, so if such a person were to suggest that the World desires war, then any such conflict would become... somewhat religious in nature. A few lords and assorted politicians might use that to inflame their support base." Caprica frowned. "We can't reveal Rainnewt's reasoning if it's based on the World's will."

I huffed. "It's based on his own interpretation of that will," I said. "I don't think he's right. I don't remember any of Miss Menu's quest prompts telling me to start a war or anything like that. He's just doing things this way because he's not very nice and because he's too lazy to find a solution that helps everyone."

"I don't think those kinds of solutions exist all that often," Amaryllis said. "But I won't disagree that Rainnewt is a fool."

"Let's put that aside for the moment," Caprica said. "Broccoli, the favor you asked of my father will put him in an interesting position. I don't think most would look down on him for ignoring the favor, though it would tarnish his reputation a little. On the other hand, he can now use that as an excuse to put more effort into finding a diplomatic solution to this entire situation. If a sylph lord or lady questions why the royal family is trying so far to de-escalate, we can claim that we're honor bound to do at least the bare minimum to find a peaceful solution."

"That's good, isn't it?" I asked.

Caprica nodded. "It is. That was a daring move, and a risky one. You basically earned a lot of political capital and spent it all instantly, which will take some of the older politicians off guard."

"What about my boon?" Awen asked. "I don't know what to do with it."

Bastion was the one to reply to that question. "Usually, the boon will allow you to ask a favor, such as what Broccoli did. Or it will allow you to borrow something from the one who has given you the boon. Asking for money outright would be possible, but it would make you seem somewhat dishonorable."

"Boons have been used to ask for assistance with political issues, to gain permission to ask for someone's hand in marriage, and for things as simple as throwing a great party," Caprica said.

Amaryllis perked up. "Someone has used a king's boon to throw a party?"

Caprica nodded. "Once. When my father was first prince. I heard it was quite the event."

"That's great," I said. "Do you want to do something like that, Awen?"

Awen frowned and glanced out of the carriage's window, her eyes seeming to stare beyond the passing buildings. "No, I think I'll use my boon for something else. I haven't decided yet, though."

"It's up to you," I said. I leaned to the side and bumped her shoulder with mine, a physical reminder that I was there for her if she needed me or if she just needed some hugs.

Awen nodded once. "I'll come up with something, don't worry. Boons don't expire, right?"

"Not quite, no," Bastion said. "But usually they're only valid with the person who issued them, and only for the issued. If you pass away, or the king leaves the throne to the next leader, then the boon's more or less forfeit. Though a new ruler might reinstate the boon, if they really wish to."

"A boon is an unnamed favor. It holds no value beyond that given by the boon-giver's honor," Caprica said. "I think there have been kings in other nations whose boons would be worthless because their word was worthless."

The carriage shook as we bounced over a sidewalk. I glimpsed the walls of the palace moving past, then the gates rattled shut behind us.

We wheeled around the entranceway and came to a full stop in front of the palace. A guard opened the door while another set a small wooden step stool next to the carriage. We scrambled out and onto the front steps of the new palace. There were a lot more guards around, I noticed. Maybe it was like that across the entire city, though? The entire guard force being placed on higher alert in case Rainnewt had plans beyond just his attack on the summit.

A nice butler sylph greeted us and led us into the palace proper. The girls and I were brought to a side passage with a large washroom. I didn't exactly need to take the warm and damp towel I was handed, but stuffing it against my face felt nice, so I didn't make a fuss.

"We likely have outfits Broccoli and Awen can change into," Caprica said. I wasn't sure if she was talking to me or to one of the servants.

"What's wrong with my outfit?" I asked. It was clean.

Caprica gestured down, and I noticed for the first time that there were cuts along the seams and a few scrapes that my Cleaning magic couldn't do anything about. Awen's dress had a small tear or two as well.

"Oh."

"The staff can sew it back together, I'm certain. They are impressively quick too. You wouldn't imagine how many dresses and uniforms need a quick bit of last-minute adjusting before an event."

I nodded along, and when a maid brought me an outfit, I slipped behind a changing screen and dressed up. It was one of those more militaristic sylph uniforms: all square angles and poofed epaulettes. It made me feel like a proper captain or something. Also, it had a skirt, which was nice.

"Okay," I said as I stepped out. Awen and Amaryllis inspected me, and I got a thumbs- and talons-up. Awen was in a pretty sundress in a pale green that was quite lovely on her. "What now?" I asked.

"Dinner with guests usually starts long before the food is served," Caprica said. "We can linger around the dining hall. There's room to sit, and finger food."

"Oh, I love finger food," I said.

"Then you'll be quite pleased to find that there's a whole host of choice here," Caprica said.

"Anything we should note before the dinner?" Amaryllis asked as we followed Caprica through the many corridors of her home.

Caprica started to shake her head, then stopped. "We don't talk about politics, religion, or the economy until after we've eaten. Usually, that kind of thing will be saved for after dessert. It's just polite, because it gives those who don't want to talk about such things an excuse to vacate the area without being rude."

"So until then, only happy subjects," I said.

"Yes, exactly," Caprica said. "You might meet my other sisters. Gabrielle will certainly be here. And my mother, of course. Though she might be off bullying Inquisitor Storm."

The dining hall was a large, plus-symbol-shaped room. The center was dominated by a large table underneath a ceiling made of windows that let in the fading evening light. The four branches had all sorts of interesting distractions, though. Benches and a piano in one, a small library in another, and even what seemed like a small games room and a smoking parlor.

Already, a few sylphs were milling around, or quietly minding their own business while sampling some sweet-smelling meats and pastries.

"A room full of important sylphs," Amaryllis muttered. "Time to put your Friendmaking to work, Broccoli."

I grinned. We didn't have much time to prepare for the evening, but it might be fun after all.

· Chapter Forty-Three ·

Dine Hard with a Vengeance

Anyone in particular we should get to know?" I asked Caprica.

"I suppose my older sister. She's . . . Well, you'll meet her in a moment," Caprica said. She was looking toward the small library-like section of the dining hall, specifically at a young sylph woman in a dark dress standing next to two older gentlesylphs.

That had to be her sister. There was a clear resemblance between the two of them. The same brow and nose, though Caprica's hair was a dark shade of brown, and her elder sister had pure black hair. "What's her name?" I asked as we crossed the room.

"Steph," Caprica said. "Though she prefers Stephania with strangers. Her middle name is Rubbottom. My parents gave her the name after a paladin who worked for father and served with mother for a few decades before retiring with honors. She hates the name."

"Rubbottom," Awen repeated. She brought her hands up to cover her mouth and hide a smile. "I think I can guess why she doesn't like it."

"Too bad, Uncle Rubrub is really nice. He gave me my first sword," Caprica said.

Stephania turned as we approached, her gaze lingering on Caprica without a change in her expression before she scanned the rest of us. "A moment, gentlemen. I imagine my sister wishes to introduce her friends."

The two sylphs bowed curtly and nodded our way before walking off while chatting to each other. I wouldn't have minded them staying. More company was always the best kind of company.

"Hello, Caprica," Stephania said.

"Steph," Caprica said. "You guessed already, but I wanted to present my friends to you." She gestured to where Amaryllis, Awen, and I stood. "This is Lady . . . This is Amaryllis, Awen, and Broccoli."

I grinned. She'd made an effort to drop all of the titles. That was actually genuinely nice. We were more than just a collection of neat titles and family names.

"A pleasure," Stephania said.

"Hi!" I said. "Do you do hugs?"

"Pardon?"

"Like this," I said before stepping up and wrapping Stephania up in a quick hug. It was the rather boring, prompt kind of hug that didn't give you much time to really enjoy the contact.

Stephania blinked at me as I broke away, then glanced at Caprica. "*These are the heroes of the day?*"

"They are," Caprica said gravely. "Broccoli and Awen here discovered the plot to blow up the old palace and everyone in it. Awen disarmed the explosives while Broccoli valiantly fought the bomber until a brave paladin showed up to assist her."

"You're skipping a few details," I said.

"Awa, I only disarmed two bombs," Awen said. "The guards took care of the rest."

"Yeah, and I barely fought Rainnewt. He's way stronger than I am, so most of my fighting didn't end up doing much more than slow him down. Bastion did most of the work."

Stephania sighed. "Of course Bastion was involved somehow. I should have guessed, with how excited you are about all of this, Caprica."

"Don't be that way, Steph," Caprica said. She crossed her arms. "I'm hardly excited by all of this either. I could have died today. Father, too, for that matter, and dozens of distant cousins and people we know as well. It most certainly would have sparked a war."

"Yes, I suppose so," Stephania said. "Why did you bring them to me, Caprica?"

"You're being rude, Steph."

"I can't find it in me to care," Stephania dismissed. "No sidestepping the question. We're sisters, aren't we? Answer me honestly."

Caprica let out a long sigh. "Because you usually have a good idea of what is going on in the city. I need to know what the nobility is thinking, the merchants. Your friends."

Stephania shook her head. "And to think you've always looked down on me for spending time with business people, rather than those of you who like to play dress-up as soldiers."

"Um, are we stepping into something here?" I asked.

"Sounds like the average sisterly argument to me," Amaryllis said. "Let me guess, you both pursued different hobbies, got pulled apart by different peer groups, and now you're both too obstinate around whatever you're passionate about to reconcile, even though both of you still love each other."

Caprica and Stephania both looked at Amaryllis for a long moment before they both shook their heads.

"Absolutely not."

"I'm afraid you're entirely wrong."

Awen and I giggled, which had them both wear the exact same expression of offended nobility.

"You're both cute," I said. "Miss Stephania, if you don't mind me saying so, I think Caprica just wants to share her new friends with someone she cares about a lot. She made sure to have us spend time with Gabrielle already too. And I think all three of us would love to be your friend too."

```
Stephania Rubbottom Sylph

Desired Quality: Someone who acknowledges her superior
intellect

Dream: To become the wealthiest sylph in all of Sylphfree
to show up her bratty little sister
```

That dream . . . was going to take some working around.

"Fine, then," Caprica said. "I really could use your help, Steph. And this is to try and head off a clash of arms. Imagine how many of my play-soldier peers will be upset if a war never happens."

Stephania rolled her eyes. "Very well. I suppose it is for a good cause. Though there are some among my own peers who are rather eager for great battles and the opportunity for government contracts."

"I can imagine," Caprica said. "They might bear investigating."

One of Stephania's eyebrows quirked up. "Oh? So this is your ruse. Come over all friendly and chatty with . . . these three bizarre characters, then find out which business sylph you can pin some of your troubles on?"

"Hardly," Caprica said. "It's just as likely that the trouble comes from the military or a radical branch of it."

"Um," I said. "Haven't we proven that Rainnewt is responsible for everything?"

Caprica shook her head. "We haven't. And even if he takes full responsibility, it's unlikely to be true. Too much has happened for it all to be orchestrated by one person. He needed to have coconspirators. Perhaps even people who are above him in terms of responsibility. It wouldn't be like the leader of a conspiracy to do the dirty work themselves."

I didn't have that impression from Rainnewt. He seemed more than capable of tricking people, but working with others over the long term was . . . probably something he had to work on.

"If you say so, I guess," I said.

Caprica nodded. "I do say so. This might be a great opportunity to weed out some tasteless opinions near the top of our society."

That didn't sound very nice. But before I could ask about it, a bell tinkled. A butler stood next to the table, a small silvery chime in one hand, a towel draped over his other arm. A team of serving sylphs had slipped into the room without me noticing and were placing plates and cutlery onto the table in the center of the room with quick efficiency. "Dinner will be served momentarily," the butler said in a gentle voice that nonetheless carried across the room. "Please, find your seats at your convenience."

Each seat had plenty of room on either side of it, and along with that, small plaques with names engraved upon them sat in front of the plates and silverware.

"Come, I imagine you'll all be near the head of the table today," Caprica said.

She wasn't wrong. Awen, Amaryllis, and I were to the head seat's right. Awen's seat was right next to the king's, with me sandwiched between her and Amaryllis. Caprica and her sister sat across from us, and I imagined those were the seats reserved for family or something.

The seats were comfy but just a bit short. I was sitting with my feet planted on the ground and my knees up a bit. The table and chairs were sylph-sized, even if they were grandiose and pretty.

The king walked in without ceremony or fanfare next to someone I assumed was a paladin until a maid rushed out and placed a second seat next to the king's, then another came with plates and cutlery for the new place setting. The queen?

Everyone but Caprica and Stephania stood, so my friends and I did the same after a moment of confused hesitation.

"Oh, don't bother, please," the maybe-queen said.

She was tiny, one of the smallest adult sylphs I'd seen, with short-cropped hair that was an exact match of Caprica's and a scowl fit for an angry schoolteacher. Her armor was definitely a paladin's, if a bit lighter than what I'd seen Bastion wear normally.

The king pulled out his wife's chair, and she rolled her eyes before sitting down.

"Good evening, everyone," the king said as he sat down in turn. The last few people still standing dropped back into their seats. The king clapped his hands in eager glee. "I heard that we have scallops from Quickwood and this very nice apple brandy from Mattergrove. And Captain Bunch?"

"Huh? Oh, yes?" I asked.

"I made sure the chefs prepared a more vegetarian meal for you," he said. "No need to worry."

"Oh, thank you! I think I can eat most things, though. I wasn't born a bun, so meats and stuff only give me a bit of a tummy ache."

The king chuckled. "Well, we wouldn't want that."

The same servants that had set the table were suddenly placing appetizers down before us, and I had to wonder if their sneakiness was some sort of cool skill.

The smells from the food around me hit, and I suddenly realized that I was starving. It was an effort not to drool like a baby bun as I picked a fork at random and gobbled up my meal. I noticed Amaryllis rolling her eyes, and some of the nobles farther down were trying hard to look composed and proper as they ate, but I didn't see the point in that.

Whenever a course was finished, the servants returned from *somewhere*—I was paying attention, and I never caught them entering the room—and placed the next meal down in front of whoever had finished.

There was a bit of small talk all across the table. The king asked Caprica and Stephania about their days. The queen said that Gabrielle was feeling better after a long day's rest but that she wanted to take an evening nap, so she'd had an early dinner. Mostly, though, everyone was too busy eating to talk.

And then, before I knew it, a butler set before me a small slice of cake that I wasn't sure would fit in my tummy. I wasn't sure I could eat it, but I was certain I'd give it a try. It was vanilla with some sort of strawberry jam on it, and it looked like something from the good kind of dream.

"I know it's something of a faux pas," the king said.

I glanced up. He was talking to me and my friends.

"But I wanted to ask a few questions, if you don't mind. Mostly about the dungeons you've managed to clear on the way here."

I opened my mouth to speak, but a talon poking my leg from under the table shut me up. "What do you want to know?" Amaryllis asked as she dabbed her lips with a serviette.

"The captain was able to repair a dungeon, correct?" he asked.

"Less repair and more rid it of a pest," Amaryllis said. "Twice, in fact. Once in the wilderness to the south of the Crying Mountains, and once again in the tiny port of Insmouth."

"We have a piece of root from that dungeon!" I remembered. "It's in the *Beaver*."

"I see," the king said. "Would you be willing to demonstrate, Captain Bunch?" he asked. "We have something of an issue at a local dungeon, and there are quite a few people who would like to see your abilities firsthand."

"Oh, sure," I said. "But after dessert."

· Chapter Forty-Four ·

Hiring a Professional Cleaner

My friends and I were spread out a bit more. This part of the dining hall had a good number of comfy chairs to slouch on, and we'd moved a few of them around a central coffee table. Or was it a tea table? I wasn't sure if they had coffee in Sylphfree. Mine was right across from the king's seat, and I had Amaryllis and Awen on either side on their own big, poofy seats.

The king was sitting on a big loveseat with wooden arms covered in carved animals and little scenes of mountainscapes. Next to him, his wife sat, still in her armor, with one leg crossed over the other. She was knitting what looked like a teeny-tiny jumper.

Caprica and her sister were sharing another loveseat, and neither looked like they were enjoying it.

"You know," the king said. "I'm not used to people making demands of me."

I frowned, then tapped my chin. "I guess that makes sense, being a king and all. But still, I want my friends to come with me if they can."

"The dungeon in question is important to our nation," the king said. "What if we determine that its location and layout are sensitive information? Sharing that with one person who has earned our trust is well and good, but several people?"

I nodded. "That makes sense."

"So you'll go on your own?" he asked.

"I didn't say that," I said. "I still want to go with my friends."

The king didn't pout—that wouldn't have been very kingly of him—but I had the impression he really wanted to. "You're very obstinate."

"I don't think I am," I said.

Caprica sniffed. "If anything, Father, you should take it as a sign of Broccoli's good nature. She is fiercely loyal to her friends."

"Well, I mostly want Amaryllis and Awen to be with me because it sounds fun, and fun should be shared."

"If it helps any," Amaryllis interjected, "Broccoli can't keep a secret from her friends. She'd spill the location of the dungeon and everything she learned about it the moment one of us asked."

"That's troubling," the king muttered.

"Secrets aren't part of a healthy relationship," I said.

The queen looked up from the jumper she was knitting. "Let the girl bring her friends. The dungeon is hazardous enough, even with trusted comrades."

"We're not sending her down there alone," the king countered. "The Knights of the Long Rest are jealous of their dungeon. They wouldn't allow strangers in without an escort at the best of times."

"I'll see if any paladins are free," the queen said.

"Or we could send some of the royal guard," the king said. "I suspect the paladins will be a bit much for this. Though . . . those who will want to see Broccoli's Cleaning magic in action might want to send their own observers."

"We can't send an entire platoon's worth of people into the dungeon," the queen said. "Let them pick one each, perhaps, make sure that they're aware of the risks, then let the Knights of the Long Rest pick out a pair of guides. At that point, you'll already be stretching the number of people you can safely send into the dungeon."

"What kind of dungeon is it?" I asked. I'd been in my share of them already. It didn't make me an expert or anything, but I imagined that I knew more about dungeons than maybe the average person.

"The Dungeon of the Lullaby Knight," the king said. "It's an hour's flight from Sylphfree, with a small compound around it where the Knights of the Long Rest are headquartered."

"A knightly order?" Amaryllis asked.

The king nodded. "We have a few."

"More than a few," Caprica said. "They're a popular way for nobles and some people to grow in martial prowess at their own pace while sidestepping the rigors of the army."

"Having so many orders fosters a good, competitive market," Stephania said. "Besides, the orders need to fund their own housing, training, and equipment. They're less of a burden on the nation's coffers."

Caprica and Stephania were glaring at each other again. Was there some animosity between the army and these knightly orders? The queen might have noticed my look, because she filled me in some more.

"The nation's army is grand and proud, but it is a literal meritocracy. The talented and hard-working rise in the ranks, regardless of their birth. Knightly orders, on the other hand, are mostly filled with noble scions. They buy their own equipment and rank themselves as they see fit. The orders are still subject to the army chain of command, though, and they need to participate in assisting the nation just as the army does. Most orders will find a niche. Occasionally, they will be built around a specific dungeon and will use that as a way to unlock a unique class and evolutionary line that allows them to better serve the nation in a specific and unique way."

"Huh," I said. So they were basically small, army-like clubs. I wasn't sure what to think about that.

"The most famous are the Wyvern Knights," Caprica said. "There's a dungeon that gives a class that allows one to tame and ride wyverns. The knights serve as an aerial cavalry alongside airships. It's a prestigious position to be in, and their membership is both exclusive and expensive to obtain."

"Ah, what do the Knights of the Long Rest specialize in?" Awen asked.

Caprica nodded at the question. "They specialize in a few areas. Mostly, they have magic that allows them to make others fall asleep. They've been used to suppress riots, and they can boost the recovery of those who are sleeping, as well as themselves when they're asleep. I think they have a few more skills, but they are somewhat secretive, and honestly, they're not the most popular of the knightly orders."

"The Knights of the Long Rest have always been close to the throne," the king said. "And their loyalty is beyond reproach. There are two other dungeons afflicted with these Evil Roots within our borders, but I trust the knights and suspect they will welcome the aid more kindly than others might."

"Neat," I said. "Well, in that case, I don't see any harm in helping. When do we head out?"

"Broccoli," Amaryllis said. "You're forgetting something."

"I am?" I asked. I really couldn't see what I was forgetting. A maid popped by and placed some cups down, then filled them with tea.

Amaryllis leaned forward and took her cup between two talons. "Payment, Broccoli. We're rendering a service to Sylphfree by not only clearing this one dungeon but by teaching them how to clear their own. Dungeons are practically priceless. If we teach them how to save their dungeons from near-certain destruction, that teaching is similarly priceless."

"Oh," I said.

"The kingdom will, of course, cover all of your expenses so far," the king said. He glanced back and over his loveseat and… and a butler was there who had absolutely not been there the last time I checked. "Could you make note of that, please?"

"Covering our expenses is a nice start," Amaryllis said. I could almost feel the greed wafting off her. "Our ship was damaged on the way in, and the costs to repair and dock it will certainly add up as we have to wait longer within Sylphfree."

The king grinned. "Of course, of course. That's perfectly understandable."

"Don't let the children step all over you just because they're small and innocent," the queen said.

"I'm not so easily swayed, dear," the king said. "How about this: as compensation for the work, each of you will be awarded fifty Sylphreen ducats."

"That's all?" Amaryllis asked.

"It's far beyond what even an expert would be paid," the king said.

"Ah, but experts can be trained and called upon from elsewhere," Amaryllis said. "Riftwalkers with World-given quests are not nearly so common. Unless you plan on using Rainnewt to do the deed, then I suspect you're not so much hiring an expert as you are hiring the only person anywhere who can help. That must have some value to it."

The king chuckled. "Very well then, I have been swayed by your incredible negotiating ability."

He'd definitely expected Amaryllis to try and squeeze a bit more out of him. But Amaryllis looked appropriately smug, so I didn't point out that she'd tripped right into the king's trap.

"One hundred gold each. Which I suspect is a bounty worthy of such a task. You will also be granted the right to take the class you earn from the dungeon, if you so choose. And I will sign a writ granting you rights of first choice on any items dropped during the excursion."

"Is that special?" I asked.

Stephania was the one to reply this time. "It's not impossible for someone outside of a knightly order to take on an order's dungeon. Usually, the order will ask for a fee, but because the dungeons belong to the kingdom first, they don't have a legal right to refuse a citizen access as long as the citizen has permission to access the dungeon. What they *will* do is force those attempting the dungeon to be escorted through it. It prevents untrained people from dying in a dangerous environment. Part of that contract gives the guides rights to anything found within the dungeon."

"Oh," I said. That didn't seem entirely fair. "Okay, well a hundred gold is a whole lot, so that seems fine to me." I could recall a discussion with Amaryllis a long while ago where she'd told me that a small airship cost about a thousand gold. We'd earn enough in one day to purchase a third of a ship! That was pretty huge!

"Wonderful," the king said. He clapped his hands, and a new butler bowed next to him and extended a piece of paper on a wooden board with a pen fixed to it. The king took the board and wrote something on the page pinned to it with quick, easy grace. He folded it up after signing it at the bottom, then the butler poured warm wax onto the front of the letter, which the king touched with a big ring. "And now it's quite official. We merely need some witnesses and your own signatures."

Caprica and Stephania both agreed to act as witnesses, which seemed fine. I guessed that three royal signatures on a contract made it pretty official.

The contract was passed to Amaryllis, who signed it, then to me.

By my will as King of Sylphfree, ruler of Goldenalden, and rightful liege of the lords and ladies of sylphkind and those within our rightful lands,

I hereby decree that the following persons have permission, officially obtained, to carry with them the classes and possessions they have rightfully obtained from the Dungeon of the Lullaby Knight: Lady Amaryllis Albatross of the Harpy Mountains, Lady Awen Bristlecone of Mattergrove, and Captain Broccoli Bunch of lands beyond the Rift.

For the inestimable task of ridding our nation of the Evil Roots which infest its dungeons, they shall each be awarded one hundred Sylphreen ducats for their brave work.

By my name,

Reggie IV G. Sylph

As witnessed by

Caprica B. Sylph

Stephania R. Sylph

I stared, pen in hand and poised to sign. "Wait, your name is Reggie?"

My friends both sighed. "Awa, Broccoli, can you not insult the king, please?"

"I wasn't!" I said. "It's just, I didn't expect his name to be Reggie. I thought he'd have a fancy name."

Caprica was notably not looking in my direction and had a hand over her mouth while her sister snickered quietly.

The king actually pouted when his wife chuckled.

"Well, so much for that," he said.

· Chapter Forty-Five ·

Away

Caprica showed us to a guest suite in the palace, where we each got our own room to sleep in. The day had been pretty long, so it didn't take long for all of us to head to bed. The next morning started with a light breakfast in the suite's shared dining room.

A few hours after breakfast, while we were still wondering what to do, Caprica returned and gathered us up. "Is there any equipment you need?" Caprica asked.

"We have some equipment at the inn," I said. "We can't go tackle a dungeon in borrowed dresses, I don't think."

"Oh, you certainly could," Caprica said. "With the number of people helping in this dive, you should be relatively safe even if you choose not to help at all. But yes, I wouldn't want to go into a dungeon without good equipment."

"I could use a crossbow," Awen said. "Maybe a war hammer? Mine is back on the *Beaver*."

"If you have a dagger I could borrow, one suitable to be held by talons . . . ?" Amaryllis said. She didn't quite end her sentence, letting it float there as an almost-question.

Caprica nodded. "Certainly. I'll poke around in the armory. We should have everything you need. Broccoli, do you have a weapon of choice?"

"I use a spade most of the time," I said.

"A spade," Caprica repeated. "Does that have any relation to why you used a broom in the arena?"

"I have a makeshift weapons skill," I said.

"Ah. There was speculation that you used a broom and dustpan as a sort of message for Francisco, not taking the fight as seriously as you could. Your explanation makes a lot more sense, knowing your personality." Caprica escorted us out of the palace to a waiting carriage. "This is where I'll be letting you go. We'll see each other soon enough, though, I'm sure. Do be safe while in the dungeon."

"You're not coming with us?" I asked.

She shook her head. "No, I don't need to face a dungeon for a while, and besides, it's . . . no place for a princess." She frowned, then carried on. "It'll only make the army folk going in more nervous. They'd no doubt insist on tripling the number of guards, and it would take twice as long to accomplish half as much. Best to stay back and maybe try to help from here."

"That sucks," I said. "I'd love to go on a proper adventure with you someday. Bye-bye hugs?" I asked. It wasn't actually a question because I was already reaching over for a hug.

Caprica chuckled and patted me on the back as I gave her a quick squeeze.

Getting back to the inn only took a few minutes of clattering along the busy morning streets of Goldenalden, then we had a quick dash upstairs to get ready for a quick dive into a dungeon. "You know, I expected a lot of things from our visit here, but I didn't consider that we might go dungeon diving again," Amaryllis said.

Awen shrugged her long coat on. "It's not that unusual, is it? We've been going through a lot of dungeons to fight those Evil Roots. I guess it's not too strange that we're taking on another one."

"I guess," Amaryllis said. She closed up the front of her own coat, then patted it down to make sure it was fit properly. "I think we've tackled more dungeons than most people will see in their entire lives, and that only in the space of a few months."

"That's because we're proper adventurers," I said with a firm nod. "We'll see a whole heap more before we're done."

"And when will we be done?" Amaryllis asked.

"Well, if Awen's uncle is any indication, then we'll be done when we're old and fat and want to spend more time talking about all of our adventures instead of having new ones."

"My father always said that Uncle would never stop. That the only way for him not to go on another big adventure is for one of them to finally be more than he can chew," Awen said. "It always worried me that, one day, he wouldn't come back to brag about all the interesting things he saw."

I gave her a side-hug. "Don't worry! I'm sure the way things are going, we'll bump into him in the field one of these days. Maybe we can hit a dungeon together? Bet he'd be really proud to see some of the things you've invented."

Awen blushed, but she nodded all the same.

We left the inn in another rush, Amaryllis being worried that we might be late. We weren't even sure where we were going, so I didn't worry too much about being late. The carriage driver seemed to know where to go, so once we jumped back in, we took off across the city once more.

It took a bit, but eventually, the carriage rolled to a stop, and the driver opened the door.

We were at one of the city's docks, the more militaristic one, where every ship docked next to a pier hanging off the edge of the mountain was one of those boxy military ships, with big ballistae and metal sides.

"Ladies, Captain," a young sylph soldier said as he moved up to the side of our carriage. He gave us a hand to help us down. "Knight-Captain Covenseeker is waiting for you by pier A8. He asked that I escort you over."

I glanced around as I stepped out. There were several levels of piers here, with some reaching way out so that much larger ships could dock. It wasn't nearly as busy as any of the commercial docks we'd been to. There were people moving things around, but it seemed pretty calm overall, very clean and orderly.

I regretted not getting a coat or something as a chill wind whipped past us. There weren't any buildings between us and the open sky to protect us from the weather.

Pier A8 wasn't too far off, a smaller pier with an all-black ship docked next to it. It wasn't a huge vessel, barely half again the length of the *Beaver*, with the same boxy build that the sylph military ships seemed to favor. The crew were already moving about, preparing the ship to take off.

A group were gathered next to the pier, sylphs in nice uniforms, some of them tugging on pipes or big cigars so that a long stream of pale smoke trailed out of their group.

The knight-captain was easy to make out, he was the one in full plate armor. He grinned and detached himself from the rest of the group to meet us halfway. "You must be Captain Bunch," he said as he shook my hand. "And Ladies Albatross and Bristlecone," he continued, this time bowing to my friends.

"You're the knight-captain?" I asked.

"Indeed," he said. His smile had his big bushy mustache twitching up. "And you three are my saviors today. Come, come, you should meet some of the others."

"Are they the ones we'll be going into the dungeon with?" I asked.

"Oh no, most of us are too far past our prime to be crawling in some old dungeon. We'll be sending younger, sharper folk down with you. They'll be better able to keep you safe, no worries. I made sure you'd be accompanied by the very best that the Knights of the Long Rest have to offer."

We reached the other older gentlesylphs and were reintroduced, then there was a long list of names and titles and ranks, so many that I lost track after the first three. They seemed like important people, though: a general, one admiral, and a few directors and members of some groups that were interested in fixing the dungeons in and around Goldenalden. We were going to be working with their subordinates.

A bell tolled, and the introductions were put off as everyone boarded the airship.

"Captain, Ladies!" a young sylph called out to us. We turned to find a soldier running over with a stack of boxes in his arms. He was sweaty and red-faced, as if he'd just been sprinting over. "Package for you, from Princess Caprica."

Amaryllis frowned and opened the topmost package to reveal a long crossbow in a box carefully crafted to hold it in place without rattling about. Dozens of bolts were strapped in there, too, ready to be used. "Caprica's weaponry," Amaryllis said. "Thank you. We'll take these off your hands."

Amaryllis handed Awen two of the boxes, then took the smallest one for herself. The last was mine—at least, that's what the little tag looped around its handle said.

"The princess also gave me this letter," the sylph said. He bowed as he presented a letter to us.

Amaryllis took it, then unfolded it unceremoniously. "Oh, she says we can keep the weapons. As long as they're boxed up, we shouldn't have any trouble with law enforcement, and if we do, we can always just complain to Caprica about it."

"Ladies!" Knight-Captain Covenseeker called out to us. "Do you need assistance?"

"We're good!" I called out. We rushed over to the airship and up the gangplank to climb aboard.

A sailor led us down a level to a smoking room, where the sylph officers were pouring over a map amidst clouds of smelly smoke.

"Did you want to see the dungeon layout?" Knight-Captain Covenseeker asked.

"Uh, can we have a copy of that map?" I asked. I didn't mind spending time with the officers—they'd been polite so far—but all that smoke was a bit much. Besides, I kind of wanted to see what was in the box Caprica had sent over. The crossbow Awen received had looked really cool, though I didn't get much time to look at it.

"The Order of the Long Rest doesn't make a habit of spreading maps of our dungeon around."

"Oh," I said. "In that case, maybe we'll look at it later? Uh, is there a room we could use maybe?"

The knight-captain seemed very understanding as he led us to a small resting room. It had a small porthole looking out of the ship and a couple of long sofas that someone small could lounge on. He told us to rest up and not to worry before heading back out.

"He's nice," I said.

"He has nothing to lose from being nice," Amaryllis said.

"What's that mean?" I asked.

"Oh, never mind," Amaryllis said. She sat on the very edge of one of the seats and opened her box. "Let's see what the princess found."

Caprica, it seemed, had found a really pretty dagger.

It was nice and long, a bit longer than the knife Amaryllis usually carried, with a blade shaped like a spread wing. It even had a few little carvings in it that hinted at feathers.

"This is gorgeous," Amaryllis said. She spun the knife around, and I noted that the handle was strangely curved. "I think this is spoils of war. No way the sylphs made such a beautiful harpy spellsword."

I used Insight on the dagger.

`Featherlight. Quick-cast dagger. Old.`

"It suits you, I think," I said.

Amaryllis nodded, then found a sheath in the box. "No hidden sheath, but I can hardly complain," she said as she stood up and strapped the knife to her hip.

"Do I go next?" Awen asked. She was practically bouncing on the edge of her seat.

"How about you do one, then I do mine, then you do your other one?" I asked.

Awen laughed. "Sure," she said before she popped open the box with the crossbow. She laid it down and very carefully reached down to touch it. "It's . . . it's a Snowlander crossbow," she said.

`A standard sharpshooter's bow. New.`

The box didn't have much by means of decoration. It was still pretty, though, nearly all metal, with a few pulleys and a folding crank. It even had a small sight that could unfold from its side. "A Snowlander weapon? From the north?"

"My uncle had something like this once," Awen said. She seemed almost reluctant to take it.

"Then you'll be just like him, right?"

She paused, nodded, then picked the weapon out of its box. "I'll use it well," she said.

I grinned. My turn!

· Chapter Forty-Six ·

Weedbane the Dandelion Slayer

I always loved opening presents. It never happened too often, which made every event where I did get a gift that much more special.

Technically, the boxes that Caprica had sent over weren't presents—they lacked the always-fun wrapping paper—but I decided to count it as one anyway. The box tagged Broccoli Bunch was as long as I was tall—not counting my ears—but quite thin, made of some sort of wood covered in leather bound in place with big knobby brass studs. It was quite long, longer than any of the other boxes by a good bit.

My tail was twitching with nervous energy, and my cheeks were starting to hurt.

"Well, are you going to open it today, or are you just going to stare at the box?" Amaryllis asked.

"I haven't decided yet," I admitted. "On the one hand, opening the box means I get the present. On the other, leaving it closed means I get to *anticipate* the present, and sometimes that's even more fun."

"You . . . you absolute moron," Amaryllis muttered. "Come on, open it up, or I will."

"No! You can't! Opening a present is a sacred moment," I said. Dropping to my knees in front of the box, I undid the two clasps holding it shut, then pulled the top open.

What waited for me within was a long wooden staff with a curve near its middle and a small handle poking out midshaft. At the end was a curved blade tucked along the side of the shaft, long and narrow and super thin, made of something that almost glowed. It was fixed to the end of the staff by a rather complicated-looking swivel mechanism, with some sort of lock on it.

"A scythe?" Awen asked.

"Huh," I said. Reaching down, I grabbed the scythe by the middle and lifted it up. The blade clunked down, and something went *snick* as it locked into place. "With an unfolding blade. Not what I expected."

"It's a gardening tool," Amaryllis said. "Or farming, I suppose. Magical too."

Magical? I used Insight on the scythe.

```
Weedbane. Ancient.
```

"Whoa," I said.

I noticed Amaryllis crouching down next to the box, and when she stood, she had a small note in hand. "A bit of history on your new toy," she said.

"Oh?" I asked. I looked around for a place to put the scythe, then handed it to Awen when she reached for it. "I want to see."

Amaryllis handed me the note.

Dear Broccoli,

   This old thing has been sitting in storage for an eternity. I believe it was gifted to a gardener who worked at the old palace, but no one has claimed it since. It should be enchanted with a few dozen old utility spells. May it serve you well in your quest to rid the world of a new sort of weed.

   Caprica

The writing was hasty but still very pretty. "So, it's old, huh."

"That's good. Older items tend to interact better with their own enchantments," Amaryllis said.

"The mechanism here's not too complicated. See, it's just a bolt that unfolds and locks the blade in place, with a little leaf spring to keep the bolt from unlatching. You just need to press in . . . here." Awen's face went red as she pressed hard on a little stub with her thumb. Something eventually clicked, and she was able to refold the scythe's blade. "Easy."

"Cool," I said as I took Weedbane back. "How do I even use this? There's a handle here, and I guess you hold this part?"

This was going to be a great improvised weapon, if the level of improvisation was equivalent to how hard it was to use as a weapon. Maybe if I planned to exclusively fight people by hitting their ankles. Or if I was fighting really short enemies.

I gave the scythe an experimental swing, then held back. It was the sort of thing that would require a lot of space to move around in, and we weren't in a very spacious room.

"Watch it with that thing," Amaryllis said. "I bet the edge is magically sharpened."

"Oh, right," I said a bit sheepishly. "I should put it away for now, at least until we arrive at the dungeon."

Putting actions to words, I fiddled with the catch—it really was hard to press in—and then folded Weedbane back into its case.

"All right. Awen, you have a present left, right?"

Awen nodded. She closed the box with her new crossbow in it, then set the second box she got atop it. This one was narrower and a bit shorter, about the length of my arm from shoulder to fingertip. She undid the clasps on the box, then flicked it open. Within, resting in some cloth padding, was a war hammer. It was boxy, with a long, square-handled hilt and a head that wasn't any rounder.

"That's a sylph hammer if I've ever seen one," Amaryllis said.

I leaned forward and used Insight on it too.

```
A sylph heavy-infantry hammer. New.
```

Awen pulled it out of the box and spun it this way and that. "I can't see anything too special about it," she admitted. "It looks almost like it was drop forged."

"If it's a plain old standard arm, then the only enchantments on it will be to prevent rusting and maybe to lighten the weapon. Both sylphs and harpies are keen on having lighter tools," Amaryllis said.

"Wouldn't that defeat the point of it being a hammer?" Awen asked. She gave the hammer a couple of experimental swings, then nodded. "It feels nice. My other hammer's handle is a bit bigger. I think it was made for a man's hand, and mine are small. This is nicer."

"Neat," I said. "Should we pack everything up and head back out? I want to ask the knight-captain about the dungeon before we reach it."

We found Knight-Captain Covenseeker in the airship's smoking space still, the gentlemanly old knight chatting up a few of the generals. He brightened when we approached. I hoped that no one noticed the aura of Cleaning magic around me getting rid of all the smoke.

"Ladies, Captain, how can I assist?" he asked.

"We were hoping to see the map of the dungeon," I said. "And maybe you can tell us a bit about it too?"

"Certainly," he said. "Rumor has it that all three of you are part of the Exploration Guild?"

"Yup," I said. Technically, Awen hadn't signed on, actually. We needed to get that rectified at some point. I was certain the local guild master wouldn't mind adding her to the rolls. "We've dived our share of dungeons before. This will be my . . . uh, sixth, I think."

"Impressive," he said with a nod. The other generals nodded as well. There was much pipe and cigar waving. "The Dungeon of the Lullaby Knight might not prove so difficult a challenge, then." With a gesture, he presented us with the dungeon map.

Six floors, each one taking up a square on the large map, with some arrows and lines showing where the floors connected to each other, and little notations pointing out facts about the dungeon.

"It is a relatively young dungeon, five floors, each connecting back to a central room." He tapped what I had thought was the first floor. "This room here. Every time you complete a floor, you return to this room, and when you re-exit the room back into the dungeon, you'll be on the next floor down."

"Does it move?" I asked.

"The dungeon? No, I don't believe so. It might well be some magical effect. Teleportation, perhaps. Though it is seamless. A portal, maybe. We had some academics study the passageways some time ago, but nothing came of it."

"Interesting," I said.

"What's the dungeon's theme?" Amaryllis asked. "Beyond sleep, I mean."

Knight-Captain Covenseeker hummed. "Difficult to say, exactly. Or rather, difficult to sum up in a single word. I believe the dungeon's main theme centers around lullabies. Perhaps dreams?"

"Oh, that sounds like a lot of fun," I said. "And it gives you a knight class?"

"It does! Nightie Knight. We're quite fortunate that the name is respectable."

"Respectable?" I asked.

One of the generals chuckled. "The poor Knights of the Dark Burst."

"Why? What's so poor about them?" Awen asked.

"The class given by their dungeon is the Flatulent Boomer class. Deadly, yes, but perhaps not a name worthy of polite company," the knight-captain said.

I held back a giggle with great effort. "Yup, that's . . . yeah. Nightie Knight sounds much cuter."

"What kind of threat are we talking about here?" Amaryllis asked. "A five-floor dungeon won't be without risks."

Covenseeker nodded. "Indeed. But you won't need to worry about any of that. We'll have some of the very best down there with us. And I've gone through the dungeon a dozen times already. Nothing will harm a hair on your heads. I promise it on my honor."

The generals all nodded and made a big show of making it look like what he was saying was very impressive.

"If you say so," I said.

"You just need to worry about showing us how to get rid of those nasty roots that settled in. Quite the pest, I hear."

"Have you tried to deal with them?"

"We sent a few younger knights down to deal with them, but they came back banged up and bruised and claiming that there was nothing to be done. Silly young boys that don't know better. We'll show them how it's done."

"Right," I said.

I glanced at my friends, who both seemed equally worried. Being confident was great and all, but sometimes the Evil Roots turned a dungeon weird, and that might mean that previous experience in the dungeon wasn't worth as much.

"Well, thank you, Knight-Captain Covenseeker. I'm sure we'll all feel very safe down in the dungeon. Do you know how long it will take to get there?"

"Another half hour, winds willing," he said. "Our little fort isn't all that far from the capital. That way if an emergency arises, we'll be some of the first on the scene."

I felt like that last part was directed to the others more than it was to us. Was he going to use this trip as a way to make the Knights of the Long Rest look better? That wasn't terribly kind.

"We'll go rest for a bit, then," I said. "Maybe get our stretching done before we have to walk all over the dungeon."

"Of course, of course."

My friends and I excused ourselves to the far end of the room, where we found some seats next to one of the only portholes on this level of the ship.

"They're clueless," Amaryllis said. "Or they're downplaying the threat posed by an Evil Root."

"How long do you think the root has been there?" I asked.

She frowned. "They sent people in. Which means they knew about it. Call it one day to learn about it, a day to send someone in, another to return to the capital and ask for assistance, then today. So at the very least, four days have passed. That's a strict minimum. I'm going to assume that the root has been active for much longer."

"That might be troublesome," I said.

Awen nodded. "We're going to have to be careful. Plus, we'll be going in with a lot of people."

"Won't that make it easier?" I asked.

"These won't be expert adventurer buns taking things very seriously," Amaryllis said. "Half the people we'll be with will be there because they're an expert of some sort or another, not a fighter. We might have to carry a lot of dead weight."

"Oh," I said

This whole expedition was starting to feel like a bit of a bad idea.

"We're just going to have to do our best, I guess," I said. "Make sure everyone that goes in comes out in tip-top shape, and wipe out the root while we're at it. Maybe they'll take the threat of the roots more seriously too?"

"We can only hope."

· Chapter Forty-Seven ·

The Knights of the Long Rest

The airship banked around and flew in a gently spiraling curve that brought us lower and closer to the ground. I squished my face up against a porthole until my nose made a mark on the glass so that I could better see the fort below.

It wasn't as big as I had imagined. Or as ancient-looking.

The fort was built up against the side of a smaller, stubby mountain. It didn't have as much of an incline as the capital, though it was pretty tall and jaggedy all the same. The fort had large walls on the edges furthest from the mountain, growing smaller as they approached the mountainside.

Part of the fort was a complex of stone buildings and two large, square towers with battlements above and arrow slits all around. Below them was the main keep, and then a wide-open landing strip, entirely covered in gravel and with a row of blinking lights down the middle.

The latter bit didn't seem to fit into the aesthetic that the rest of the fort was going for, though Knight-Captain Covenseeker had said that the dungeon wasn't all that old, so perhaps the entire fort was relatively young too.

The airship slowed down for its final descent, and I saw sylphs jumping off the sides with long ropes trailing after them. Those were slid through big eyelets on the ground, then hooked onto winches that were powered by ground crews.

The ship lurched as we finally touched down, and I pulled back from the porthole just as a rig with a staircase was rolled up next to us.

"All right, everyone," Covenseeker said, his voice booming through the room. "We've arrived. One at a time, gentlebeings."

The older sylphs got off first, and then my friends and I followed after them. We climbed up to the deck, then moved to where the ramp I'd seen was being affixed to the ship's side.

When we arrived on solid ground again, it was to find a row of four sylphs all decked out in plate armor with swords by their hips and proper, knightly helmets tucked against their chests. They saluted in unison on the barked order of a sylph in armor similar to Knight-Captain Covenseeker.

"The Knights of the Long Rest are ready, sir," the knight said.

Knight-Captain Covenseeker stepped up, looking more serious than he had all day, and returned the salute. "Noted, Lieutenant. Is the team assembled?"

"Yes, sir," the lieutenant said. He turned and gestured toward the keep. "The squad is assembling in the dive room, sir. All guests to the fort are accounted for."

"Well done," Knight-Captain Covenseeker said. He spun around to face all of us. "Gentlebeings, please follow me. We will find rest and respite in the main tower. Captain Bunch, Ladies, please follow the lieutenant."

The gaggle of generals and officers toddled off under their cloud of cigar smoke, leaving us with the lieutenant and the four stiff-backed knights.

"Hello, sir," I said with a nod to the lieutenant. "And hi to the bunch of you too!" I added for the knights behind him.

The lieutenant didn't seem to know how to react. Poor guy, had no one ever been friendly to him before? "Ah, hello, ma'am. You must be the expert."

"How did you know?"

"The, ah, ears, ma'am."

I almost reached up to touch them but held back. "I guess they are a defining feature. Well, it's a pleasure to meet you. Will you just be escorting us to the dungeon?"

"And through it," he said. "My name is Lieutenant Petalwrought. I'll be your guide today."

"I'm Broccoli, and these are my friends, Amaryllis and Awen. We'll be in your care, Lieutenant Petalwrought."

The lieutenant nodded once, then glanced away, as if he couldn't meet my eyes. "Ah, if it's not too impertinent to ask, ma'am, do you have any training in dungeon delving? The reports I received were light on details."

"My friends and I have gone through half a dozen dungeons," I said. "We're not experts, but we've tackled a few together, and a couple with bigger groups. I don't think any of us have been in an expedition this big, though."

Amaryllis cleared her throat. "The knight-captain seemed . . . perhaps a little less than aware of the dangers brought on by the Evil Roots. Have you explored the dungeon since?"

"I went in with two knight-recruits. We barely made it out alive," the lieutenant said. "It's a run I've done frequently. The dungeon has changed in the last few weeks. It's become far less hospitable. Not that it was ever entirely safe, but some floors had puzzles that could be solved nonviolently."

"That's really unfortunate," I said. "What about the others? We're going down as a whole group, right?"

The lieutenant nodded, then gestured toward the keep. "Shall we head to the dive room? I imagine the others will be growing impatient."

"Sure," I said.

We started across the courtyard while sailor sylphs ran about taking care of the airship. The other knights followed behind us in two neat rows of two. "We'll be going down with four experts."

"I thought there would be more," Amaryllis said.

"I . . . may have overstepped my position a little," Petalwrought said. "But I vetoed any member that didn't have at least basic combat training or experience. I had to promise that the rest could come down once the bulk of the threat is handled."

"That might be for the best," Amaryllis said. "The dungeon will only get harder as the days pass. Having to watch over deadweight will make it even more of a challenge."

"We shouldn't call people deadweight," I said.

Amaryllis huffed. "If their presence harms us more than it helps us, then that's what they are. We know how to fix this issue. They're just coming along to see how it's done."

"You're making us sound like big heroes," I said.

"Isn't that exactly what we are?" Amaryllis asked. She sounded genuinely confused.

I considered it. "I don't know? I don't think so. We've just been having fun, mostly. Sometimes we stop by to help people, but it's not a big deal."

Amaryllis shrugged. "Your reputation is going to catch up to you eventually, Broccoli."

"It's not a bad reputation," Awen assured me.

The front of the fort was enclosed so that the only way in was through a corridor leading to the front door. I imagined it was to make it harder for people who could fly to sneak up on the entrance from above.

He opened the door for us, and we moved through a long corridor. The keep was all gray walls and flickering magical sconces, with a bright red carpet laid out on the floor the only concession to comfort.

In my opinion, the place could really use a more homey touch, maybe some flowers, a photo or two hanging off the wall? The lieutenant led us through a room at the far end, then through an armory, where armor hung off racks next to swords and shields and other weapons. The room smelled like oil and leather.

"This way," he said.

Just past the armory was a very strange room, mostly because I wasn't sure if it was a room. The ground was all stone, but not quarried stone, just the sort of uneven rocks you'd find outside, though a path had been worn through them. The walls ended unevenly, with the floor being at a bit of an angle. The path through the room went off to the side, then down, where the stones had been rearranged into steps. At the bottom were a few sylphs and a cave opening.

"Is that the dungeon?" I asked.

"It is," Lieutenant Petalwrought said. "The keep was built around it, as you can see. Difficult to do, on account of the land around the dungeon's entrance, but we managed."

I nodded along. "Why not remodel things a bit?"

"You can't," Amaryllis said. "Not entirely. Messing with a dungeon's entrance is just a bad idea all around. Besides, the entrance is more like a portal. If you dug behind it, you'd just find dirt and rock, not some tunnel or whatever."

"Oh, right," I said.

"Everyone!" Lieutenant Petalwrought barked. "These are the experts the capital has sent over. Please, let's all greet each other, then check our gear. Then we'll be off into the dungeon."

I nodded, then waved to the group. "Hello. I'm Captain Broccoli Bunch of the *Beaver Cleaver*. I'm the one who has magic that can break Evil Roots."

"I'm Amaryllis Albatross, thunder mage."

"Awa, I'm Awen Bristlecone, um, mechanic?"

The four sylphs glanced at each other, then one stepped up—a small sylph woman. Small for a sylph, that was. "Aria Lightspring, magical researcher, Army Division of Sciences." She nodded to us quite firmly. Aria had an army uniform on, but over that, she had rigging with a bunch of tools and a backpack that seemed loaded with stuff. A sword hung by her hip, and I noticed a buckler on the side of her pack.

"I'm Erin Winterhand," another of the sylphs said. "I'm with the Department for Dungeon Protection. We work to ensure that the nation's dungeons are safe and secure and well documented." Erin bowed to us. He had gear that I'd first associate with adventurers: a pack, a few knives, a short spear, and an assortment of armor that was definitely not part of an official kit. He also needed a bit of a shave.

"Lucille Rosenfell," the next said. "Mage." She had robes on, a big hat with a bit of a cone in its center and a badge affixed to it, and a staff. Definitely a magic-user.

"And I'm Bron, Bron Talldance," the last said. He was a big boy, all muscle covered in a thick gambeson. He was grinning at us. "I'm with Magical Games and Sports. Don't reckon I'd usually be here, but I can swing a mace as good as any, and I know my share about plants and the like."

"Hello, everyone. I hope we'll all have plenty of nice experiences in the dungeon together," I said.

The lieutenant nodded. "And I'm Lieutenant Petalwrought, but you all know me already. These four knights will be accompanying us in the dungeon. They will be keeping you safe, but down there, what I say is law. You have an idea, you pass it by me first. Understood?"

I nodded, and there was a chorus of "understoods" from some of the others.

"Good. We haven't been given nearly as much time to prepare as I would want, but I suspect giving that root more time would only make things worse. Perhaps speed is of the essence here. Nonetheless, we'll be going through the dungeon slowly and carefully."

Everyone gathered up in a tighter group, though it was clear that we weren't all comfortable with each other yet.

"All right, I'll take the lead. First room should be safe, but I have my doubts," Lieutenant Petalwrought said. He pulled out his sword, and all four knights did the same.

My friends and I scrambled to grab our gear. Awen slid a bolt into her bow, Amaryllis tested the sheath of her dagger, and Weedbane snicked open. That got a few weird looks. I brought the scythe up so that the blade hung over my shoulder. "We're ready," I said.

Without much fanfare, we started into the dungeon as one big group.

```
You are entering the Dungeon of the Lullaby Knight.
Dungeon level 12-14
Your entire party has entered the dungeon.
Seal dungeon until exit?
Dungeon left unsealed.
Any person can enter dungeon instance.
Any person can exit dungeon instance.
```

This was it. I could feel the tension radiating off everyone else as we marched down a deep, dank tunnel, where the light was dim and . . . and where a faint song hung in the air, too quiet to be made out but definitely there.

· Chapter Forty-Eight ·

A Full Bedspread

The dungeon's main room, the one that was supposed to lead to every floor, looked like a bedroom.

A cute bedroom at that. There was a small desk to one side, a child's bed on the other, and a bookcase filled with toys and baubles tucked away next to another doorway. The room was quite big, more than large enough for all twelve of us to step in.

"This isn't what I was expecting," Amaryllis said. She knelt down and poked at a teddy bear, casually left on the floor atop a colorful braided carpet. "I thought this would be more . . . knightly."

Lieutenant Petalwrought chuckled. "You'd think that, yes. The Knights of the Long Rest try not to advertise the fact that our dungeon is themed in such a childish way. Though I would beg all of you not to lower your guard. The teeth on the monsters we will be fighting are more real than any nightmare, and their magics are potent. Moreso now."

I nodded as I glanced away from the bookshelf. Every book on there looked like a children's book of rhymes and nursery songs. "Where do we go from here?" I asked.

The lieutenant pointed to the door ahead of us. "Right through there. That'll open onto the first floor. On leaving the floor, we will be back in this room here, and we can re-exit the dungeon, but you cannot leave the floor until it is complete."

Aria, the magical researcher, perked up at that. She tugged a small notepad from her backpack and started scribbling. "Has that changed at all since the introduction of the invasive species?"

"You mean the strange plants?" Lieutenant Petalwrought asked. "No, I don't think that rule has changed, but . . . Ah, you will see one of the changes that have occurred once we're passed the first floor."

"Evil Roots," I said. "That's what the quest prompts about them call them."

Aria and the others looked at me. "There are quests relating to them?" she asked.

"Oh, yeah. The World really doesn't like these root things. I don't know if they're like a sickness or, like you said, an invasive species, but they're bad news. They'll suck up all the mana in the dungeon too. I don't know if they've ever killed anyone that way, but I wouldn't be surprised."

Aria jotted down a few more things. "No wonder the crown wants this dealt with so quickly."

"It's a big old problem is what it is," Bron said. "So, we moving on?"

"In a moment," Lieutenant Petalwrought said. "First, we go over the first floor's rules and how to get past it. Then we decide on a formation and some contingencies. We won't have time to discuss these things on the floor itself, not if we intend to pass it unharmed."

Everyone seemed to take his words seriously, and he gave us a grateful nod.

"The first floor is a trial by combat. This dungeon has never shied away from those. The floor is shaped roughly like an arena, though the footing is hard to travel upon. If you have a difficult time walking, try skipping your way forward. It will make more sense once you're on the floor itself."

"What is the combat against?" Lucille, the wizard sylph asked. She adjusted her grip on her big staff. "Any known weaknesses we can exploit?"

Petalwrought nodded. "There are two types of adversaries. The edge of the arena is lined with creatures we've identified as blankifolds, though of a strange and perhaps unique variety."

"What are those?" Aria asked.

"Large creatures made of magical, cloth-like material," Amaryllis said. "They envelop people, smother them, then eat them."

The lieutenant nodded. "These are made of a quilt-like material. If you stray too far to the edge of the arena, they will ambush you. They might move toward you regardless. They are weak to fire or anything else that cloth would be weak to. Piercing attacks will harm them, though not very well. Crushing attacks are useless. Your best bet is to try to cut them apart. They aren't much stronger than a blanket, truly. If they capture you, try to make yourself bigger. Spread your arms and legs apart. They will have a difficult time enveloping you that way."

That was kind of spooky.

"The main adversary on the floor will be in the center, a child's bed mobile."

"A what?" Erin asked. He'd been pretty quiet so far, but I could tell he was listening.

"It's a device that hangs over a bed, with small objects attached to toys on it. It spins, to distract a baby," the lieutenant said. "This one will have five creatures tied to it. Usually knights, warriors, perhaps lions or bears. You need to defeat all five to defeat the mobile, and on doing so, the door to the next floor unlocks."

"So," Lucille said. "Walk in, stay close to the center, defeat the floor boss, then move on?"

"Ideally, yes."

I raised my hand. "Has the Evil Root infected anything here?"

"Not the last time we explored the floor," he said. "But that may have changed."

"Formation?" Erin asked.

"I will challenge the floor boss with two knights. The other two will guard you," the lieutenant said. "I know that some of you are capable fighters, but I'll ask that you focus primarily on keeping yourselves and your comrades safe. The floor boss is unable to leave a certain set area, so they shouldn't be a risk to you. Though on occasion, the floor boss has had forms capable of using some sort of magic. I'll warn everyone if that's the case."

"That's a lot of risk you're shouldering mostly on your own," Amaryllis said.

"All of the knights here have faced this dungeon before. Several times each on our own. We should all be capable of taking on the floor boss, and with three of us working together, it shouldn't be an issue," the lieutenant said. "But, if there is trouble, then we'll back out of the boss's range and regroup. Everyone understand?"

Nods all around, and then Lieutenant Petalwrought moved over to the door at the end of the room, half turned, and pointed to two of the knights.

"You two after me, then the group. The other knights take the rear. Keep your eyes open and your weapons sharp."

He opened the door and slipped in.

We followed a moment later, filing into a long corridor with pastel walls and a carpeted floor. It was lit only by a dim, warm light coming from the end of the hall. When we exited, it was onto a soft, padded floor, covered in a strange, cloth surface. It took looking around at the entire pattern of the floor to figure out that we were on a quilt—a quilt on a huge bed.

I jumped up and down, feeling the ground bounce below me.

It wasn't quite like being on a trampoline. Those had a lot more bounce than this. This was more like jumping atop a pile of blankets. There was a lot of give but not much pushback.

The floor was square, with walls covered in pretty wallpaper that had giant teddy bears and animals on it, though the wallpaper seemed scratched and weatherworn in places, and I could tell that some parts were stained.

The middle of the room rose up to a big hill. Or maybe it was less like a hill and more like a huge blanket with something beneath it. Atop that hill, with a massive chain leading way, way up into the darkness where a ceiling should have been, was a mobile.

It was tilted really hard to one side, so that the lowest of the items on it was resting on the hilltop, as if it were a discarded toy.

"Look," Awen said. She was pointing off to the side.

I looked, but couldn't see what she was pointing at. The floor was all quilted patterns, different bits of cloth of different colors, all laying next to each other in neat little squares.

Then I noticed some of those squares moving.

"Oh, I see them," I said.

A quilted blankifold, level 10. Stalking.

They didn't look all that dangerous, but then, they were magical killer blankies, and I wasn't sure what to think of that.

"We have . . . That's a knight on the hill," Lieutenant Petalwrought said. "So, knight, elephant, shooting star, sheep, wizard."

I glanced along the circle of the mobile. There were indeed five ropes hanging from it, with a stuffed elephant, a big plush star, a sheep, and a robed wizard toy. They were all bigger than I was, which made it hard to really pinpoint the scale of things.

I did notice one other thing, though. "Wait!" I said.

"Yes?" the lieutenant asked.

Pointing at the mobile, I tried to gesture to the chain holding it up. "There's a length of root around the chain. Do you see it?"

"I see it," Amaryllis confirmed. "That means that the floor boss is likely corrupted."

"Do you know what that will mean for those of us fighting it?" Lieutenant Petalwrought asked.

"I don't," I said. "It might even be easier. Sometimes the root makes enemies in a dungeon a bit stupider. They go berserk and will attack even if they should be cautious. And sometimes they'll ruin their own floor puzzles. We went through an undead dungeon once, and a lot of the undead were unable to move because they had roots growing through them."

"Interesting," Aria said. She scribbled something down. "Would you say that the root hampered the dungeon more than it made it more dangerous?"

"Uh. I think so? When we cleared the main root in that dungeon, the dungeon monsters started attacking the remaining roots. Like an immune system."

"A what system?" Aria asked.

"The thing that allows your body to fight off infections and illnesses," Lucille said. "It's what makes you feverish to burn off an illness."

Aria muttered something while writing that down. "If that's the case, then these roots truly are antagonistic to the dungeon itself."

"More on that once we've cleared the floor," the lieutenant said. "Stay here and watch out for the blankifolds."

The two knights with the lieutenant stepped up, swords whispering out of their scabbards while the two that remained stood on either end of our group, facing outward.

I shifted to the side so that I had more room, then held onto my scythe. I didn't quite know how to use it yet, but I wanted it close by if anything jumped out at us. Still, most of my attention was on the oncoming fight.

The three knights climbed up the hill, shields raised and ready, swords in high guards next to them, ready to plunge into anything that came too close.

The mobile above shifted, tilting back, and with that motion, the knight on its nearest end rose off the ground and stood. It was a toy knight, with jointed arms and legs and a body made of wood. Even its sword was more of a wooden plank, with some rough cuts along it to give it an edge. It raised a shield by its side, a large kite shield, almost as tall as it was, and its helmeted head rose up to stare at its oncoming foes.

"Awa, reminds me a little of that puppet dungeon," Awen said.

"Did that one have an Evil Root within it?" Aria asked.

"No, just puppets," Awen said. "I think that might have been worse, actually. They're kind of scary."

"You find them scary?" Amaryllis asked.

Awen blushed to the roots of her hair. "Awa . . . no?"

Amaryllis crossed her wings. "Why didn't you say anything?"

"I, ah, didn't want to disappoint you. Since you like them so much?" Awen asked.

I held back a giggle, then patted Amaryllis on the back. "It's okay. I still love you, even if your hobby is scary."

"It is not!"

"Maybe we should be paying more attention, you know?" Bron asked.

"Ah, right," I said. Time to get our heads into the game. No goofing off now!

· Chapter Forty-Nine ·

Lay Them to Rest

Lieutenant Petalwrought fought the toy knight with grace and skill. He reminded me of Bastion, though his stance was lower, and he struck with more force and slid back with less finesse. A different fighting style, but one that wasn't too far away, then?

The toy knight swung its wooden sword around with big, sweeping arcs that unbalanced it and sent it spinning. Even though it was clumsy, I still had the impression that it was dangerous. The toy's arms were pretty long, and that wooden sword, even if it wasn't very sharp, was still heavy-looking. The lieutenant and his two companions made sure never to be close to it, not even trying to block the blows with their shields.

The blankifolds around us shifted closer, like curious dogs chasing a scent.

Lucille raised her wizard's staff, then pointed the end of it at the nearest one. "Permission to burn it out?" she asked.

The nearest knight considered it for a moment. "Granted," he said.

A whooshing ball of fire raced out of the end of Lucille's staff, hotter than anything I could produce by far. It splashed against the monster, then stuck to it, the fire almost acting like a liquid.

The blankifold squirmed, but it was mostly made of fabric, and cloth wasn't exactly the most fireproof of materials.

Unfortunately, the floor was also made of fabric.

"Oh, that's annoying," Lucille said. She waved her staff around, and I felt the air grow dry as the air shifted in her direction. A ball of water formed, and she fired it out ahead in a big wave that splashed over the burning blankifold and the quilted floor around it.

Water hissed and smoke rose. When it cleared, the fire was gone, and the blankifold was very much dead.

`Ding! Congratulations, you have burned out a quilted blankifold, level 10!`

`EXP reduced for fighting as a group!`

"Huh," I said.

"Got experience for that?" Amaryllis guessed. I nodded and she continued. "It's normal. Big parties like this are pretty terrible for leveling, though. The experience isn't much, and it's split too many ways."

"That's why you need to make up for it by eliminating more targets," Lucille said. "Though perhaps let's not use fire."

"I'm not great with ranged options," I said. "Not unless cloth monsters are weak to Cleaning magic."

Bron chuckled, a deep, booming sound. "No, I'm afraid not."

"They're coming this way," Erin said. He pointed with the tip of his spear at the blankifolds, who were, indeed, coming our way.

I squinted. No they weren't, actually. They were all moving, but not all toward us. A lot of them were shifting carefully toward the middle of the room, to the hill where the lieutenant was fighting.

The toy knight was looking worse for wear. An arm had been clipped off at the elbow, and a whole leg was missing. Its sword was gone, too, so all it could do was hop on one leg and try to kick the knights around it.

Soon it would be replaced by another one of the toys on the mobile.

"They're surrounding the lieutenant," Aria said. "Is that normal behavior?"

One of the knights guarding our group swore. "It happens," he said. "We need to form a circle around the hill."

"Let's do it right, then," Bron said. "Everyone can fight here, but we should space out our best fighters to provide uniform protection. Captain Broccoli here's the important one too."

"Agreed," the same knight said.

They hatched a quick plan. Everyone would form a ring around the boss fight, far enough to be well out of range of the fighting atop the hill. The set-up was simple enough. I was going to be sandwiched between the two knights, which was a little annoying, then clockwise from there, it was Amaryllis, Bron, Aria, Lucille, Erin, Awen, and finally back around to the knight that was on my right.

It took a bit for those on the far end to get to their spots, but the blankifolds were slow movers, and we had plenty of time to position ourselves and plenty of room to move in, too.

I swiped my scythe through the air a few times. Weedbane was going to be tricky to use. The angle on the blade was all wrong for slashing, and it was a bit top-heavy. The pole being crooked also made it hard to hang onto it.

A blankifold undulated its way closer to me. One of the knights stepped out toward it.

"Ah! Wait, can I get this one?" I asked. "This is a new weapon I still need to figure out, and I'd rather do that with something easy."

The knight paused, then glanced at the blankifold. It was only level ten, and he was right there. "As you wish, Captain," he said. He stepped back but still kept his sword by his side.

I grinned as I stepped up. The blankifold would be tricky to fight normally—they seemed to like staying low to the ground, with only the edges of their surface touching the quilted ground.

The blankifold must have seen me coming . . . even if it didn't have eyes. It reared up, the cloth behind it bunching into a springlike fold, then the entire creature shoved itself toward me.

I swung Weedbane to meet it. The tip of the scythe poked into the middle of the cloth, then the blade moved through the blankifold as if it weren't even there.

With a quick side-hop, I moved out of the blankifold's path, letting it flop onto the ground where I'd been standing. It was cut but not dead. I guessed that it didn't really have internal organs, so I'd have to chop it up some more if I wanted to defeat it.

Swinging the scythe around, I spun my entire body to put more strength into my next swipe. Weedbane sang as its blade cut the air, and just like that, the blankifold was split in half down the middle.

`Ding! Congratulations, you have chopped up a quilted blankifold, level 10!`

`EXP reduced for fighting as a group!`

"Oh, that's sharp," I murmured as I stopped my spin.

It seemed as though I'd have to fight in quite a different way if I wanted to use Weedbane. My spade just needed me to bonk things with the flat end or chop them with the sharp bits. Weedbane could only scythe through things along a very close arc. Anything farther away, and it was more like a long pickaxe.

"Interesting weapon," the knight said.

"Thanks, I think," I said. "It's a bit weird."

"Weird isn't bad," he said. "Experienced fighters probably won't know what to think of someone carrying that around."

"They'll probably just think I'm weird," I said. I turned as I heard a clanking behind me. The mobile was turning, dragging up the body of the toy knight, which was very much broken. The elephant slid into place, then it trumpeted loud and clear from its felt nose.

"Watch your footing!" Lieutenant Petalwrought shouted.

The elephant reared up, then brought down its plush forepaws with a thundering *boom*. The quilted land rippled out in a wave from the elephant, staggering some of the others, but I was able to hop up and hug my knees to my chest, letting it pass under me.

I landed with a bounce, the plush terrain still wobbling.

Glancing back, I saw the lieutenant dart in and chop the elephant apart, foamy clouds of white stuffing flying all over as the elephant's stitching was chopped up.

The mobile creaked again even as the lieutenant backed away.

The shooting star descended, and immediately, I felt a warmth hit me even as the room grew brighter.

The star flew in widening circles, faster and faster. That lasted as long as it took for the lieutenant to slap the shooting star out of the air.

I didn't even get to see how it fought, which was a little disappointing.

What was next? The sheep?

The mobile shifted, and a fluffy sheep landed on the ground.

I noticed a few of the others fighting off blankifolds, so the perimeter was holding. Lieutenant Petalwrought would have plenty of time to deal with the sheep.

I yawned and lowered Weedbane's pole, leaning against it.

"Stay awake, everyone!" Lucille shouted from across the arena. "There's a sleep-inducing effect at work!"

"Really?" I asked. Then I stifled another yawn. It was a strong yawn, the sort that brought tears to your eyes. "Oh, yeah, I guess so."

The sheep was harder for the lieutenant to hit. His two knight companions ended up helping him. Mostly, it just hopped around a lot, and when they struck it, any blows against its fluff just bounced right off, with a noise like someone smacking a pillow.

Speaking of pillows, I felt like I could really use one.

I smacked my cheek a few times, then shook my head until my ears hurt from wiggling around too much. I had to stay awake!

Eventually, the lieutenant skewered the sheep with a swift strike, and I felt a warmth leaving me. It was as if someone had just gently removed a blanket I was snuggling with. It didn't snap me back awake, but it did remove that sleepy influence.

The mobile moved, stuttered, then jerked down.

The last one to defeat—the wizard.

That one was scary. It was a magic-user, and the toy wizard was wrapped up in thin, viny tendrils.

It raised both of its arms, and I felt mana shifting in the air around it. A spell?

Then the Lieutenant stepped up to it and casually lopped its head off, then both arms, then the legs, then he cut the mobile's strings and chopped the body in half before it could hit the ground.

Parts of the wizard flopped to the ground.

Ding! Congratulations, you have put the Sleeper's Mobile, level 12, to sleep!

EXP reduced for fighting as a group!

"That was easy," Amaryllis said.

Lieutenant Petalwrought nodded, then began to check his sword for nicks. "The wizard's the most dangerous of them all but the easiest to defeat. It doesn't move, and it's relatively weak. Its spells take a long time to cast as well, but they are deadly. It's a good lesson for recruits to learn." He sheathed his sword with a click. "The floor's done. Is everyone well?"

No one was injured. The others had taken out a few blankifolds here and there, but there weren't that many of them in the room, not compared to the size of our group. I dismissed the EXP notifications and joined the others near the center. "Where to next?" Aria asked.

"That way. The door should be unlocked for us to return to the starting room," the lieutenant said.

Aria nodded, then dropped to one knee next to the wizard. "This one had some roots on it."

"And I noticed that the mobile was functioning a little worse than usual," the lieutenant said. "The sheep is usually more of a challenge, and the mechanism jammed before the wizard came down."

"I noticed that too," Aria said. She took a few notes, then fished a small vial from her pack, into which she placed a length of the root with some tongs. "That'll do for now."

As a group, we started toward the far end of the arena. I bounced a bit. Now that the area was safe, I could participate in some good, wholesome bed-jumping. My friends rolled their eyes or giggled—Amaryllis and Awen, respectively—but the others in the group didn't seem to mind at all.

Maybe it was because I was a bun? Buns were bouncy. It was just the way they were.

"What's the next floor like?" Aria asked.

"We'll go over it in a moment," the lieutenant said. "Suffice to say, it won't be as easy as this one."

· Chapter Fifty ·

Knight-Light

The room beyond the end of the floor was the same room that we'd found at the entrance of the dungeon. There was even the dungeon's exit at one end, just casually waiting for us. There were a few small changes, though. The bedroom's wallpaper now had a small pattern along the bottom that looked like entwined roots. The bed in the corner was undone and messy, and more toys were scattered across the floor.

Otherwise, it was pretty much the same as the room we had entered through. Which was, of course, impossible unless the dungeon was doing some very silly things with physics.

Lieutenant Petalwrought pulled out a small box from a pocket tucked on the inside of his armor. It clinked, glass tapping against glass within the small wooden box.

"You're each going to want to drink one of these," he said as he undid the clasp holding the box in place and opened it.

Within were twin rows of glass vials with cork stoppers. He plucked one out and turned around to show it to us.

"These will keep you awake in the next part of the dungeon. We don't usually allow the use of these, since staying awake through your own will is a good test of a knight's resolve, but we are not here to test that."

I used Insight on the vial he was holding, just out of curiosity.

`A potion of wakefulness. New.`

"May I?" Lucille asked. She pinched the bottle the lieutenant held, brought it close to her eyes, then opened it and sniffed near the neck. "It should be safe," she said. "Unless the person who made it is far better at making poisons than I am at detecting them. What are the side effects, lieutenant?"

"Occasionally, the potion will work too well," he said. "You might have a difficult time sleeping tonight. That's not too unusual. The potion will keep you awake, but it won't sharpen your senses. You might have an unpleasant evening. Otherwise, I would suggest a more fibrous diet tomorrow."

We each took a vial, then downed them one at a time. There were lots of grimaces going around and a few grossed-out coughs.

"It also tastes exceptionally vile," Petalwrought remarked as he took his own.

I shuddered at the taste. It was like the worst sort of cough medicine but somehow a hundred times more bitter, and it was sticky on the way down, clinging to my throat and burning a bit. Once it hit my tummy, I felt a wave of wiggly energy sweep through me. I wasn't sure if I felt more awake or not.

Lieutenant Petalwrought closed his box, still with a couple of vials left, then tucked it away while he spoke. "This next floor is a maze. It isn't an overly difficult one most of the time. The path out will be illuminated by small lights affixed near the floor. They are usually spaced apart in such a way that you can always see the next one. It's the spaces between the lights that are dangerous."

"Can we make our own light?" Amaryllis asked.

"Some of this floor's adversaries shy away from light, while others are attracted to it. On average, I would recommend we light our way. There are two types of monsters in the room. One has never been seen—they attack with long, multi-jointed limbs that are relatively fragile. You can break them easily, but they have a lot of pulling power. They will ambush you in the dark, trying to grab you and drag you away. Their main body will never approach the lights, however."

"Creepy," I said.

"Indeed," he said. "The other enemies are large . . . large teddy bears. Wearing a knight's armor and raiment. They will attack you more honestly and are attracted to any lights within the maze."

"Cute," I added.

The lieutenant chose not to comment. "We'll be going in with a three-two formation. I'll be at the head with two knights, our guests in the center, and the other two knights will take care of the rear. We will be staying very close to each other. Do not stray."

We nodded, then Lucille raised a hand. At the lieutenant's nod, she asked her question. "Any types of magic or abilities we should avoid?"

"Not really, no, though you don't want to use any abilities that will hamper the others' visibility too much or slow the group down," he said.

Bron grunted. "What about them arms in the dark? Any way of knowing they'll be coming at us?"

"They are quiet, though you might hear a scuff or shift before they appear. Generally, the arms will go for members who are separated from the group or who are on the edges. Any other questions?"

"I have one," Aria said. "Have the roots changed anything? Especially with this floor of the dungeon?"

"Good question. I hadn't thought to mention it, but we've noticed some . . . corruption on the teddy bear knights. As well as roots entwined around the joints of the arms. They behave mostly the same. Perhaps a little more aggressively than before."

"Thank you," Aria said with a nod. She jotted that down in her book, then stuffed it away.

"Any more questions?" he asked.

"Ah, um, how long is the maze?" Awen asked.

Petalwrought shook his head. "Hard to tell. It's never the same length twice. We tend to measure them by the number of lights we cross. Usually somewhere between five and twelve."

There didn't seem to be any other questions after that, so we organized ourselves into the formation we'd be diving into the second floor in. Lieutenant and knights at the front, more at the rear, and my friends and the researchers and others bunched up in the middle.

It was pretty cramped, so I folded in Weedbane's blade, just in case. I could still use it to bonk stuff with the blade folded—it was still a heavy stick with a metal bar in it, after all.

Petalwrought opened the door we'd use to enter the room. This time, it led into a poorly lit corridor. "If you have magical lights, now's the time to use them," he said.

Two of the knights summoned little wispy balls of light, then Lucille cast a spell that made her staff glow. Not hard enough that it was difficult to look at, but still bright. She leaned it up onto her shoulder, and it cast a circle of soft light around us.

I summoned my own little lightball and held it up next to me while a few of the others did the same.

We were a well-lit group as we moved through the narrow corridor, then finally through a wide door at the end of it.

The first I saw of the maze was a passageway whose proportions were all off. The ceiling was too high up and the walls too far apart. Wallpaper covered everything but the floor with dancing teddy bears and knights and fantastical creatures. They were all really big, though.

The maze stretched out before us, with a few side passages just barely visible in what little light reached them, and way off in the distance was a circle of light with a glowing device in its middle.

"That's a night-light," I said.

"Hmm," was Petalwrought's reply.

The night-light was shaped like an elephant, and I suspected it was made of something like glass, with an incandescent bulb within. Were those kinds of lights more common than I thought on Dirt?

By unspoken agreement, none of us rushed ahead to the night-light. We walked with careful steps, the only sound filling the dark our footfalls, the clink of the knights' armor, and our breathing.

Slowly, quietly, we crossed the distance with every eye scouring the darkness for motion and danger. My big ears swiveled this way and that as I tried to spot anything before it came at us, but I couldn't hear anything.

And so we arrived at the first night-light.

The knights moved past the light and formed a cordon within the lit area. "Everyone accounted for?" Lieutenant Petalwrought asked. He made a point of counting every head. "Good. Where's the next light?"

"Sir, that way," one of the knights said. They pointed into the dark. I squinted that way and could make out a faint light in the distance. It was clearly just some light illuminating a wall, not the night-light itself. That had to be around a corner, but I couldn't see where the corridor turned.

"Same formation," the lieutenant said. He shifted things around so that he was back at the front of the formation with two knights by his sides.

More darkness, though this time we weren't moving parallel to the pattern in the carpet. I hadn't even noticed that it had a design of interlocking squares until we weren't moving along it.

Our lights illuminated corner walls, and when we finally arrived at the light the knight had pointed out, it was obvious that it was just an intersection. The night-light itself was farther down.

I glanced back at the last light. It was far away from us and flickering.

Was it getting darker?

There'd be no retracing our steps if we had to.

"This is spooky," Awen muttered.

I nodded. "Yeah," I whispered back. This didn't feel like the kind of place made for loud voices and laughter.

We started toward the night-light, then stopped when the lieutenant raised a fist.

I aimed my ears at the dark. The hairs on the back of my neck rose as something shifted. The sound was an echo, distant . . . maybe. Or maybe it was coming from just around the corner, and we had no way to know that a corner was even there.

"Onward," the lieutenant said.

We reached the next light with a collective sigh.

Safe. For now.

The light flickered, barely noticeable with all the lights we held but still there.

"We're perhaps moving a little too slow," the lieutenant said. "Next light?"

"I see it," Bron said. "Left a ways and forward. Something's near it, I think. Can't rightly tell."

The next light was down a long, narrow corridor. The lieutenant went ahead, and since he couldn't walk with his knights by his sides, they were split up so that they'd be mixed in with the rest of us.

The hallway was so narrow I could touch both walls without having to stretch my arms. It made the lights we were collecting feel too bright, especially as the wallpaper had a slightly reflective quality here.

The images were all of plush animals, some of them being held by long hands with too many fingers and joints. Roots clung to some of them, like nooses around their necks.

We crossed a few openings as we pushed forward—long passages into the dark that our lights couldn't illuminate the whole of.

We were nearly at the next night-light when something crossed before it.

There was no missing that the light had dimmed. It brought all of our attention up and forward and onto the large form waddling past the light.

The corridor widened, which was probably for the best.

The creature pacing next to the night-light saw us coming with its giant beady eyes. It was a teddy bear, like the lieutenant had said. Bands of iron encircled its big belly, and it had an open helmet squeezed onto its plush head.

A long sword was held by its side in a plush hand. It looked as sharp as any sword I'd seen.

"Two of us will take it on," the lieutenant said. "The rest of you pay close attention to the dark. It wouldn't be beyond a grasper to use the distraction to grab someone."

The lieutenant and one of the knights stepped up.

That left the rest of us just outside the safety of the night-light's glow, in the near-dark that seemed harder and harder to ward off.

That's when I started to hear a shuffling, a shuffling that was growing louder by fits and starts.

· **Chapter Fifty-One** ·

Unbearable Arms

Something's coming," Bron said. "Somethin' big." He spun his mace around in a little circle, loosening his arm to strike.

The rest of us huddled closer. It was probably not ideal for a fight. Swords needed room to swing, and magic needed clear lines of sight. But the other option was being farther from the others and closer to the dark. Had our little pool of light gotten smaller? It might've been my mind playing tricks on me, but it seemed like our glow wasn't reaching as far.

I tried to brighten my lightball, but I don't think it helped.

My eyes darted around, and my bun ears swiveled this way and that, searching for the source of the noise. I couldn't pinpoint it at first, except to say that it came from my right. Then I heard a faint snap, like someone cracking the joint of their finger. But that was from above.

"Above us!" I said. My little lightball shot up into the dark and zipped past something white and skeletal lurking in the abyss.

Amaryllis and Lucille fired two spells in the same breath. A fork of lightning was followed by a spray of glimmering icicles that chilled the air in their wake.

The arm flinched back, a hand big enough to grab me around the waist twisting and writhing as Amaryllis's magic worked into it, and then the icicles thumped into what little flesh it had.

Something screeched, far, far away, and the hand disappeared faster than something that big should have been able to.

"Was that the thing in the dark?" I asked.

"Looks like it," Bron said.

"Guard up, ladies and gents," Erin said gruffly. "I'd rather not get caught by that thing."

Aria hummed. "Anyone else notice the roots on it?" she asked.

I shook my head. I hadn't seen anything like that. Then again, it was only visible for a moment, and then my vision had been ruined by Amaryllis's lightning. I was still blinking back my night vision. Idly, I reformed my lightball in my free hand and held it up.

Ahead of us, Lieutenant Petalwrought was finishing up with the big teddy bear knight. The big monster was missing some stuffing already and looked worse for wear. The knights harried it, one taking to the air, another lunging for the bear's waist while Petalwrought slashed forward, meeting the bear's sword with his own.

I winced as the bear was chopped apart. It fell to the ground with a soft thump, and the knights regrouped and eyed the dark around them.

The night-light chose that moment to flicker.

"Reform," Lieutenant Petalwrought said. "We need to move out. We don't have a lot of time to lose."

We caught up with the group, and our formation returned, the knights on the edges and rear, the rest of us in the center providing what light and help we could. Lieutenant Petalwrought pointed ahead to another distant light.

"We need to move a little faster, make up for lost time," he said.

"What happens if we're slow?" I asked.

"Then the night-lights wink out, and you need to find your way out of the maze without them." He glanced back, and his eyes were hard within his helmet. "We do not want to do that."

"That would have been good to know earlier, sir knight," Amaryllis muttered.

I swallowed and nodded.

"Are there any other things we should know?" Amaryllis asked.

"There's a way to avoid fighting the bears. You need to sing a lullaby—it'll put them to sleep," he said.

"Then why didn't we do that?" I asked.

"They're not a great challenge, and we all need to sing. I don't know if all of you know lullabies, and singing as a group isn't an easy task."

We started moving, so I set aside my arguments for the moment. The corridors narrowed again, but we weren't as far from this night-light as we were the last.

This one was unguarded, but Lieutenant Petalwrought didn't seem amused when we arrived. The light flickered. "We're still not moving fast enough," he said. "Let's work up to a light jog until we reach the next one. We can alternate walking and jogging."

"I see the next one," Bron said. "Off thataway." He pointed, and following his finger, I noticed a faint glow in the distance.

"Good eye," the lieutenant said. "Let's not dillydally. If you find yourself unable to keep up, speak up. We won't go faster than our slowest. We can redistribute packs."

Again, we took off. The distant light wasn't the night-light, not directly. As we jogged closer, it became clear that the light was around a corner. There was a small staircase, tight enough that we had to step up two by two, then the floor widened and kept widening until I couldn't see any walls except for one way out in the distance, with the night-light on it.

We started jogging over to the light, but of course, we didn't all jog at the same speed. Our formation thinned out a little in the center, though we were still well within each other's lights, and the knights kept their circle around us the entire time.

I was glad that I'd spent the last month and a bit being so active. Before coming to Dirt, if I'd tried to run this much, I think I would've collapsed.

Still, I was looking forward to the next night-light, for the small pause it would bring. I was more looking forward to being off this floor. The maze was scary in the same way that the long shadows lurking under your bed were scary. Worse, even. These shadows had actual hands that wanted to reach out and—

Aria screamed. Just a short wail that was cut off with an *oomph*.

Spinning, I looked for the scientist, but she wasn't where she had been before.

The formation stopped, but at different speeds, so we ended up spread even farther apart.

"That way!" one of the knights said.

He rushed into the dark, sword bursting into light with a brilliant glow.

I bounded after him. "Amy, keep everyone safe!" I called over my shoulder. Not including Awen was probably rude, but I was already a dozen bun hops away and had to focus on moving.

More mana went into my lightball, creating a greater circle around me.

Shouting came from behind, but I focused my hearing forward, toward the knight, and toward the sound of bone scraping on floor.

The knight closed in on Aria, and I saw the glow of his sword illuminate the struggling woman. One of the hands had grabbed her, a thick finger grasping around her neck, the others around her middle. Sylphs were smaller than humans, likely lighter too. They'd be easier to drag away.

The knight grabbed Aria by the hand, and his added weight slowed them down. Then he hacked at the hand with his glowing sword.

I rushed past them.

Weedbane opened with a dangerous *snick*, and I pushed mana into it until the scythe glowed an eerie white.

My slash passed through the bony arm holding Aria with the same difficulty it would have cutting through a single blade of autumn grass.

Another distant screech, from far, far away in the dark.

"Oh, oh." Aria gasped, eyes wild and movements frantic. "Oh, that . . . that was . . . that was awful." She flung the hand off her, though it looked like a few fingers had been hacked off already.

"We need to get back, *now*," the knight said. "They might try to grab all three of us next."

"Okay," I said. I tossed Weedbane to the knight, who caught it midshaft out of reflex, then I scooped up Aria, careful not to squish her wings. "Come on! We can still see the night-light!"

We shot off, the knight easily keeping up with my sprint despite his armor and the added weight of my scythe.

"Y-you can put me down," Aria said between bounces.

"I will," I promised. "Just as soon as we're back with all the others." It wouldn't do to put her on the ground now when we were still in the open and one of those creepy hands could swoop back in to grab her. "How did it grab you?"

"I don't know," she said. "I was keeping up with the others, but I'm not used to running quite so much. I wasn't looking up, actually. Then it was around me and . . . and pulling me away."

I tsked. "How rude! I'm glad you're safe."

We met up with our friends before reaching the night-light. They must have seen us heading to the night-light. Somehow, it was hard to see them until we were almost upon them, even with all the lights hovering above and around the group. A quick headcount showed that everyone was there.

"How is she?" Lieutenant Petalwrought asked.

"I'm fine," Aria said, voice only wavering a bit.

"Good. Captain Bunch, can you carry her to the next light? We'll regroup there. Come on, everyone, double time it. No spreading out!"

We ran to the next light and arrived just as it started to flicker. Only twice, but the second time it turned off, it stayed off for a full second. It felt like a very long second.

I set Aria down on her feet, then brushed off her clothes, putting a bit of Cleaning magic into it to remove the dust and scuffs she'd gotten from being dragged. "There, nice and safe," I said.

"Thank you," she said. Then she fetched her notebook out with a huff and scribbled something in the quick, sloppy handwriting so common to doctors and scientists.

"Let's tighten our formation," Lieutenant Petalwrought said. "We don't want to lose anyone else who happens to be on the edge. Knights, I expect you to pay more attention, please. Though this failing is my own."

That was nice of him to say, taking the worry off his subordinates' shoulders like that. We spotted the next night-light a bit farther out. It was much closer than the last had been, but it was flickering already.

"I know I said we would walk to the next, but I can't help but feel as though the lights are deteriorating faster than usual," the lieutenant said.

"Then we'll move faster than usual too," Lucille replied.

We set off at a fast jog for a minute, then the lieutenant raised a fist, and we slowed to a brisk walk. It allowed those of us in worse shape to catch their breaths. As soon as the next minute was over, the lieutenant waved ahead, and we jogged once more.

The on-off cycle continued until we were close enough to the next light to see that it wasn't unguarded. Two bears, both of them a bit to the right of the light itself. One looked like it was covered in roots, the big vines wrapped around its arms and armor making it hard for it to move at all.

"I see the next light already," Lieutenant Petalwrought said. He pointed to two of the knights. "You and you, peel off, distract. The rest of us will run straight by. Rejoin the tail and send the rearguard forward."

The plan went off without a hitch. The two knights waylaid the bears while we ran by, directly toward the next night-light. Then the knights disengaged from the bears and caught up with us in a matter of seconds. Our formation reformed with two fresh knights at the front, and the two unharmed bears gave up on their chase as soon as we were out of the range of the lights.

"There it is!" Bron said. "I see it. There's a door thataway!"

Next to the night-light was, indeed, a doorway. Our pace quickened without anyone having to say anything, and even those of us struggling from the run found a second wind.

I kept expecting an ambush, arms reaching out to grab us at the very end, but nothing of the sort happened.

"Well done, everyone," Lieutenant Petalwrought said as we reached the last light and the door. "Now let's get off this World-forsaken floor."

· Chapter Fifty-Two ·

Childish Fears Grow Up to Become Adult Fears

This was our third time in the bedroom that linked the entire dungeon together. I was growing used to the room, I guessed, though it had changed again.

The bed wasn't just undone, it was missing its blankets and sheets, and the mattress was stained and gross. The walls too. Water damage made the pretty wallpaper peel in places and rot in others. Mold was sneaking up along the floor, and the entire room smelled damp and unclean.

I couldn't resist letting some Cleaning magic leak out. It spread across the room and brushed aside some of the worse stains and cleaned out the mold. I didn't want anyone getting a cough while we were down here, and the room smelled much nicer after a minute or so.

We caught our breaths after the long run on the last floor. Aria slumped to the ground and splayed her hands out behind her, and Lucille leaned against one of the walls. Even my friends looked a bit winded, though we were recovering quickly enough.

Lieutenant Petalwrought cleared his throat. "The next room shouldn't be as difficult," he said. "Does anyone have a timepiece?"

Bron did. He pulled it out and tossed it to the lieutenant, who caught the device out of the air.

"We've been in the dungeon for just over an hour. I think we're due a small pause. We have some supplies if anyone needs to eat. Don't forget to drink as well."

"I'd love some tea," Lucille muttered.

"Ah, I can help with that," I said. I could be helpful! I plopped my pack down and pulled out my tea set. It was a necessary part of my adventuring kit, after all. I prepared some tea for everyone, though I only took a tiny cup for myself. Dungeons didn't have bathrooms, and while it was an easy walk back up to the surface, I didn't feel like challenging that maze room again.

Once everyone was relaxed and sipping at warm tea or lukewarm water, the lieutenant straightened his back and cleared his throat for attention. "Two floors remain before we meet the dungeon's boss. This next one is perhaps the easiest floor in the dungeon, at least for some. It's generally a combat-free floor, just a challenge to test your bravery, and so far you all seem more than brave enough to pass this trial."

I puffed out my chest, even if the compliment was a bit silly. I wasn't that brave, I just wasn't afraid of much.

"What's the challenge on this floor?" Lucille asked.

"Not another maze, I hope," Erin muttered.

The lieutenant chuckled. "Nothing so complicated. It's a series of rooms, each with a bed and some sleeping amenities. To get to the other side, you need only crawl under the bed. Eventually, you'll find yourself in a corridor, though the dimensions are never the same. That's where you'll encounter your greatest fear."

"Our greatest fear?" Awen asked.

The lieutenant nodded. "I have only heard of a few who have been injured on this floor, at least physically. The fear will be illusions and light and sound. Not real. Just keep pushing forward. Ignore the fear or face it, as you wish. Once you've crossed the corridor, you'll come upon a doorway into a hallway. That is where we'll all gather before returning to this room."

"Can more than one person go under the same bed?" I asked.

He shook his head. "No, it's one at a time. There are multiple rooms, so we'll all have a bed to crawl under. Fears rarely change, so I know that the knights and I will be facing the same challenges as we have before. The first time is unpleasant, but always remember that it is only an illusion. It will not actually hurt you."

"You've already said that some people were injured," Amaryllis pointed out.

Lieutenant Petalwrought nodded. "Yes. Usually by their own magic. On occasion, a recruit has tripped over their own sword."

One of the knights jokingly elbowed the other. I couldn't see the face of the poked knight, but I could feel the embarrassed glare directed at his companion.

"You won't be injured by the challenge itself. Scared, perhaps, but not injured. I promise."

There wasn't much else to do once we were done drinking. I refused the offer of crackers from Bron—they looked way too dry—and then I repacked my tea set, nodding to Lucille's muttered thanks.

We didn't form up as we continued into the next room. Lieutenant Petalwrought stayed at the front, but he said that we didn't need to worry about any adversaries in this next part of the dungeon. Still, it was clear that he was checking his corners and watching for trouble anyway. He was nothing if not diligent.

Awen slid up next to me as we squeezed into the next floor. "Broccoli," she asked in a low voice that wouldn't carry.

"Yeah?" I asked.

"Can . . . can I get a hug before we split up? I . . . I don't know what my fears are, but I think it would be easier to face them, ah, with a hug?"

I grinned and bumped my shoulder against hers. "Always," I said. "You, too, Amaryllis."

Amaryllis was just behind us. She scoffed. "As if I need such things. Though I imagine that I would be wasting my time if I insisted otherwise instead of just humoring you."

"That's right," I agreed.

The first room was . . . a room. A little space with a desk, a shelf with some knickknacks, and a bed.

One of the knights was picked to go first, to show us how it went. The bed wasn't all that big, but he squeezed his pack through the opening, then dropped onto his tummy and shimmied through.

The room had a door that led into another bedroom, this one much bigger, with a bed fit for two in the middle. "Any volunteers?" the lieutenant asked. "I'll be going last."

"Might as well," Bron said. He dropped, then rolled under the bed. When I leaned down to see under it, he was gone, and I could see clear out to the other side. Was there a trapdoor or something?

We continued into the next room, and this time, when the lieutenant asked for volunteers, Awen was the one to step up. "Awa! I'm going to go next, please. Just . . . want to get it over with."

"Fair enough," he said.

Awen turned toward me, and I pulled her into the best hug I could manage. "You'll be fine," I said. "Remember, no matter what you see, no matter what scares you, Broccoli Bunch will be there for you on the other side, okay?"

Awen nodded. "Thanks," she said with a return squeeze.

She snuck under the bed and was gone soon after.

We crossed two more rooms, losing as many members along the way, one of them a knight, before we came upon a bedroom fit for a princess. "Well, this one seems good enough for me," Amaryllis said.

I grinned and shared a hug with her too.

Under the bed she went, with a lot of grumbling along the way about the indignity of it all.

I waited until I couldn't hear her anymore, then checked under the bed. No Amaryllis.

"She'll be fine," Aria said. "I'm sure all of your friends are as brave as you are. There's nothing to worry about."

I smiled back at her. "Thanks," I said.

The next room saw Lucille squeezing under a rather fine bed in a humble little room. She didn't want hugs.

And then we came upon a teeny-tiny bedroom, one small enough that it was tough for everyone to squeeze in. "Ah, one of these," the lieutenant said. He was glaring down at the bed.

It was a children's bed, all nice and neat and covered in a colorful bedspread. "What's wrong with this one?" I asked.

"Not much room under the bed. It's hard to squeeze in, even for a sylph."

I shrugged. "I'll go this time," I said. I was sure I could pass through. "But, ah, can someone take my scythe? He's a bit big."

Erin volunteered to hold my scythe for me, with a promise to give it back as soon as we met again.

I dropped to my knees, took off my pack—which was fortunately squishable enough to fit into the space—then I crawled in on elbows and knees. It really was a tight fit. As I pushed in, I had to exhale hard to make space for my chest to fit, and even then it was rather uncomfortable. I was regretting picking this bed when I finally scooted forward a little and found myself no longer under the bed.

With a bit of a wiggle, I pulled myself out of the tight space, then tugged my pack out while I eyed my surroundings. It was a great empty space, dark, with deep, branching silhouettes nearly blocking out a faint, pale-blue light coming from somewhere ahead I couldn't see.

I created another lightball, then raised it high so that I could see better.

The room was filled with roots.

They crisscrossed from every direction, big brown ones as large as trees and some no bigger than my pinkie. I poked one of the roots with my foot. It thunked. So they weren't just illusions, then. I shouldered my pack and looked for a way through the maze of roots. I didn't find a way to walk through it, but I did find a way to slip between the bigger roots.

Was this my greatest fear? A room choked by Evil Roots? It was more annoying than scary, honestly.

I rolled through a hole and flopped onto the ground on the other side of the roots, then paused as I heard someone groaning above.

It was Amaryllis, and she was nearly stuck trying to squeeze her way through the roots. I tried not to giggle at the look on her face, and that had her glancing up and finding me in the dark. "Well, will you help me or just stand there gawking?" she grumped.

I laughed and climbed up to help her down. She was quite stuck, actually, but we managed to wiggle her through. Mostly, that meant me putting some weight on one of the roots so that it moved aside and made enough room for her to pass.

"Are you okay?" I asked. I patted her back free of dust. A bit of Cleaning magic whipped away some of it too. Did that mean this was the real Amaryllis?

She sighed. "I'm fine. I didn't think we could rejoin each other in here. The lieutenant didn't say anything about it."

"He didn't," I agreed.

Amaryllis's eyes narrowed. "Are you the real Broccoli, then?"

I shrugged. "I know I am, but then I don't know if you're the real Amaryllis. The lieutenant also said that the illusions in here couldn't hurt us. Uh, I know you're physical, though."

"Corporeal. The word you're looking for is *corporeal*."

I grinned. Whether or not it was the real Amaryllis didn't matter, I figured. I'd treat her as a friend, and that was that.

"Come on, there's a weird light that way. I bet that's the exit."

"Yes, you would run toward the first shiny thing you see," Amaryllis grumbled.

I laughed, the sound lightening my heart in the face of the darkness and the roots. I gave her a hand to slip through two of the bigger roots.

"Broccoli," she said once she was on the other side. "Come here, please." There was a strange, worrisome note in her voice. I hurried to push through, and when I did, I found myself confused.

We were on a hillside? There were still roots all around us, and it was mostly dark, but only on the edges.

In the center was a ravine, with a slope before us and one just a little ways away. The image, the illusion, faded on the edges. It still felt familiar, somehow.

Then a group of cervids materialized from thin air at the far end, and with them, an Amaryllis that was trussed up and tied.

"Oh." It was the only sound Amaryllis made.

Was this . . . was this that time she was kidnapped? When I rescued her? Wait, was this her greatest fear, rather than mine?

"It'll be okay," I said as the scene continued. "I'm here, you're fine."

"I know," she said. "But still."

We probably shouldn't have stopped to watch, but neither of us moved, not even as a smaller, bunny-ear-less Broccoli showed up, looking . . . looking like a much younger, less confident me, one who desperately wanted to save the only sorta-friend she had made so far.

· Chapter Fifty-Three ·

Past Tense

Amaryllis and I didn't move.

The Broccoli illusion planted herself on one side. The cervid mercenaries on the other.

I knew what would happen. This was all a vivid memory, still. We'd . . . or the illusion of me would talk. The cervids wouldn't be completely unhelpful.

Amaryllis, the illusion across the rivulet, glared at her captors, then she spared the illusion Broccoli a softer look. Almost as if thanking her for being there.

This was the moment where Amaryllis really became my friend. Before this, we . . . well, we weren't getting along that well. I had been trying hard to convince her to be friends, but maybe I was trying too hard. I had been desperate for friends back then. A new world, a system I didn't understand, magic that was strange and bizarre and wonderful.

Then, just as we were starting to become closer, Amaryllis was kidnapped.

I had already decided that she was a friend, I think.

The illusion-Broccoli argued with the cervid mercenaries, and it got pretty heated. She looked defeated—even sad, in her oversized beige gambeson and tipped-back helmet.

The old me whistled, and Throat Ripper landed atop the hill next to Broccoli. He was as big as I remembered, all bones and armor. Even now, as strong as I'd become compared to all those months ago, I didn't think I could fight him on an even playing field.

A small army of skeletons followed, the illusions forming out of swirling light to stand atop the hill beside illusion-Broccoli. The cervids across from them looked nervous now.

The back and forth continued.

I remembered what would happen.

The cervids would toss out a smoke bomb, to distract and blind illusion-me. Then I'd wash it away with Cleaning magic. The cervids would decide that it wasn't worth fighting, and they'd toss Amaryllis down. Then they'd leave, and I would get to reunite with Amaryllis. I think that was the moment that really solidified everything for us.

The smoke appeared as the cervid leader said something that I couldn't hear, then it was cleared and—

My breath caught in my throat, and I heard Amaryllis gasp.

In reality, in my very vivid memories, Amaryllis had been tossed down to roll into the creek.

In this illusion, her head was wrenched at an impossible angle, her snapped neck deformed around displaced bone, and the leader kicked her down the hill. She rolled, stopping halfway down in a tangle of loose legs and wings. Her eyes stared across the hill, confused, unblinking.

"No," I whispered, hands jumping over my mouth.

The illusion faded, first at the edges, breaking apart like sand caught in an unfelt wind, then working toward the center until all that was left was . . . was Amaryllis's corpse.

"No, no," I whispered. That . . . that was . . . But it hadn't happened, it wasn't real, it was . . . Was it Amaryllis's fear?

I turned to my friend, expecting to see her as shocked as I felt.

Instead, she was furious.

"Typical," she spat.

"What?" I asked.

Amaryllis's talons balled up, and she glared at the fading illusion, then at me. "I said typical. That's probably what should have happened back there, isn't it?"

"No, it isn't what happened at all," I said. "It's okay, Amaryllis, it never happened. You're fine, we're both fine." I reached out to hug her.

She stepped back, out of hugging range. "It's not what happened, but it's probably what will, isn't it? Broccoli Bunch, always charging headlong into trouble. Like I said. Typical."

"What?"

Amaryllis brushed me off. "I've seen enough of this. I'll make it back on my own."

"Amaryllis?" I asked. "What's wrong? Are you okay? It's okay to be scared."

"I'm not scared, you idiot. I've just realized that your stupidity will be the literal death of me." She turned, and the emotions in her eyes were conflicted. Anger, but sadness too. "I'll figure out how to get out of here on my own. I don't need you, nor do I want you."

I stood there, frozen and confused for a few long seconds.

"No!" I said "No, it's not like that." I didn't know what it was even like, but, but things were confusing and weird and . . . and she was gone.

Had I stood around for too long?

I couldn't even hear where she went. All I found around me was darkness and roots, and the faint light ahead that, hopefully, showed me where the exit was.

I swallowed, then carefully wrapped my arms around my middle. It helped with the shaking.

Once I felt a little more calm, I gathered up my determination and pushed forward. Amaryllis . . . needed help. Probably. Maybe seeing that had scared her a lot more than it had scared me, and being afraid alone was a thousand times worse than being afraid with someone next to you.

The wall of roots didn't make pushing forward easy. I had to crawl over and under them, sometimes taking my pack off to be able to squeeze through the few gaps I found. It was after flopping out of one of those and landing tail-first on the other side that I discovered that I wasn't alone.

A disheveled Awen was standing nearby, eyes wide and teary until she saw me. "Awa? B-Broccoli?" she asked.

"Awen?" I bounced to my feet, then looked around. Another wide clearing in the roots. The light ahead was much closer now too. Just a bit more. "Are you okay?" I asked.

She nodded, then swallowed. Her arms rose, and I gladly gave her a hug. I needed it, too, I think. "I was scared. I saw things and . . . yeah," she said.

"It's okay," I said. "I'm here."

The hug ended too soon. Awen felt strangely cold. She must have been really spooked.

"Awa, I thought that . . ." she started, then stopped.

A mist was filling the room again, transforming it into a whole new scene.

It was a nice room, well appointed and richly decorated. I noted a piano in a corner, some bookshelves with hardcovers and a window overlooking a pretty courtyard. Then chairs and sofas formed, and I recognized the place.

This was in Mattergrove, in Awen's home.

The people in the seats were easy to recognize too. Amaryllis, Abraham and his friend, even Awen and her parents and brothers.

"This is when we met," I said.

Awen nodded, but she continued to look at the scene.

Things happened as I remembered them. We talked a bit, there were introductions, and then I gifted Awen my old wand. She flushed and looked happy, and I thought the scene might not be so bad. Then Amaryllis and my illusion left, walking in place while the scene flowed past them. The illusions talked for a moment, with just a few gestures. I didn't look so different than I did now, I don't think. The ears and tail were conspicuously missing, though.

Then illusion-Awen came around, and we greeted her again.

This was the part where we went off. The part where I basically kinda-sorta kidnapped Awen.

Instead, the illusion-Awen shook her head, teared up, and ran back up the staircase.

Illusion-Broccoli glanced at illusion-Amaryllis. They shared a shrug, then headed out.

"No," I said. "That's not how it happened at all. I'm really not liking the illusions in this place."

"M-maybe that's how it should have worked out, though," Awen said.

I spun toward her. "What do you mean?"

She didn't meet my eyes. "This life we lead, it's dangerous, Broccoli. So dangerous. I was kidnapped by pirates! I nearly died in the Insmouth dungeon! Those bombs the other day—a twitch, and I'd be dead. I . . . I would be safer back home. Maybe I should never have followed you."

"I . . . No, you're my friend, my best friend. I love having you on our adventures."

"Awa! You do, but they're not for me, Broccoli. Don't you understand?"

My breath caught, and I felt something nasty in my chest, as if a fist were gripping my heart. "But . . ."

"I'll see you later, Broccoli," Awen said. She moved on toward the light. "I think I need to think."

I watched her go, then shook my head and ran after her. "Wait!"

She jumped over a root, slipped past another, and then . . . and then was gone.

I stopped, feet heavy as my heart.

Leaning back against one of the roots, I paused to catch my breath and steady my pulse. I had to blink a lot.

Was I a bad friend?

I pushed forward, because I didn't know what else to do.

The roots proved as much of a challenge now as they did earlier. That meant I had to squeeze through even more of them. How had Awen and Amaryllis left so quickly? Or was the floor making it easier for them than for me?

I winced as my hips got stuck between two roots. Had I been eating too well while in the capital?

With a wiggle, I managed to squeak past, though I'd need to take a moment to fix the fur of my tail.

Congratulations! Through repeated actions, your Proportion Distortion skill has improved and is now eligible for rank up!

`Rank C costs one Class Skill Point!`

I stared at the prompt, then smiled a little.

"Thanks, Mister Menu," I said. "It's nice of you to try and distract me."

The light got brighter, and between one root and the next, I found myself in front of a door in a recess that had glowing walls around it. The door was simple and plain but still really inviting. I stumbled over to it, then opened it up.

There was a hallway beyond, wide and plain, with doors set about a meter apart. It reminded me a little of a motel corridor.

People were milling about aimlessly in the corridor. Aria, Erin, some of the knights . . . my friends.

I swallowed thickly and moved over to them trying not to drag my feet. Awen looked a little shaken, and Amaryllis was standing with her back real straight and a frown on her face.

"Uh, hey, guys," I said.

Awen turned toward me, then crashed into my chest. "Broccoli," she said, though it was muffled.

I returned the hug. She felt much warmer.

"Hey, I'm sorry," I said. "You, too, Amaryllis, I'm really sorry."

"What are you on about?" Amaryllis asked.

"I . . . I'm sorry I brought you with me! And that you've been through so much danger and pain and fear! And for all the kidnappings! And the times you nearly died! And . . . and . . ." I couldn't go on. I felt tears bubbling up.

She looked confused. "What are you talking about?"

I sniffled. "H-huh?"

"Where is all this coming from?"

"We . . . we talked. About . . . all the danger I've dragged you into."

"No, we didn't?"

I blinked, still hugging Awen, but now also very confused. "So we didn't meet in the room with all the roots?"

"Oh, there were plenty of roots, but no Broccolis," Amaryllis said.

Awen sniffed. "You were in mine."

"Oh," I said.

"You died."

"Uh." I blinked again. "Pretty sure I didn't."

Amaryllis sniffed. "Obviously, whomever you saw in there with my likeness wasn't me."

"So you're still my friend?" I asked. "You're not angry at me?"

"I'm angry that you'd think so little of me that I'd abandon our friendship," Amaryllis said.

I grinned. "Does that mean you'll give me a hug?"

She rolled her eyes, then gave me a hug, and everything was okay and nice and warm. Awen giggled after a bit, then I joined in, too, because laughing made the scary less scary.

Eventually, the hug broke, and my friends both looked better. I probably did too. Awen wiped her face clean, and Amaryllis's shoulders slumped a bit. I glanced around and saw that just about everyone was back. The lieutenant was missing, but he'd said he would be the last to go, so that was probably nothing to worry about.

"Hey, girls?" I asked. "I think we should talk to the others."

"What about?" Amaryllis asked.

I shrugged. "Just, you know, stuff. Maybe to distract them? Some don't look like they had it easy in that last room." The knights all looked pretty okay. I guess that they had all been through the room before, so they knew what to expect. Arin looked all right, and Lucille stumbled out of a room looking more angry than afraid.

Erin, though, looked a bit shaky, and Bron was still missing, as was one of the knights. Just saying hi and maybe giving them a quick hug might make things better. Amaryllis nodded, and Awen did too.

"Hey, everyone," I said, loud enough that they all could hear. "I'm making tea again. Anyone want some?"

· Chapter Fifty-Four ·

Counting Sheep

Is everyone well?" Lieutenant Petalwrought asked.

He was the last to arrive in the hallway that connected all of the corridors together. Still, despite that, he didn't look ruffled or bothered at all. He just went around and checked on everyone, then stood by the door at the end of the hall with his back straight and his eyes hard.

"That floor can be quite the challenge for some. I'm glad to see that everyone is still on their feet and that the floor didn't break any of us. I'm impressed. We will take a moment to relax again before moving on to the next floor."

"What's on the next floor?" Lucille asked.

Lieutenant Petalwrought crossed his arms. "The fourth floor is challenging. We will be fighting wave after wave of sheep."

"Cute, fuzzy, fluffball sheep?" I asked.

The lieutenant blinked. "No, demon sheep."

"Cute, fuzzy, fluffball demon sheep?" I hoped.

The lieutenant ignored me. "Their main attacks are straightforward charges and magical bleats."

"Magical bleats?" Lucille asked.

"The magic takes on two forms. One of them is a magical blast that imparts physical force. Think of it as similar to an air-blast spell. They can knock you off your feet, though they are not exceptionally powerful. They will try to trample you if you're prone. The second aspect of their magical attacks is that they will put you to sleep."

"Will the potions we took negate that?" Amaryllis asked.

"To a great extent, yes," Lieutenant Petalwrought said. "Though the potion isn't perfect, and enough concentrated magic can knock you out all the same. Less-focused attacks will still distract and weaken you."

"How do we fight them?" Erin asked.

"They'll be coming in waves over a fence-like barricade. Once we've defeated enough, the fence falls and we can move on to the next area.

Usually, there are three fences, but there can be more. I believe that the number depends on the number of participants and their respective levels, though we never quite pinned down the exact pattern."

So, we'd have to fight some sheep, then we would move on to the final floor. That seemed easy enough.

"As for the method. The knights and I will form the front line. The sheep will always come from the same direction. If you can provide ranged support without harming any of us, then I'd encourage you to do so. The sheep's faces and legs are their weak points. Their bodies are covered in a thick layer of wool padding that makes it difficult to cut them. A sufficiently sharp stabbing or piercing attack can push through their armor. Their horns are also quite tough. They can parry some attacks with them."

The others asked a few more questions, and eventually, we settled on a formation that we'd take once we were on the fourth floor. Petalwrought was at the front and center, a pair of knights on either side, and then the rest of us behind. He even had us stand in that formation while in the hallway.

Awen was going to use her crossbow, Amaryllis her magic, and the rest of us would help with what ranged magic we could manage. Erin and Bron both volunteered to be at the back, where they could run in and counter any sheep that made it past the knights.

I wasn't sure if I'd be able to help much. Cleaning magic wasn't going to counter a charging sheep. I had fireballs, though, and I imagined those would be pretty effective if I could set their wool on fire.

"All right," the lieutenant said. "Let's move out. We don't want to let the potions wear off too much."

The bedroom that connected every floor together was as I remembered, though again it was in worse shape. The water stains on the walls before had darkened, and the floor and bedding were moldy and rotting. Something dark was dripping from a crack in the ceiling.

A putrid stench hung in the air, thick enough that I instinctively flared my Cleaning aura. It helped a little, but the smell seemed to keep manifesting, like it was enforced by the room itself.

We didn't linger there for long. The lieutenant stood by the door to the next floor, then did a quick check of his equipment. The other knights did the same. Erin had given me Weedbane back in the hallway, so I checked the scythe's staff and blade for any nicks. Then I shifted my pack to make sure it was on snug and helped Amaryllis with hers.

"Everyone ready?" Petalwrought asked.

There were nods and "yes, sirs" all around.

He opened the door, and we filed out after him.

The floor was like a long tunnel. Big cliffs stood on either side, made of jaggedy rocks that towered above. The sky wasn't a sky at all but looked more like a painted ceiling, with little glow-in-the-dark stars placed between fluffy, night-darkened clouds. The stars glowed enough to see—it wasn't bright, though, so a few of us sent out our magical lights again.

"There's the first fence," Lieutenant Petalwrought said.

The fence was . . . a fence—some wooden boards held up together to form a wall that was just a bit shorter than I was from toe to ear-tip. We couldn't see past it, not with the way the boards were pressed in. It looked like an ordinary fence, painted with stars and suns and moons to make it livelier.

"Roots," Aria said.

I followed her gaze to the base of the fence. She was right—roots were poking through the boards.

"The last few times we ran the dungeon with the roots in it, they didn't seem to change much," Petalwrought said.

A rumble sounded from beyond the gate, like a small stampede of horses clopping through muddy ground.

The knights spread out in a wall before us, shields up, swords ready. The rest of us ran to our spots. I had a place in the middle, not too far behind the lieutenant, with both of my friends by my sides and then Aria and Lucille on their side.

The fence shook as a hooved foot clacked atop it, and then a sheep was jumping over the fence. Another followed a split second later, then another.

I was expecting a little sheep. Sure, the lieutenant had said demon sheep, but in my mind, they had been waist-high fluffballs with widdle horns.

These things were nearly as tall as the sylphs before us, with huge, curved horns that swept around their heads and came to a point next to their faces. Glowing red eyes locked onto us, and the front row of sheep bleated.

I gasped as a burst of air slapped me back a step while a loud *baa* sounded in my ears like someone blowing on an airhorn.

Then the world went woozy, and I felt my eyes growing heavy. I almost fell to one knee, but the act of falling snapped me awake, and I regained my balance. I pushed some Cleaning magic around my body. It helped, I think.

Right! I was supposed to be helping!

I concentrated and formed a brace of fireballs. The knights met the sheep's charge and it broke against them, sheep snarling and bleating as the mass tried to press forward. "Range!" Petalwrought shouted.

With a flick of my arm, I cast my fireballs at the sheep.

Lightning and a fiery whip cracked through the air from Amaryllis and Lucille, and I heard Awen's crossbow twang.

The sheep bleated again as the magic and projectiles hit them. Fur caught fire, and the sheep were pushed back and off the knight's shields.

It was enough for the knights to mount a counterattack.

"Keep firing!" the lieutenant ordered while his sword hacked and slashed at the sheep before him.

They were tough. A few attacks bounced off their woolly covering, and I noticed that large roots were tangled into the wool. It made it even harder for attacks to get through.

Finally, the first of the sheep went down. That freed up a knight, who immediately ran to help one of his comrades. With more attacks suddenly turned onto the other sheep, they quickly fell, each disappearing as a mist of whitish fog as they lay on the ground.

"Well done," Lieutenant Petalwrought said as the last of the sheep died.

We all got a nice little dose of experience points—the sheep were level twelve!—but my attention was more on what had landed on the grassy ground where the sheep faded. "What's that?" I asked.

"Ah, loot," the lieutenant said. He picked up a bundle of what looked like . . . yarn? "You can make some excellent clothes from this. It's spun already and, from what I've been told, of superlative quality."

"Does your order make clothes?" Amaryllis asked.

"We've had a member or two who can, over the years, but no, for the most part we sell these off to raise funds. The drops aren't so common that they're worth farming. Mostly, they serve as a nice reward."

"Can I keep that sample?" Aria asked. "For science, of course."

The lieutenant shrugged and tossed her the bundle. "Any injuries?"

Once everyone confirmed that they were fine, we moved toward the fence as a group. A strong kick from Petalwrought was enough to knock the entire thing over with a loud whump.

The other side of the fence was the same as this side. Was the grass a little greener? I checked back and forth. I couldn't tell, but maybe? It was certainly closer to our goal.

"Same formation," the lieutenant said. "The number of sheep usually increases with each fence. If we started at five, then it's possible we'll have too many to hold back at the front."

"What do we do, then?" I asked.

"Mister Talldance, Mister Winterhand, if you would be so kind as to watch the flanks?" the lieutenant asked Erin and Bron. They both nodded and stepped up to the sides, weapons at the ready.

As soon as we crossed the middle of the open space, the thumping of hooves sounded again. Sheep sailed over the fence, landed heavily on this side, then charged right at us.

They were met with steel and magic.

Sweat slid down my brow as I focused on flinging as many fireballs ahead as I could. They weren't doing much, individually, but with a large number of them, I was at least shaving the wool off one sheep's side.

This group went down like the last. First one fell, then that dominoed into the entire group collapsing.

"Check your health and mana," the lieutenant said. He was just a little sweaty, too, I think. Hard to tell with his helmet on. "If you're low in health, we have some ointments and potions. We broke out the good stock for this mission. If you're low in mana or stamina, we can pause for a moment before pushing forward."

Mana: 85/145

My mana tended to go up by a bit more than one a minute, I think. It wasn't exact. "I'm still good for another fence, I think," I said.

"Likewise," Amaryllis said. "But time saved now might repay later, especially if the challenge will grow fiercer as we continue."

"Two minutes to rest, then," the lieutenant said.

That wasn't much at all, but it would have to do, I supposed.

I stretched and resisted the urge to use just a little bit of Cleaning magic on myself. I could go a few minutes without wiping off my sweat. I wondered if I was growing to have a phobia of dirtiness? Would I still hug a friend if they were stinky?

I looked at Amaryllis with narrowed eyes until she turned to stare at me. "What?"

"Nothing," I said.

"All right, everyone," the lieutenant said. "Let's keep moving. We're almost to the end."

We stepped up to the fence and kicked it down.

It was supposed to be clear on the other side, at least until the next wave of sheep came after us.

Instead, an abomination was waiting. It looked at us with six baleful eyes, then, after taking in a deep breath, it blasted out a warbling scream.

"BAAAAA!"

· Chapter Fifty-Five ·

Sheepish

The monster's first mouth stayed open, revealing rows of teeth far too sharp for any sheep. Its bleat continued, pushing a wash of too-warm air past our group. All along its sides were some roots wrapped around its wool. Some were loose, and they wiggled with the bleating.

I shielded my eyes from its breath, then coughed as I took a whiff of it.

These demon sheep didn't brush their teeth often enough.

I pushed a surge of Cleaning magic ahead, forming a shield against the stench. It was a little difficult. The bleat was making me tired, I think.

Then the demon sheep's second mouth opened wide, and it bleated. "BAA!"

The third mouth opened a moment later and joined in the scream with a powerful bleat of its own.

Soon, the three *baas* harmonized, becoming a single loud tone that was impossible to ignore. The blast of air grew stronger, and I felt my shield of Cleaning magic straining.

"Hit them!" the lieutenant ordered.

I blinked. It was hard to keep my eyes open. Hit them? Hit who?

My hand lowered, and I felt my Cleaning shield start to fizzle out on the edges. It stank again . . . but I didn't see why it mattered.

I brought my hand up to cover a yawn, then let it drop.

Everything was so heavy.

Maybe we could retreat a little? I didn't like fighting anyway.

A loud *snap-crack* sounded, and I felt the hairs on my arms rising as Amaryllis let loose with a powerful blast of lightning. The air burned, and the stink from the sheep's breath was replaced by the stench of burning wool and seared flesh.

The bleats grew stronger but took on a pained tone.

The world went black, like shutters closing across my sight.

Oh . . . those were my eyelids. I was . . . supposed to keep them open, right?

Thunder sounded again.

I got an eye open and saw Lucille toss a fireball ahead, but it was slow and weak, entirely unlike her previous attacks. And I saw Awen raise her crossbow from the corner of my eye. She was swaying, almost drunkenly, but she gritted her teeth and glared ahead. The crossbow twanged, and a bolt bristled out of the one the sheep's heads.

One of the three voices was silenced.

Then the lieutenant and Erin were charging ahead. They hit the three-headed demon sheep all at once, clobbering and slicing into it with more violence than skill.

I swayed. Blinked, then refocused. The bleating had stopped, and with it, the urge to sleep faded.

Looking around, I saw two of the knights laid out on the ground. Lucille was on one knee, eyes closed, and Aria was hunched over, breathing even.

I shook my head to push away the miasma of sleepiness. "Is everyone . . . okay?" I asked. The lieutenant and Erin seem to be finishing off with the monster.

"They're likely just asleep," Amaryllis said. She moved over to Lucille, then extended a wing to the sylph to help her onto her feet.

"Awa, that was scary," Awen said. "No one told us about any sheeberus monsters in here."

"Yeah, I guess the lieutenant forgot," I said. I moved over to the knights who had fallen over and shook their shoulders with a shoe. That woke them up. They were surprisingly spry in their full suits of plate and were able to roll up onto their feet all on their own.

"Did I fall asleep?' Aria asked as I woke her up.

"Just a bit of a nap," I said.

She rubbed at her face, then looked around in a panic before finding her notebook on the ground next to her. "That creature! It was covered in roots! Is that a natural evolution of the dungeon that became corrupted, or did the corruption lead to that specific evolution? I need to document this. If that kind of monster doesn't appear after we've cleared the roots out, then it could mean . . . Well, I don't know what it could mean, which is why I need to write this down."

"Uh-huh," I said. She was rambling, but that probably just meant she was doing all right.

I glanced up at the lieutenant and found that he was wiping his sword clean on the woolly fur on the three-headed sheep's back.

"Is everyone okay?" I asked again.

No one asked for help, and everyone was either on their feet or climbing up. No injuries that I could see, just lots of blinking and people rubbing at their faces. One of the knights removed his helmet and emptied his canteen onto his head.

Lieutenant Petalwrought stood taller, the monster at his feet dissolving into that strange dust that all dungeon creatures turned into once they were defeated. "This was a serious miscalculation on my part," he said.

"Are these creatures typical here?" Amaryllis asked.

"No. I've never seen its like," he said. "But we should have been better prepared to tackle unknown threats. We weren't, which is why this one has taken us off guard. It looks like some mixture of three of the normal sheep we have to deal with, combined into one larger abomination. The World acknowledges it as a new, single creature."

I blinked, then brought up Mister Menu and looked for the experience drop from the fight.

Ding! Congratulations, you have sheared a demon sheeberus, level 16!

EXP reduced for fighting as a group!

"Do you think there will be more like it?" Aria asked.

"I have no way of knowing," the lieutenant said. "We'll have to find out the hard way. Let's take two minutes to catch our breath. Check your equipment. Do whatever you need to do to stay awake."

I didn't quite know what to do, so I did some stretching. I didn't want to end up with a pulled muscle, and it would help me stay awake. At least, I hoped it would.

Two minutes passed in a blink, and we reformed the same formation as earlier. "If we see one of those large ones, we charge in. They're powerful enough to be a major threat. I want them off the field as soon as possible," Lieutenant Petalwrought said. He spun his sword around, stepped up, then planted a boot against the next fence.

It crashed down with a heavy whomp, and we moved into the next area with slow, cautious steps.

A distant bleat was the first sign the next wave was coming. Then the first sheep were sailing over the wall. No big ones, but a lot more of the little ones than last time.

I flung some fireballs ahead, smacking one of the sheep dead in the face hard enough that it stumbled into a roll and was trampled by the sheep coming up behind it. Then the sheep were on us, and the knights raised their shields and met their charge with a wall of steel.

Bolts and spells flew out ahead, swords were swung, and Erin and Bron came around the flanks to prevent the sheep from encircling us.

Things were going pretty well.

Then the fence at the end crashed outward with a heavy bang, revealing two of those big sheep. In the distance, more thumping sounded.

The next wave, already? Had it triggered on its own?

"Tighten up!" Lieutenant Petalwrought shouted. We squeezed closer together. "We need to hit them before they start using their sleep magic on us."

"Counter?" one of the knights asked.

The lieutenant hesitated, then nodded.

The four knights and the lieutenant raised their shields up, then aimed their free hands toward the sheep battering at the front lines. They blasted some sort of magic forward. I could feel it, but it was otherwise colorless and hard to make out, like a heat haze.

A few of the sheep slumped down, asleep.

Of course the knights had sleep magic of their own!

"I can get to one of them!" I said.

"You're our VIP," the lieutenant said.

"I won't be very anything if we lose here," I countered.

Amaryllis cursed under her breath, using some very unladylike words. "Fine. Give it your all, everyone. No point in holding back here!" Having said that, she reached her hand out to the oncoming sheep, then grunted before slippery spikes of lightning shot toward them. I had the impression she was using a lot less finesse than usual and was instead focusing on pouring as much magic into the spells as she could.

It worked. A few of the bigger zaps took out some sheep all on their own, and those that didn't die right away were staggered or knocked out.

Lucille joined in, and I saw Awen lowering her crossbow, a focused look on her face. Soon, large glass caltrops appeared in her hands, and she flung them over and ahead of our group.

I nodded, bunched my legs up close, and launched myself out and over with a huge bounce that carried me up close to the ceiling.

One of the heads of the sheep I was aiming for turned up. "BAAAA!" it blared.

I grit my teeth and weathered the blast of wind. There was no falling asleep, not while in the air. I couldn't afford that.

Weedbane snapped open, and I spun my hips around so that I twisted in the air. The scythe's point swept right into and through the coarse, root-covered fur on the sheeberus's back. It made a pained sound even as its white wool was stained red.

I landed, a bit awkward with the weight of the scythe pulling me aside. I wanted to swing again, but then the sheep moved.

For something so big, it could move pretty fast, at least with short bursts. One of the heads swept down and rammed me in the chest, sending me stumbling. I had to crawl away from its hooves as they came clattering down in an attempt to squish me.

Weedbane couldn't help here, it was too big . . . One of the sheep faces dipped down, maw open wide with crooked teeth ready to bite. I grabbed it by the neck and held it away from me. This . . . wasn't the best position to be in.

Then the sheep bleated at me, and I felt things grow a bit hazy. This wasn't too bad. It was warm, and I was on the ground. If I let go, maybe the sheep would be like a big blanket . . .

I blinked hard, then pulled at the sheep's magic. My own was running low, so I'd borrow some from the sheep monster. It felt as if the veins in my arms were going to burst.

I had to get rid of that magic, now.

So I did. I turned the magic into a tiny fireball, then another and another and another blooming all over its body. The sheep recoiled at the constant onslaught of fireballs, but I didn't let go of it. I planted my feet against its chest so that it couldn't kick at me, then pulled at its magic even more. That meant more tiny fireballs zipping around and smacking into the sheep's faces and underbelly.

The sheep's three heads bleated, and it stumbled back and wrestled itself out of my grip. It looked pretty rough there.

I rolled to my feet, kicked Weedbane up, and caught it out of the air.

Two slices later, and the sheep was down.

I glanced back. The second wave had rushed past and was hitting the group while the other big sheep had thundered past and was busy fighting the lieutenant at the front of the group. Blood ran down the sheep's chest from where the lieutenant had savaged its throats. When it tried to bleat, only a wavering, gurgling noise issued forth.

I tightened my grip on Weedbane, then rushed back. The sheep at the rear of the formation never saw me coming, focused as they were on trampling the knights holding them off.

With the sheep falling left and right and a few of the knights being freed to move more, the fight turned from a desperate defense to a quick and dirty offensive. The knights focused on the biggest sheep, taking it down with ease once they outnumbered its heads. The others took out the stragglers, with Erin and Bron moving around to make sure that those sheep that had fallen asleep were well and truly done.

And then the big sheeberus fell, and the fight ended.

Bing bong! Congratulations, your Cinnamon Bun Bun class has reached level 13!

Stamina +10

Flexibility +5

You have gained one Class Skill Point

· Chapter Fifty-Six ·

Nightie Knight

Is everyone okay?" I asked once again.

It was pretty clear that not everyone was in the best of shapes. One of the knights knelt down and removed the plates over his leg. A bit of blood was there, and I suspected that one of the sheep had stomped his foot hard enough that the armor hadn't protected him entirely.

Erin was sporting a nasty black eye, and Bron had a shallow cut through his gambeson right over his short ribs. The sheep did have horns—had one of them poked him in the chest?

"I'm out of mana," Lucille said. She slumped back onto the ground and leaned against her still-upright wizard's staff. Her face shone with sweat, and she looked exhausted.

"We'll take however much time we need," Lieutenant Petalwrought said. "At least we've reached the end of this floor. No combat for a while."

I glanced ahead. I hadn't noticed earlier, but the fence the sheep had knocked over was the final one. The room ended at a wall with a doorway in its middle. The end of the floor? I relaxed a bit. If that led back to the bedroom that connected every floor together, then we'd be safe for a little bit.

But then, we had the boss fight coming up.

It was a little selfish of me, but I still checked on my friends before anyone else. Awen was stifling a yawn while carefully recranking her crossbow. Amaryllis looked stern but a bit disheveled too. Her feathers were all tussled up and swept back.

"Are you guys okay?" I asked.

"We're fine," Amaryllis said. She waved me a bit closer, and I walked over, expecting a hug. Instead, she bonked me on the helmet with the back of a talon. "What were you thinking? Bouncing ahead like that? I saw you flop over and thought you were about to be crushed. You dumb bun."

"Hey! I made it out of there just fine," I said.

"If you had been injured, then no one here would have been able to help you," she said. "Think of what that would do to Awen."

"Awa?"

"Exactly," Amaryllis continued. "If you were hurt or had died because of some overgrown sheep, then she would be inconsolable. Then I'd have to deal with her crying, and I'm the last person we want dealing with that kind of useless emotional outburst." She took a deep, deep breath, then let out a big huff. It was the sort of huff that outright admitted that she was projecting her emotions onto someone else.

I hugged her. "Thanks for worrying about me," I said.

She carefully returned the hug, with much grumbling and half-hearted attempts to say that she wasn't. I opened the hug up a bit, making room for Awen, who joined in as soon as she could hastily put down her crossbow.

Congratulations! Through repeated actions, your Hugging Proficiency skill has improved and is now eligible for rank up!

Rank D is a free rank!

"Oh, nice!" I cheered. "My Hugging Proficiency skill finally went up a rank."

Amaryllis sniffed. "So, that's why you kept hugging us so much. We're just here to grind your skills, are we?"

I laughed. "Sure! Let me grind my hugging skills on you some more!" I squished my cheek against hers and wiggled until she squirmed out of my grip.

"Well, it's good to see that your moods are difficult to bring down," Lieutenant Petalwrought said.

I let go of my friends, and all three of us stood up straighter. It was a bit embarrassing to be playing around while others were still hard at work. "What can we do to help?" I asked.

"There's not much to do now," he said. "Just relax, recoup your mana as best you can, and if you have any wounds, then now would be a good time to let others know. Every knight, myself included, has taken some courses on how to apply first aid in the field."

I shook my head. I was fine. I might have lost a couple of points of health in that scuffle earlier, but I wasn't hurting any. My mana was very low, but that would fix itself if we just waited a little while. "What's our next step?" I asked.

"We'll move on in just a minute. I think Aria is inspecting some things and taking notes. Once she's done with that and everyone is able to move again, we'll continue on to the next room. I'll brief everyone on what to expect from the dungeon's boss there."

I nodded. "Okay then."

Aria finished with her note-taking next to the sheeberus's body, then rejoined the group just as one of the knights finished helping another back into his armor. He had a small gash that they'd bandaged up. The armor was dented, but it still looked usable.

I don't think anyone had expected to meet as much resistance as we'd found on this floor.

Once everyone was ready, we moved on.

The bedroom was . . . disgusting. The bed was a rotting mess, the walls were caked in mold, and the entire room stank of rot. Roots were poking through the walls, and dark sludge was steadily dribbling from the ceiling and pooling in one corner. The floor was clearly uneven, with parts of it bowing upward and a definite slant to it, as if the entire room was to one side.

The air reeked so badly that my stomach was roiling. The other party members didn't look much better, and even the Lieutenant seemed taken aback.

I instinctively sent out a flood of Cleaning magic, then remembered I was trying to replenish my mana and forced myself to hold back. In seconds, the air was once again nearly unbreathable.

We spread out across the room. Despite our exhaustion, no one sat down. We even gingerly avoided the walls.

"I'll make this quick. I believe some congratulations are in order," Lieutenant Petalwrought said. "This dungeon is one of the more challenging ones, at least for its level. Few floors can be solved without violence, and those that can are no easier for it."

"The next floor is the last?" Aria asked.

The lieutenant nodded. "The boss floor. As soon as we cross that door, we'll be facing the dungeon's boss." He gestured to the only door in the room other than the one we'd come in from.

"What's the boss like?" Aria asked.

"His name is the Nightie Knight. Same as the initial class you gain from the dungeon."

I pressed a hand over my mouth to keep the giggles in. "That's such a cute name," I said.

"Yes, well, in any case," Lieutenant Petalwrought went on while ignoring me. "The Nightie Knight will come out of a large building. He rides upon a steed and will charge across the floor in an attempt to hit anyone that might challenge him. His lance will stun anyone it hits, and his steed can easily trample you if you're not careful to avoid it."

"Is it alone?" Amaryllis asked.

"He is, yes. In all honesty, the Nightie Knight was never a great challenge. The previous floor is usually much more difficult, if only because facing many weaker foes can overwhelm you where a single stronger opponent can be kited and fought more directly."

"So what's the plan then, Lieutenant?" Erin asked.

"The knights and I will form a wide cordon near the center of the room. I would suggest that everyone else split apart. Be ready to move aside when the Nightie Knight charges your way. His turning radius is relatively large, so it's easy to avoid him if you start moving early. Magic is effective, as are most ranged attacks. Take out his steed and he'll become a greater, though less mobile, threat. Dodging him when he's charging around the room is less dangerous than fighting him one on one."

"So we just pelt him with magic and win?" Amaryllis asked.

"Essentially, yes," Lieutenant Petalwrought said.

"Sounds . . . easy?" I tried.

The lieutenant made a so-so gesture. "It's not a difficult boss. I've fought him entirely on my own before. It's a rite of passage within our order. It's not an easy fight either. The boss moves quickly and hits hard. One blow from his lance and you will be knocked out, either from the hit itself or from the powerful sleeping magics he employs. Likewise from any strikes once he has been unseated."

The lieutenant fielded a few more questions about terrain and tactics we could use, but in the end, we pretty much decided to fight the Nightie Knight in the safest way possible: bombard him from range and hit him when he got close to the knights.

After a good twenty minutes of breathing through my nose as little as possible, most of which were spent in quiet as we all just worked to refill our mana and stamina, the lieutenant stood taller and stretched his back out. "I think it's time," he said.

We filed in behind him, and I noticed that everyone was a lot more comfortable with being close to each other than we had been at the start. It was wonderful what a few hours of near-death could do for making friends.

Petalwrought had described the boss room as a big field surrounded by stone walls, but he had failed to mention the fact that the field was a farmer's field. Big stalks of what I think was wheat stood in neat rows, and a beaten-dirt path led all the way up to a big stone windmill with motionless sails.

It would probably have looked like an idyllic scene if it weren't quite so dark and if the earth weren't broken up by invading roots the size of tree trunks.

At least it just smelled like earth, rather than an open landfill.

The sky above twinkled full of stars, and a big crescent moon sat big and plump above, casting everything in pale blues so that even if it was dark, we could still see pretty well.

"The Nightie Knight will come from the windmill," Lieutenant Petalwrought said. "Avoid the crop field. The footing isn't great, and the wheat will cut your visibility."

The windmill creaked, and it looked like it wanted to turn, but it was held in place by a thick root that wound its way up the stone side of the building. That didn't stop the double doors at the front from banging open.

Golden light spilled out onto the fields where the knights and the lieutenant were spreading out.

I hurried to find a place to stand away from anyone else, just like he'd asked, and I noticed that Amaryllis and Lucille were both preparing to cast some pretty big spells.

My breath caught as the boss moved out of the windmill with a heavy *clip-clop* of hooves on dirt.

The Nightie Knight was a short man on the back of a mule. He held a two-by-four tucked under one arm and a garbage lid strapped to the other. His armor was a resplendent set of baby-blue pajamas decorated with little teddy bears and sheep. He had a long, floppy nightcap.

Amaryllis snorted.

"Don't underestimate him," Petalwrought warned.

"Oh, no worries," Amaryllis said. "I'm not underestimating him. I'm merely mocking his sense of fashion."

I pouted. That looked pretty comfy, though.

The Nightie Knight raised his wooden lance, and his mule brayed into the night.

"Roots!" Aria said. "There's roots all over him."

I squinted into the dark, then flung a little lightball ahead to make things clearer. She was right. The Nightie Knight was covered in roots all around his body, like cords holding him tight. They kept his legs gripped to the side of the mule, and as the steed moved forward, it became obvious that the roots were making it harder for it to move at all.

The knight charged . . . only it was more of a limping trot.

"Fire!" Lieutenant Petalwrought shouted.

Amaryllis and Lucille fired off twin blasts of lightning, followed soon after by Awen's crossbow twanging into the night.

I joined in with a brace of sticky fireballs, which splashed against the knight and its mule.

The fight was on!

And then it was over.

We all started as the boss flopped to the ground and turned to dust.

I blinked.

"Huh."

· Chapter Fifty-Seven ·

The Root of the Matter

"Hold!" Lieutenant Petalwrought called out with one arm raised.

Everyone held their positions, though I think most of us looked around for a trap of some sort. Was a second boss going to appear? A bigger, badder boss?

I kept searching, but there was nothing suspicious. The boss room was quiet except for a slight wind that rustled the grass and wheat, and the sporadic creaking of the windmill. Finally, Amaryllis broke the silence. "This isn't normal, I take it?" she asked. "That the boss died this easily?"

Had the boss really died? I checked Mister Menu real quick to confirm it.

Ding! Congratulations, you have sent Sir Napwashad the Nightie Knight, level 16, to his eternal slumber! For defeating a dungeon boss, bonus EXP is gained! EXP reduced for fighting as a group!

Mister Menu had another notification for me after that one.

Dungeon cleared!

All adversaries within the Dungeon of the Lullaby Knight defeated.

All bosses defeated.

Broccoli Bunch, Cinnamon Bun Bun, level 13, Wonderlander, level 4, is awarded the Nightie Knight class.

All class slots filled.

Replace current class with Nightie Knight?

Replacing one of your current classes will reset your level to 0 in that class.

No, thank you. Although, of all the class options I had, this one was one of the most interesting. Maybe I'd take it as a third class. Though with the way my leveling had slowed down, that wouldn't be for months.

"It's really the boss," Lieutenant Petalwrought confirmed. "Knights, stay here, guard everyone. Erin, Bron, could you follow me? We'll verify that the exit is still cleared."

Everyone let out a sigh, and some of the tension left us. I think we were all hyped up for a big battle, but that wasn't going to happen. I was . . . a little annoyed, but I pushed that away. I didn't need to be worried or annoyed at not having to fight. If anything, it was a good thing.

I had to admit that I was a teeny tiny bit hooked on the thrill of doing crazy dungeon stuff though. It was a ton of fun.

I moved closer to my friends while folding Weedbane back up. "That was unexpected," I said.

"It was," Amaryllis said. She looked a bit distracted, though.

"Is everything all right?" Awen asked.

Amaryllis nodded. "Oh, yes, it's fine. I leveled up my Thundere class. Level thirteen."

"Oh, same as me!" I said.

She nodded. "I suspect Awen won't be far behind. There's a tendency for people who work together and face the same challenges to eventually reach the same level threshold."

"Is thirteen a big number for you?"

"No, nothing special, just another step forward. It's nice to see some growth, though. I might push some of my skills up a rank."

"Oh, I'm thinking of doing that too. I have a Wonderlander skill that I'd like to see become a bit stronger. It might be fun!"

"Hmm," Amaryllis said.

Awen shrugged. "I'm pretty happy with our growth so far. It's a lot more than I think anyone expected from me . . . except maybe Uncle."

I laughed and pulled her into a hug. "If that's the case, then I'll expect you to hit level one hundred and be the strongest person ever!" I said.

"Oh no," Awen said, monotone. "Now I'm going to have to live with your crushing expectations instead."

I laughed some more, then settled down as I saw the lieutenant leaving the windmill "It's clear," he said. "More roots, but the door to the main room is accessible."

"Where's the dungeon core?" I asked.

He tensed up for a moment, then relaxed. "It's back here. In the bedroom that links everything together. Come on, everyone. Unless there's anything anyone here wants to verify?"

There wasn't, though Aria did shuffle her foot through the ashes left by the boss when he faded away. "Any drops?" I asked.

"Can't see them if there are any," Aria said.

"The boss here only drops things on occasion," one of the knights said.

"It's usually pajamas. They're comfortable enough. Help you rest well. Sometimes his lance will stay. It's really just a piece of lumber, though."

"Oh, that's . . . Well, it's something," I said.

"I suspect if this dungeon were open to the public, it wouldn't be all that popular with delvers," Bron said.

"Because the drops are all kind of . . . uninteresting?" I asked.

"That, and it's real tough. The best dungeons for dungeon delvers are those that are low risk, easy to work through, and have good rewards. Cloth is . . . Well, it's not bad. Good clothes take a lot to make, I'm sure. Some of it can be pricey, but it's hard to justify risking your life to maybe fetch a pair of pants and some yarn, ya know?"

I nodded along. "I don't think I could become a dungeon delver."

"We delve two to three dungeons a month," Amaryllis said.

"Yeah, but never the same one twice. I'm in it for the new experiences. I think the sense of wonder might wear away if you visit the same place twice, you know?"

We entered the windmill. The interior was all old wood and dust, with what looked like several half-floors above, where I could see the mechanism for the mill held in place by big wooden beams. A huge grindstone sat in the center, an imposing slab of carved rock that forced us to walk along the edges of the room. Roots were using the beams above to hang in place and had definitely clogged things up by jamming themselves in the gears and wheels.

"This way," Lieutenant Petalwrought said. He was next to a door, which opened up onto a familiar bedroom.

"That'll lead us out of the dungeon?" I asked. "And to the core room?"

"Both, yes," he said.

We followed him in. The same bedroom since the start of the dungeon, only this one had cracked floorboards with thick roots shoved in between the wood, making everything uneven. A large root had plowed through one of the walls, and dirt spilled out from the floor-to-ceiling rent as though we were underground, even though a window right next to it showed a pretty view of some nighttime fields.

Was this the first bedroom-room with a window?

The wretched miasma of rot and mold felt like it was trying to choke me to death. Fetid water ran down the walls, and the only reason the floor wasn't a swamp was because it was seeping out through the cracks made by the roots. The bed frame had literally rotted out and collapsed, while the dresser had fallen over, spilling sodden nightclothes through the mud.

"There's an extra door here," Amaryllis said past a handkerchief over her mouth.

I looked around, and she was right. The other bedrooms all had two doors. One to enter, one that led onto the next floor. This one had a third.

It was blocked, though, by a large root that was pressed right up against the door.

"That's how to get to the core," Lieutenant Petalwrought said.

I stepped over to the doorway placing a hand on the root.

"Maybe stand back a bit?" I requested. "I'm going to clear out this root."

"Please describe the method you will use for this attempt?" Aria asked. She had her notebook out already.

"Mostly, I'm going to blast it with a lot of Cleaning magic. If it's like the last few roots, then it'll kind of . . . disintegrate? Uh, Lieutenant, the Evil Roots will definitely not like that. They might try to fight back."

His eyebrows rose, then he looked around the room, which had a number of roots in it. "Will they try to grab us?"

"No, at least, I don't think so. They might move. Mostly, they'll spawn these terrible plant monsters that'll try to eat us."

"Uh." The lieutenant looked a lot more on guard now.

"But only if there are any seed pods!" I hastened to add. "And we haven't seen any of those yet."

"Everyone, on your guard," he said. His sword came out, and the knights did likewise. "What's the plan once the path is cleared?"

"Is the core right on the other side of this door?" I asked.

"It should be, yes," he said. "It's in a rather vulnerable place."

"All right. Then I'll clear a path to the core, then wash everything around it. Aria, if you want to take notes, that'll be the time."

"Lucille, I'll want your expert opinion," Aria said. "You know magic better than I do."

Lucille nodded at that, then refocused on me.

I took a deep breath, then checked my mana.

`Mana: 87/145`

Not perfect, but more than I'd had to work with on other occasions. And once we were in the core room, I wouldn't lack any mana. "Oh!" I said as I remembered. "In other dungeons, the dungeon itself might react to the roots breaking."

"React how?" the lieutenant asked.

"Monsters might respawn suddenly. We don't have to go back through any of the rooms again, right?"

"No, the exit is right there," he said.

"How do monsters react?" Aria asked. "I've never heard of a dungeon respawning creatures while people were still in an instance."

"They'll reappear and attack the roots. I don't know if it'll be enough to clear the entire, ah, infection. But they'll attack the roots instead of not reacting to them at all," I said.

"It's not too dissimilar to a body's reaction to an allergen, in a way," Amaryllis said. "A sort of immune response that the dungeon can only use once the grip of the roots is broken away."

"Any other questions?" I asked.

At the lack of response, I nodded, then turned to the root. "Whelp, here goes," I said. I pressed my hand against the root, then focused on my magic. My improved Way of the Mystic Bun let me feel the mana running through the root, but it was . . . surprisingly weak? I could move someone's mana in their body, but it felt like every last bit of mana in the root was zipping away—or maybe it was being used up as quickly as it came?

I supposed that made a sort of sense.

Cleaning magic erupted out of me in a condensed storm. It coursed across the room, stripping mold off the walls, wiping the windows clean, removing every stain from the blankets and what was left of the mattress in the corner. The room's smell, of dust and staleness and rot, was wiped away by a fresh breeze that left the place smelling like spring and freshly cut wood. Except for my closest friends, some of the others even took a step back, shifting uneasily as my magic wicked away sweat stains and grime. The knights wouldn't need to polish their armor today!

Then I concentrated the magic back into the root. I grunted as the magic didn't quite want to take hold, but I was a stubborn bun, and no root was going to dirty this place up under my watch.

The smaller sprouts sticking out of the root disintegrated. The floor creaked as some of the roots poking through the boards blackened and fell apart. And then the big root before me twitched under my hand and seemed to try to pull back.

"No way, buster," I cursed.

My mana dropped like a stone, but I didn't care. I drove my magic into the root like railroad spikes hit with a sledgehammer, one after another. The root creaked, parts of it turning to powder along fault lines, letting great chunks of plant flesh slough off.

And then the root couldn't support its own weight, and it snapped apart down the middle, both halves thumping to the floor.

I let out a long sigh, then wiped my already-clean brow.

Mana: 9/145

Close one! But I still had a tiny bit in the tank. "That's one root down," I said. "Or enough to let us through, at least," I said.

". . . That was impressive," Lucille said. "I have only had a few chances to see Master Rank magic at work, and it's rarely in so specific and narrow a focus for a magical skill."

"Ah, well, thanks! It happened entirely by accident!" I said.

With that, I tugged the door to the core room open, then winced at what I saw.

A wall of roots. Hundreds of tiny ones all braided together to form a barrier that I could hardly see past. Bigger ones filled in the space around those, and through that web, only faintly visible past a canopy of leaves sprouting from the roots, was the dungeon's core sitting atop what looked like a pile of blankets in a baby cradle made of stone.

"This is going to take some work."

· Chapter Fifty-Eight ·

Uprooted

The moment I was able to sneak my hand closer to the core in the center of the core room, everything became a lot easier. Enough ambient mana was present that my mana reserves refilled faster, a point every ten seconds or so instead of one a minute. That just meant I had more mana to pour into Cleaning magic.

I pressed my free hand up against one of the little roots blocking the entrance. It fell apart as my Cleaning magic got to work. The root snapped, and I moved on to the next one below it.

"Is there anything we can do to help?" Lieutenant Petalwrought asked.

"I don't think so," I said. "Sorry! I'd love to have some help, and if there was something I could ask for help with, I would, but . . . Yeah, this is just going to take a little bit."

Another root snapped, and I noticed the entire body of the Evil Roots shifting very slightly. Did it know that I was harming it? I asked myself, not for the first time, if the Evil Roots could think. If they could, did they know that they were hurting the dungeons they were grabbing onto?

My mana bounced up and down as I waited for it to refill a bit, then I used it all up on cutting apart the roots blocking the entrance. Eventually, I had a space that was big enough to crawl through. "I think I'm going to climb through," I said.

"A dungeon's core is high in mana," Lucille warned. "Unless you're spending all of it, constantly, then there's a very real chance that you can hurt yourself."

"Yeah," I said. "But that's what I plan on doing. Flood the entire room with enough Cleaning magic that the Evil Roots don't have a choice but to fall back. It's easier to do if I can use the core's own magic for it. Besides, look, it's regrowing."

I tugged on one of the smaller roots and showed it to the others. The tip of it was still a little raw where my magic had cut through it, but it was turning a paler shade of green, and it looked as though the root was growing back.

"Interesting," Aria said. "Its growth rate must be spectacular. That's . . . perhaps two or three millimeters a minute, at a guess. I'd need a ruler and some way of marking its progress over time to be certain."

"The roots cover a large portion of the entire dungeon," Amaryllis said. "They would need to grow quickly to do that. I imagine various parts of the root network grow at different paces."

"I'm going to write so many papers from this," Aria said with obvious glee. "Lady Albatross, Lady Bristlecone, you've experienced other dungeons plagued by these roots, correct? Ah, good. Could you tell me about them? Maybe how those . . . infections . . . differed from this one?"

I listened with half an ear as my friends related their stories of the other dungeons we'd explored together. Aria took notes, of course.

Once I had an opening that was wide enough, I climbed up into it after tossing my pack aside and handing Weedbane to one of the knights. I had to slip my head and shoulders in first, then I hoped that the sylphs behind me were all gentlemen as I squeezed my hips through the passage.

I landed in a roll on the other side and found the ground covered in those big flat leaves that the roots seemed to only grow around a core. Were they like leaves facing sunlight, but instead of sunlight they were fixed on the core?

Did that mean that the core was radiating mana directly? It did glow a bit.

That was worrisome. I didn't know that much about radiation, but I recalled it being pretty scary, and usually, if it was radioactive enough to glow, then seeing it wasn't good for you.

Well, an issue for later.

I pushed out a wash of Cleaning magic around me, breaking up a circle of the leaves, then as more and more mana gathered in me from being closer to the core, I started to fill the room with Cleaning magic.

It was like I was a filter, sucking in the ambient mana and then pushing it out in a form that was able to harm the roots.

The leaves all across the room withered. Simply flooding the room with Cleaning magic wouldn't be enough to clear the bigger, thicker roots, but I suspected it was a start.

I could either destroy the roots on the edges of the room and work my way in, or I could clear those grabbing onto the core directly. It only took a moment's thought to come to a choice. The core was basically an important part of the dungeon, so removing the roots there would make the dungeon feel a bunch better.

I had to work carefully. I didn't want to strike the core itself in case it broke, but it was surrounded by roots. So, I carefully cut through the roots leading up to the core. Judging by how the roots on the walls flinched, they didn't like that one bit.

Once they were detached, it was pretty easy to peel some of the roots off the core just by tugging on them. A few were wrapped around tight enough that I had to let some ambient Cleaning magic brush up against them until they loosened and I could tear them off. After a few minute's work, the entire core was clear.

"There you go," I muttered to the dungeon. "Nice and freed up." For some reason I couldn't help but think of the dungeon as a cute animal caught in a fence.

The . . . taste of the mana in the air changed. I paused as I felt at it to be sure it wasn't a bad change.

Then . . . then nothing happened, so I started blasting.

Big gouts of Cleaning magic splashed against the walls and ceiling and floor, burning away the root's infection until big clumps of root fell down with heavy thumps all around the room.

Some of the roots tried to squirm away, others seemed to try and reach out to grab me, or maybe the core behind me, but they were slow-moving, and when they met even more Cleaning magic, their efforts turned to nothing.

Soon enough, I walked along the edge of the room, splashing magic onto errant bits of root on the floor.

The room was much nicer without big vines clinging to the walls. It was a sort of nursery, with pastel walls and clean wooden floors. Unfortunately, there were holes in the walls, and the floors were warped, but I had the impression that that wouldn't last for very long. The dungeon, or at least the core, was free of the roots, so it had an opportunity to heal.

Quest completed!

Trim the Cruel!

The core is saved!

"I think that's it," I said as I left the dungeon's core room. My mana was topped up to max and then some, but I was leaking an aura of Cleaning magic that would chew away at the excess.

Lieutenant Petalwrought carefully stepped into the room and walked around it once. I had the impression that he was trying not to wince at the clinks and clangs of his armor as he moved with careful reverence. "It seems clear," he said as he exited the room. "Will the roots perish now?"

"I don't know," I said honestly. "I think they might. The last dungeons started to fight back against the roots. I don't know if that means that they'll all win against them."

"But if the dungeon's fighting back, then it has a chance," Erin said. "We've delivered it a dose of medicine. I imagine the rest is up to the dungeon itself."

I nodded. "That's how I think it works. I got a quest update. It said the dungeon's saved. I don't know if that means just for now or if it's a permanent thing."

A few of the others were giving me a look at that. I think it might have been the mention of the quest. If they treated the World as something very important, then getting a message from it was pretty important too.

"We'll have to trust you, then," the lieutenant said.

"I mean, you should verify anyway. Maybe send someone down tomorrow to see if there are any more roots poking into the room," I said.

He nodded. "I'll inform the knight-captain and the other knights."

"I might want to see that," Aria said. "If the roots are still here tomorrow, then there's a chance they'll be falling apart, or degrading. Even if they're completely gone or remain as they are, I'll want to see. It'll be important to know moving on . . . and for my papers too."

"Speaking of higher-ups," Amaryllis said. "We should head out. I'm somewhat tired of being in a dungeon, and I think we're due a payment soon for services rendered. Though I imagine we'll only see that once we're back at the capital."

Everyone seemed to agree with that. I think we were all a bit tired. What time had it been when we entered the dungeon? Early afternoon? I couldn't even begin to tell what time it was now. Some of the floors had felt like they went on forever. Had we been here for a couple of hours or nearly a whole day? I couldn't even guess by feeling how sleepy I was.

"The exit is right through here," Lieutenant Petalwrought said. He walked over to the last unopened door in the bedroom. "Before we go," he said with a hand on the handle, "I want to say that it was an honor working with you all. Though most of you come from varied backgrounds and occupations, you all comported yourselves with dignity."

I knew that pride wasn't a very nice emotion most of the time, but I still puffed out my chest at his words. "Thank you. I'm glad we all got to become friends."

There were a few chuckles, and Awen bumped her shoulder against mine.

Then the door was opened, and we filed through it. A tunnel awaited us on the other side. Just a few meters in, and I recognized it as the same one we'd used to enter the dungeon. And then we were out.

A lone knight, in only half the armor as the others and with a spear by his side snapped to attention as he saw us entering the room. "Sir Petalwrought, sir!" he said at volumes that might have been a bit much for indoors.

"Hello, squire," the knight said. "Can you inform the knight-captain of our success?"

"Yes, sir!" the squire shouted back. "Right away, sir. The knight-captain is in the upper debriefing room, sir."

That was a lot of sirs. This boy took himself very sir-iously. I giggled, then worked hard not to laugh when Amaryllis shot me a look. "Never mind. It'll just make you angry if I explain."

She rolled her eyes

"I believe everyone but our knights should come," the lieutenant said. "Unless you gentlemen have anything important to add?" he directed the last to the knights.

They shook their heads, and I imagined they were all eager to get out of that armor and into a bath. One of them handed me back Weedbane, and I thanked him with a cheery smile before tucking the scythe on my shoulder.

"Very well then. Please follow me once more, everyone," the lieutenant said.

We moved through the castle and past a small courtyard at the back. The sky was that dark blue that only came about when the sun was about to set, which answered one of my questions, at least.

Too tired to chat, we tromped up the stairs to the next floor, where a bunch of generals and important riffraff were waiting for us.

· Chapter Fifty-Nine ·

Sizing Up the Future

I'd expected the meeting with the generals to be kind of boring, and I wasn't wrong at all.

The generals, who had been drinking and smoking cigars earlier, decided to act a bit more professionally, and so they met us in a meeting room where we all sat down. Lieutenant Petalwrought reported on our entire excursion through the dungeon in short, clipped sentences while sitting as if his back were locked in place.

Once he was done, Aria delivered a very preliminary report. There were lots of words used whose meanings I wasn't sure of, and the generals spent a lot of time nodding even though I was pretty sure they didn't understand any better than I did.

Then it was my turn. I bounced on my seat as I explained how I cleaned up the core. I used as many gestures and examples as I could. The generals seemed more confused than not when I was done, but Amaryllis and Awen were smiling, so I decided it probably didn't matter.

"Well, that was . . . educational," the knight-captain said. He stroked his mustache, then nodded. "I believe we are quite done here for the moment, gentlemen and ladies. I'm aware that the sun has set already, but our magnificent navy has no fear of flying in the dark! The generals and I will deliberate for some time still, but those of you who wish to return to the capital may prepare yourselves for the flight back."

With that done, we left the meeting room.

My friends and I stayed back for a bit to say bye to our new friends. I hugged everyone, even Erin and Bron and Lucille, who seemed a bit worried about getting hugged—which was quite silly, but I kept the hugs short so that they wouldn't be uncomfortable—and then Lieutenant Petalwrought insisted on shaking my hand, even after I offered him a hug.

"It was a pleasure working with all of you," he said. "I'm genuinely glad that the dungeon has been cured of its ills. Hopefully, it will be restored and in proper order soon enough."

"I hope it feels better too," I said.

We milled around for a bit, but eventually, I think my friends and I all felt a little weary—not tired, not sleepy. We'd taken some potions to keep awake, and judging by how bouncy I felt, I wasn't going to be sleeping anytime soon.

We left the knight's little castle and crossed the training yard back to the sylph warship, which was still anchored in place. The sailors we passed were mostly sitting back and relaxing. A few were even snoozing away next to the crates and boxes they'd unloaded when we arrived.

My friends and I climbed aboard the ship, and when no one met us on the main deck, we went down a level back to the room where we'd waited on the way over.

I found the cot in the corner of the room, spun around, and flopped onto it. "Ah, that was a long day," I said.

"It was," Amaryllis agreed. She sat down to my right, scooted back, then folded her legs up under her.

Awen hopped onto the other side, then she squeezed herself closer to my side. I leaned to the side, ears flopping atop her head and chin on her shoulder. "It wasn't a bad day," she said. "The last couple of weeks have been . . . busy, but not bad."

"Yeah, I guess so. I'm looking forward to getting back to adventuring though. Politics isn't for me, I think."

Amaryllis sniffed. "Yes, I suppose you'd say that. Perhaps we can take the long way back home. I've always wanted to visit the north."

"Oh," Awen said. "I'd like that. I . . . I would like to get stronger too. I only leveled up once in the last couple of weeks, and that was today."

"Right!" I said. "We'll get even stronger, then. I need to level up my hugging skills, and . . . Oh, I have a skill I want to put a point into as well."

It had been a little bit since I'd looked at my growth.

Name	Broccoli Bunch
Race	Bun (Riftwalker)
First Class	Cinnamon Bun Bun
First Class Level	13
Second Class	Wonderlander
Second Class Level	4

Age	16
Health	145
Stamina	160
Mana	145
Resilience	55
Flexibility	75
Magic	35
Skills	Rank
Cinnamon Bun Bun Skills	
Cleaning	S - 07%
Way of the Mystic Bun	C - 17%
Gardening	D - 41%
Adorable	D - 100%
Dancing	D - 100%
Wonderlander Skills	
Tea Making	D - 100%
Mad Millinery	D - 94%
Proportion Distortion	D - 100%
General Skills	
Insight	C - 100%
Makeshift Weapons Proficiency	C - 24%
Archeology	D - 29%
Friendmaking	C - 79%
Matchmaking	D - 68%
Hugging Proficiency	D - 57%
Captaining	E - 89%
Cinnamon Bun Bun Skill Points	1
Wonderlander Skill Points	3

General Skill Points	3
First Class Skill Slots	0
Second Class Skill Slots	0
General Skill Slots	3

Way of the Mystic Bun was proving to be a great skill at its new rank. Otherwise, not much had changed with my Cinnamon Bun Bun skills. Maybe I could put that spare point into one of them? Or was it cleverer to wait for Cleaning to be ready to become even more powerful?

My Wonderlander skills were coming along nicely too! I was going to get a new skill in a couple of levels. I couldn't wait! I was definitely going to put more points into Proportion Distortion. Sure, it wasn't the most useful of skills, but it sounded fun!

Mad Millinery was only growing slowly. Maybe I had to start trying on more hats? I'd try to remember to visit another hat store.

Insight was at its maximum. Friendmaking was getting close too. If there was ever a general skill I wouldn't mind using some of my precious slots on, that was it. Hugging Proficiency, too . . . I was really grinding that one.

But in any case.

Congratulations! Proportion Distortion is now Rank C!

Proportion Distortion

Rank C - 00%

The ability to fit in and fit out. You can now use magic to help you grow up or grow down!

I tilted my head as I tried to figure out what that meant. The tilting moved me a bit away from Awen and made my ears flop in the other direction, onto Amaryllis.

I poked at the skill. The way it was phrased sounded like an ability that I could use on myself. Was it like when I had used Jumping to jump around?

Closing my eyes and pinching my tongue between my teeth, I felt around myself with my magic. It was something that I wasn't too used to yet. I bet that to someone raised on Dirt it would be second nature.

I found a switch eventually. It was kind of buried in the pit of my tummy. I poked at it with some mana, and it sent a tingle across my entire body, like a shiver.

Interesting.

"Hey, Amaryllis?" I asked.

"Yes?"

"Can you hurt yourself with your own skills?"

Amaryllis thought about it. "Yes, but not usually directly. A light application of creativity could turn a harmless skill into a danger, of course. You had a skill that let you jump around. It didn't harm you, but it didn't prevent you from jumping off a cliff either."

"Right," I said. "I'm gonna try something."

Before Amaryllis could protest, I shoved a healthy heaping of mana into the swirly thingy in my tummy.

Everything around me shifted. I felt magic clinging to me and my clothes, then that tingly feeling returned, but way stronger.

And then my friends and the room around me became much, much bigger.

"Whoa!" I squeaked.

My friends jumped, both of them turning to look where I was, or rather, where I'd been. They both looked down at the same time.

Their expressions couldn't be more different. Amaryllis stared in utter confusion before frowning. "You moron, what have you done now?"

Awen gasped, then reached down with hands that were very, very big. She grabbed me under my arms, her hands big enough that her thumbs touched. Then she lifted me up before her and held me out at arm's length.

I wiggled, especially when one of my ears flopped down before me and I had to shove it aside to see.

"Tiny," Awen said.

When she hugged me, I laughed. It was weird being hugged when Awen was so much bigger.

When the hugging ended, Awen placed me on her lap. "What did you do?" she asked.

"I tried my new skill," I squeaked while I worked to push my ear back. It seemed as if I'd made myself small, but my ears hadn't changed in size at all. So they were as big as usual, but since I wasn't, they were now about as long as I was tall.

That was going to be tricky to work with. Though maybe it had just been me using the skill wrong. I needed to practice!

I dropped off Awen's lap, then ran to the edge of the cot. Awen gasped and reached out for me, as if to stop me from falling off the edge. It was farther down than it had been before, but she didn't need to worry. I stopped pouring mana into the thing in my tummy, and with a snap, I returned to my normal size . . . probably. I was now standing on the edge of the cot, head almost banging against the ceiling.

I'd need to be careful not to bonk myself with the skill.

"Well, that was something," Amaryllis said. "Why is it that you always end up with the most bizarre abilities?"

"I just say yes to anything I stumble onto," I said.

She smacked herself in the face. "Broccoli," she said with the same tone she usually used for calling people idiots.

"Let me try to do the opposite," I said.

"The opposite?" Amaryllis asked. "You'll make yourself bigger?"

"Yup," I said.

"No," she shot back.

I blinked. "No?"

She shook her head. "No. Not indoors. Certainly not onboard a ship, no matter how close to the ground we are."

"Ah, right, that makes sense," I said. "Whelp, in that case, I'm going back to being small. I want to see if I can get small enough to fit into a pocket."

"How about you don't experiment with a new skill so carelessly?" Amaryllis asked instead.

"Could you keep it up all night?" Awen asked. "Like a plushie . . . but warm?"

"Uh, I don't think I can," I said. "It uses up a lot of mana. I'm not sure how much, but at least a point per second, maybe a bit more? I bet it'll get better with practice, though!"

"That's unsustainable," Amaryllis said.

"Yes, but it's fun," I shot back.

Amaryllis rolled her eyes. "Broccoli, you're just so . . . Broccoli."

"Hey! I'm not a noun you can just toss around like that."

And so we bickered, and we joked around, and we unwound ourselves after a hard day's work.

I think we'd done a pretty good job in Goldenalden. We'd foiled Rainnewt's evil plans, helped people learn how to break Evil Roots, and hopefully, stopped an entire war from happening.

I was pretty proud of what I'd done.

That pride wouldn't distract me from more adventuring, though! I couldn't wait to hop back aboard the *Beaver Cleaver*, join up with some of my other friends and crewmates, and head off to the next great adventure!

About the Author

RavensDagger is a Canadian writer who wants to make people smile. The best way to do that, he has found, is by pecking away at the keyboard and hoping for the best.

Podium
DISCOVER
STORIES UNBOUND
PodiumAudio.com